Praise for Mary Burton

BURN YOU TWICE

"Burton does a good job balancing gentle romance with high-tension suspense."

—*Publishers Weekly*

"Scorching action. The twists and turns keep the reader on the edge of their seat as they will not want to put the novel down."

—*Crimespree Magazine*

HIDE AND SEEK

"Burton delivers an irresistible, tension-filled plot with plenty of twists . . . Lovers of romantic thrillers won't be disappointed."

—*Publishers Weekly*

CUT AND RUN

"Burton can always be counted on for her smart heroines and tightly woven plots."

—*For the Love of Books*

"Must-read romantic suspense . . . Burton is a bona fide suspense superstar. And her books may be peppered with enough twists and turns to give you whiplash, but the simmering romance she builds makes for such a compelling, well-rounded story."

—*USA Today*'s *Happy Ever After*

THE SHARK

"This romantic thriller is tense, sexy, and pleasingly complex."

—*Publishers Weekly*

"Precise storytelling complete with strong conflict and heightened tension are the highlights of Burton's latest. With a tough, vulnerable heroine in Riley at the story's center, Burton's novel is a well-crafted, suspenseful mystery with a ruthless villain who would put any reader on edge. A thrilling read."

—*RT Book Reviews* (4 stars)

BEFORE SHE DIES

"Will keep readers sleeping with the lights on."

—*Publishers Weekly* (starred review)

MERCILESS

"Burton keeps getting better!"

—*RT Book Reviews*

YOU'RE NOT SAFE

"Burton once again demonstrates her romantic-suspense chops with this taut novel. Burton plays cat and mouse with the reader through a tight plot, credible suspects, and romantic spice keeping it real."

—*Publishers Weekly*

BE AFRAID

"Mary Burton [is] the modern-day queen of romantic suspense."

—Bookreporter

DON'T LOOK NOW

ALSO BY MARY BURTON

Near You

Burn You Twice

Never Look Back

I See You

Hide and Seek

Cut and Run

Her Last Word

The Last Move

The Forgotten Files

The Shark

The Dollmaker

The Hangman

Morgans of Nashville

Cover Your Eyes

Be Afraid

I'll Never Let You Go

Vulnerable

Texas Rangers

The Seventh Victim

No Escape

You're Not Safe

Alexandria Series

Senseless

Merciless

Before She Dies

Richmond Series

I'm Watching You

Dead Ringer

Dying Scream

DON'T LOOK NOW

MARY BURTON

This is a work of fiction. Names, characters, organizations, places, events, and incidents are either products of the author's imagination or are used fictitiously.

Published by Montlake, Seattle

www.apub.com

ISBN-13: 9781542021456
ISBN-10: 1542021456

Cover design by Amanda Kain

Printed in the United States of America

DON'T LOOK NOW

PROLOGUE

Austin, Texas
Tuesday, March 23
10:15 p.m.

"Call out for help, just like we practiced." He pressed the phone to the woman's face.

She moistened her dried lips and said, "Help me, please. He's going to kill me."

He cocked a brow, reminding her there was more to the script.

"Please save me."

Satisfied, he ended the call, removed the battery from her phone, and tucked both in his pocket. He grabbed the wadded cloth, shoved it back in her mouth, and pulled the plastic bag over her head. She moaned and struggled to free her face from the plastic and her hands from their bindings.

His very first one, he had been too afraid to kill. The second one he'd murdered quickly because he thought death would satisfy this nagging desire. But he had been plagued by disappointment. That was why this time he had resolved to savor the experience like a fine cigar.

As he suspected, her slow, steady suffocation intensified his sexual pleasure. The writhing of her muscles. The twitches in the hands and legs bound tight with black corded rope. Her panicked expression amplified by the plastic bag. She was fighting to breathe, endure, and survive. It was a remarkable battle, given her lifestyle. Endurance was embedded deep in everyone.

He pulled the bag off her head, gave her time to inhale deeply and for the color to return to her face. He covered her face again and delighted in her renewed struggle. He repeated the process three more times.

Each time he zeroed in on her pleading, desperate, and frantic eyes, his erection hardened like it had when he was a teenager. Overcome with a craving he could no longer control, he had pushed inside her. The first time, he had come quickly and rolled off her as she'd panted for air. The second time, he had lasted longer, and this third time he'd decided he could repeat this process over and over forever.

But time was running out. Better to leave while the getting was good. There would be a next time. Not with this one, but another—of that he was sure.

He yanked on jeans, a black pullover shirt, and athletic shoes. He knelt beside her and tightened the bag's drawstring around her neck. Her breasts heaved up and down faster. He gently smoothed his hand over her naked body. "I like it when you fight."

She stilled but watched him closely under hooded eyes.

"This is better than anything I'd dared imagine." The first time had been good, but *this* was fantastic.

This intentional experience was akin to Dorothy stepping out of Kansas's gray prairies into the vibrant Technicolor world of Oz. Daydreams never captured the feel of tense flesh, the scent of nervous sweat, or the truly rapid rise and fall of a woman's chest. The mind had nothing on reality.

He liked this new world, and he did not want to return to the black-and-white realm. This journey was a one-way ticket, and this experience needed to be repeated. The risks no longer mattered. What mattered was duplicating *this* high.

He straddled the woman and angled her face so that their gazes met. She strained her head up, pressing the soft white skin of her face against the thin plastic. The gag in her mouth made it impossible for her to speak, so she moaned her one last plea for her life.

"You and I are the same in many ways. As much as we try to convince ourselves we're in control of our addictions, we're not. It's just too powerful," he said. "You understand, right?"

She shook her head, attempted to scream, and expended the last of her oxygen. He tied the drawstring in a bow, double knotted it, and rose on his knees. He lifted her and laid her on a large piece of plastic. He rolled the bottom edge of the plastic over her feet, wrapped the right edge over her, and tucked it in under her body. As she groaned and moved her head from side to side, he gathered the opposite section, tucked it under the other side, and tightly swaddled her. Next, he covered her face, muffling her waning screams.

He reached for a roll of packing tape and yanked a length of it from its spool, the firm jerk echoing in the abandoned room. She flinched. Her struggles resumed, but they were slower and sloppier.

Round and round the tape went, encasing her thin body around the midsection, feet, neck, and finally her face.

Her moans had softened to a dull mewing, and her muscles spasmed only involuntarily now as she consumed the last traces of the oxygen. Like a flickering light bulb, her filament glowed red with the last relics of energy before going dark.

Rising, he wiped the sweat from his brow and stepped back. The cool-night-air temperatures would rise back to the unseasonable nineties tomorrow, and the heat, combined with the magnifying effects of the plastic, would melt her flesh and sinew at an accelerated rate. Left alone here in this old house, she would turn to mush in a matter of weeks. Of course, there was the risk she would be found sooner rather than later. This old house, chosen for several sentimental reasons, had been sold, and the new owner planned a renovation and flip. Given the growing market in Southeast Austin, crews would arrive within weeks.

Really, he needed only about a week, maybe eight days. By then she would be unrecognizable, and it would take DNA to identify her, if that were even possible. Girls like her generally were not in DNA databases.

He rubbed his hand over his sweat-damp hair, glanced at his fingers, and saw the slight tremor. He chalked it up to this euphoric high, which now wielded a crushing power over him.

CHAPTER ONE

Tuesday, March 30
10:00 p.m.

The call from dispatch was a jolt to homicide detective Jordan Poe's system. After a fifteen-hour shift, she had arrived home, eaten a quick dinner, and settled on the couch to watch a movie. She had immediately fallen asleep.

Now, as she bolted up to the shrill ring, she shook off the sleep and reached for her phone. "Detective Poe."

"Detective, a woman's body has been found in Southeast Austin." Dispatch rattled off familiar cross streets and an address less than ten blocks from her house.

"Tell me." Jordan cleared her throat as she moved toward the kitchen through her darkened house, illuminated by only the television screen's light.

She listened patiently as the dispatcher told her about the discovery of a woman's body. No details about manner of death, but the body was in an advanced state of decomposition. Translation: the smell would saturate anything porous that came within fifteen feet. Full PPE was suggested.

She made a strong pot of coffee, and as it brewed, she brushed her hair, refashioned it into a bun, and splashed water on her face. Ten minutes later, coffee in hand, she pushed out of her front door, wearing yesterday's clothes. She slid behind the wheel of her SUV, parked in a small gravel driveway by her bungalow. She had inherited the one-story, fifteen-hundred-square-foot house from her mother twelve years ago, and she had spent a lot of that time renovating it. Many of the homes on her block still had their original owners and had not been updated. But the rush of newcomers to Texas had discovered the East Austin neighborhood with wooded lots, and it was a matter of time before the elderly residents sold.

When she arrived on the scene ten minutes later, she had drained her coffee and convinced herself she was not exhausted.

The one-level ranch was painted a mint green. It was surrounded by a chain-link fence encircling a yard filled with tall weeds. Across the street was a heavily wooded empty lot that had turned into a dumping ground filled with discarded tires, an old stove, and piles of brush.

Four cop cars were parked along the house's curb, their blue lights flashing in the darkness. A forensic van was parked in the short driveway, and two techs were setting up a tent and table. Normally the techs used tents to shield them from the hot Texas sun, and seeing as the sun had nine more hours before showtime, the setup told her they expected to be here well into tomorrow.

Before her mom, little sister, and she had moved to Austin, they had lived in Boston. She remembered the snow had come up to her waist on her sixteenth birthday, and the January air was so cold the windchill drove the temperatures below freezing. That was the day her mother had mumbled something about "being done with this shit," and the three of them had packed the family's blue Subaru and driven to Austin.

The day's growing heat brought her back to the moment. She noticed there were still no reporters on the scene yet, and she was relieved. Crime in this area was standard, but sooner or later the press would catch on and this would all get more chaotic.

She rose up out of her vehicle, grateful to stretch her long, stiff legs. She was craving a good workout, but that was going to have to wait.

Jordan's low-heeled boots, dusted with dirt from yesterday's crime scene, crunched against the freshly graveled street as she moved toward the back of her SUV and opened the hatch.

Shrugging off her jean jacket, she tugged on the lightweight PPE suit over a black T-shirt and worn jeans banded by a leather belt. Next it was shoe coverings and latex gloves.

She looked up at the ramshackle ranch. A sign in the front window indicated it was marked for remodeling by a developer who had done dozens of projects in the area over the last year. No doubt, the landowner hoped to sell the property to a newly relocated young professional willing to pay a premium.

A couple of forensic technicians wrestled a large light up the two concrete front stairs and into the house. After a moment, they reappeared, faces grim as one plugged a long extension cord into a generator. A press of a button and the generator jolted to life, and the interior of the house lit up.

A deputy moved toward her. He was tall, lean, a bit gangly, but he had the look of a guy who would fill out.

She guessed he was in his midtwenties.

"Detective Poe?" he asked.

"That's right. And you are?" Hints of her Boston accent drew out the last word.

"Officer Wilcox." They shook hands. "I was first on the scene." His face was stoic, but his fingers flexed involuntarily. Easy to control reactions on the face, but there was always another body part that gave the nerves away.

First seconds on a scene were precarious and tense. And if you should be so unlucky as to come across a suicide, murder, or infant death, the emotional gut punch was inevitable. "When did you arrive?"

"Two hours ago. The renovation crew chief called it in. He's still in his truck. Not happy about having to wait for a detective."

"We all could think of better things to do, including the victim."

A slight smile tweaked his lips. "That's for sure. The crew chief figured the dead person was a squatter or drug addict who had died. It's not rare in this area."

"I was told the victim is female."

"That's right."

"Any idea of the cause of death?"

"Offhand, I'd say suffocation. But who knows? It's nothing like I've ever seen." He shifted his feet and flexed his fingers.

"How long have you been on the job?" she asked.

"A year."

This scene likely was now in the officer's Book of Firsts. All cops had a book like that, and no matter how full it got, there was always room for a new horror. "Okay. Let me have a look."

"Want me to come with you?" Officer Wilcox asked.

"Stay in the yard. Fewer people in the house, the better."

His relief was palpable. "Understood."

She slid her mask over her face and crossed the gravel driveway, and as she climbed the two front porch steps, the scent of decomposition hit her hard. She stopped, raised her hand to her nose.

"Jesus," she muttered. Her first year on the job, she had swabbed Vicks under her nose but learned menthol did not conceal rot. These days, she sucked it up, knowing the brain would cancel out the smell after a few minutes.

"Detective Poe!"

She turned toward Andy Lucas, the senior forensic technician in the department. He was short, had a round face and belly, and his ink-black hair showed no signs of graying despite his recent fiftieth birthday.

"Andy."

"When you get inside, follow the yellow cones to the body. There's a lot of dust in that room, so I have a prayer of getting a shoe impression."

"Roger that."

"Hey, and thanks for the case of beer," Lucas said.

"A man only turns fifty once."

"Thank God," he joked. "Took me days to get over the surprise party."

She had helped host the event, which was just as much a department morale booster as it was a celebration of Lucas's half-century milestone. Because she did not drink, she had left early, but the stories, some of which were pretty damn funny, still circulated two weeks later.

She stepped over the extension cord, walked heel to toe beside the yellow cones, which led her into the small main room. Artificial light shone on faded rose wallpaper peeling off old shiplap, four barred broken windows, and clumps of hay nestled in shadowed corners.

She moved toward the illuminated area and the victim. Female, with a slight frame, and naked, she was wrapped in a thick layer of plastic. Her hands were bound, and there appeared to be a bag over her head and a gag in her mouth.

The manner of death stirred memories Jordan had worked hard to forget. Closing her eyes, she drew air into her lungs, her desire to avoid the stench overruled by the need to breathe fully. Tight bands of anxiety squeezed her chest. She closed her eyes, pushing away the past and allowing her mind to settle. This was now. Not two years ago. And she had nothing to worry about.

Slowly, her thoughts collected, and she opened her eyes. Chalk up another experience for her Book of Firsts.

As she did at all fatality scenes, she mentally reclassified the dead person from *Human* to *Evidence*. This woman could no longer speak, but her body still might have secrets to share.

The body was badly decayed. Gases had already built up in the belly and burst through the skin, leaving a real oozing mess encased in the plastic. The covering around the body had slowed the bugs attracted to decomposing flesh, but a few had found a small opening and begun nature's work. Another two weeks and there would not have been much to find.

The plastic bag over the victim's head was secured in place with a thin drawstring tied in a double-knotted bow.

Jordan had responded to a couple of accidental autoerotic asphyxiation deaths. The people who played this dangerous game cut off oxygen to the brain, sexually stimulated their bodies, and then, seconds before orgasm, released the bag or neck restraints. The rush of oxygen was supposed to heighten the pleasure, but the trick was to remove the bag or rope in time. In both prior, unrelated cases, the victims had been men. One had worn a belt around his neck, whereas the other had chosen a thin cord. Each had passed out before the big O and suffocated to death.

Even if this woman had started this dangerous trek willingly, it was clear she had not been alone at the time of her death. Had the dead woman's sex partner panicked and wrapped and dumped the body?

At this stage it was impossible to tell the victim's ethnicity. Her skin appeared to be brown, but Jordan knew that could be from decomposition. Her hair had been icy blond, but the color looked as if it could be found on any drugstore shelf.

Age was another detail that was hard to call. But if Jordan had to guess, she would have said the victim was young.

Footsteps behind her had her turning to see Andy and the other tech, Marsha Brown, enter the room. In full PPE, they looked more alien than human.

"We'd like to get started on the footprints," Andy said. "They'll be the first ruined."

"Sure, go ahead," Jordan said.

"Are you sticking around?" Andy asked.

"Just standing back and observing."

As Jordan backtracked her steps to the front door, she imagined other motives behind this killing. With the border 220 miles away, human trafficking was common here. Though coyotes raped and sometimes killed their victims, they generally discarded the bodies on a barren patch of earth in the open sun. Some might take the time to cover the remains with a little dirt or brush, but she had never seen any wrappings this elaborate. Drug dealers and pimps were not strangers to violence, but they rarely went to such lengths with their dead, unless they were sending a message.

The house was marked for renovation, so whoever had left Jane Doe here had known she would be found eventually. Maybe he wanted her found. Maybe it was a sign of misguided respect or contrition for what he had done. Maybe it was a message to someone. Or maybe he simply wanted his work displayed.

But until she could find out more about the victim's identity, any stab at motive would be conjecture.

Her attention was drawn back to the bound hands tied with precise, tight knots. Like the drawstring, they were double knotted.

Jordan guessed the killer had played with the tension on the bag before he killed her. How many times had he brought her up to the point of death and then carefully loosened the drawstring so she could suck in enough oxygen to stay alive? Had she been a willing participant or a victim? Jordan had seen a lot of crazy shit over the years, but her money was on murder.

Had she been the killer's first victim? Had he been playing out this erotic scenario for months—if not years? The thick plastic wrap and packing tape, even finding this location, required planning.

Forethought. Jordan remembered the woman she had found bound, gagged, and struggling to breathe two years ago, when she'd still been a patrol officer. She'd saved that one, but she had been minutes away from losing her.

"Christ," she muttered. "What do the footprints look like, Andy?" she asked. "Any idea how many sets?"

"From what I can see, there're the deputy's prints as well as another set."

"Only one other?"

"Yep. The contractor smelled the decomposition and didn't enter the house."

"We can assume they are the killer's prints, and he likely carried her in here?" Jordan asked.

"She's barefoot and has small feet. I don't see any prints like that." Andy killed the big light, and they were plunged into darkness before he shined his flashlight over the dusty floor. Shadowed footprints appeared. "We lost a lot of the killer's initial foot strikes near the body, but in the corners and around the perimeter we have traces of his footsteps. Lucky for us the place has been abandoned for a while, and the dust was thick."

Picturing the scene, she imagined a killer carrying in his unconscious victim. That gave him time to get his plastic, tape, and whatever other toys he had brought to this party. By the time the victim had woken up, she would have been naked and immobilized with rope and perhaps under the weight of his body. How long had her struggles to live lasted? Minutes? Hours? Days? For the victim, time must have stretched for an eternity.

"I'll leave you to it," Jordan said. "The medical examiner can take the body."

"Right. Should have a report in a few days, week at the most."

"Thanks."

Tightness fisted in Jordan's chest as she stepped onto the porch. The eyes of the four other deputies settled on her. How many bets had been placed on the newest homicide detective's reaction? She squared her shoulders and slowly walked down the steps and crossed to the forensic van.

She wanted to rip off the PPE and scrub the stench off her. Suddenly, the protective gear reminded her of the plastic encasing the dead woman. But again, she moved slowly, drawing her gaze up to the nearly full moon before she removed her mask. There were enough women in Texas law enforcement so she was not an anomaly, but freaking out at a crime scene earned any officer a black mark, regardless of gender.

She dumped the gloves and booties, and then the suit, in the disposal bin. There was no breeze to cool her skin, but with the outer layer shed, she felt lighter.

As she crossed back to her vehicle, she saw Officer Wilcox eyeing her. It was a matter of time before he churned up the courage and asked whatever question was on his mind.

She kept moving, opened the back of her SUV, washed her hands with sanitizer, and from a cooler grabbed a bottle of water as Officer Wilcox approached. She handed the first bottle to him and took a second for herself.

She twisted the water bottle's top open. "What's on your mind, Officer?"

"I've seen shootings and car accidents. But nothing like that." Absently, he scraped the water bottle label with his thumb. "This killer took pleasure in what he did."

"You're right. Some kill for sport, Officer." As he drew in a breath and nodded slowly, she added, "It takes planning to find the woman, this location, and assemble the supplies." She raised the bottle to her lips, savoring the cool liquid in her mouth. "Even if the killing was meant to be a lesson, this killer enjoyed his work."

CHAPTER TWO

Monday, March 11
Two years ago

It was 2:00 a.m. when Jordan parked on the dark corner of Seventh and Red River Streets in downtown Austin. By day, it was a safe enough area where tourists, artists, and hipsters congregated. But at night, drug dealers and sex workers moved out of the shadows and plied their trades openly. Austin was like most cities: bad things happened in the light of day, but they thrived at night.

She moved toward an alley where a man had been shot dead two nights ago over a twenty-dollar squabble. A week before that, two junkies had overdosed.

Jordan wore faded jeans, a graphic T-shirt, and scuffed boots. She was not carrying her badge and had swapped her sidearm for a small .38-caliber revolver strapped to her ankle.

She moved past a brick wall covered with a large mural of a grinning jester, his white teeth amplified by a red background. At the corner, a tall blonde wearing black leather and white sneakers leaned against a signpost. Her name was Stacey, and she was a sex worker. Jordan had crossed paths with Stacey several times when she worked undercover narcotics. Stacey could be funny, and when she was not too loaded, her street smarts zeroed in on trouble faster than most.

Jordan walked up to Stacey and made a point to keep her body language relaxed. People down here could smell fear and desperation.

Stacey knew Jordan was a cop but judged her to be fair because Jordan never razzed her or the other women, and often had a couple of twenties when they answered her questions.

"What brings you to my neck of the woods?" Stacey asked.

"I'm looking for someone." Jordan pulled a picture of a young woman from her pocket. The woman was twenty-two, looked like she was much younger, but given her current lifestyle, her youth would fade fast. Soon, she would age beyond her years. For now, she remained slender, her blond hair soft and natural.

"You mean Avery?" Stacey asked. "Is she in trouble?"

"No trouble. I'm afraid she's using again. I want to help her."

"How do you know her?" Stacey asked.

This was the point where Jordan was not sure if honesty was the best policy. She considered a half dozen well-worn lies but found them tired and less convincing than the truth. "She's my sister."

"No shit." Stacey shook her head but did not look shocked. She had seen it all. "You got a junkie for a sister?"

"She wants to get better. She had a setback."

Stacey pulled a cigarette pack and plastic green lighter from her large patent leather purse. She removed a cigarette and lit the tip. "Don't we all?"

Jordan's sister, Avery, had moved in with her six months ago, full of resolve to get clean. They had been down this road before, but Jordan had not given up hope, so she'd welcomed her sister back into the house.

Hours ago, Jordan had been doing the laundry, and thinking she would help Avery out, she'd scooped up the dirty clothes off her sister's bedroom floor. She had found a baggie of white powder in a shirt pocket and confronted Avery. The two had fought bitterly, and Avery had stormed out.

Stacey inhaled and blew out smoke as she studied the picture. "She was here an hour ago. I tried to talk to her, but she was just looking to score."

"Do you know from who?"

"I ain't looking to get anyone arrested. I don't need trouble."

"I'm not looking to arrest anyone. *Who* tells me the quality of what Avery bought and where I might find her."

"She was asking about Walker," Stacey said.

"Marco Walker." Walker had dated Avery once. And he was the reason she had started using.

"That's right."

Jordan tucked the picture back in her pocket. "He still living down the street above the El Dorado bar?"

"He is, but I didn't tell you nothing."

"Thanks, Stacey." She handed her the fifty bucks that was supposed to get Jordan to payday. It was going to be peanut butter sandwiches for the duration.

Jordan moved down the dark street, past the unlit alleys. Music from a bar drifted out an open window. A man and woman were laughing across the street. And in one alcove two grunted and groaned as they went at it.

A three-story building sat on the corner. There had been a bar on the first floor until it had closed last year. On the second and third floors were apartments that saw a lot of resident turnover.

She climbed the stairs to the third floor, removed the gun from her ankle holster, and knocked on the door. Inside, music pulsed loudly. Anywhere else there would have been a noise complaint. She tried the doorknob. It was unlocked.

Carefully, she pushed open the door. She spotted a stereo on a side table, and she crossed to it and shut it off. Her ears throbbed in the silence.

There were two bedroom doors, and she opened the first. On the floor, she found a mattress covered with rumpled sheets, discarded clothes, and trash.

She moved to the next bedroom, and when she opened the door and flipped on the light, she immediately spotted the woman lying on her side, facing the opposite wall. Her hands were bound, and she sounded like she was gagging.

Jordan rushed toward her, rolled her on her back, and found herself staring into her sister's vacant eyes. Tucking the gun in her waistband, Jordan removed the gag tied around Avery's head.

Avery's eyes were wide, her pupils dilated, and she was choking. Jordan arched Avery's neck, opened her mouth, and checked her airway. She swiped her finger inside Avery's mouth and felt plastic. She reached in deeper, grabbed the foreign object with her fingertips, and pulled it out.

Avery sucked in a full breath, her chest rising and falling.

Jordan's hands trembled as she raised her sister to a sitting position. "Avery!"

Avery coughed, and when she focused on Jordan's face, tears welled and spilled down her cheeks. "I'm sorry."

"I know. I know. I'll call an ambulance."

"No, please. Just get me out of here."

"Who put the plastic down your throat?" Jordan struggled to contain her anger. Her sister needed help, and someone had taken advantage of her weakness.

"I don't know." Her voice sounded hoarse, scratched.

"Did Walker do it?"

"I don't know. Maybe. Maybe a friend of his."

"Did you get any names?"

"No," she cried. "I just remember Walker handing me the needle and tying me up. I'm sorry. I'm so sorry."

Jordan pulled Avery into an embrace. "Okay. It's okay."

Avery's body shuddered with sobs as she gripped the sleeves of Jordan's T-shirt. "I'll never do this again."

"I know. I know."

This latest setback hit Jordan hard. She thought about what it would cost for another stint in rehab. And then the endless days of wondering whether Avery had used again.

But Jordan would do what she had done since their mother died. She would put one foot in front of the other and find a way forward out of the darkness.

CHAPTER THREE

Monday, April 12
8:00 a.m.

Jordan arrived at the police station. She considered stopping in the break room for more coffee, but when she heard the collection of cops talking, she moved directly to her cubicle. A string of sleepless nights had left her in no mood for conversation.

Nearly two weeks after the female body had been found in the abandoned house, it had not yet been identified. That was not surprising. There were a lot of Jane Does in the world who never ended up reclaiming their real names. But the Jane Doe wrapped in plastic continued to bother Jordan. She had had too many nights since when she'd woken up, overcome by a suffocating sensation.

Jordan wanted to believe she cared about all her homicide victims, but some carried more weight than others. To date, there were three who never strayed far from her mind. The old woman beaten to death for the five dollars in her purse. The three-year-old girl struck by a hit-and-run driver. And the fifteen-year-old star football player shot behind the school bleachers. She'd solved all those cases. Brought all the killers to justice. And though the judge had wielded hefty sentences in each case, the victims had never left Jordan.

Only when she was really tired, say after a thirty-six-hour stint on a case, their presence was all the more acute.

This latest victim, Jane Doe, had officially joined her trio of lost souls. But so far, Jordan was not any closer to finding her killer.

There were all brands of evil, but killers like this one, the ones who tortured their victims and displayed them like a proud cat leaves a newly killed mouse on a doorstep, gave cops nightmares. If this was his first kill, Jordan would bet money it was not going to be his last.

***

At the crime scene, she had spent an hour interviewing construction manager Manny Bennett, and he had mentioned that he was behind schedule.

"Demo on the house was supposed to begin days ago," Mr. Bennett said. "We've got more properties than we can handle. I should have been here last week."

"Do you keep any surveillance cameras on-site?" Jordan asked.

"We don't bother until we start moving construction supplies onto the property. There's no point guarding a run-down house."

"How long has the house been vacant?"

"Two years. The property has been in bankruptcy courts since then. We bought the house a month ago, but my crew only stuck our company's sign in the front yard two weeks ago, so everyone on the block knew we were coming sooner or later."

"Any trouble with squatters?"

"Sure. One of the reasons I came by tonight was to put new locks on the doors. Now that we're ready to move forward, I didn't need an uninvited guest setting a fire to stay warm or trashing the house further."

Mr. Bennett's background check had cleared. No arrests or priors, and he had been with his current employer for ten years. He was married with three kids.

Jordan's phone rang, pulling her thoughts back to the blotter on her desk, the doodled circles, and the blinking light of line one. She picked it up. "Detective Poe."

"Detective, this is Dr. Faith McIntyre with the state medical examiner's office."

Jordan's chair squeaked as she leaned forward. She had called about Jane Doe's autopsy status several times. The doc was always polite, but women like Jane Doe often ended up at the bottom of the priority lists. "Dr. McIntyre."

"I've done the autopsy of your Jane Doe. It's taken me several days to write up the report, and I apologize for the delay." To Dr. McIntyre's credit, she cared about all the bodies she examined, even the ones without names.

"Any idea of the cause of death? We're all assuming asphyxiation on this end." Jordan picked up a pencil and began to draw more circles.

"As you know, the decomposition is advanced, so much of the soft-tissue evidence has been lost. But X-rays did not show any broken bones, and the U-shaped hyoid bone, often fractured during strangulation, is intact. There was a hairline fracture on the back of her skull. It wasn't enough to kill her, but it would have knocked her out."

Dr. McIntyre continued, "After we stripped off the outer-layer wrapping, as you said, we found a plastic bag around her head. There was a drawstring, and it was cinched pretty tight. My guess is that's what killed her."

"Any identifying marks on the body?"

"Three tattoos, including a bird, the name *Billy*, and a cross. She was also wearing a crescent moon necklace. Small and delicate."

Jordan scribbled notes into her case notebook. "What about sexual assault?" she asked.

"The vaginal tissue was fairly degraded, but I did find the presence of semen. It's also not in great shape, so I doubt there'll be any viable DNA. But she did have sex shortly before she died." Papers flipped in the background. "Her stomach was nearly empty. I doubt she'd eaten that day."

"What about ethnicity and age?"

"White female in her late teens or early twenties. She was about five foot two, and she had blond hair, which does not appear natural."

Not a lot, but now she had details to share when she called the missing person department.

"I also ran a toxicology test," Dr. McIntyre said. "I'm still waiting on the results. They should be back soon, but it appears she had track marks on her arms."

"If she's been arrested, there's a chance her DNA is on file."

"Agreed. We'll send it all to your forensic department."

"It's a start."

"Good luck, Detective. Keep me posted on any arrests."

"Will do, Dr. McIntyre."

Jordan hung up the phone and immediately dialed the missing person department.

"Detective Rivers," a woman said unhurriedly after three rings. Detective Marla Rivers was a transplant from Florida, newly divorced, in her early thirties, and good at her job.

"Detective Rivers, this is Jordan Poe with Austin Police. I work homicide."

"Right. Haven't spoken to you in a while."

"Been busy."

"How's the homicide department?"

"Can't complain." Jordan was making a name for herself and did not hide her ambition to rise up the chain. "Have you heard about the Jane Doe found two weeks ago wrapped in plastic?"

"Sure. You identify her?"

"No. Medical examiner gave me a brief description. Female, late teens or early twenties, fake blond, five-two-ish. I was hoping you might have reports on someone like that." She also listed off the tattoos.

"I have several missing person reports, but most don't fit that age range. I'll see if any new cases have come in. We get new ones all the time."

Jordan knew that in the United States, more than six hundred thousand missing person cases were filed annually. But of those, 99 percent were solved or canceled. The person either returned home or was located dead or alive. "Send me whatever you have. I need to start somewhere."

"Sure. The files will be on your desk by tomorrow."

"Thanks, Detective Rivers."

She hung up and checked her watch. She had an hour to get to the courthouse for a bail hearing. She had been following this case since it had come across the wire last week. The defendant was Marco Walker, Avery's ex. He was being held on manslaughter charges. He claimed he had accidentally killed his current girlfriend during an argument when she had taken a swing at him, and he had pushed her. She had fallen, hit her head on the edge of a fireplace, and died instantly.

Jordan's heeled boots clicked in the hallway as she moved to the elevator and down to the lobby. In her car, she bristled at the heat, wondering what the hell the air temperatures would be like in August. She quickly turned on the engine, and the AC dutifully spit out hot air. She gave it a few impatient seconds to cool before she backed out of her space.

As Jordan pulled onto the street, her phone rang. It was the café where Avery worked, which meant Avery had likely lost her phone again. Not good, or safe. Adding to her worries was the call itself. It had been over two years since Avery's last overdose, but Jordan always feared this was the day it would all fall apart again.

Avery was twenty-four. She worked at the Austin City Café forty hours a week and sold her mixed-media paintings at fairs and on street corners. She got by, was staying clean, but the girl's life always remained on the edge. Like their mother had been, Avery was a free spirit. Jordan had tried to convince Avery to move back in with her, but Avery remained determined to live on her own.

"What's up?" Jordan asked.

"Today is Mom's birthday."

She knew that, or at least had remembered two days ago that today was *the* day. But this morning she had overslept and, in the rush, forgotten it. "I know."

"You forgot."

"I did not."

"Are you coming with me to the cemetery this afternoon?"

"I'd like to."

"I hear a *but* . . ."

"I have no idea when I'll get out of court. I'll call you as soon as I'm free," Jordan said.

"My shift at the café starts at three, and I work until ten. We've made night runs before."

"I know. I'm just not fond of the dark." Jordan paused at a red light, tapped her finger on the steering wheel.

"Face it; it would have appealed to Mom."

"I'll pick you up at the end of your shift, and we'll have a soda and toast Ma."

"Sounds good."

"Everything all right?" Jordan asked. "You have that tone in your voice."

"What tone?"

"If I told you that, you'd change it. What's going on?"

"Just feeling down, I guess. Mom would have been fifty-five today. Sucks she's dead."

Jordan's chest tightened a fraction as she imagined alarm bells clanging. "Are you doing okay?"

"I mean, I'm not great, but I'm not doing anything stupid. I swore I would never do that again."

Addiction shattered promises all the time. "I know. And you're doing so well."

"You're sounding like a mother again."

When their mother had died, Avery had been twelve and Jordan twenty-two. She'd scuttled her plans for law school and joined the Austin Police Department. It had offered decent pay, good benefits, and stability in their lives.

Avery had been at that perfect storm of raging hormones and middle school, and their mother's loss had toppled her out of balance. As hard as Jordan had tried to steady her, she could not seem to keep her sister on course. By fourteen, Avery was drinking booze and smoking pot. She'd met Walker when she was twenty-one, started using the hard stuff, and nearly died. She had been clean for two years, but it seemed just like yesterday.

Jordan wanted to remind Avery that Walker was on trial for manslaughter but did not want to stir trouble. She needed to loosen her grip. "Sorry about that."

"I'm good. Really," Avery insisted.

"I'll see you tonight at work."

"Deal."

She hung up, shaking the unease that had crept under her skin, and found her way to the courthouse. She parked, located her courtroom, and took a seat in the back. The room was almost empty. She recognized the parents of the dead woman, Mr. and Mrs. Sanchez, sitting behind the prosecution's table. There was no one sitting behind the defendant's table except one man.

His shoulders were broad, and he was wearing a white shirt that stretched over what looked like muscles on muscles. She had seen the type at the gym. Guys who turned the workout into a kind of religion. Working shit out for the most part.

His bearing told her he was law enforcement, and she would bet money he was wearing a Texas Ranger star. Those guys were tall, muscular, well over six feet, and they had a don't-screw-around-with-me air. Given a different setting, she might have inquired about his name, searched for a wedding band, and asked him to help her out with her yearlong sexual dry spell.

But they were in court, and she kept wondering why a Texas Ranger cared about Marco Walker.

A man wearing an expensive suit took a seat at the defendant's table seconds before Walker was escorted into the room. The suit was Harold Sunday, Walker's attorney. The two nodded to each other, but neither spoke.

The bailiff announced Judge Trace Martin, everyone rose, and the side door opened to a tall rawboned man wearing a black robe. Martin's salt-and-pepper hair and mustache set off his deeply tanned skin, and when he sat, he surveyed the room carefully. This judge had a reputation for going tough on domestic abuse cases. Mr. and Mrs. Sanchez were lucky to have Judge Martin.

The prosecutor introduced himself as Victor Ingram. Harold Sunday stood, said good morning to the judge, and then swept the courtroom with his gaze. He locked eyes with Jordan, nodded, and then sat back down. Sunday was a sharp lawyer, and his specialty was getting the bad guys out on bail.

Jordan had crossed paths with Sunday two years ago when she was still with narcotics. He had waited for her outside the courtroom and, flashing his million-dollar smile, told her she was pressing her luck. She had ignored him. The next morning, she had found a dozen strangled rats on her front lawn and her tires slashed. Nothing could ever be linked to Sunday, but she knew he had been behind it.

The judge sat, and so did everyone else in the courtroom. As the ranger took his seat, he looked back at her. She guessed he had seen Sunday's nod and wanted to locate the recipient.

Jordan looked at the ranger, raised a brow in question. His frown deepened, and he turned.

Harold Sunday painted an unflattering picture of the victim, Elena Sanchez, and documented her drug issues as well as her public fights with her boyfriend. Sunday claimed that the single blow Walker landed on his girlfriend had been in self-defense. She had stumbled back and struck her head on the stone hearth. She was dead before the ambulance arrived.

Jordan knew it could not be that simple. She believed that Walker had been planning to farm out a drug-addled Avery to one of his friends two years ago, and she would bet he had done the same with Elena. Jordan had met up with Elena on Sixth Street a month ago and warned the woman to find a new man. Elena had looked nervous, worried that someone would overhear Jordan and she would later pay a price. She had all but run from Jordan.

The judge went through a lot of preliminary legal talk and finally got to the point of the hearing. "After careful consideration of the facts, I'm setting bail at two hundred thousand dollars."

The sum sounded high, but for Walker, finding a bail bondsman and the required 10 percent down payment would not be hard.

Jordan shifted in her seat as Mr. and Mrs. Sanchez gasped. A jolt of anger shot through her, and keeping her emotions in check was a struggle. It was not fair. Walker belonged behind bars. He should not be able to walk until his day in court. Elena should be alive.

Walker's shoulders slackened with relief while Mrs. Sanchez wept softly.

"Mr. Walker, until such time as you can arrange bail, I'm remanding you to the city jail," the judge said.

Jordan sat so still. She was pissed. But she shoved it down deep and, after the judge left the room, walked up to the Sanchezes.

"Mr. and Mrs. Sanchez," she said, aware Walker and Sunday could hear her. "I'm Detective Poe. I've been following your daughter's case. I'm sorry for your loss."

Mr. Sanchez wrapped an arm around his wife's shoulders. "*Sorry* does not do us any good, Detective. That animal will be out on the street. He should be in jail."

"It's bail. The charges are still pending."

"He'll be long gone over the border before his time comes," Sanchez said. "He'll get away with murdering our only child."

"No, he will not." Jordan handed them her card. "If you have any questions, feel free to call me. I'll call you as soon as I know more."

"Thank you," Mrs. Sanchez said.

As Jordan turned to walk them out of the courtroom, she caught the triumphant glimmer in Walker's eyes. He winked at her and puckered his lips into a kiss. Sunday's gaze followed Walker's. Amusement twinkled in his blue eyes before he nudged his client out the side door.

Anger and resentment burned Jordan's gut. How would she have handled herself if Avery had died?

She walked the couple to their car in the lot, offered more condolences, asked if there was anything she could do.

Mr. Sanchez said, "I could kill that man. He deserves to die."

Mrs. Sanchez laid her hand on his arm. "Don't say that."

"Why not, Constance? I could *kill* him."

"He'll stand trial," Jordan said.

"You don't believe that any more than I do. There won't be justice until Walker is dead. And I hope I'm there to see him draw his last breath."

"You don't mean that, Pete," Mrs. Sanchez said. "He's upset, Detective."

"I know. But you must let the police handle this."

Mr. Sanchez turned, got into the car, and started the engine.

"Will there really be justice for Elena?" Mrs. Sanchez asked.

"I hope so," Jordan said.

When they pulled away, she squared her shoulders. She understood wanting justice for a loved one. Walker had gotten away with hurting Avery, and with the Mexican border only 220 miles from Austin, he could easily be in the wind by tomorrow.

"He's not going to run." A man's deep voice was directly behind her.

Turning, she recognized the man from the courtroom, and he was now wearing his white Texas Rangers hat and mirrored aviator sunglasses. "And you are?"

"Ranger Carter Spencer."

"Detective Jordan Poe." As they shook hands, she noted his palms were rough, his grip strong. "How can you be sure he won't run, Ranger Spencer?"

"I've charges of my own pending. They'll be filed within forty-eight hours."

"Well, Ranger Spencer, I hope your charges will keep him behind bars. Left on his own, it's a matter of time before someone like Elena Sanchez dies again."

"He'll stand trial for her death."

She thought about the crime scene pictures the investigating officer had shown her of Elena Sanchez's body lying beside the hearth. Elena had been a pretty woman and looked as if she had been in good health. But Walker preferred finding the young, healthy ones and introducing them to drugs. He had lured Avery onto that same dark path, and her sister was simply lucky. If Jordan had been five minutes later . . .

"Do me a favor and put Marco Walker away for a long time," she said.

"I will."

"We haven't crossed paths before," she said.

"Been in El Paso and Houston. Moved back to Austin two years ago."

"How's that going for you?" Spencer was a good-looking man. No wedding band. And if not for this terrible timing, she might have knocked the rust off her limited flirting skills.

"I grew up here."

"Changed some in the last few years, hasn't it?"

"Yes, it has."

Her phone buzzed in her back pocket. She reached for it and saw her boss's name. "I've got to take this."

"Sure." He touched the brim of his hat. "Good to meet you, Detective Poe."

"Same to you, Ranger Spencer." She was already raising the phone to her ear as she turned. "Captain Lee, what can I do for you?"

"There's a body."

If he had known today was Walker's bail hearing, either he had forgotten or the newest murder had shifted it down the priority list. Likely the latter. "The body's in an abandoned house on the east side of Austin, five blocks from the first Jane Doe. Body's wrapped in plastic. Victim appears to have died of suffocation."

Though she had foreseen this trend, she felt no satisfaction. "I'll be there in fifteen minutes."

"Jordan, if this is the same guy, then we could have a real problem," Captain Lee said.

"Two weeks between kills is a quick turnaround." Most serial killers—and neither she nor Lee would dare utter that moniker yet—had a cooling-off period. They needed time to process, come down off the adrenaline high, and relive the crime. Only when the memory was worn out and threadbare did a killer like this go hunting again.

"Let me get to the scene, and I'll see what we're dealing with," she said.

"If it's the same guy, I'm not delaying," Lee said. "I'm calling the Rangers."

"Don't be so quick to hand it over. Let me get to the scene."

"Call me within the hour."

"Right."

She shoved her phone in her pocket, and her pace quickened as she approached her unmarked vehicle. Within feet, she noticed the long scratch along the driver's-side door. Shit. Her car had been keyed. Her first thought was Sunday. If he had not personally done this, he had found someone to do it for him.

She glanced around the lot for any security cameras and found none. "You'll have to try harder, Sunday," she muttered as she opened the door.

The Jane Doe case felt really personal, and for that reason alone she would not let it go.

CHAPTER FOUR

Monday, April 12
11:00 a.m.

The forensic team was on scene when Jordan arrived at the old house in Southeast Austin. Like the first murder scene, this house had a sign in the front yard for a local real estate development company announcing work would begin April 15 on this property. Again, the killer would have known crews were scheduled to be at the house and the body would be found.

This house was a ranch, one story, and painted a fading gray. The yard was overgrown, and a tree in the front yard drooped long branches over a rusted oil tank once attached to the house.

She donned full PPE gear before she climbed the stairs, pausing long enough to introduce herself to the uniformed officer. She recognized Sergeant Dave Saunders. He had been on the force thirty years, and when she had been in uniform, she had been under his command. "Sergeant Saunders."

"Detective Poe."

Each time he said *detective* there was a hint of humor and also pride in his tone. She had risen through the ranks quickly, but few questioned her work ethic or skills. "How are Alicia and the boys?"

"Doing fine. And Avery?" Saunders had arrested Avery four years ago for being drunk in public and called Jordan, told her he would not file charges as long as Avery entered drug rehabilitation. He was one of many who had helped save her sister's life.

"She's well. Working in a café and selling her art. Clean two years."

He nodded. "Well, the world does turn, doesn't it?"

"It does." A spotlight turned on in the house, catching her attention. "Better get to work."

"It's a bad one."

"Thanks for the heads-up."

She entered the brightly lit room. The walls had been whitewashed so long ago they looked gray. There was an old couch that had several burn patches on it, and she imagined someone sitting there smoking and dropping a crack pipe. Beyond the main room was a kitchen filled with garbage and covered in decades of grease. To her right were two doors that appeared to lead to what had been bedrooms.

She followed the yellow crime scene markers toward the first bedroom, where her gaze went directly to the body wrapped in thick plastic like an Egyptian mummy. This victim had blond hair, but her face and belly were bloated with decomposition gases, distorting her features and figure. Her hands were bound, and there was a gag in her mouth. Under the large outer wrap was a plastic bag covering her head. A drawstring was tied in a neat bow.

Lights from a digital camera flashed as Andy Lucas moved around the body, shooting pictures. "She's been dead about two or three days," he said, continuing to shoot.

"And she resembles the first victim."

"Yes, she does."

Jordan moved closer to the body, squatted, and studied the bloated features under the plastic and the tape bound tight around her body. "Two for two," she said quietly.

"Yeah," Lucas said. "Not good."

"What about shoe impressions?" she asked.

"A few. They look similar, but I'll have to put the images under the microscope."

She looked out the bedroom window toward a small garage on the property. "You'll check the garage?"

"On the list. We're going to be here for a couple of days," he said.

She examined the bedroom window locks. They were fastened. "Fingerprints?"

"Sure, but there have been plenty of people in and out of this house. Could be anyone."

"Any hits from the prints you pulled at the first scene?" she asked.

"Ran 'em all through AFIS. A couple of hits, but both guys have been in jail the last year. My guess is they used the house to crash."

In the dry Texas heat, fingerprints produced by the human body's natural skin oils could last for a long time.

"Okay." As she turned to leave the room, she imagined the departmental and media storms this death would cause. One Jane Doe could go unnoticed pretty easily. Even the strange manner of death would not have been enough to keep Jordan on the case. Her captain would assign her the next homicide, and this investigation would be relegated to her free time.

But two Jane Does killed in a similar manner could not be dismissed. "Thanks, Lucas."

She left the house and at the forensic van quickly pulled off the PPE. The hot sun mingled with a gentle breeze but did little to cool her skin. She fished her phone from her back pocket and dialed. Her boss picked up on the second ring. "Captain Lee."

"Do you want the good news or the bad news?"

"Give me the bad," he said.

"The woman was killed in the same manner as the victim found on March 30."

"And the good news?"

Jordan shook her head. "She's been dead about two or three days, which will give Dr. McIntyre something more to work with. We might be able to identify this one, which will be a start."

"Jesus," he muttered. "I can feel the heat from the brass and press scorching my skin now."

"I'll put a call in to Dr. McIntyre and ask her to open up her schedule for this one."

"I'm going to make some calls myself. We need to get a handle on this fast. This case won't slip gently into the night."

"I'm on it, Captain Lee. Give me at least a few days to run down leads."

"That's a lifetime during a case." Another phone rang in the background. "I've got to go."

"Sure." As Jordan hung up, she was annoyed by her boss's impatience. He understood that investigations took time, and she had an excellent closure rate.

She called Dr. McIntyre, landed in voicemail, and left a message for her. Next she began the tedious task of speaking to the neighbors. Most cases were solved not by fancy forensics but by cops hitting the pavement and asking lots of questions. She paused at her vehicle and washed her hands with wet wipes, brushed her hair, and spritzed with perfume. Smelling like decomposing flesh never helped break the ice.

She crossed the street and found herself facing three homes. Two had been renovated, and one looked as rough as the crime scene house. She opted for the latter.

She crossed the yard of cut wire grass, past an overturned bird feeder and a collection of neatly stacked bricks that matched the border of a garden filled with pink skullcap flowers.

Curtains in the window to the right of the front door flickered, and Jordan's hand automatically went to her sidearm. She crossed the porch, knocked on the door, and stood to the side.

A chain scraped on the inside, and a couple of locks clicked. The door opened to an elderly woman. She was heavyset, had pinned her white hair back in a thin bun, and wore a blue housecoat. "You with the cops, ain't you?"

"Yes, ma'am." Jordan removed a card from her back pocket and handed it to the woman. "Detective Jordan Poe. I'm investigating the crime scene across the street. What's your name, ma'am?"

"Ruth Penn." The woman dropped her gaze to the card and flicked the edge with a bent finger. "They were supposed to fix that house up in a week or so. We're all glad. It's nothing but a rattrap for druggies."

"How long have you lived here, Ms. Penn?"

"Forty-seven years. Lived here with my husband for most of 'em. We raised five kids here."

"And your husband passed?"

"Two years ago."

"I'm sorry for your loss."

The old woman shrugged. "We had a good run."

"Did you see anything at that house that might have caught your attention?"

"People come and go out of there all the time," she said. "Even when they put up the 'No Trespassing' signs, no one cared."

"Anyone been there two to four days ago?"

"I saw a car circling the block about that time. I'd never seen it before, so I kept an eye out. Driver circled a few times and then left."

"Did you get a look at him?"

"He was wearing a ball cap and sunglasses, so it was hard to tell. But I did get the license plate."

"Did you?"

Mrs. Penn nodded, proud of herself. She reached in the pocket of her housecoat and pulled out pink readers before turning to a stack of papers by the front door. She riffled through the advertisement flyers, store receipts, and bills. "I know I wrote it down."

"Take your time," Jordan said.

Mrs. Penn hunted through the bits of paper, scratched her cheek, and adjusted her glasses. Finally, she produced a short grocery store receipt with numbers and letters scribbled along the margin in red ink. "Here it is."

Jordan accepted the slip of paper printed at the corner store down the road. Milk, a candy bar, a pack of cigarettes, and the scribbled license plate. She read the scrawled handwriting and the three letters and three numbers. "Is that an eight or a three?"

Mrs. Penn homed in on the number in question. "An eight. I've never been good at closing those loops."

"What kind of vehicle was it?"

"A blue pickup truck. It was an older model. Had a big scrape down the side."

"Why did you think it didn't fit in this neighborhood?"

"Because I've never seen it before. When you're retired, you get to know the street in front of your house. There's a rhythm. When a truck circles your block real slow and pauses in front of the house across the street, it's impossible not to notice."

"This area is starting to change," Jordan said. "Lots of new people coming and going."

"Sure, I've seen new people driving around, looking at houses. But this guy drove slow and stopped in front of that house."

Jordan fingered the receipt dated April 8. "Do you remember what time of day?"

"I remember exactly. *Live with Kelly and Ryan* had just ended, and I was rising to make a cup of instant decaf. I was waiting on the kettle and strolled to the door. That's when I saw the truck. Made three passes about ten a.m."

"And the driver never got out?"

"Not that I saw. He could have come by during the show, and I wouldn't have noticed."

Jordan studied the letters and numbers, reminding herself the eight was not a three. "And the driver has not come back?"

"Not that I saw."

"What time do you go to bed?"

"Ten p.m., like clockwork. I thought I'd stay up late after I retired, but too many years of a routine is hard to break."

"I get it. I'm like that."

If the driver had returned after 10:00 p.m., he could have parked in the garage, carried his victim inside, killed her, left, and Mrs. Penn never would have known. "If you think of anything else, Mrs. Penn, would you call me?"

"Sure. I'll call."

"Who lives to your right and left?"

"On the right is a guy who does something with computers. Works long hours, but he's pleasant enough when I see him. Says he's going to fix his place up when he gets the time. To the left is Mildred Harris. Her son just moved her to a nursing home."

"Okay." She got the name of the software engineer. He might be the kind of guy who was up late.

"What's going on in that house across the street? Too many cops for it to be a squatter or a druggie."

"A woman was killed."

"How?"

"Can't say yet."

"Can't or won't?"

"A little of both." A wry smile tipped the edges of Jordan's lips. "You're sharp. I appreciate that. Wish we had more people like you in the world."

The compliment did its job, and Mrs. Penn seemed to forget about asking more questions. "We all got to do our part."

"Thank you again."

"Keep me updated, Detective Poe. This is my home, and I want to be safe."

"Yes, ma'am. I'll do that."

***

Jordan got away from work at 9:30 p.m. She had run the blue pickup truck's plates, discovered it had been reported stolen eight months ago, and the owner, Owen Franklin, was currently serving time in jail. A BOLO had been issued for the vehicle, but if this killer had used a stolen truck, he likely was not driving around in it. The software engineer next to Mrs. Penn had been in Seattle for the last two weeks.

She barely had time to grab a bundle of red carnations from a convenience store and arrive at Avery's café by 10:00 p.m.

"You made it." Avery picked up the carnations off the passenger-side seat, sat, closed the door, and clicked her seat belt in place in one continuous move.

"You had your doubts?" Jordan asked.

"Your job has a habit of popping up at the worst times."

"I'll send a memo to the criminals."

"Ha ha." She fingered the red carnation with the most wilted petals. "At least you picked her favorite color."

"Ma and her red nails. She said they made her feel pretty."

"She was pretty," Avery said. "I like the way you call her *Ma*. Reminds me we were from Boston."

Avery had been six when their mother had packed them up and moved to Texas. Her deep drawl made her sound as Texan as any twenty-four-year-old born in the state, whereas hints of Jordan's Boston accent always made her stand out. She was a hybrid creature who did not quite fit in Texas or Boston.

A cool evening breeze blew in Jordan's window as she drove through town to the small cemetery north of Austin. It was miles beyond the edge of the city, but at the time had been all Jordan could afford. She pulled through the stone entrance and wound her way to the top of the hill where the cremated bodies were interred. Jordan shut off the engine, and they both stared into the long lit room filled with hundreds of tiny boxes that all contained someone. Neither one of them was in a rush to go inside.

"What was the case that almost made you late today?" Avery asked.

Jordan's sister normally did not care about murder, but conversations about their mother were always charged with strong emotions. Avery had been only twelve when their mother died, and she had not witnessed the darker side of Donna Poe's addiction. Jordan remembered countless days of putting her mother to bed at 3:00 p.m. and making sure Avery had done her homework and gotten a hot dinner. Even to this day, she still had trouble containing her resentment, which always came twisted with the fear that Avery would succumb to drugs again. So, murder won as the conversation starter.

"A homicide. A woman was suffocated on the southeastern side. It'll be on the eleven p.m. news." The media rush had begun about 4:00 p.m. with a couple of reporters, and by the time she'd left the scene an hour ago, there were three news vans and several other journalists.

"How did she suffocate?" Avery asked.

Jordan allowed a breath to leak out over her lips. "Someone put a plastic bag over her head."

"Shit." Avery pressed her fingertips to her temple, against the vein that pulsed when she was tired. "Wasn't there another woman like her about two weeks ago?"

Jordan stared up at the bright stars. "Yeah. How did you hear about her? There wasn't much media coverage."

"I heard about it at the café. We get a lot of cops there. And don't worry, nothing sensitive was discussed. It was just the basic facts found in a press release."

"Okay."

"It's a horrible way to die," Avery said. "That feeling of needing air and not being able to get it is terrible."

Jordan had learned she had been less than a few minutes behind the man who had shoved the plastic into Avery's mouth. Avery always said she did not remember much about the man or why he had done it.

"Are you sure you're okay?" Jordan asked.

Moonlight caught the curls framing Avery's face. "I'm not as fragile as I look."

Jordan always listened with two sets of ears. One as a sister, the other as a cop. "When is your lease up?"

"Next month, but we've been through this." Avery now sounded exasperated.

"Okay. I won't push. But know the door is always open."

"I know. Thanks."

They both got out of the car. Thick clouds now covered up the full moon, and if not for the lights in the remembrance hallway, it would have been pitch black.

Like with all visits to Ma, they talked about the good times and sidestepped the bad. Neither of them mentioned the accident. Jordan had always known some of the truth behind it, but when she'd become a cop, she'd pulled the accident report and learned that their mother's blood alcohol had been three times the legal limit. The lack of skid marks at the scene showed their mother had never braked before she'd run her car into Lake Austin. She was either too drunk or it was intentional. The autopsy revealed she had been alive when she'd hit the water and had drowned.

Maybe that was why Jordan hated confined spaces and kept her car windows cracked when she drove.

"This is a hell of a way to spend a birthday," Avery said.

The sound of her sister's voice brought Jordan back to the moment and the echo of their footsteps over the stone floor.

"I know."

"Mama would have hated it. Why are we here?"

"It's what you always want to do."

"I don't want to do this anymore," Avery said. "Seeing her name carved on that metal plate is getting harder, not easier."

"Why?"

"I got off the junk. And I can't mask my bitterness anymore. I got free of it. Why couldn't she do it for us?"

"She wasn't as strong as you."

"But she had two kids, for Christ's sake. If you can't get clean for your kids, what does that say about you?"

"Like I said, she wasn't strong. And we all have the potential to break if the right combination is dialed up."

"You don't break."

"Maybe my combination hasn't been dialed yet," Jordan said.

Avery tucked the flowers into the small vase by their mother's name. "You have to make me a promise."

"What's that?"

"Don't die."

There was real fear in Avery's voice that Jordan had not heard since her sister was really young. "I'm not planning on it."

Avery looked at her sister. "You think that woman who was suffocated planned on it?"

The image of the dead woman's face, bloated and distorted, rushed into Jordan's mind. The victim might have gone with the killer to turn a trick, get high, or both, but she certainly had never bargained for the horrors unleashed on her. "No, I don't think she did."

"No one plans the bad stuff, Jordan. But it's out there waiting for us."

CHAPTER FIVE

Tuesday, April 13
8:00 a.m.

Jordan was on her fourth cup of coffee when she arrived at the medical examiner's office. Sleep had eluded her last night, and when she finally put her head on the pillow at 1:00 a.m., her mind ping-ponged between the faces of the two victims and her sister. A nightly replay of crime scenes was not anything new, but tossing her sister into the mix was. Blame it on the cemetery visit.

She showed her badge at the front desk and rode the elevator down to the basement. The routine was strangely rote. Her long hair was always pulled back and twisted into a bun, so it was a matter of putting her purse and jacket in a locker, slipping on a surgical gown, gloves, and a mask before she made her way to the whiteboard on the wall, which stated Jane Doe / Poe was in suite 101. Got to love the rhyme.

When Jordan pushed through the door, her focus zeroed in on the table where the victim's sheet-clad body now lay. Her vision narrowed, and she forgot everything except the god-awful smell and the outline of the woman's body under the sheet.

There was an imperceptible shift behind her, not quite a footstep or sound but a change in the air pressure. When she turned, Ranger

Spencer stood in the room. She took a defensive step back. His expression telegraphed a mixture of curiosity and maybe humor. He had caught her off guard, and he knew it.

"Ranger Spencer. What brings you here?" Jordan asked.

His hair was thick, black, and cut short on the side, and the longer layers on top were slicked down. He had shaved, but she suspected by lunchtime a thick stubble would cover his chin.

He nodded toward the body. "Your boss, Captain Lee, asked me to attend."

"What the hell? This is my case." Frustration soaked each word.

"He's asked for the Texas Rangers' help. He's afraid he has a serial killer, and he wants all hands on deck."

"I'm perfectly capable." As tempted as she was to string together a half dozen expletives, she paused. The trick was to sound confident and not defensive. "It's not been twenty-four hours."

"Fourteen days if you count the first one, assuming she's the first."

There had been moments in Jordan's career when she'd faced real trouble. Ranger Spencer was certainly not an armed assailant lurking in an alley, but he was not here simply to help. He was going to take what was hers.

Dr. McIntyre entered the room. She was a tall woman with thick blond hair pulled back in a ponytail. She moved like she came from money, but she was also approachable. Jordan had seen the doctor answer hard questions asked by family members seeking answers about a loved one's death. The doctor always kept her explanations to the point and factual, but her tone was also soft. She was married to a Texas Ranger, so Jordan suspected she did not have an issue with Spencer's presence.

"Good morning, Detective Poe and Ranger Spencer," Dr. McIntyre said.

"Morning," Spencer said.

"Good morning," Jordan said.

Dr. McIntyre flipped on the overhead light and angled it over the body. "Before you ask, Detective Poe, there's no word on the first victim's DNA."

Jordan had called the lab twice and had gotten the tried-and-true story of backlogs and understaffing. "I'll call again."

"Let me call the lab," Spencer said. "I'll let them know we have a second case. That'll move it along."

Jordan drew in a breath, shoving down her frustration. A word from a ranger could magically speed up the labs. "Terrific."

"We might have better luck identifying this victim," Dr. McIntyre said. "Her fingerprints are intact."

Her technician entered the room and opened the sterilized instrument packet before removing the sheet.

Since Jordan had joined homicide last year, she had found the autopsy the least appealing part of the job. The body, already violated by violence, was about to be torn apart in a manner that always left her stunned. The older detectives accepted it as a matter of course, and she hoped one day she would as well. In the interim, she kept her emotions in check. A startled or visibly sick detective did not instill confidence. And with Spencer here, she did not so much as shift her feet or flex her fingers.

The body was bloated and already starting to discolor, but now that the plastic was removed, Jordan had her first unobstructed view of the dead woman's face. She saw traces of an attractive woman under a twisted expression reflecting the victim's last minutes. Her lungs would have been heaving, her head swimming, and her muscles cramping as she struggled to breathe. Like drowning, she would have fought to move, free herself, and suck in air. Just like Avery.

"The subject is a Caucasian female, five foot two, one hundred pounds with blond hair." Dr. McIntyre pointed her finger to the loose skin dangling near the elbow. "There's some evidence she used drugs.

However, her teeth appear to be in good shape, suggesting the substance abuse was not extensive."

Rigor mortis had come and gone, so that when Dr. McIntyre went to the head, the neck muscles were pliable enough to turn right and left. The doctor noted there was bruising on the victim's jaw and a wound on the back of her head. "She was struck with a blunt object just above the base of her skull."

"Like the first one," Jordan said.

"Yes. Very similar wound patterns."

"That's how he subdues them," Jordan said.

Mrs. Penn had said nothing about hearing a woman scream. And there was only a single set of footprints leading into the house. She had been unconscious when he'd carried her inside.

"Any theories on the weapon?" Ranger Spencer asked.

The doctor inspected the wound more closely. "Like I said, blunt. There're traces of wood in the flesh," she said. "A baseball bat? A two-by-four?"

Ranger Spencer nodded. "A bat is transportable and not illegal."

"Nothing resembling a weapon was found at either scene," Jordan said. "Presumably there would be traces of the victim's blood on it."

Dr. McIntyre continued the external examination, noting two tattoos, an old scar, and several broken fingers on the victim's right hand. "These are most likely defensive wounds."

Next, the doctor opened the chest cavity with a Y incision. The body's slipping skin peeled back easily from the chest and belly. The internal organs appeared healthy, normal weight considering the decomposition, and there were no other wounds or bleeding that suggested additional trauma. A vaginal examination produced semen samples.

"The first semen samples from Jane Doe #1 were badly degraded, but there might be some DNA similarities to suggest it was the same man," Dr. McIntyre said.

Jordan would bet a month's pay the DNA from the semen would be a match. This had to be the same guy.

However, her beliefs or gut feelings were not evidence. And tunnel vision was a dangerous thing in police work. A cop who narrowed her focus often missed critical details that did not fit her theory. Her gaze dropped to the victim's slim wrists, bruised by restraints. It was hard not to make a hasty judgment.

The room was hushed and somber, with only Dr. McIntyre's classical music filling the silence. There was none of the easy cop banter between Jordan and Spencer. If she had been working with another detective, she would have made conversation about his weekend plans, the wife, the kids, anything to defuse her tension. People on the outside did not understand a cop's ability to chat about everyday life when faced with an autopsy. But they all needed ways to blow off steam.

When the autopsy was complete, Jordan and Spencer thanked the doctor and retreated to the locker room. Each silently stripped off their gown, gloves, and mask and washed their hands.

"Where do you go from here?" Ranger Spencer asked her.

He understood investigations and the natural order of things. She could have quipped that he should use his detective skills and tell her, but she simply said, "Forensics."

"I'll meet you there."

"I can give you a full report," she said.

He lifted his hat off the locker shelf and carefully traced the worn leather strip rimming the base. "There's something about seeing it for yourself. Details get lost in the translation."

"Let's be straight with each other, Ranger Spencer." She met his direct, dark gaze, which was as unwavering as a rattler's. "Have I been pulled from the case?"

"I'm here to consult."

He was here to take the case. Her boss was going to toss this football to the Rangers, who had more budget and reach across the state. "Well, until I see the papers with my own eyes, I've got a case to work."

***

Spencer did not consider himself a poacher. He did not go out of his way to stick it to another cop, especially one as competent as Detective Jordan Poe. She had been on the homicide team for only a year, but her closure rate was impressive. And before homicide, she had made a name for herself in drug interdiction.

But he was not here to protect feelings or let anyone down gently. This case had landed in his lap because he had worked two different serial killer cases. The first had been in Houston. Killer had drugged his victims, raped, and then strangled them. That killer, a truck driver, was now serving life without parole. The next three linked murders he'd investigated were in El Paso. Three Hispanic women had been beaten to death, their bodies dumped on the side of the highway, before he had tracked the killer down. Guy was a local pastor. Shit, the preacher had looked as pure as the driven snow when Spencer had arrived in his church office and placed the cuffs on his wrists.

Yes, Poe had an impressive closure rate, but according to Captain Lee, she had never tracked a killer like this.

Neither he nor Detective Poe spoke as they moved to their vehicles. He removed his hat, tossed it on the passenger seat, and started the engine. He knew the way to the forensic lab but followed Poe. Several times he had to run a yellow light to keep up with her. Was she trying to lose him? When he caught up to her at a stoplight, she was talking. He would wager big dollars she was complaining to her boss. He sure as hell would have been.

She beat him to the forensic lab and parked at the far end of the lot. He slid into the spot near her and got out of his car, then settled his Stetson on his head. In the distance a police siren wailed down a street. Poe strode toward the front door, leaving him behind as she moved with confidence. Her legs were long, her posture erect, and her gaze on the front door.

He easily overtook her and reached for the door, paused, and waited, then opened it as she approached. "Who are we meeting with?"

"Andy Lucas," she said as she stepped inside. "He's the forensic technician who has worked both scenes." As he followed, she walked toward the elevator doors and pressed the up button as if she had a grudge against it.

He'd been born and raised in Austin, but he had not lived here since he was eighteen, twenty-two years ago. Over the last two years he had familiarized himself with the new streets, the patrol officers' names, even the best places to get decent barbecue, but there was always something new to learn.

Six months ago, he had purchased a house twenty miles north of the city, where land was still affordable, and there he could take off the badge and be himself in his downtime. His tenure with the Department of Public Safety as a patrol officer and then the promotion to the Rangers had kept him on the move for the last decade. Austin was his last duty station, and he looked forward to putting down roots.

The elevator doors opened, and Detective Poe stepped past him into the car. He followed. He was a big man and knew his shoulders and braced legs took up a good bit of surface area, but he had always seen his size as an advantage. Most took a step back to give him room in tight spaces. Poe did not.

This close, he noticed those long legs brought her up to his shoulder, or roughly five nine. She kept her makeup sparse, but high cheekbones and full lips did not require much paint. He guessed she was in her early thirties, but her gaze displayed more life experiences than most had at her age.

The doors opened, and they made their way to the forensic lab, where she spotted a shorter man with a rounded face and belly. When she smiled at him, it was genuine, and it softened her angled features. Spencer noted faint crow's-feet feathered at the edges of her eyes, suggesting she either laughed often or squinted into the Texas sun too much. He was inclined to believe the latter.

"Andy, I'd like you to meet Texas Ranger Carter Spencer. Spencer, this is Andy Lucas, head of our forensic team."

Spencer extended his hand. "Officer Lucas."

Lucas's grip was strong and his gaze measured. "Good to meet you, Ranger Spencer. I don't think we've crossed paths before."

"I've been back in Austin a couple of years. Worked mostly drug cases."

"How do you like Austin?"

"I grew up here, but it's changed. There're streets and housing developments where they did not used to be. But Austin and I have been getting reacquainted," he said.

Detective Poe reached for her phone and glanced at the screen. Impatient, she appeared to be filling the time until Spencer and Lucas's meet and greet was over.

Lucas glanced at her and did not appear to be surprised by her vague irritation. "Let's have a look at what I have so far."

They followed him to a large room with a sizable light table in the center. There were two piles, and both contained plastic wrap, packing tape, and strips of knotted cord that had been cut. "We took these from both crime scenes. On the left is the evidence from the first scene and on the right, the second. Same brand of plastic, tape, and cord. This killer sticks with what works for him. All of this can be purchased at a hardware store or online and is going to be difficult to trace."

Spencer studied the evidence bag containing the cord restraints. They had been secured to the victim's hands with a constrictor knot.

Once in place, it would have been almost unbreakable. "He put a lot of thought into this murder."

Jordan squared her shoulders. "I spoke to the neighbor who lives across the street from the second crime scene." She updated him on the pickup truck circling the house and its status.

"He scopes out his kill houses beforehand. He's organized. Likely stashes his supplies there as well," Spencer said.

"Any sign of a blunt object?" Detective Poe asked. "Last we spoke you said no."

"Still correct," Lucas said. "We went over every square inch of the house and found nothing with blood on it."

"You said you had shoe impressions from the first scene," she said.

"Athletic shoes, size ten." He moved to a computer screen and pulled up an image of the shoe impression. "This was taken at scene number one and"—he pressed another key—"this was lifted at scene number two." Another press of a button and the images appeared side by side. "It's a Nike athletic shoe. Nothing remarkable about that, but if you blow up the image, you will see a noticeable nick on the outer side of the right foot. Shoes that have been worn enough develop their own unique print."

"Meaning it's the same shoe at both scenes," Detective Poe said.

"Correct."

"What about surveillance footage near the two murder scenes?" Spencer asked. "Beyond that one neighbor, were there cameras?"

"No cameras within five blocks of the first scene, and three blocks from the second," Detective Poe said. "I was surprised there were not more doorbell cameras."

The average person appeared on camera footage up to two hundred times a day. "If this killer had scoped out this area, then he would have noticed that. Supports the assumption that he doesn't want to be caught," Spencer said.

"He's having too much fun," Detective Poe said.

She was right. This killer's very brief cooling-off period suggested he could be on some kind of binge killing spree. And the murders were not going to stop until they caught him.

"What about fingerprints or DNA from the scene?" Spencer asked.

"There are fingerprints at both the first and second scenes. The prints at the first scene weren't usable, but we lifted a really good palm print from the second location's front door," Lucas said. "Just put it in AFIS, so we should have an answer soon."

"So why get sloppy the second time around?" Detective Poe asked. "He's not only left possible fingerprints, but he chose a location that was destined for renovation within days."

"Arrogant or sloppy? At this stage, it doesn't matter. Let me know if you get any hits on the print," Spencer said.

Spencer's phone rang. The display flashed Captain Lee's name. Turning from Detective Poe and Lucas, he raised the phone to his ear. "Ranger Spencer."

"Any progress?" The question frustrated Spencer. Lee was a cop, and he knew cases like this did not solve themselves overnight.

"No, sir." Spencer generally tacked *sir* on when he was annoyed.

"I'm getting pressure to hold a press conference," Captain Lee said.

"Who's pressing this?"

"The mayor. Several local media outlets want a statement. The bodies were found in two areas marked for urban renewal. Turns out the same guy has the contract to renovate both sites. He feels like he's being targeted and has friends in the governor's office."

"I believe Detective Poe spoke to the site manager, Manny Bennett. What's the developer's name?"

"Michael King," Captain Lee said.

King had been touted in the press often in recent weeks for his energy-efficient new houses and buildings. "I'd like to talk to him."

"I already have," Captain Lee said. "He has no idea why his properties have been singled out."

"Still, I want to talk to him," Spencer said.

"Let me put this bluntly. King has influential friends, and you and Detective Poe do not have reputations for tact."

Spencer looked back toward Detective Poe and caught her staring at him. She did not look away. "We'll play nice. Sir."

"First the news conference. Then you can talk to King."

Politics was a fact of life. In his younger days he'd bucked when faced with it, but now he saved his energy for the fights that mattered. And politics could be useful if handled correctly. "When?"

"Two hours. And Detective Poe needs to be there. I want this to look like a partnership between the Rangers and Austin Police. We need a show of unity."

"Where?" Spencer asked.

"Austin Police Department's conference room. The public information officer is setting it up now."

"There's still not much to say," Spencer said.

"I understand. But the image of you two standing side by side will be a visual sign of accord."

"Sure." He hung up and crossed back to Detective Poe, who he already had guessed ranked cooperation low on her priority list. "Your boss wants a press conference."

"Why?" she asked.

"Bodies were found at sites being developed by the same man. Press is ready to tell the city we have a serial killer in Austin."

She arched a brow. "So, we go make nice and play a little politics."

"Can you do that?" he asked.

A small smile tugged the edges of her lips. "I guess we'll find out."

CHAPTER SIX

Tuesday, April 13
1:00 p.m.

When Jordan returned to her desk, the missing person files were waiting for her. She sank into her chair, shifted her sunglasses to the top of her head, and slurped the remains of a soda from a drive-through meal.

There were six files in all, and according to a note from Detective Rivers, the women had gone missing in the last two months. Two were Hispanic, which she immediately set aside based on Dr. McIntyre's physical assessment of the victims. Of the remaining four, one was African American, which she also set aside. She looked at the three remaining profiles: Susan Wallace, Tammy Fox, and Rhonda Simms. The first two missing women were nineteen and twenty. Rhonda Simms was thirty-nine, short, and heavyset. She did not fit the profile of Jordan's two Jane Does.

She thumbed through Susan "Susie" Wallace's missing person report. She had last been seen in downtown Austin near Sixth Street. No known history of sex work. Had moved to Austin from Houston and failed to come home one night after she and her roommate went barhopping. The roommate, Sonya Jefferson, had filed the report eight weeks ago.

Tammy Fox's profile was almost identical. She lived close to Susie and had last been seen leaving her job as a waitress at a local bar, the Saloon, on Seventh Street last Friday. Her report had been called in by her boss.

Jordan flipped through the files and looked at the pictures of the missing women. Susie had red hair, but she could have dyed her hair blond like Jane Doe #1 or #2. Tammy's hair was blond, like both Jane Does, but given the timeline of her disappearance, she could only be the second victim.

When Jordan had been assigned to patrol, she had worked the downtown district near Sixth or Seventh Streets. On any Saturday night, it was flooded with tourists, students, and businesspeople looking for a good time. And there were plenty of drug dealers and sex workers to help them enjoy whatever pleasures they sought.

She keyed in on the bar where Tammy had worked. She remembered the Saloon well. Once she had dragged an underage Avery out of there. Her sister had argued that she was fine and had screamed that Jordan had embarrassed her. Five seconds later, Avery had puked in the alley.

Those had been tough days with Avery. Jordan had been in over her head. In her late twenties, she was not prepared to parent a troubled, defiant teenager. One of Avery's counselors had recommended that Jordan see a therapist herself. She had laughed at first but relented when too many sleepless nights were eating away at her. The therapist, Dr. Rogan Malone, had been a pretty chill guy and was an expert in substance abuse. He had been a sounding board and had offered advice when asked. She had visited him almost weekly for four years. As she learned in sessions, Avery's problems were a symptom of something bigger. The loss of their mother had marked them both. Jordan coped by working too much, whereas Avery abused substances. Both sisters had no close relationships, and both had a habit of choosing unavailable men.

A year ago, Jordan and Rogan had run into each other. She had still been reeling from Avery's near suffocation, and because they no longer had a professional relationship, she'd found a way to justify their brief affair. Rogan had understood her romantic track record and should have predicted that the relationship would not last. Still, he had seemed surprised when she ended it after a month.

She glanced at the clock. Time to get down to the press room. She pulled her hair out of its bun, combed it out, and repinned it. She grabbed lip gloss from her desk drawer, applied it while peering into a small mirror, and then pulled on her jacket. She arrived in the conference room ten minutes before the show.

Spencer and Captain Lee were already there and talking. The ranger did not look happy, but then she doubted he ever did. She made a mental note to ask around about him.

Television reporters had come from all the major local stations. For the newspapers, the *Statesman* and *Chronicle* were represented. This was more attention than any of her other cases had ever received.

Captain Lee motioned her forward, and he positioned her on his left and Spencer on his right. Jordan squared her shoulders, tried to accept this was part of being a cop, but impatience jabbed her.

Captain Lee cleared his throat. What followed was a rehash of the few scant details they had cobbled together. Young women. Petite. Strangled. Wrapped in plastic. The detail he left out was the plastic bag over the victims' heads. Cops often left out a detail that only the killer knew. It could be the ace in a cop's pocket.

Spencer spoke next. He assured everyone that the Texas Rangers were the lead on this case now. More updates would follow.

Jordan was not called to the podium, which basically told her she was officially sidelined. In all honesty, the spotlight was not her happy place, and she preferred working in the shadows. The less she was noticed, the more effective she could still be on this case. If either man had assumed she was backing away, he would be incorrect.

"Detective Poe, do you think this killer will strike again?" The question came from an evening television reporter, Angela Richards.

If Jordan and the reporter were friends, she might be honest and say he would. But to admit it publicly not only would create worry in the community but also could be laying down a challenge to the killer. "Our focus remains on solving the two cases we have now. And as I always do, I advise everyone to take the standard safety precautions when they're in public."

Though true, it was basically an unsexy comment too boring to garner any headlines.

After the press conference ended, the reporters came toward the podium as if to get a juicy off-the-record comment, but Lee only thanked them all and ushered Jordan and Spencer back behind closed doors.

She waited for Spencer to leave before she turned to Lee. "You're taking this case from me, Captain Lee?" Jordan asked.

Annoyance and hints of regret flashed on his features. He did not want a fight. "It's better for all of us if the Rangers take over."

"Why? You haven't given me a chance," she said. "We haven't even identified the bodies."

"You show promise, but there's no substitute for practical experience in fieldwork," Captain Lee said.

"Then let me work with Spencer," she said. "We can partner for the duration of this case."

"It's not your case anymore, Detective Poe. Let it go."

"That certainly would make it easy for you, wouldn't it?" she said. "If the Rangers fail, there's no blowback on you. If I fail, then it looks bad on you."

"Detective Poe," Captain Lee warned. "Don't press this."

"My closure rate is one of the highest in the department," she countered.

"It's a done deal, Detective Poe." Captain Lee was just as stubborn, and she would have more luck beating her head against a brick wall than arguing for this case. "I understand you're frustrated. Take the rest of the day."

Her teeth clenched, she said, "I don't need a break."

"Cool off before you cross a line with me. I'm your boss."

She was digging herself into a hole, and if it got much deeper, she would be riding a desk for the next six months. "Sure."

When she left Captain Lee, she was furious. Christ, this was not the Dark Ages, when a female detective was an oddity. But Captain Lee was a political animal by nature, and his agenda extended far beyond her sex and this case.

"What's the deal with the press conference?" The question came from Detective Leo Santiago. He had been transferred to homicide eleven months ago. He worked hard, was motivated to close cases, and was easy to work with.

"You saw it?"

"We all did." Santiago had served in the marines before joining the Austin Police Department. They had the same rank, but he was several years younger. He was a paint-by-numbers guy who liked his shirts starched and ties fastened tight. He also had a perfect smile that got him the pick of the ladies.

"Then you know as much as I do," she said. "Rangers have the case. Win some, lose some."

"Spencer's one of the best."

"Let's hope he gets justice for those women."

She grabbed her purse, left Santiago standing by her desk, and crossed the parking lot in quick, clipped steps. When she reached for her car door handle, she hesitated and tipped her face to the sun. Drawing in deep breaths, she considered her options. She could go home and work out in her garage gym, or she could stop by the Saloon and find out what the manager knew about Tammy Fox.

In her car, she switched on the engine, opened her window a fraction, and waited for the air-conditioning to kick in. It was 3:00 p.m. The Saloon likely was not open, but if it was the same manager she remembered, the crew was prepping for the evening. There was also Susie's roommate, who had called in the missing person report. Jordan opted to start with Sonya Jefferson, the roommate, who according to the missing person report also worked evenings at the Saloon.

She easily found Susie's apartment building in East Austin. It had seen better days, but she guessed the rent was manageable in a city with exploding rates. She entered the front door and climbed to the second floor. She knocked hard on the door, but there was no answer. She pulled a business card from her pocket, scribbled *Call me*, and shoved it in the doorjamb.

It took her thirty minutes to find parking near the Saloon on Sixth Street. Though it had been fashioned to look like an Old West saloon, it was new construction. There had been a lot of rehab in the city in the last few years. Old had been torn down for the new.

The front door was locked. She banged on it. The lights were on inside, but she did not see anyone. She knocked louder. Finally, a man appeared from a back room and shouted, "We don't open until five."

She pressed her badge against the window. "Got some questions for you."

The man muttered under his breath and, pulling a bar towel from his shoulder, crossed the room and opened the lock. The guy was midsize with a rounded belly, and he wore a lightweight plaid shirt, jeans held up with a tarnished rodeo belt, and brown cowboy boots.

"I'm Detective Poe."

"Do I know you?" he asked.

"You're Dustin Tate. The bar manager."

"How do you know that?"

"Found my sister here five years ago. Underage and drunk."

Mr. Tate held up his hands. "Shit. I've not seen your sister."

"I'm not looking for her. And I'm not here to make trouble. Just have a few questions. May I come inside?"

"Yeah, sure." He stepped back, glancing at the clock as if her visit were already costing him time he did not have.

Jordan pulled out a picture of Tammy and another of Susie. "These two women went missing recently. Do you recognize either of these women?"

"I know Tammy. I called the police when she didn't show up for work last Saturday. That's not like her."

"What can you tell me about Tammy?"

"She's worked here for about six months. Friendly. Customers like her. Not like her to flake."

"You're a very conscientious employer."

"What's that mean?"

"Girls like Tammy come and go from hourly jobs like this one. You called her in as missing within forty-eight hours."

"Like I said, she worked hard, seemed to keep her nose clean. I was thinking about offering her more work."

Tammy had also been beautiful, and it did not hurt to have someone like her flirting with customers. "You two have something between you?"

"I keep the business and personal stuff separate." He shifted his feet, rested his hands on his hips. "I don't want to know what my employees do, and I don't want them knowing my business."

"It's not a crime to date an employee. She was of legal age." She leaned forward. "I'll ask everyone in this bar if you two had a thing, if I have to."

"Fine, we had been going out for a couple of months. But I don't need that getting around."

"Married?"

"In the middle of a divorce. Don't need to fuel the fire."

"Fair enough. What about surveillance footage?" Jordan asked.

"It goes back about a month," Tate said. "Guess you want me to pull it?"

"That would be helpful."

"That's hundreds of hours of footage."

"I got the time," she said.

"My bookkeeper does all the computer stuff, and she won't be in until later. I'll have her call you when she has the disk."

"Thanks. What's her name?"

"Marian Dawson."

"Great."

"Do you really think Tammy is in trouble? I thought maybe she had started using again and needed help."

"That could be the case. But I have a couple of Jane Does at the morgue. Tammy fits the general description. It's a long shot, but she could be one of them. What about Sonya Jefferson?"

"She works nights. She was in last night. Has the next two days off."

"You have her number?"

"I'll have the bookkeeper send it to you."

"Thanks."

He shook his head. "Too many girls come here thinking it's all going to be fun and adventure."

"And it is, until it's not."

"Speaking of which, how's your sister?"

"Sober. Living a good life."

"One of the lucky ones."

"So far, yeah. Thanks, Mr. Tate."

Jordan left the bar and, in her car, started her engine as she stared down the block. Killers, like anybody else, were creatures of habit. They not only had their favorite types of victims but were also partial to murder methods and hunting grounds.

***

Casey Andrews folded the job application as she left Thompson's Market on Sixth Street. She was feeling good about herself. Clean sixty-one days and on the verge of getting a real job. The store owner, Mr. Rawlings, had liked her. She could tell by the way he had trouble hiding a smile when he talked to her.

She was good looking, and it might be an unfair advantage to the others applying, but she would take whatever she could get. As she crossed the street, she thought about the NA meeting that was going on right now. It might not be a bad idea to stop in.

As she moved down the street, she spotted Marco Walker. He leaned against a wall and was talking to a young woman, who looked strung out. She had heard he was in jail. *How did he get out?*

She turned to cross the street.

"Casey!" Marco shouted. "You're not going to visit an old friend?"

If she was going to be working at Thompson's Market, Marco would see her often, and he could make her life difficult. Better to make nice and not rock the boat.

Gripping her purse strap, she turned to him, smiling now. "Marco."

He strode toward her, his gait relaxed. Nothing ever seemed to rattle the guy. "I haven't seen you lately."

"I thought you were locked up."

"Was, and now I'm not."

"Well, glad you got out. Be seeing you." She turned.

"What're you doing down here?" Marco fell in step beside her.

"Getting a job."

He snapped the application from her hands and read it. "You're going to be a shopgirl." He was laughing at her.

"Something like that." She grabbed the application back.

He looked her up and down, leering, reminding her of what she had traded for her last hit. "I can see you being a shopgirl. Good customer service."

She gripped her purse tighter. "Thanks."

"I'm heading to a party. Do you want to come?"

"No, thanks. I need to catch my bus home."

He sniffed, looked from left to right. "Let me give you a ride. No need to take the bus."

"That's okay."

"I insist." His tone sharpened. "Unless you think you're too good for me."

She did not need the trouble. And a ride was not going to kill her. "Sure, Marco, that would be nice."

"That's my girl." He removed a key fob from his pocket, clicked, and the lights of a black Mercedes winked. He opened the door and waited like a gentleman for her to take her seat.

The interior was filled with the new-car smell, and the seats were super soft. Marco always did like the good stuff. He slipped behind the wheel and started the engine.

"Got something for you." Before she could respond, he tossed a baggie filled with a white substance on her lap.

"What's this?"

He grinned. They both knew exactly what it was.

"I don't want it."

"Just keep it. For a rainy day."

This was the time to open the car door, get out, and leave the bag behind. But as she stared at the white powder, an old hunger rose up in her. Her mind shrank from the job, her sobriety, and the future to the small baggie. She slipped it in her purse, promising herself she would flush it down the toilet as soon as she got home.

Marco pulled into traffic. "That's my girl."

CHAPTER SEVEN

Tuesday, April 13
4:45 p.m.

Jordan had learned that Tammy Fox had also worked part-time at Thompson's Market near the center of town as a cashier before taking the job at the Saloon. Jordan was in Thompson's at least once a week but could not picture the woman.

When Jordan pushed through the front door of the grocery store, small bells rang overhead. The store carried the exotic grocery items, expensive cuts of meat, and name-brand spices that appealed to the newest residents in the area. There was also an extensive take-out section, which came in handy after a long day. The prices stretched the bounds of her pay grade, but food was one luxury splurge she could justify. Fifteen dollars for a small cut of salmon and twenty dollars for exotic cheeses. These were the kinds of foods Avery loved. The kid had always rolled large, and she had never been quite happy with Jordan's discount take-out pizza or five-dollar all-you-can-eat Chinese food buckets. But when Jordan had brought home Thompson's takeout, Avery had been front and center.

Jordan strolled past the cashier, a young guy who was about nineteen or twenty, and went toward the prepared-food section.

A man came from the back room and smiled at her over the sparkling display case. He was a stout man, midforties, with strong hands and a full chest that filled out his white T-shirt and white apron. "Detective Poe. Good to see you. What can I get you?"

"Hey, Mr. Rawlings. I'll take a rotisserie chicken." Organic cost thirteen dollars for a small bird. But it was enough to feed her twice or her and Avery once.

"Coming right up."

He picked a fancy container and set a fresh chicken in the bottom before sealing it up. "Can I interest you in a side or two?"

"How about the roasted potatoes?" Another side and she would be eating peanut butter and jelly for the next week.

He handed the package to her in an upscale plastic bag she would probably save and use for something because it was too nice to toss away. "Here you go."

"Thanks," she said. "Hey, I have a question, Mr. Rawlings."

"Shoot."

A wry grin tugged her lips. "I've been assigned a missing person case." Not technically true but close enough. "The woman's name is Tammy Fox."

"Tammy. Good kid. If you're investigating, she's not been here in a couple of weeks."

"I was hoping if I spoke to people she knew, I might jog some memories."

He leaned on the glass display top. "A solid worker," he said. "Talked all the time about making a home here. I was thinking about promoting her to assistant manager. She got me into donating the store's extra food at the end of the day to the shelter."

Avery had spent time in the nearby shelter. She had just turned eighteen and decided Jordan's rules were too harsh. "And then she quit?"

"Yeah. It came out of the blue. She said she could make better money cocktail waitressing and would have more time for her artwork. I hated to lose her, but the kids who work here never stay long."

"Did she have any friends?"

"Kids who've stayed at the shelter and other artists."

"Where was she from?"

"She never said, but I think she had a substance-abuse problem. She was never high here, and it seemed like all that was in the past. I didn't think her move to the Saloon was a good idea."

Junkies fell off the wagon all the time. Years of sobriety could be wiped out with one bad choice, which could tip them into a death spiral. For all Jordan knew, Tammy was in a flophouse with a needle in her arm. Or she could have moved back to wherever she came from. Impulse control could be an issue for addicts.

She pulled a business card from her pocket. "Can you call me if you think of anything? I'd like to find her."

"I hope you do find her. Be nice to know she's doing okay," he said as he came around the counter. "Let me walk you to the front. I want to tell the cashier that your order is on the house."

"You don't have to do that."

"I want to," he said easily. "It's the least I can do."

As they approached the register, he said to the kid, "Richie, this is Detective Poe. She's looking for Tammy."

The kid swiped back a thick lock of hair. "Wow, I didn't know she was missing."

"Did you know her well?" Jordan asked.

"Sure, we sometimes took our breaks together, and I helped her deliver our extra food to the shelter."

"Richie or I still coordinate the deliveries," Mr. Rawlings said.

"Mr. Rawlings, did you make deliveries with Tammy as well?" Jordan asked.

"Sure. She liked going. Half the time, she knew a few of the residents, and they chatted while we unloaded."

"Did she ever talk about herself?" Jordan asked.

"Not to me," Rawlings said. "What about you, Richie?"

"A little," Richie said.

"And?" Jordan prompted.

"Feels weird talking about her," Richie said.

"I'm trying to help her," Jordan said.

"She had a boyfriend in Houston. She broke up with him, and that's why she came to Austin. To get away. He used to hit her."

"Did you get a name?"

"She never would say. And she only talked about him once. Then she seemed to catch herself and didn't say more."

"Did she do drugs?"

"She smoked cigarettes, but that's all I saw."

Cigarettes elevated the dopamine levels in the brain, which calmed the nerves. Jordan knew some addicts and people with mental illness smoked regularly as a form of self-medication.

"Did she ever talk about leaving?"

"No," Richie said. "In fact, we were supposed to go to a movie. It was an artsy kind of thing. She was into art. She would set up her easel on Sixth Street and sometimes sketched people for money."

Avery had done the same. Maybe the two had crossed paths.

Jordan showed them both a picture of Susie Wallace. "Either of you ever see her?"

Both men studied the picture, and both shook their heads. "We haven't seen her," Rawlings said.

"Never," Richie said.

"Call me if you think of anything." She handed another card to Richie.

The kid glanced at the card and frowned. "It says you're with homicide. Do you think she's dead?"

"I hope not. Either way, I want to know what happened to her. If you two should hear from her . . ."

"We'll call," Rawlings said.

"Thanks." She left the store, and as she approached her car and saw the long gash, she thought about Sunday and Walker. "Bastards."

The inside of the vehicle quickly filled with the scents of herbed chicken and roasted potatoes. She checked her phone, saw no messages from anyone she had left a card with, so she decided to drive home. Good day to get a workout in.

Ten minutes later she pulled into her gravel driveway and grabbed her purse and food. Out of the car, she looked around the yard, realizing it needed cutting. She could not remember the last time she had been home early on a workday. Well, she could at least knock out the yard today.

As she approached the front door, she heard the beat of music. Avery was here? The arrival of her sister was welcome, if not unexpected. Right now, silence would have left her to her own thoughts.

Smiling, she wondered if her sister had smelled Thompson's chicken and roasted potatoes. "Avery, is that you?"

When she closed the front door, the music stopped.

"Yeah, thought I'd stop by."

Avery had not stopped by for two years. After the last time she had used, she had moved out, needing to tackle sobriety alone. She had found a sober house and focused on restarting her life. Jordan had hated it that Avery was not home, but Avery had insisted. In time, she had gotten the job at the café, saved her money, found a small room to rent, all the while staying clean.

As much as Jordan liked the idea that her sister was here, an alarm bell sounded. "Everything all right?"

Avery appeared around a corner with a dish towel in her hand. She wore loose athletic shorts, a Texas T-shirt, and her blond hair pulled up in a ponytail. "Can't a sister visit a sister?"

"Yes, but . . ."

"Just needed a little grounding. Family time."

To ask if this had anything to do with the Jane Doe cases risked chasing Avery off. "Fair enough. Where's your car?"

"Lent it to a friend. He dropped me off here and said he'd bring it by in the morning."

Sounded like a simple explanation, but Avery had lent her car out before to friends who needed a clean ride to pick up drugs. "Good to have you."

"What are you doing home early? Has the world come to an end?"

"No. Got booted off a case, and the boss thought I needed a quiet afternoon to collect myself."

Avery arched a brow. "Detective, did your temper show?"

"A little."

Jordan removed her sidearm and locked it in the drawer of a handmade entrance table she had found in Fredericksburg a couple of years ago. "I come bearing food."

Avery surveyed the bag, and her eyes filled with questions. "For you to shop there means it was a rough day. It's crazy expensive. And you only treat yourself when times are tough."

"I was asking questions about a missing girl at the Saloon and also Thompson's Market and thought I'd buy dinner. The storekeeper gave it to me for free."

"Who were you asking about?"

"Tammy Fox."

"Seriously?"

"You know her?"

"Yeah. We went to meetings together. She's also into art."

"When's the last time you saw her?" Jordan asked.

"Over a month."

"What is she like?" Jordan asked.

"She was struggling the last time I saw her."

"Struggling with sobriety?"

"That and making money. She left Thompson's and took a job at the Saloon because it paid better. I didn't think it was a good idea. Bars are too tempting on a lot of levels. She said it was only temporary, but it takes only a second to stumble.

"I can ask around, if you like. There're people out there who won't talk to you but will confide in me."

Jordan's first reaction was to say no. She did not like Avery being exposed to her work. Then she reminded herself Avery had lived more in her twenty-four years than most young adults. "That would be great. Any and all help is welcome. But please be careful."

"I'll be careful." Avery took the bag and glanced inside. "This looks amazing. Better than the frozen pizza I was considering cooking for us. You really need to go to the grocery store."

"I just rarely have the time." Jordan shrugged off her jacket and hung it in the entryway closet. "Serve us up a couple of plates, and I'll change."

"I saw Mr. Rawlings at the food bank the other day," Avery said. "Seems like a good guy."

"Seems?"

A half smile quirked her lips. "You know I have trust issues."

Jordan laughed. "Join the club."

In her bedroom, Jordan stripped off her boots, shirt, jeans, and bra, which she swapped for shorts and a T-shirt. She would eat, cut the grass, and then go into her garage and work out on the CrossFit system she'd had installed last year.

Avery set up two place settings and folded paper towels for napkins. "I thought given the takeout from Thompson's, we should make it special."

"I could do that." She went to the refrigerator and grabbed two sodas. Another late-afternoon anomaly, but why not? She'd sweat it off cutting grass.

They each served up a healthy portion of chicken and potatoes. Avery took a bite and closed her eyes, moaning softly. "So good. You've made my day."

"Glad I could make somebody's."

"So, what case got you in hot water with Captain Lee?"

"The boss gave my case to the Rangers. He thinks we have a serial killer."

"As in Tammy was killed by someone like that?"

"Maybe. I don't know. She fits the profile."

"Tammy worked at Thompson's Market."

"I know. How was that?"

"I guess fine. She never said." She stabbed a potato. "Why would Lee give your case away?"

"The ranger in question has experience in cases like this. The captain doesn't want an unsolved serial killer case on his record."

"I can't think of anyone other than you who would want to solve it more."

"I can't, either, but in the end, the captain's opinion is what matters."

"Sucks."

"Yep."

"Can't you run fingerprints or DNA or something on these bodies?"

Jordan pushed a potato around with her fork. "Not enough of the first one left to get a fingerprint. And DNA takes time. We might have better luck with the second."

"Dental records?"

A slight smile tugged at Jordan's lips. "I'm rubbing off on you."

Avery shrugged. "Maybe."

"If we can get a name, then we can search for and then request dental records to confirm an identification. If either victim had a dental implant, we could trace the serial number. But neither has had serious dental work done."

Avery was quiet for a moment. "Why wasn't there enough left of the first victim?"

"That's not dinner conversation."

"It is in this house," Avery said easily.

Jordan had tried not to bring her work home, but that was impossible on the really tough days when a case troubled her as this one did. "This topic is better suited for an empty stomach."

"You don't need to baby me."

"I know." Suddenly memories of the dead woman wrapped in plastic transposed with the day she'd found Avery suffocating to death. "By the way, have you found your phone?"

"What makes you think I lost it?" Avery asked.

"I'm a detective."

"It's in my apartment, somewhere. I'll find it." Avery jabbed her fork in a potato and stared at the spud jutting from the end. "What do you think about me joining the police academy? I know I make art and work in a café, but neither job pays much, and one day I would like to make a difference."

Jordan pictured her sister wearing a uniform. It did not jibe with the streak of blue in her blond hair or her multicolored peasant top. "What brought this on?"

"I see what you do. You help people. And I know there're forensic artists. I thought I could mingle art and the law."

"It's a very structured training routine."

"It'll be an adjustment, but change is good, right?"

Jordan studied her sister. "This isn't a trial balloon, is it? You've put a lot of thought into joining the academy. It's why you're here tonight."

Avery ate the potato and took her time chewing it. "I've read up on what it takes to be a police officer. My history of drug use could ruin it all for me."

After the last couple of days, Jordan had not thought there was much that could surprise her. But there it was. "You've been sober two years."

"Plus one month and two days."

"You're really serious."

"Yeah. The plan was to work at the café until mid-August and then apply to the academy. The pay is decent, and it comes with benefits. I can't stay on your health care forever."

"How long have you been thinking about this?"

"A few months. But if I can't overcome the drug thing, it's academic."

"You don't have a police record."

"Thanks to you, but I did use. That question is front and center on the application."

"I can put in a word." She doubted there was much she could do. Two years clean was impressive, but drugs were a hurdle she doubted the department would overlook. "Nothing ventured, nothing gained."

"Can't work in the café forever."

Hard not to respect ambition. "Fair enough. I'll make calls if that helps."

"Thanks."

"I'm proud of you."

Avery shrugged, but there was a lightness about her Jordan had not seen in a while. "How did the victims die?"

Jordan sat back, slowly picked up her fork, and then detailed some of the facts.

Avery's gaze was unflinching, but the color in her face faded a little. "Do you think they'll ever be identified?"

"I don't know. I hope so. I'll send an email tonight to the medical examiner and tell her about Tammy Fox."

"What about the ranger? You going to tell him?"

She thought about standing at that press briefing, feeling more like window dressing than a cop. This was not the first case taken from a detective and turned over to the state. But it was a first for her, and it pissed her off.

"If Dr. McIntyre can match Tammy Fox to either Jane Doe, then the doc will tell Spencer. If there's no match, it doesn't matter."

"I thought you were a team player?" Avery asked.

"This isn't a game of kickball, and I'm not begging anyone to let me play on their side."

Avery regarded her with curiosity. "This doesn't sound like you. Why does this case bother you so much?" Before Jordan could answer, Avery cocked her head. "It's personal because of what happened to me."

"Cases aren't supposed to get personal, but as you'll find out if you become a cop, they sometimes do." Jordan rose and grabbed a second soda from the refrigerator. "Do you think back to that night?"

"Sure. More often than I should." Avery set down her fork and sat back. "I was feeling so good about myself that night. I hadn't used in months. I thought this was the time I would get and stay clean. And then Walker showed up. He always has a way of making you feel foolish if you don't do what he wants. He gave me the drugs, and I put them in my pocket. I had no intention of using them."

"And I found them. And we got into a hell of a fight."

"I took off, found Walker, and the next thing I know, I'm on the floor of that apartment, and he's tying me up."

"Did he shove the plastic in your mouth?"

"I don't know. I passed out. When I woke up, I couldn't breathe."

"Had Walker done anything like this before to you?"

"No." She looked up as if trying to control her emotions. "I thought I was going to die, and then you appeared out of nowhere. Why did you come looking for me?"

"I was worried. You were so angry when you ran off, and I felt terrible."

Questions could trigger bad memories, and normally she shied away from the past with Avery. But given the two dead Jane Does, looking back was necessary. Jordan sat quiet, trying once again not to imagine what had happened before she had arrived. "It's in the past."

"Yeah," Avery said. "The past."

***

Jordan had spent the next two hours cutting the grass, edging the yard, and digging up several plants killed by drought. Next, she had worked out for more than an hour. After a hot shower, she had fallen into bed, her body exhausted. Avery had asked to stay the night, and Jordan had readily agreed. Her sister was in her old room, sleeping. Safe and sound.

This should have been a night when Jordan slept well and hard. Instead, she stared into the darkness, worrying over her sister's safety and wondering if it really was wise for Avery to ask questions on the street about Tammy. They both knew the world where Tammy and Walker lived was dangerous and full of traps to trip her up.

Then she reminded herself that Avery looked good, and she was thinking about the future. She wanted to help, and she was here. Both were firsts.

But Jordan's mind would not turn off. This case amounted to dozens of puzzle pieces that had yet to form a clear picture.

Jordan shifted to her side, punched her pillow, and then rolled on her back.

Instead of counting sheep, she inventoried her puzzle pieces. The two corner pieces were the two Jane Does, each kidnapped, sexually assaulted, and suffocated. The other pieces were drug issues. Each, like Avery, had a history of drug use and had lived or worked in Marco Walker's territory. These fragments might not fill in the center of the entire picture, but right now they felt like they belonged somewhere.

It made sense to pay a visit to Marco Walker. She could confirm he had not jumped bail. And if she could keep her cool, she could ask about the missing women, who shared too many similarities with Avery, and maybe find out why the hell he had tied her sister up two years ago.

Maybe if she could keep her cool. Controlling her temper with Walker was a big damn ask right now.

CHAPTER EIGHT

Wednesday, April 14
2:30 a.m.

Casey had not intended to take the drugs. She had planned to ignore Walker and had nearly thrown the baggie away a dozen times. Then she had texted her friend Missy, who told her she would be crazy to toss it. And each time the little bag dangled over a toilet or sink, she could not bring herself to dump it.

Walker: Did you try it?

Casey: No.

Walker: But you want to. I know you, girl. What would one time hurt?

Casey: I've been clean for two months.

Walker: You can handle this. Live a little.

When Casey did not respond, he added, I can hear your brain working.

Casey: I want to be good.

Walker: You are good, baby. Park in the alley, like you used to. It's safe there. And I'm close if you need me.

Casey: Maybe.

Maybe she had been expecting a moment like this all along. Otherwise, why keep two phones—one for her mother and the one Walker had just texted on.

She should toss the second phone and the drugs. But there were still thirty-three minutes left on the dealer phone, and it seemed wasteful to toss it. And sobriety was hard, and she never knew when she might need a break from the stress. Walker had once called keeping a stash hedging her bets.

When she finally crossed a mental line, she sneaked out of her mother's house, called an Uber, and rode into Austin to Seventh Street. Out of the car, she saw a couple of sex workers on the corner, talking to potential clients. Music from a bar pulsed.

"Casey, is that you?" one of the girls shouted.

Casey did not respond.

"Good to have you back, girl." Laughter rumbled around them. "Walker is going to be glad to have you back."

Gripping the handle of her purse, Casey walked toward the old building where she used to hang out. It was an abandoned retail store. The racks, counters, and display shelves had long been stripped, and in their places now were crates and a few mattresses. A few people huddled in corners, each staring at her, but she kept her gaze averted, her purse clutched tightly to her body. She found an empty corner, sat, and pressed her back to the wall. She unfurled her fist and stared at the powder. She could handle one hit.

One hit will not hurt.

Just one.

You can handle this.

Her drug counselor, Dr. Malone, always said the devil's voice was so sweet it could convince anyone of anything. He had warned against listening.

But she did not see the harm in using this one time.

Just once, and then she would be back on the straight and narrow.

It took less than five minutes to heat up and inject the drug into her vein. Immediately, it hit her system, and her head fell back against the wall.

Suddenly, she felt safe here. She was far from her mother, and if anyone saw her now, they would not give her a second glance.

In the darkness, she was protected as the world drifted away. She felt so good. At peace. Like her old self. Yeah, she had broken her sober streak, but that did not seem so terrible right now. She would get back on track first thing tomorrow. Time began to slip away, and her eyes drifted closed.

Someone jostled her, and when she looked up, she was staring into the eyes of a man she did not recognize. He was wearing a black bandanna over his face, but his eyes were vivid and sharp. Maybe it was the devil come to check on his handiwork.

"A little birdie told me you were here," he said.

His voice was smooth and soothing.

"Go away," she said.

"How does it feel?" he asked. "Do you feel whole? Satisfied?"

She shrugged, suddenly hating to be seen like this. She tried to focus her blurred gaze. "I don't know what you're talking about."

"I know the feeling. Once you've tasted pure pleasure, you can't think of anything else. I've tried to stop, but I can't."

"I can stop."

"No, you can't. We're the same, you and me."

"No."

"It's time we go."

"I'm not going anywhere with you."

He took her by the arm. His fingers bit deep into her flesh as he hauled her to her feet.

She staggered. "I don't want this. It was a mistake."

"You can't help yourself. And neither can I."

"Leave me alone."

He pushed her forward. "I want to. But I can't."

The edge of determination in his voice reminded her of herself. "No."

She stumbled a couple of steps forward. Time to get the hell out of here. Another step and she heard the rush of air seconds before she felt the crushing blow on the back of her head. Her world went black.

***

Spencer had worked late, not pushing away from the desk until after 2:00 a.m., when he finally decided he would be no good to anyone if he did not get a few hours of sleep. So he had driven the thirty minutes north and pushed through the front door of his home. After a shower, he lay in bed, only to discover sleep did not come as easily as he had hoped. When it finally came, it was a light, restless sleep, filled with tangled images of two dead women and Jordan Poe.

When he rose with the sun, he was firing on a few more cylinders as he stood, coffee in hand, at the back window of his Liberty Hill home. He stared out over the patchy green grass, firepit, and large mesquite trees now shrouded in a thick layer of fog. The house itself was rough and likely had not been updated since the eighties, but it had come with land. Though the house and land required his time, neither made him feel guilty nor reminded him of his failures.

He refilled his travel mug and, on his phone, checked local media sites for any coverage of the case. Two stations and the papers had picked it up. The reporters had spit out the basic details given at yesterday's meeting. One article featured a picture of him at the podium, Lee and Poe behind him. Poe was looking at him, and her expression was intense. If looks could kill.

Another article had gone so far as to describe the bodies being wrapped "King Tut" or "mummy" style. They were the kind of monikers that boiled a case down to a noun that was easy to picture but missed the mark on a number of levels. Still, if a nickname prompted someone to call the new tip line with a legitimate lead, it would be worth it. Tip calls were rarely productive because people misread what they saw; there were crackpots and, his very favorite, the psychics. But the one diamond in the rough would make the hours of confused, crank, or crazy calls worth it.

Next he checked email, scanning quickly until he spotted one from Detective Poe to Dr. Faith McIntyre. Poe had copied him.

The doctor's reply was addressed to both Jordan Poe and him. *Detective Poe, I just received the arrest records for Tammy Fox and Susan Wallace and will cross-check their DNA and fingerprints against the two Jane Does. I'll update you soon on my findings.*

He was not surprised Jordan was still working the case, but he did not like it.

He hit "Reply All" and ordered the DNA and fingerprint findings directed to him. "I'll give you this one, Poe," he said. "But that's it."

Irritated, he dropped his gaze to the crime scene photos from the first Jane Doe "Mummy" murder. He had not walked that crime scene yet, and now that the case was his, he needed to see it for himself. The department had put a hold on renovation on the property, but the longer he lingered, the angrier Mr. King would get, and the likelier the crime scene would be compromised.

He grabbed his hat and strode toward his vehicle. He drove southeast toward the initial scene where Jane Doe #1 had been found. In early-morning commuter traffic, the drive took him thirty minutes. When he arrived in Southeast Austin, the sun was already warming the morning air and burning off the fog. Out of the car, he settled his Stetson on his head and carried the crime scene photos in a manila folder. He strode across the dirt and scrub grass toward the old house. The crime scene tape had been ripped off the front door and dangled in a slight breeze. It was impossible to contain a crime scene unless a uniformed officer was posted on-site, and given the staffing constraints, that was not possible.

He opened the door, and stale air, still ripe with decomposition, rushed toward him. He opened the folder and compared the image of the wrapped naked body lying on the wide-plank wood floor to the empty room before him. This house was similar to the second scene, and given the mode of murder, the killer had already decided on a distinct pattern and victim type.

He walked the room, his footsteps thudding against the wooden floor. In the distance, traffic mingled with the shouts of someone calling for a friend.

Rubbing his chin, he squatted by the stain on the floor left by the decomposing body and compared it to the picture taken by the forensic technician. In several of the shots, Jordan Poe stood in the background, her arms crossed, her face grim. She did not strike him as a tender soul, but he sensed this one troubled her deeply.

Rising, he flipped through the pictures to the second scene. The two crime scenes were damn near interchangeable. He had submitted the case details to the FBI's ViCAP and CODIS systems, hoping this killer had struck in another jurisdiction or had had his DNA collected. No matches yet, but that could change.

He walked out the back of the house toward a small garage. Lucas had documented tire tracks and identified them as all-terrain tires, which could very well fit the blue pickup truck a witness had spotted near the second crime scene. If the truck was an older model, it would not have GPS and would not be trackable. He hoped, given the BOLO issued on the truck, that the killer was rote enough to keep using it.

He pictured the killer parking in the garage, pulling the unconscious victim from the bed, and carrying her into the house. In the quiet of the night, he would have several hours of privacy to toy with his victim.

Spencer passed back through the house, locked the front door, and returned to his vehicle. He called the Austin Police's missing person division and found his call routed to Detective Marla Rivers. They traded quick introductions, and he got to the meat of his call.

"I need a rundown on two missing person cases that interested Detective Poe: Tammy Fox and Susan Wallace."

"Sure." Papers shuffled and computer keys clicked. Detective Rivers gave him an abbreviated version of what were likely slim case files. "Was Detective Poe able to link either of these cases to her Jane Does?"

"The medical examiner is looking into it now," Spencer said.

"What else can I do for you?" Ringing phones in the background mingled with the edge of irritation in her voice.

"Text me pictures of each woman."

"Consider it done."

"And if Poe requests any more information linked to these two murders or any missing women like these Jane Does, let me know."

There was a long pause. "Sure."

He ended the call, and seconds later his phone dinged with a text. It was from Rivers and contained the pictures of the two missing women. Immediately, he discarded one but keyed in on Tammy Fox. Poe might be onto something.

***

Jordan's forced respite ended with an 8:00 a.m. call. Dispatch asked her to respond to a possible suicide by hanging. The body had been found in an East Austin apartment. All suspicious deaths fell under her job description, and it was up to her to evaluate the scene. She would report her findings to the medical examiner, and after Dr. McIntyre conducted her autopsy, the doc would make the final call on whether the death was a homicide, suicide, or undetermined.

When Jordan arrived a half hour later at the run-down apartment building, two marked cars had secured the scene. The building was divided into segments, each section containing twelve units, four on each floor. An exposed center stairwell linked the different levels.

Out of her vehicle she slung her badge around her neck, crossed to the first uniformed officer, who had already strung yellow crime scene tape in front of the master stairwell. "I'm Detective Poe with Austin Homicide."

"Yes, ma'am," he said. "Officer Murphy. The scene is in apartment number 3-B. The next-door neighbor, Alana Stone, called it in. She lives in 3-A."

"What's her story?"

"Spent the night doing coke with the dead man. She said about four in the morning she realized she needed to come down from the coke and mellow. She went back to her place for a beer and fell asleep for a couple of hours. She woke up, realized she left her phone at the male's apartment, and returned. Door was open; she went in and found the dead man hanging from a light fixture."

"Where is Ms. Stone now?" Jordan asked.

"Rescue squad took her to the hospital. She was in rough shape."

"Tell the hospital to hold her until I see her."

"I'll ask. But you know how it goes. If they need a bed and she doesn't, out she goes."

"Tell the hospital I insist. Does the dead neighbor have a name?"

"According to the wallet on the table . . ." The officer glanced at a small notebook, the likes of which most cops carried. "Marco Walker."

"What?" The name was not that common, and given the law of averages . . . "Are you sure?"

"Face is bloated, but it matches the driver's license picture."

She reached in her pocket for latex gloves and a mask. "Let me have a look."

Taking the stairs quickly to the third floor, she moved down the gray, dingy hallway covered with peeling paint. A door opened behind her, and her hand went automatically to the weapon on her hip as she pivoted. An older man with tousled graying hair, a stained tank top, and worn jeans glared at her.

"What the hell is going on? I can't get any sleep."

Jordan stepped toward him and introduced herself. "And your name?"

"Dan Lawson."

"Have you been here long?"

"A couple of months."

"You know the guy in 3-B?"

"He just moved in two days ago."

Like pulling teeth. "He any trouble? Anyone have an issue with him?"

"He had a hooker in there yesterday. The two made a hell of a racket. But beyond that, I don't know anything about him."

"What about Alana Stone? You know her that well?"

He rubbed the stubble on his chin. "We've had a few beers."

"She must know the man in 3-B. I hear she partied with him, let herself into his place, and found him dead."

"Alana ain't shy about going through unlocked doors and grabbing what she needs. Where is she?"

"Hospital." She scribbled his name in her notebook and asked him to stay away from 3-B. At the front door, she ducked under the yellow tape and stepped into the apartment. It was the furnished kind, with a drab, careworn sofa and two matching chairs, a small efficiency kitchen with a tiny refrigerator, a twenty-inch television, and a small café-style table with one chair. There were men's clothes on the floor along with dozens of beer cans and a pizza box with three half-eaten slices remaining.

Hand on her weapon, Jordan moved toward the bedroom and stopped in the doorway when she saw Marco Walker's body hanging in his room. The second café chair was lying on its side just behind his feet, which hovered several inches from the carpeted floor. The base of the light had pulled away from the ceiling.

He was dressed in jeans but wore no shirt, leaving his tattooed chest and belly bare. The bloating and contorted face staring back at her had little in common with the smirking one she remembered from the courtroom. A part of her was glad he was dead. And another resented him for taking his secrets to the grave and not spending the next twenty years in prison. Memories of Mr. Sanchez's postcourtroom threat whispered in her ear.

"I hope you didn't do anything stupid, Mr. Sanchez," she muttered.

Behind the body was a bed dominated by a mattress and box spring covered with rumpled sheets. There was a nightstand, and on it were an empty money clip, a handful of coins, and a ring of keys. The two bedroom windows overlooked a brick wall. No sign of a suicide note.

To her right was a bathroom. The plastic trash can contained several used condoms, and a faint line of white powder dusted the gray countertop. Water dripped from the showerhead.

The clank of footsteps, rattling equipment boxes, and muffled voices signaled the arrival of the forensic team. She greeted Andy Lucas and Marsha Brown, who, like her, were pulling long days.

Lucas set down his box and looked up at the body as he knitted his gloved fingers together. "The fun never stops, does it?"

"No, it does not."

"What do you know about our boy here?" Lucas asked.

"I saw him alive and well in court two days ago. He made bail."

Lucas studied the man's face closer. "Charged with killing his girlfriend, right?"

"That's right."

"Only a lucky bastard would have made bail so fast."

"His good fortune came wrapped in an expensive suit. But looks like his attorney wasn't here to save him this time," she said.

Lucas opened his bag and removed a digital camera. He clicked a couple of test shots, checked the exposure. "You're welcome to stick around."

"I'll let you do your thing. I'm headed to the hospital to talk to the woman who found him. Let me know if you find a suicide note."

Once she talked to Alana Stone, she would return to Walker's building to knock on doors. And a visit would have to be paid to Mr. Sanchez.

She waved to the uniformed officer and stripped off her gloves and mask. In her vehicle, she pulled away and reached for her cup of coffee. What remained was cold.

***

Minutes after 10:00 a.m., Jordan arrived at the hospital and went to the main reception desk, showed her identification, and asked for Alana Stone. The woman had been transferred from the ER to a room on the third floor.

As she crossed the lobby to the elevator, the familiar scents and sounds of the hospital coiled around her. As a uniformed officer, she had followed her share of ambulances to the ER and seen the blood pool at the emergency-room staff's feet as they struggled to save a gunshot victim. The facility's surfaces had been cleaned to the point of gleaming, but she always had the urge to bathe after being here.

The elevator door opened, and she pressed the third-floor button with her knuckle. When the doors closed, she inhaled slowly, reminding herself it was a short ride.

At the second floor, two nurses in scrubs stepped on and selected the fifth floor. They were chatting, carrying coffee cups and glazed doughnuts. The doors opened on the next floor, and Jordan excused herself as she pressed past them.

She showed her identification to the charge nurse, introduced herself, and learned Ms. Stone was stabilized. There was no uniformed cop by her door, but an empty chair suggested the officer had stepped away.

Inside the room, the television light flickered on darkened walls and the woman lying in the bed. Her pale wrist was handcuffed to the bed railing. Though Ms. Stone had reported the body to the police, her intoxicated state and inability to answer basic questions had made her a person of interest. There had been a few times in Jordan's career when the guilty party had called in a crime, believing the cops would buy their story more easily.

Ms. Stone's body was still and her jaw slack. If not for the slow rise and fall of her chest, she would have looked dead.

Jordan pulled up a chair beside the bed, scraping the metal against the floor, and then in a loud voice said, "Ms. Stone." The eyelids fluttered, but she did not move. "Ms. Stone!"

Her eyes opened, sparking with surprise and fear. "What?"

"Ms. Stone, I'm Detective Jordan Poe with the Austin Police Department."

"What?"

Jordan repeated herself several times, filled a glass of water for the woman, and turned up the lights. "I need to talk about Mr. Walker."

"What about him?" Ms. Stone drank thirstily from the water cup Jordan held to her lips.

"You called the police about him this morning."

"Did I?" Ms. Stone's eyes closed.

Jordan set the cup down and clapped her hands loudly.

Ms. Stone's eyes opened, but she still appeared dazed.

"You spent last night partying with him," Jordan said.

"He wanted to have fun. Said he'd give me a bunch of free shit."

"As in cocaine and fentanyl?"

"Maybe."

"How long were you with him last night?"

"I don't remember."

"Think, Ms. Stone. What time did you leave him? Or did you?"

Thin brows knotted. "I left him about three or four a.m. He had a friend come over, and I didn't like him."

"Who was the friend?"

"I don't know," she said. "He had business with Walker."

"What kind of business?"

"Didn't ask. The guy was giving Walker cash as I was leaving."

Jordan remembered the empty money clip and wondered if Lucas would find cash in the apartment. "What did the friend look like?"

"Medium, dark hair, quiet."

That description could belong to thousands of men.

"Did he have a name?" Jordan asked.

Ms. Stone was silent.

"I don't care about your drug use, Ms. Stone. Or if you turned tricks. I want to know what happened to Mr. Walker."

"I was flying high when I left. I had to leave early for work." Her eyes widened as if she remembered she had a job. "I think I'm late for work now."

"You're not in any shape today to go."

"I have to call. Where's my phone?"

Jordan slipped on gloves and rummaged through a nightstand, where she found an unused Bible. She then moved to the closet, where she discovered Ms. Stone's phone bundled in a plastic bag along with a thin dress, necklace, bracelet, and hoop earrings. "I'll call your work for you. Just give me the name."

Ms. Stone mumbled a number and Jordan called it. The manager of a fast-food joint answered, and Jordan explained the situation. The man on the other end did not sound happy but accepted the explanation.

"All clear, Ms. Stone."

The woman relaxed back against the pillows.

"Ms. Stone, I need you to tell me more about the second man."

"I don't know shit about him. Seriously."

"Can I look at your photos on your phone?" Jordan asked.

"Sure."

Jordan opened the photos app. There were several pictures of Ms. Stone and Walker taken last night. The final image provided a glimpse of the second man, but his face was turned, and he was wearing a ball cap. He appeared to be midsize with dark hair, which fit the description Ms. Stone had given. She wondered whether surveillance cameras in the area of Walker's apartment had recorded a blue pickup truck. "Can I forward these pictures to my phone?"

"What? Why?"

"They're images of a crime scene."

"Sure."

Jordan sent the images to her phone. "Ms. Stone, I'm contacting my forensic department, and I'm going to have them send a tech to collect your phone."

"Why?"

"They might need to look it over."

"Why?"

"You were the last person who saw Mr. Walker alive."

Ms. Stone moistened her lips. "But I didn't do that to him."

"Do you have a pimp? Was the second man your pimp?"

She looked away. "No."

"You sure about that?"

"I'm solo now."

"Do you have a boyfriend? Someone who might not like you with Walker?"

"No. It was just Marco and me having fun. And then creepy new guy."

"Did Mr. Walker make any comments about killing himself?"

"No, he was riding high. Happy. Was glad to get the money. Said he could supply more." Her eyes drifted closed.

Jordan clapped her hands again. "Ms. Stone, how did the second man and Mr. Walker get along?"

"Fine, I guess."

"What does *fine* mean?"

"They weren't yelling. But not exactly friends."

"But they knew each other?"

"Yes. The other guy reminded Walker that he still owed him."

"Who owed who?"

"Walker owed the guy."

"Money?"

"I guess."

A quick knock at the door and Jordan rose. The missing uniformed officer entered. He was scowling, his hand on his weapon until he saw Jordan's badge. She introduced herself, told him about Ms. Stone's bag of belongings, and asked him to keep them secure until the forensic team arrived.

"I'll be leaving soon," the officer said. "I'm only authorized to be here until you arrived."

"Fair enough." When she turned to tell Ms. Stone she might return, the woman was already asleep. "Has anyone visited Ms. Stone?"

"Her lawyer. A Mr. Harold Sunday. And because she was an overdose, the hospital drug counselor, Dr. Malone."

Malone made sense, but Sunday would not waste his time on someone like Ms. Stone unless she had a pot of money or had information he wanted. "Harold Sunday? You sure about that?"

"Very."

"Thanks."

Out in the hallway she informed the front desk of what was happening regarding their patient's belongings and headed to the elevator. She was tempted to leave immediately. Christ, she hated hospitals.

She owed Rogan Malone a visit. Despite their failed romance, he had spoken to her witness and needed to be interviewed. On the elevator, she hit the button for the sixth floor, the psychiatric unit. Like it or not, the past was reaching out of the shadows yet again.

CHAPTER NINE

Wednesday, April 14
12:00 p.m.

Jordan moved down the familiar hallway to the office door at the end. The nameplate read **Dr. R. Malone**. There was no **In Session** sign displayed, so she knocked.

"Enter."

She pushed open the door and found Dr. Rogan Malone behind his desk, his head bent, his brow furrowing as he stared at a stack of forms. "Still hate the paperwork?"

His scowl dissolving, he looked up and rose. "Jordan, it's been a while."

She moved into the space. There was not anything remarkable about Rogan Malone's office. Laminated wood shelves were crammed full of books, the oriental carpet's loose weave was worn, the couch could be lumpy in several spots, and the window overlooked the parking lot. It always smelled faintly of cigarettes, though Rogan denied he smoked.

But this was the space she had run to when Avery's problems had gotten out of hand. She had been desperate to save her sister and deal with the growing panic that had tightened her chest like a vise. In this space, the troubled world had vanished long enough for her to see the solutions.

But that was before Jordan and Rogan had slept together. Since then, she had not been here and was surprised to discover the office still soothed her nerves, even if his presence did not.

He came around the desk and gave her a hug. The familiar scent of his soap, even the cigarettes, eased the edginess that had been coiling inside her since she had seen the first Jane Doe.

Rogan was midsize, had brown hair, and once in a candid moment joked he needed to lose fifteen pounds and get to the gym more often. She thought the extra weight made his face pleasantly round, and his self-deprecating humor charming.

"You look terrific."

"Thank you."

"What brings you to my neck of the woods?" he asked.

"Came to ask you about Ms. Stone. She was brought in this morning."

He regarded her closely. "I can't talk about patients; you know that."

"Of course," she said. "But she's attached to a suspicious-death investigation, and I was wondering if she said anything that could help."

"I can't say, Jordan."

"Sure, I get it."

"I'm glad you stopped by. You look good." He motioned with his hand for her to sit in one of the two office chairs angled toward his desk. She took the one on the left, like she always did. He took the other because he never liked having the desk separate him from his patient.

"Have you ever counseled Ms. Stone before?"

He chuckled. "You're still stubborn."

"It's all I know."

"Fair enough. But I still can't answer."

"How have you been doing?" she asked.

"Good. As you can see, still plugging along."

She knew very little about his personal life, and that was for the best. Cut ties. Clean breaks.

"Looks like you still hit the gym," he said easily.

"Put one in my garage. It's my meditation."

Grinning, he shook his head. "As I have said, the gym is for the body, not the mind. Meditation is mind exercise."

Jordan laughed, holding up her hand. "I tried it. No can do."

"I won't ever stop reminding you."

"I know." Her mind shifted to the Jane Does. "You remember Marco Walker?"

"The drug dealer. I hear he hanged himself."

"Ms. Stone told you?"

He shrugged.

"Does he still like to get the young, pretty girls hooked so he can traffic them?" Avery came to mind. Jordan had tried to talk to her sister about being trafficked, but Avery refused to discuss it.

"He had no reason to change."

"What about an attorney named Harold Sunday?"

Rogan frowned. "He's Walker's attorney and sometimes represents some of the girls arrested for prostitution. He can be violent from what I've heard."

"How so?"

"Walker used the girls to pay off his debts with Sunday. Sex for legal defense."

That was not a surprise. Would Sunday be the kind of guy who took the sex too far? "Can I run a case by you?"

"As long as it's not a patient."

"It's not."

The smile in his eyes faded, and she sensed a mental shifting of the hats between personal and work modes. "Ask away."

"I have two Jane Does . . . or did."

"Did?"

"My boss turned the case over to the Texas Rangers. The two murders are related, and he's worried I'm in over my head. Which, for the record, I'm not."

"Politics does make the world go around."

"Maybe, maybe not."

"So, why're you asking me about a case that you were removed from?"

"I've seen some nasty crime scenes. But these two have to be the worst."

"Can I ask how the victims died?"

"I'm not saying anything the press hasn't heard. They were sexually assaulted, held for an undetermined time, and wrapped in thick plastic. They were smothered to death."

"Damn."

"Yeah, it was a quiet, cruel violence that I've not seen before."

"And you want to know why a killer would do something like this?"

"I do."

He steepled his fingers, resting his elbows on the arms of his chair. "That's a hard one."

"Both bodies were packaged in the same manner. Hands bound, gags in the mouths, naked. That's nothing new to the streets."

"But the plastic is."

"I've seen wrappings used to help dispose of a body, but not as a manner of killing the victim."

"Suffocation is slow and induces a great deal of fear. The air in this room is about twenty-one percent oxygen. We both would experience impairment if it dropped to ten to fifteen percent, and then we'd feel panic. Death occurs at eight percent. Were either of the women strangled?"

"Hard to tell on the first because of the state of decomposition, but there were no signs on the second. And both hyoid bones were intact."

"The plastic is a form of entrapment."

"It would also allow the killer to easily watch the victim die," she said.

"As you must know, some killers are excited by the pain of their victims. And plastic is an easily accessible, fairly untraceable weapon. No ballistics or knife wounds that can be traced back to the killer. You would have to find the original roll of plastic and match the raw edge of your sample with the last cut."

"That works when I find the killer," she said. "Tell me what I don't know."

"Your guy is smart. That kind of killing requires planning. I'd say he's clearly excited by erotic asphyxiation. Does he have a type?"

"He likes blondes. Small boned. Young."

"Blond, like you?"

"Maybe. But I'm not small boned or that young."

"You're also not easy to subdue and control like these victims. Do you think he's finished?"

"If I had to bet the farm? No."

"Does this case remind you of Avery?" he asked.

Her body stilled, and with great care she crossed her legs and threaded her fingers. She had confided many details to Rogan when she'd seen him as a patient. "A little."

"That's why you're still working the case. It's personal."

"All cops have a case that hits too close to home."

"You'd had many when you worked in the narcotics division."

"Can't run from your fears," she said.

"You run directly toward them. Then and now."

"This case found me."

"And it was also taken away, but you continue to chase it. You're still trying to save Avery."

"This is becoming a little too much about me." Unease scraped under her skin, prompting her to rise.

He stood. "I can do some research on the topic of autoasphyxiation, known in my circles as sexual heroin. Maybe I could find something that would offer some insight."

"I would appreciate it if you have the time."

"I'll make the time. This is fascinating in a macabre sort of way."

"Thank you, Rogan. I appreciate the insight."

"I doubt I said anything you didn't already know."

"Always good to bounce ideas off of people."

To his credit, he did not ask if they could get together for lunch or coffee. Maybe they really were back to being friends.

***

Minutes later, Jordan was in her car, the sticky humidity blowing in her partly opened window. She dialed Sunday's number and waited.

"Mr. Sunday's office," a young woman said.

"This is Detective Jordan Poe. I'd like to speak to Mr. Sunday."

"He's in a meeting."

"I'll be on his doorstep in ten minutes if he doesn't get on the line right now."

"Hold."

She listened to nondescript music as the scenery along I-35 passed her.

"Detective Poe," Sunday said. "What do I owe the pleasure?"

"I understand you are representing a Ms. Stone."

"No, I am not."

"You were seen in her hospital room this morning," she countered.

"Paying a visit to a friend."

"When's the last time you saw Walker?"

"In court." He chuckled softly. "You sound tense."

She thought about the long scratch along her car door. "Defense fees for a manslaughter charge must be expensive."

"What are you getting at?"

"Just seems to me if a guy owed you a lot of money, and he couldn't pay, you might get impatient. You might want to send a message to others like him."

"What's that supposed to mean?"

"Where were you at four a.m. this morning?" she asked.

"In bed with a very pretty woman. Where were you?"

"Did the woman have a name?"

"I didn't get it."

"Get it."

"Am I being charged?"

"No."

"Ah, but you sound angry and hungry for an arrest." He chuckled. "You're tense. Know what an uptight woman needs?"

"I'll see you soon, Mr. Sunday." She hung up before he could respond.

As she drove, she unrolled her window more, uncaring that the air was heating up the interior of her car. She was glad to be on the open road, if only for twenty or thirty minutes. When her exit came up, she was almost disappointed. But the real world was always waiting.

She took the exit and wound through San Marcos near Texas State University. Following a familiar route, she located the Sanchezes' small one-story residence, located on a cul-de-sac. It was a typical suburban home.

"I could kill that man. He deserves to die," Mr. Sanchez had said to Jordan. His wife had laid her hand on his arm and told him he did not believe that. *"Why not, Constance? I could* kill *him."*

Jordan parked and walked up the stone sidewalk to the front door. She rang the bell and stepped to the side. Resting her hand on her weapon was protocol, but it felt more like an insult in this case. Still, she was here alone, and precautions mattered.

The front door opened to Constance Sanchez, the welcome in her gaze turning questioning. "Detective Poe, what brings you here?"

"I came to talk to you and your husband. Is he here?"

"Yes, he's in the kitchen making chili. Please come in."

Inside the house, painted in buttery yellows, the rich scents of tomatoes, onions, beef, and cumin greeted her.

"Is there a problem?" Mrs. Sanchez asked.

"We need to talk." Jordan's direct tone indicated this was not a social call.

"Of course."

They passed down a hallway filled with pictures of Elena Sanchez. A smiling infant in pink, a little girl on Santa's lap, a ten-year-old dressed for soccer, the young woman in a bright-blue prom dress, and the high school graduate ready to take on the world.

They found Peter Sanchez at his gas-burning stove, leaning over a pot of steaming chili. Her stomach rumbled, and she realized she had not eaten today.

"Detective Poe is here," Mrs. Sanchez said.

Mr. Sanchez reached for a small bowl and ladled in chili. "First you try my chili. I bet you haven't eaten today."

"I have not." She accepted the bowl, scooped up a spoonful, and blew on the hot liquid before tasting the rich flavors. "Amazing."

"Not too much salt?" he asked.

"Perfect."

"My husband always has something cooking on the stove, and his culinary skills are good therapy."

Cooking was his escape from the memories waiting for him each time he walked down the hallway of his house. "I can taste your devotion in the cooking."

"Eat," Mr. Sanchez said.

She understood this was his process. He was building up the nerve to hear whatever it was she had to say.

"Are you going to eat?" she asked.

"I eat while I cook." He rubbed his rounded belly. "Constance says I'm getting fat."

He poured coffee for himself and his wife, and both sat across from her. "You work too hard," he said. "Time to stop and smell the roses."

She chuckled. "You're right." Hungrier than she thought, she ate the entire bowl. As she dabbed her mouth with the napkin, she raised her gaze to them.

"Have you come to check on us?" Mrs. Sanchez asked. "If you're wondering if Marco Walker has been hassling us, do not worry. We have not seen him."

"Walker is the reason I came." Carefully, she rearranged the napkin in her lap. "He was found dead in an apartment this morning. He hanged himself."

A rushed breath escaped Constance's lips. Her husband sat back as if he had just dropped a heavy weight. They stared at Jordan, waiting for the details.

"When was the last time you saw Mr. Walker?" Jordan asked.

"In the courtroom," Mrs. Sanchez said.

"That true for you as well, Mr. Sanchez?" Jordan noted he was another man with a midsize frame and dark hair. Ms. Stone had said the new man had given Walker money and said he *owed* him. Though Walker did owe the Sanchezes, she could not imagine Mr. Sanchez faking any kind of camaraderie with Walker.

The initial shock vanished from his face. "Yes, of course. Constance and I came home after the bail hearing. We have not left the house since."

"Why would he kill himself?" Mrs. Sanchez asked.

"That's what I'm trying to figure out," Jordan said.

"Did he leave a note?" he asked.

"No," Jordan said. "At least we've not found it yet."

"You don't think he killed himself, do you?" Mr. Sanchez asked.

"I'm not sure. I'm waiting on the autopsy. But I wanted you to hear the information from me first."

"We appreciate that," Mrs. Sanchez said.

"She's also trying to figure out if we had a hand in his death," Mr. Sanchez said. "We have a strong motive."

"It's my job to talk to anyone who might have had an issue with him," Jordan said. "And you said you could kill him when we left the courthouse."

"He was upset, of course," Mrs. Sanchez said. "We lost our baby girl. It was too much to see Walker go free."

"I understand that. And there're days when I don't like my job because it forces me to have conversations like this."

Mr. Sanchez's gaze sharpened. "I'm not sorry he's dead, but I would not have sullied my hands with his death. I know God will mete out justice."

"Now he'll get to do it a lot faster," Jordan said.

"There must be other people that hated Marco Walker," Mr. Sanchez said.

"That's what I'm trying to determine. We know he was partying with a woman who lived next door. She had a record for prostitution and drug use. According to her, they parted ways about four in the morning, and then she came back about six a.m. to get her phone."

"Model citizens," he said.

Jordan let the comment pass and took a moment to carefully fold and lay her napkin by her bowl. "Did Elena ever mention any of Walker's friends? Any that might have felt threatening."

Mr. Sanchez scoffed. "They were all threatening."

"Did she ever mention if Walker had trafficked her?"

Mrs. Sanchez raised her hand to her mouth. Tears welled in her eyes.

Mr. Sanchez was silent and then: "She never said anything about that to me. Constance, this would have been a conversation a girl has with her mother."

Mrs. Sanchez swiped a tear. "There were men who tried to take advantage, but she said Walker kept them away from her."

"Okay."

"Are you saying that monster gave my daughter to other men?" Mrs. Sanchez asked.

"I have no evidence he did. I'm here only because I wanted to have this conversation with you out of respect. When the medical examiner's report comes in, I'll touch base."

Regardless of how she felt about the couple and their loss, if either had killed Walker, there would have to be a reckoning.

"Thank you," Mrs. Sanchez said. "You have been very kind to us. And we know it is not your fault that Walker got bail. We were just shocked and upset the other day."

"I know," Jordan said.

Jordan rose, as did Mr. and Mrs. Sanchez. Mrs. Sanchez found a smile, but her husband stood back, his expression stoic.

In the car, Jordan slid on her sunglasses, turned on the engine, and opened her window, letting the hot, dry air warm her chilled skin. She truly felt for the couple. She could have been them two years ago, standing in a courtroom screaming for justice and grieving her sister's death.

She drove through the Sanchezes' small working-class neighborhood and up I-35, finding the traffic unusually light. Her phone rang. "Detective Poe."

"It's Detective Rivers. Missing persons."

"Detective, what can I do for you?"

"I've been thinking about the missing person cases I sent over to you."

"You know the Texas Rangers are conducting the investigation now."

"I know. And Ranger Spencer will be my next call. Right after lunch."

A smile tweaked the corner of Jordan's lips. Seemed Spencer had ruffled more feathers than her own. "What do you have?"

"A young girl was just reported missing by her mother. The young woman spent the night at her mother's home last night but was gone when the mother and sister woke up. The mother got worried and started making calls to some of her daughter's friends. No one has seen Casey, so she called me."

"Casey?"

"Casey Andrews. She's nineteen, blond, and has a prior issue with substance abuse."

"She's been gone less than twenty-four hours?"

"But she fits the profile of the two Jane Does at the morgue. Hence the call. Could be nothing but doesn't hurt to share information."

Jordan switched lanes. "Can you send me her photo?"

"Sure. I know the mother wouldn't mind a visit from the police. She's pretty upset."

"Send me the mother's home and work addresses. I'm on it."

CHAPTER TEN

Wednesday, April 14
3:30 p.m.

When Spencer heard about Walker's death, he drove directly to the crime scene, and when he arrived, the medical examiner's technician was waiting for him. Jordan Poe was the investigating detective on the case.

He hurried up the three flights of stairs, working his fingers into latex gloves. On the third floor he noted the cop standing outside the door and the flash of a camera in the room.

When he reached the room's threshold, the two medical technicians were standing in front of the body, which had been placed on an unzipped body bag. There was a rope still coiled around Walker's neck.

As Spencer entered, the techs moved aside and gave him his first good view of the body.

Spencer stared at Walker's body, searching for signs that this was not a suicide. The body itself showed no visible signs of trauma other than the hanging, but that would be for the medical examiner to determine. Walker's bare feet were a dark blue, an indication he had been hanging when his heart stopped, and the blood had settled to the lowest part of the body.

"When did you cut him down?" Spencer asked.

"About five minutes ago. Detective Poe gave us the go-ahead to do what we needed."

"Where is Detective Poe?"

"She's following up with Alana Stone, the woman who found the body. Ms. Stone was sent to the hospital to be treated for an overdose."

Two years of investigating this drug-trafficking case was coming to a halt. He had been close to arresting Walker, and if he had, he would have used the potential jail time as leverage to get the name of his supplier.

Spencer left the room and was on the phone to Detective Poe before he reached his vehicle. The call rang three times, and he was waiting for voicemail when he heard, "Detective Poe."

"This is Ranger Spencer."

"What can I do for you?" Detective Poe asked.

By the sound of it, she was in a car. "Walker."

"Died this morning, but you know that, right?"

"You know I'm investigating him for drug trafficking. You could have alerted me."

"Nothing to report yet."

He rolled his neck from side to side. "This isn't a game."

"Good, because I'm not having fun. I just left the Sanchez house and had to float the idea that they might know something about Walker's death."

"Did they?"

"I don't know. They had good reason. But they normally wouldn't be the types to kill."

"He hanged himself."

"Maybe."

"Why do you say that?"

"Witness, a Ms. Alana Stone, said he was riding high last night and had just gotten paid," she said.

"Who paid him?"

"Don't know. I do know his attorney, Harold Sunday, visited Ms. Stone in the hospital."

"This doesn't mean his mindset didn't turn on a dime."

"You're right. But I suspect you know a lot more about him than I do. In the interest of sharing, do you think he's the kind of man who would kill himself?"

"No."

"You were investigating him for drug trafficking."

"He's the smaller fish that leads to a whale."

"Maybe the whale wanted him quiet for good," she said. She recapped what Ms. Stone had told her about the second man in the apartment.

"Was the second man Sunday?"

"I don't know. He says he was with a woman about that time." She hesitated.

"Do you believe him?"

"I don't know. But Sunday and Walker were tight. I heard Walker got young, pretty girls hooked on drugs and trafficked them. Not a stretch to say that Sunday bought sex from the women."

He leaned against his car, letting the heat bite into the pain in his right thigh. He had been shot ten years ago during a highway traffic stop. The bullet had torn through muscle, which still stiffened when he was burning the candle at both ends.

"Do you have proof?"

"I'm off the case. That'll be your job to find it."

"I always get the sense with you there's more."

"I'm tracking down a few missing person cases. Might not lead anywhere, but it's a hunch."

"If you find anything that connects them to the Jane Does, call me."

"Sure. Also, the uniforms are canvassing for surveillance cameras around Walker's apartment," Jordan said. "When we have something, I'll call."

"I expect nothing less."

"Do the same if you find out what happened to the Jane Does."

Her direct order told him what he suspected. The Austin Police Department might have relinquished the case, but she had not. "Will do."

***

Jordan ended the call with Spencer and, out of the car, walked into the small hardware store. Her teeth were clenched. The ranger's graveled voice rumbled in her head. And for some reason she was always on edge after they interacted.

The hardware store was kind of a throwback to the stores her grandfather back in Boston talked about. People greeted you at the door, answered questions, and walked you to an item on the shelf.

Inside, she passed the front register, where a woman in her early fifties was ringing up a guy in jeans and a worn UT T-shirt. Instead of falling in line, she drifted to the back of the store. A young man, not more than eighteen, came up to her wearing a red apron. "Can I help you?"

"Do you have any plastic wrap?" she asked.

"Sure. Aisle six."

"Thanks."

The kid followed her. "You have a particular project in mind?"

"Thinking about doing some painting. I like home repairs."

"Nice. Have you picked a color?"

"Not yet." She entered aisle six and stared at the collection of tarps and light plastic wrap she had used plenty of times when she'd painted her house.

"We carry a decent selection of colors, and we can order anything."

"Thanks." She looked at a packaged square of heavy-duty plastic. She hefted the parcel. The weight felt about right.

"That's not really good for painting," he said. "It's meant to be a barrier, like if a window got broken or a roof had a hole."

Or if a body needed wrapping. "This all you have?"

"Yes, but we can order anything."

"That's good to know. Thanks. I'll be back."

"Sure."

Jordan's killer would have chosen a store like this. He could have defaulted to an online purchase, but they left credit card trails. And box stores took cash but had cameras and lots of employees.

"Hey, is Dot Andrews working today? I have a few questions for her."

"Why?"

Jordan held up her badge. "Nothing major. Just a few questions."

"She's working the front register."

"Great. Thanks."

She made her way back to the front door. The man in line was gone, and the woman had shifted her attention to aligning bottles of energy drinks stacked by the register.

"Dot Andrews?" Jordan asked.

The woman turned. She was smiling, but dark smudges hung under her eyes, and the frown lines around her mouth were etched deep. "Yes?"

Jordan held up her badge. "I came to talk to you about Casey."

Mrs. Andrews looked sideways and dropped her voice. "Have you heard anything?"

"No, ma'am. I just spoke to Detective Rivers, and I wanted to follow up. Is there somewhere we can talk?"

"Sure." She produced a walkie-talkie from her red apron pocket and pressed the side button. "Ken, can you cover the register? I need to take a quick break."

The radio squawked back, "Sure."

Ken was the young kid Jordan had been talking to, and as he approached the register, Mrs. Andrews led Jordan through the store and out the back to a small picnic table covered by a sun-faded red umbrella.

They sat at the table, and Jordan pulled out her notebook. "Do you have a recent picture of Casey?" She wanted to compare it to the one Rivers had sent her.

"Sure." Mrs. Andrews fished a phone from her pocket and held up the image.

Jordan stared at the pretty smiling face. "When is the last time you saw her?"

"Last night. She's been staying at home for a few weeks. She's trying to find a job and get her life back on track. But she snuck out of the house last night."

"She's not been gone that long. Why did you call the cops?"

"I know the people she hung out with before. They're dangerous, and I was afraid she had slid back."

"Slid back?"

"Drugs. She got in with a bad crowd when she was about fifteen. But that's all behind her now."

"How long was she into drugs?"

"On and off a couple of years. She used cocaine mostly."

"And you're sure she was clean?"

"She swore to me she was."

"Drug users can be very convincing, Mrs. Andrews."

"I know. I've been fooled before. But she seemed right. And then she vanished."

"Why would she do that?"

"I know she was struggling. Finding work these days is hard. She was losing hope."

"Does she have friends or a boyfriend?"

"She dated guys but mostly went out with friends in groups, you know?"

"Can you give me a list of her friends?"

"I never met them. I'm telling you what she told me."

"Any contact information would help."

Mrs. Andrews reached for her phone and scrolled through her contacts. "I called her friend Mary Pat. They went to high school together, and they still keep up. Mary Pat hasn't spoken to Casey in over a year. Neither has her former roommate Missy Stapleton."

"Favorite places to hang out?"

"Downtown Austin, where all the kids her age go."

"What did she do for a living?"

"She worked as a waitress at Buzz's but got let go. She was looking for another job, one that maybe paid more and had hours during the day. She was saving for a deposit on an apartment." Mrs. Andrews dug her thumb into pink, chipped nail polish on her index finger. "Where do you think she could be?"

"What is Casey's cell number?"

"She has two phones. One for friends and family and one for her dealer."

As Mrs. Andrews recited the two numbers, Jordan programmed them into her phone. "How long has she had these numbers?"

"The personal phone for about a year. She's had the drug one a few years. I told her to get rid of the drug phone. Hanging on to it keeps the idea alive that she can call her dealer and score again."

"Ever heard of a guy named Marco Walker?"

"No. Who is he?"

"No one to you. Is there a question I can ask her that no one else could answer?" If this case went public, calls would flood the station.

"Her teddy bear's name is Max."

"Max. Okay."

"You think you can find her?"

"I don't know, but I'll keep asking around." She removed a card from her pocket. "Call me if Casey contacts you."

"Sure, of course." Tears welled in Mrs. Andrews's eyes. "Thank you. I'm at my wit's end."

"I can't make any promises, but I'll ask around about her." Casey could be holed up in an apartment with a new guy, in a flophouse with a needle in her arm, hanging out with a friend her mother did not know. There was no way of telling.

Jordan thanked Mrs. Andrews again. Back in her car she pulled up Casey's phone number and pressed send. Nothing ventured, nothing gained. The call rang three times and then went to voicemail. *"Hi, this is Casey. You know the drill!"*

"Casey, this is Detective Jordan Poe," she said. "I'm with the Austin Police Department, and I'm following up on a missing person case your mother filed on your behalf. Call me. Doesn't matter what day or time." She called Casey's second number and left a similar message.

Jordan sat in her car for a moment, watching a red pickup park in front of the hardware store. Ken met the customer on the curb with a flatbed of two-by-fours, and the two loaded the supplies in the bed of his truck. Life went on. Did not matter who died or who was hurt, the world kept marching. She had resented the world's resilience to pain and suffering after her mother died and then when Avery had her troubles. How could people laugh when her world was crumbling? But it did, and in her worst times, Jordan had realized if she did not buck up and take care of business, Avery would quickly be a forgotten statistic.

Jordan considered calling Spencer and updating him on this visit, but she really did not have much to say. The city was full of missing girls. Still, Casey's history, stomping grounds, and physical appearance made her a target for this killer. She dialed Spencer's number, which went to voicemail. "This is Detective Poe. Call me tomorrow. I might have something for you."

***

Spencer strode down the hallway to his captain's office and found Ranger Henry Manchester on the phone. His scowling expression came with the job, along with the cheap desk and the paperwork. Spencer had noted that the higher the rank, the deeper the frown. It was why he had avoided any substantial promotions. He liked being on the road, logging the miles, chasing cases. Henry, who was a year older than Spencer, had joined the Department of Public Safety at the same time Spencer had. Both had played ball at UT, and both had wanted to track down bad guys for a living. More than a few times, they had sworn never to give up the real work of law enforcement. No paper pushing for them.

But Manchester's story was a classic. Fell in love, married, had a couple of kids, took on a mortgage, and then went through a divorce. Going up the ladder paid the growing bills that followed kids and divorce.

Manchester hung up and raised his gaze.

"Good news or bad news first?" Spencer asked.

"Bad news." Manchester squared his shoulders.

"Marco Walker is dead. He was found this morning hanging from a light fixture in his apartment." His tone was easy, but he was not chill about this. He was pissed.

Manchester spit out a rare expletive. "You've been working that drug case for two years."

"And now the little bird who could have sung for us is gone." Chasing Walker was the reason he had moved back to Austin.

"And the good news?" Manchester asked.

"The case is being investigated by the Austin Police Department. The detective is Jordan Poe."

Manchester sat back in his chair and folded his arms over his chest. "The one you pissed off?"

"She's a big girl. We all know how the game is played. But yeah, she's annoyed."

"Why's her involvement in the case a good thing?"

"She thinks Marco Walker was murdered."

"You just said that he hanged himself, correct?" Manchester asked.

"Yes."

"Why does Poe think Walker was murdered?"

"According to the woman who found him dead, Walker was on top of the world."

Manchester sat back.

"Also, no suicide note. And Poe spoke to a witness who said a man visited Walker as she was leaving about four a.m. She's a solid cop. I'd be foolish to ignore her instincts."

"It would take someone strong to heft Walker's body up."

"I've spoken to Dr. McIntyre, and she's doing the autopsy on Saturday morning. She might find something. And we're canvassing for security cameras and other witnesses."

"Okay. It might lead somewhere. Find out who killed Walker, and you might get another lead in your drug case." He reached for a file. "What about the Jane Doe murder cases?"

"Thanks to Poe, she's identified a woman who might be one of our victims. The woman has fingerprints on file for an arrest for drug possession."

"Poe to the rescue again. Maybe you shouldn't burn that bridge."

"I don't burn bridges," Spencer said.

"Bullshit," Manchester said.

***

He was careful to manage his addiction. Like a good addict who used clean needles, he paid attention to the details, because careful planning kept him in control.

That was why he always took the battery out of all the women's phones. They were GPS monitoring systems, and the perfect device to lead cops right to his doorstep, so he kept them powered down, memory cards removed. His silent collectibles reminded him of the women who had carried them and considered them their mini safe spaces that guarded against all bad things. You could be talking to a friend while crossing a dark alley, but comforting conversations did not protect anyone from him.

Smiling, he inspected the latest one. It had a pink cover studded with rhinestones. Curious, he picked up the device's battery and put it inside. He could indulge for only a minute or two, but he wanted to know who was looking for his little toy in the basement. Better to know who was chasing you.

The screen came alive, and a picture of the young woman appeared. In the photo, she arched her head back and gathered her lips into a pout. He typed in the passcode his new friend had kindly given him.

There were a half dozen messages. Most were from her mother. He listened to all of them. Casey's mother was worried about her darling. She feared she was making bad choices. Which was exactly what she had done.

And then there was a message from Jordan Poe. The detective stated she was looking for Casey and wanted her to call.

Startled to hear the detective's voice, he removed the battery and reconsidered the moves he had made over the last four weeks. He had been careful. Always avoided the cameras, kept his face hidden just in case he missed one, and he selected women who would not be reported missing right away.

And still Poe was sniffing on his trail.

If he were prudent, he would stop. At least for a little while. Let the case cool. The news cycle changed so fast. He would play with his toy for weeks or months while the world forgot about her and the murdered women.

Detective Poe would find Casey, eventually, but it would be too late.

***

Casey lay on the floor, her body numb, her lungs greedily drawing in air. He had come to her, masked, his dark eyes glaring at her with laser focus. When he'd told her to undress, she had refused. He'd hit her hard, knocked her to the ground, bound her hands, and put the bag over her head. Slowly, the lack of air had robbed her of will, and when he'd reached for the waistband of her pants, she had not fought. She had lost count of how many hours he'd toyed with her.

Finally, he had left her, hands bound and half-naked. She had grabbed her pants, pulled them on, and pressed her back against the cinder block wall.

Curling her feet up, Casey hugged her knees close and let her head fall back against the concrete wall behind her. Tears welled in her eyes, spilled down her cheeks, and then she wiped them away. Crying would not get her out of here.

She practiced a deep-breathing exercise she had learned in counseling. Inhale two breaths. Exhale four breaths. She tried to imagine the rolling hills to the west and the beaches of Galveston Island to the east.

Remembering her second cell phone, she hurriedly checked her pockets. He had taken one cell phone but not the second one hidden in the folds of her jacket.

On a floor above her, she heard a door open and keys jangle. She sat up, knowing he was coming. She had a good idea of what was going to happen. Living on the streets almost ensured it.

With a trembling hand, she fished out her phone. She noted the missed calls. Several were from her mother. The other number was not familiar. She listened to her mother's message and teared up again. Her throat tightened.

"Mommy, I'm sorry."

The footsteps grew closer to her door. She shoved the phone back in her pocket and wrapped the folds of her jacket over her breasts. She held her breath as the doorknob twisted and the door opened.

CHAPTER ELEVEN

Wednesday, April 14
11:30 p.m.

Jordan sat in her dark living room, staring at the stone fireplace and the painting of the wild horse above it. She had repointed the fireplace herself, and the picture had cost her an arm and a leg at an art gallery in Fredericksburg. She did not regret the scars on her fingers from the stonework or the months of brown bag lunches that had paid for the art. Both were a source of pride.

She checked the time on her phone. Avery had said she was spending the night here again. She was due in a half hour, and Jordan was not sure why she was waiting up for her twenty-four-year-old sister, who was perfectly capable of getting herself home.

It was not like there was a curfew in Casa Poe. But since she had stood in the abandoned house and stared at the first Jane Doe, Jordan's worries for Avery had resurfaced. She was going to do her best to hide her concerns from Avery. Jordan resented people hovering, and Avery was no different. However, Jordan was the older sister, and in the universe, the first one out of the womb had claim to certain rights and privileges. Worry was one of them.

Headlights swept over the living room as Avery's car pulled in the driveway. The fifteen-year-old sedan's engine chugged to a stop. Home thirty minutes early. Not typical but maybe one of the other guys in the café had closed up for her. "Take the wins where you get them," Jordan's old boss used to say.

Rising out of her chair, she carried her half-empty cup of decaf to the kitchen sink, poured it out, and moved to her bedroom. She closed her bedroom door as Avery entered the front door. Lying in bed, she listened to her sister's less-than-delicate footsteps as she flipped on a light and rummaged in the refrigerator.

Jordan lay back on her pillows and stared at the white plaster ceiling. All the chickens were home to roost, a rare event indeed, so she closed her eyes and willed sleep to take her.

But slumber refused to be bossed. It would come when it damn well pleased, and she could wait.

As tempted as she was to check her phone, viewing the screen's light was a recipe for insomnia. So, as she listened to Avery move about the house, she counted not sheep but the names of missing women. Tammy. Susie. Casey. And she tried not to picture any of them wrapped in plastic, struggling to breathe.

***

Jordan was in a dead sleep when her phone rang. She sprang up fully awake, a trick learned after twelve years on the job. She glanced at her display. The name did not register at first. Was she still sleeping? When the phone rang a third time, she picked up. "Detective Poe."

Silence was the first response. Jordan swung her legs over the side of her bed. "Is someone there?"

The caller was still quiet, but distinct breathing was detectable. It was fast, panicked.

"Who is this?" Jordan demanded.

"This is Casey."

Jordan stood up quickly, stepped on a book she had left by her bed, and stumbled before she righted herself. "Where are you?"

"I'm not sure," she whispered.

"What's that mean?"

"I'm in a basement. It's dark."

"Your phone has been off."

"He took the other one. He doesn't know about this one."

Jordan had been visible on the news at the conference. Anyone who had paid attention knew she had worked the Mummy case. Casey might not be truly missing and could have given her phone away, or it could have been stolen. There were so many variables when dealing with addicts.

"Please," Casey said.

"Who is Max?" Jordan asked.

"Max." She dragged out the word as if it pained her. "He is my teddy bear."

Not solid proof but enough. "I'll come get you."

"Hurry. I can hear him moving around, and I only have thirty-two minutes left on my phone."

"I'm sending you a Find a Friend request," Jordan said. "Accept it."

"Okay."

Jordan sent the request. "Do you see it?"

"Yes. I accepted it."

"Okay."

"I have to hang up," Casey said quickly. "He's coming downstairs again."

The line went dead.

Jordan clicked on her bedside light and winced against the brightness as she grabbed the jeans and shirt she had draped over a rocker in her room. Dressed, she shoved her feet into boots and dialed another number.

He answered on the first ring. "Spencer."

"This is Jordan Poe. I received a call from a missing girl. Casey Andrews. She says she's been kidnapped. I think her case is connected to the Jane Does."

"The case you mentioned in your voicemail?"

"Yes."

"How do you know it's legit?"

"Missing persons told me about her case. I followed up this afternoon, and her mother gave me her phone number as well as the name of her childhood teddy bear. This person knew the toy's name was Max."

He cleared his throat. "And now she's called you."

She hurried across her room, attached the gun holster to her belt, and shoved her weapon inside. "I added her phone numbers to Find a Friend. I have a signal."

"Send her location to me."

She sent what she had to him. "She's twenty-five minutes from my house."

"Thirty-five from mine. That's pretty far from the last two houses."

"Maybe he's changing it up after the news conference."

"I'll call the local deputies' office. Do not engage alone."

The order made her bristle. "I know how to handle myself."

"Wait for me. I'm on my way."

Jordan raced out of her house and to her car. She backed out of her driveway, narrowly missing Avery's car, and drove down the darkened streets of her neighborhood. The scenery was familiar, but she was driving so fast now it was little more than a blur. Above, the crescent moon and stars were vivid, bright in a clear sky.

South of the city Jordan saw her exit coming, but she barely slowed. Her heart racing, she was already fearful this was a ruse, and she was going to find Casey Andrews dead.

Her phone rang, shrill and demanding, and when she saw Spencer's name, she cursed the intrusion. "Detective Poe."

"Where are you?"

"Three minutes out." Casey had only a handful of minutes remaining on her phone.

"Deputies are five minutes out."

Two minutes' difference. Did not sound like much, unless you were trapped in plastic. "Understood."

"You and I both know this could be a trap. There're plenty of nutjobs out there that would like nothing more than to take a cop down."

She slowed and turned down a small road that led toward the hills. "I hear you."

"Do you?"

"I don't have time for this, Spencer. Just get your ass here."

She ended the call as she stared at her maps app. She was fifty feet from her next turn, so she jammed on the brakes, listened as the gravel kicked under her tires, and made the turn on what felt like two wheels.

She killed her lights and followed the gravel driveway toward a small house that was completely illuminated. She stopped her vehicle and shut off her engine. Casey's phone had minutes remaining.

As she sat watching the house, she searched for any sign of Casey or whoever was with her. There were no other vehicles that she could see, but an outbuilding on the edge of the shadows was large enough to hide one.

She checked her time. Three minutes. Glancing over her shoulder, she scanned the horizon, hoping for the lights of another cop car.

Her nerves twisted tighter, making it impossible for her to sit. She switched off her dome light and then opened her door. Rising up out of the car, she did not fully close the driver's-side door.

Drawing her weapon, she moved along the driveway. In the distance an owl hooted. She was out here alone. Backup was minutes away, but in her world that was the difference between life and death.

She moved up toward the small stone steps that led to a narrow porch. Tall windows gave her a view of a worn couch, a set of antlers hanging over it, and a coffee table. There was a kitchen off to the side, two doors that must have led into bedrooms, and a back door.

The layout of the house was similar to the other murder locations, and if this was a hoax, it was elaborate.

Thud.

The sound echoed from inside the house.

She paused, tensed, and listened.

Thud.

Crouching, Jordan moved toward the window to the right of the front door and pressed her back to the aging wood siding. She peered inside but did not see anyone.

Thud.

She shifted her position to the left and looked toward the kitchen. That was when she saw the feet wrapped in plastic.

Thud.

Bound feet jerked like a mermaid beached on land. She looked toward the driveway but did not see the flash of cop car lights.

"Shit."

Jordan tried the front door and discovered it was unlocked. She carefully pushed it open, pausing to look left, right, even up. There were no signs that there was anyone else in the house.

The bedroom doors were closed, making them the wild cards. She hurried toward the first, threw it open but saw nothing except cobwebs and an old cast-iron bed with no mattress. She hurried to the second door, pushed it, and inside saw empty boxes, a broken chair, and bags of trash.

Thud. The sound was softer now. The clock ticked faster.

Jordan moved along the wall, looked in the kitchen, and got her first full look at the woman. Her hands and feet were bound, she was gagged, and her body was fully wrapped in the thick plastic that had killed the other two women.

Wild eyes peered through the clear wrapping up at Jordan. Desperate, terrified, Casey moaned loudly, her screams muffled by the gag and the plastic.

Jordan rushed toward her, her heart pounding against her ribs with bruising strength. "Casey, is there anyone else here?"

Casey shook her head and strained her hands against the rope, using what reserves she might still have. Jordan holstered her weapon and knelt beside Casey.

Jordan's first instinct was to tear at the plastic covering Casey's face, but it was thick and double layered. She reached for a small pocketknife she always carried and flicked it open. The desperate hope in Casey's gaze was palpable.

Police sirens wailed in the distance, and the lights of a cop car flickered faintly on the walls.

Jordan punctured the plastic near Casey's shoulder with the knife tip and quickly pulled it upward, slicing the synthetic wrapping easily. She skimmed the blade past Casey's left ear and up to her scalp. She nicked the woman's cheek above her ear, but the little trickle of blood was a small price.

Jordan reached the top of Casey's head, wiggled fingers in the opening, and peeled back the layers. Oxygen rushed Casey, and her nostrils flared as she greedily sucked in air. Her face appeared thinner than in her pictures, and her lips were tinged a light blue.

"It's okay; I got you," Jordan said.

She pushed back the remaining plastic from Casey's face and, for the first time in a long while, felt like she had cheated death.

Next came the gag. It was a white T-shirt material, wadded into a tight ball and shoved deep in her mouth. Jordan grabbed the cotton and pulled it free. Casey coughed and tried to moisten dried lips with an even drier tongue.

"It's okay," Jordan repeated.

Casey sucked in a breath, letting out a scream that sounded more animal than human.

The police lights on the walls grew brighter. They'd be here in a minute or two.

"You're safe."

"No," Casey croaked. She shook her head, and her gaze shifted from Jordan's face to a point just over her right shoulder. She yelled out a warning.

Jordan's skin tightened as she reached for her gun. The barrel had barely cleared the holster when she heard a man say, "Too smart." And then she felt a blunt object strike the back of her head with a savage force.

The pain was bone rattling and lit up all the pain receptors in her body. Her grip on her weapon slackened, and her body crumpled. She fell onto her side, hitting the wooden floor hard.

Jordan looked over at Casey. Wide, desperate eyes blinked back tears. Fear and sorrow ricocheted toward her.

That was the last image Jordan saw before her world went dark.

***

"You didn't wait. Shit! I knew you wouldn't wait," Spencer growled.

He slowed as he passed Jordan's empty vehicle parked near the house. He gunned the engine and did not hit the brakes until he was just feet from the porch. Behind him the lights of the deputies' cars grew brighter as he reached for his weapon.

In the distance, tire wheels sped over dirt as he leaped over the steps onto the porch and moved toward the open door, the soles of his boots striking hard, as two deputies sprang out of their vehicles, weapons drawn. Both advanced behind him as he pushed through the front door. His gaze swept left and right. In the distance he heard wheels scraping over a driveway.

His first instinct was to pursue, but it vanished when he saw the plastic sheeting discarded near the small kitchen. He raced across the dusty wide-plank floor and around the corner.

That was where he found Jordan Poe.

She lay on her side, her head haloed in a pool of blood, her body so still and lifeless. His first reaction was anger toward her attacker and also her. It was not logical for him to be mad at her, but there it was.

He holstered his weapon and knelt beside her, pressing his fingers to her throat. He did not detect a heartbeat. His world narrowed to his fingertips and his search for any sign of life.

As a deputy approached, he shouted, "Call for an ambulance! If there's a med flight available, even better. And search the grounds for the missing woman and the killer."

The deputy immediately ordered medical assistance and search crew deployed as Spencer repositioned his fingertips against the soft skin of her neck, now speckled with blood. His fingers grew slick as he rooted around for any sign of life.

"Why the hell didn't you wait another minute? Just one damn minute."

And then he found it. The beat was faint. Erratic. But it was there.

"Hang in there, Jordan. Do not leave. Do you understand? Do not leave."

He ran his hands over her chest, abdomen, and back, searching for other wounds. There did not appear to be any injuries other than the gash on the back of her head.

Her face grew paler by the moment. "Jordan!"

She did not move or respond to the sound of his voice.

"Jordan! The paramedics are on the way. Put some of that goddamned stubbornness of yours to work and hang on."

"Ambulance is fifteen minutes out," the deputy said.

The wad of plastic behind Spencer appeared to have been sliced in two. Beside it were discarded T-shirt material and a billy club. "Casey was in the plastic, wasn't she, Jordan? You saw her and ran inside."

She made no audible response. There was only the faint gurgling of her labored breath. He rubbed his hand on her arm, hoping human contact would keep her rooted to this earth. The world narrowed to just the two of them.

"How much longer for the ambulance?" Spencer shouted.

"Ten minutes out!" a deputy said.

"Is there a med flight?"

"Med flight is on another call. They're sending the rescue squad."

"We have ten minutes, Jordan," he said. "Ten lousy minutes."

What the hell was it with time? It could be recklessly fast and make him beg for more of it. And, in times like this, so unbearably slow.

CHAPTER TWELVE

Thursday, April 15
3:00 a.m.

Spencer knelt over Jordan, bracing as helplessness and anger collided inside him. She lay so still, and the pool of blood seeping from the gash in the back of her head kept growing. He knew head wounds bled profusely and often looked worse than they were. What bothered him was that she was not moving or responding to the sound of his voice. Versed in the basics of field medicine, he knew the longer someone was unconscious, the more dire the injury.

"Detective Poe," he said, lowering his face close to hers. "I need you to open your eyes."

Her eyelids fluttered slightly, but she did not open them.

"Detective, you have to wake up. We need to find Casey."

If she by some miracle opened her eyes, he was not going to let her do anything but wait for the paramedics, who were now about five minutes out. He mentioned Casey only because Jordan's persistence on these cases told him she was the type to rally more for someone in trouble than she was for herself.

"Jordan, Casey needs you."

Her fingers twitched, and he took it as progress. "The other deputies are searching for her now. We can't find her. Either she was able to get up and run away, or whoever brought her here took her away."

Eyes rolled under her lids.

Distant sirens echoed in the night. The paramedics. Finally. The wide-open spaces of Texas were stunning, but reaching a location like this often took too long.

The phone in Jordan's pocket rang, and he fished it out. The number had no name attached to it. He answered the call. He took her hand in his, squeezed her fingers tight. "Ranger Spencer."

There was silence on the other end.

"Who is this?" he demanded.

The line went dead. He forwarded the number to his phone and then called the dispatcher's office. When the operator picked up, he gave his badge information and the caller's number with orders to trace it.

Spencer checked the Find a Friend app, searched Casey's number, and discovered the phone was not sending a signal. He scrolled through Jordan's recent calls, noting the call from Casey Andrews that came in around 2:00 a.m. Jordan had picked up, and the call had lasted for a little over a minute. Whatever was said, it had propelled Jordan out here immediately.

There were also other text messages from Avery Poe, Detective Marla Rivers, and Constance Sanchez.

Avery Poe: Where are you?

Detective Rivers: Call me.

Constance Sanchez: We need to talk.

As he tucked her phone in his pocket, the paramedics arrived and pushed through the front door. He gave Jordan's hand an extra squeeze and then rose, making room for the two paramedics.

"What happened?" the first paramedic asked.

"She sustained a blow to the back of the head. I can't find any other injuries."

"Right."

Spencer's gloved hands were slick with her blood. Though tempted to remove the gloves, he paused and burned the memory into his brain. This kind of moment had happened only one other time in his career. A sheriff's deputy near El Paso had been shot point-blank while assisting the Rangers with the delivery of a warrant. Other deputies had apprehended the suspect as Spencer had knelt next to the thirty-three-year-old man and watched him die.

"You better not die, Jordan Poe." He stepped out onto the porch. The sky was clear, and the stars winked bright in the ink-black sky. He had the sensation of ice-cold water spreading in his veins.

"Ranger Spencer."

The man speaking was one of the two deputies who had arrived seconds after he had.

"Did you find anything?" Spencer asked.

"Footprints and tire tracks," he said. "Whoever assaulted Detective Poe appears to have run out the back door to a large shed."

"Are there one or two sets of prints?"

"Looks like one, but in the dark it's impossible to tell. We'll have to get more light out here."

"The footprints led to the shed?"

"That's right, sir. And whoever ran to the shed had a vehicle parked there. There're tire tracks leading out the back of the property."

"I thought I heard someone drive off. Any idea what direction?"

"There's a paved road about a quarter of a mile from here. The driver made it to the road, but after that it's impossible to tell if he went east or west."

"Mark the footprints and tire tracks. We need to save everything we can." A lot of the evidence inside the house, if there was much, was being destroyed now by the paramedics. But that was how it went. Life before anything else.

He had been on the job long enough to savor enough wins to keep going, but there were more days twisted up with losses. All his years on the job weighed heavily on his shoulders now.

Inside the house, he heard the paramedics count to three and then raise the gurney and carry it down the few steps. Pausing, one kicked a lever, and the wheels dropped and snapped into place. A medic raised an IV bag as the trio rolled toward him.

Jordan's head was now wrapped in white gauze, but already her wound was bleeding through.

"What's her status?" Spencer asked.

"Breathing. Still not responsive to voice commands or pain stimuli," the paramedic with the raised IV said.

The other rescue worker did not stop moving toward the rescue squad truck. "She'll need an MRI and other tests to determine what damage has been done."

Spencer matched their pace. "Where are you taking her?"

"Dell Seton Medical Center at UT in Austin. It has the best trauma medicine in the county."

"Right. Thanks." That put her thirty minutes from the emergency room. Enough time for a brain bleed to do serious damage.

He would follow as soon as he could, but for now his best work would happen at the crime scene. Jordan would have done the same.

As the ambulance's back door closed with one paramedic at Jordan's side, the other slid into the front seat. The lights and sirens flashed, and the vehicle raced toward the darkness.

Spencer stripped off his gloves and swapped them for a clean pair. He walked toward Jordan's car and discovered the driver's-side door ajar. Her keys remained in the ignition. She had come in, lights out no doubt, and eased out of her car. What had compelled her not to sit tight and wait? She was stubborn but not reckless, so something had triggered her.

Her purse had fallen to the passenger floor, and he slid behind the wheel and picked it up. He opened her wallet, noted her home address. He was not sure whom to notify and realized he did not know if she was married or living with someone or, God help her, had children waiting for her to come home. He punched her home address into his phone. He would stop by the house and notify her family. Shit. If he had been five minutes faster.

The forensic van arrived, as did three other cop cars behind it. He strode toward Captain Lee, who climbed out of his cruiser. Stubble covered his chin, he was not wearing a tie, and his legs moved as if his knees hurt. Most Texas boys had played football in junior high, high school, and, in some cases, college. By their midfifties, every tackle showed in their strides.

"What the hell happened?" Captain Lee asked.

"Detective Poe called me, told me she had received a call from a missing girl, and she came out here. She called for backup but beat us all here."

"Drives like a bat out of hell." He rubbed the back of his neck. "Passed the rescue squad on the way in. How is she?"

"Unconscious."

Captain Lee cursed. He rested his hands on his hips and sucked in a breath before pursing his lips. Spencer read the body language. The captain was doing his best to lock down his feelings.

Spencer spent the next few minutes updating Captain Lee on what he had found. The tire tracks, the footprints, and the discarded plastic expertly sliced up the middle.

Lee cleared his throat. "Same guy that killed the Jane Does?"

"It looks like it," Spencer said.

"How the hell did Jordan get in contact with the victim?"

"She called her cell. Either spoke to her or left a message. The return call came around an hour ago."

"I want every available body out here."

"Already on their way."

***

Casey tried to twist out of her captor's iron grip as he dragged her back to her darkened room. Each time she struggled to break free, his fingers tightened in a bruising hold.

"How the hell did she find you?" he growled.

"Let me go, please," she begged.

He opened the door and shoved her inside. He reached for the bag that held her clothes and searched each article until he found the phone in her coat pocket. "Two phones. Very clever."

"Please, let me go."

"I'm not done with you yet. We have to finish."

"Finish what? Are you going to wrap me in plastic again?"

"Of course. We'll have to start over from the beginning."

The beginning. He had played with her for hours before he'd taken her to the house. She was not sure she could live through that again.

The door slammed hard. And the small light bulb above her head went out. She was plunged into darkness.

She ran her fingers over her face, remembering the weight of the plastic, the blistering panic, and the desperate hunger for air.

The detective had cut into the plastic. Air. Precious air had filled her lungs. She'd believed she had been saved. And then he had reappeared and moved so swiftly Detective Poe had not had time to react. He had raised a club and hit her hard on the back of the head. Triumph had glimmered in his gaze as he'd watched the detective go down hard on the floor.

In the distance police sirens wailed. She had prayed he would panic and run and leave her to the cops. But he had sliced up the remaining plastic and pressed the knife to her neck.

"I'll kill you if you make a sound. Understood?"

Casey had nodded, knowing his was not an empty threat. He would have gutted her right here. "Yes."

He had lifted her easily and tossed her over his shoulder and then scooped up the bag containing her clothes. Stunned, she had wrestled against her restraints but had been too weak to fight.

Now as she sat in her darkened cell, naked and cold, she drew in a deep breath and tried not to think about Detective Poe's blood pooling around them both.

"I'm sorry." Casey drew her feet up and hugged her knees close to her body. "I just wanted to live."

CHAPTER THIRTEEN

Thursday, April 15
7:30 a.m.

Spencer pulled up in front of a small ranch in an established neighborhood. An older yellow sedan with a few flower decals attached to the bumper sat in the driveway. The sedan must belong to the sister. From what Captain Lee had told him, Jordan had one sister, Avery Poe; no boyfriend; and no children.

Jordan's keys felt heavy in his hands as he strode toward the front door, painted a deep orange. The color was unexpected, a little quirky considering Jordan Poe's intensity. The peephole in the center and the heavy-duty lock and door hinges were practical security measures that fit her personality.

Drawing in a breath, he knew the day would never come when visits like this were anything less than excruciating. By rights, Captain Lee should have made the notification, but Spencer felt as if this was his responsibility. If he had been faster, Jordan would have been fine and Casey safe and sound. Rolling back his shoulders, he rang the bell.

Inside, footsteps hurried over what sounded like hardwood floors. Security chains scraped out of their holders and then a moment's hesitation as someone must have thought twice and checked the peephole. He stood back, giving his viewer a good look at him.

The door opened to a woman who looked like a younger, shorter version of Jordan Poe. Her hair was lighter, streaked with blue strands, and it draped around her shoulders in a tangle of curls, but the eyes and nose were almost identical to Jordan's.

"I'm Carter Spencer with the Texas Rangers."

"I've heard about you," the young woman said. "I'm Avery Poe. If you're looking for my sister, she left early this morning. I don't know where she is."

"Your sister was injured last night," he said carefully. "She's at Dell Seton."

Her curious expression shifted to alarm. "Was she shot?"

"No. She was struck on the back of the head by an unknown assailant. She was still unconscious the last time I saw her."

"Jesus," she said, running trembling fingers through her hair. "How? Where did this happen?"

"She's been chasing a killer we believe is a serial offender."

"I know about the case. I thought you took it over."

"I did. But your sister kept working the case."

She shook her head. "That would be Jordan."

"I can drive you to the hospital."

"No, I'll drive myself."

Avery shared her sister's fearless, independent vein. "There are too many unknowns at this point. Your sister received a call from a missing woman, who we haven't found yet. I don't know if the killer set your sister up or she surprised him. It would be safer if I drive you."

The first reactions at times like this were shock and fear. And then the brain kicked into gear. Schedules were hurriedly rearranged. Priorities shifted, and most of what had been important turned trivial.

"Okay, you can drive me. Let me grab my purse." She grabbed a leather satchel purse from a small table in the foyer and shoved her feet into worn Birkenstock sandals. She locked the door behind her, and he followed her toward his car. Avery paused when she saw the empty spot in the driveway where Jordan must park.

He handed her Jordan's keys. "Her car is with the forensic team. We'll return it as soon as it's processed."

"God," she muttered as she twisted her fingers around the keys.

Soon, they were both in the front seat, and he was driving toward the hospital.

"How could this guy target Jordan?" Avery asked. "She's not reckless or stupid."

"We know the victim was able to contact Jordan and asked for help. I don't think the woman was working for the killer, but time will tell."

"I heard her leave the house after two a.m. But that's the way it's always been with her job." Avery gripped the keys tighter. "Where the hell was backup?"

"The deputies and I were minutes behind her. We think when she arrived on the scene, she decided to investigate."

Avery shook her head. "I've told her a million times not to be a hero."

He tightened his hands on the wheel. "I've been in situations like that before. It's hard not to act."

Both sank into a heavy silence as he drove to the hospital. When he pulled up to the emergency room entrance, he put the car in park. "Go on inside. I'll park and then meet you."

"Is she still in emergency?"

"She was. I don't know where she is now."

"You saw her, right?"

"Yes."

"What am I going to be facing?"

"It was a blow to the back of her head. I detected no other injuries."

Avery dropped the keys in her purse and reached for the door handle. "Right."

"You okay?"

"I have to be."

Out of the car, she walked through the sliding glass doors and vanished into the hospital.

***

Spencer had remained at the hospital for several hours. When the doctors took Jordan into surgery, he realized he was of no help to anyone, sitting around and waiting. His focus shifted to his job and finding Casey Andrews.

He decided to visit the Austin Police Department's missing person division. Removing his hat, Spencer walked into the Austin Police Department station and went directly toward Detective Rivers's office.

When he knocked on Detective Rivers's door, she was on the phone, but as soon as they made eye contact, she ended the call and rose.

"You must be Ranger Spencer," she said.

"That's right, Detective Rivers. We need to talk about Casey Andrews."

"I've been pulling everything I know about her since Detective Poe's attack. Have you heard how Jordan is doing?"

"She was in surgery when I left."

Rivers drew in a lungful of air as she dropped her gaze to the file on her desk. "I assumed you would be by, so I've gathered everything I know about Casey Andrews. Detective Poe said she was going to talk to the girl's mother, Dot Andrews, and I assume she followed up."

"I've not had a chance to debrief Detective Poe, but I hope to soon." He had no idea when Jordan would be able to process case information, but for her sake, he wanted everyone to believe she would recover.

He thumbed through a contact list. At the top was Dot Andrews, and below that was Missy Stapleton. "Who is Ms. Stapleton?"

"Casey's former roommate," she said.

"Have you spoken to Ms. Stapleton?"

"I've put several calls into her cell phone, but she has not called me back. She has a history of drug abuse. According to Casey's mother, Casey moved out when she decided to get clean."

Casey fit the profile of so many missing women. Their transient lives meant critical time could pass before alarm bells were sounded. If not for Dot Andrews, weeks might have passed before anyone thought to look for Casey. "I'll find Ms. Stapleton."

"Understood."

"What can you tell me about Tammy Fox?"

"She's originally from back east. She still has an uncle in Maryland. She also filed a restraining order against a boyfriend in Houston."

"Any word on where he is?"

"Prison. Convicted of armed robbery three months ago."

"I'll need copies of her case file as well as files for Susan Wallace."

"Of course."

He leaned close, knowing he towered over her. "Search your records back about ten years. Find me the files of all the missing persons who resemble these women."

"I'll get on it now."

"And Detective Rivers, next time you have a lead in one of my cases, you call me. Don't go behind my back again." His voice was low, level. "Understand?"

She raised her chin a notch. "Yes, sir."

Jordan's injury had burrowed under his skin, scraped against his nerves, and left him spoiling for a fight. It was better he left now than unload his frustrations on Rivers.

In his car, he checked the address for Missy Stapleton and drove to the small rental house in East Austin. The house was one level and made of an earth-color stucco. The front yard was littered with trash, unused tires, and several cars.

Hand on his weapon, he walked to the front door and banged on it with his fist. When there was no response, he struck the door again, determined to wake up every damn person in the house. Finally, a curtain covering a window fluttered, and the front door opened. The woman standing there was petite with bleached-blond hair. She wore a tank top that showed off a bee tattoo on her arm and cutoff jeans.

She raised her gaze to the star pinned on his chest, her annoyance softening. "Texas Ranger. What's going on?"

"Are you Missy Stapleton?" he asked.

"Yes." She shifted her weight back and forth.

"You haven't been answering your cell phone."

"Ran out of minutes. Why are you here?"

"I have questions about Casey Andrews."

Her eyes narrowed. "I haven't seen her in weeks. Maybe a month." She slipped her hands into her pockets. "We both worked at the same place but different shifts. We were supposed to get coffee soon but never could settle on a time."

"Why did she move out?"

"She's on this new clean-and-sober kick."

"And that's not for you?"

She hesitated. "I want to be. And will be one day. But now's not the best time." She glanced at her bare toes painted with red polish. The big toe's polish was chipped.

"I'm trying to find Casey. Did she ever mention anyone that might be bothering her?"

"Her drug dealer was hassling her the other day. He had tempted her with a baggie of drugs. She took it but said she couldn't toss it."

"You said you haven't seen her."

"It was a text." She reached for her back pocket and produced a phone sporting a blue rhinestone case.

"Can I see your recent text exchanges with Casey?" Spencer asked.

She hesitated. "Sure."

April 13, 7:00 p.m.

Casey: Saw Walker.

Missy: And?

Casey: He gave me a sample.

Missy: Bring it by, girl. We can celebrate.

Casey: I should toss it.

Missy: Give it to me if you don't want it. Crazy to waste anything.

"Do you know Walker?" Spencer asked. When she hesitated, he asked, "Marco Walker?"

"Yes," Missy said. "He deals drugs."

"Any idea why she was back in his area?"

"She lost a lot of friends when she got sober. When someone gets clean, they get a little full of themselves. They become kind of a buzzkill. When no one wants to be around them, they get lonely and start to miss their old life. When they return to the streets, it's a matter of time before Walker appears."

"Why is Walker so popular?" Spencer asked.

"He gives freebies if you're willing to trade sex with him or one of his friends," Missy said.

"Tell me about these friends," Spencer said. "Any one of the friends not get along with Walker?"

"Walker pisses a lot of people off. He often makes promises he doesn't keep. Most can't do anything about it, but some can."

"Tell me about the people he can't charm," Spencer said.

"I make it a point to keep away from those guys. I don't want to end up hanging from a rope in my house like he did."

Casey had vanished hours before Walker had hanged himself. If Walker had passed Casey off to a friend, he would have had to have done it on the thirteenth or fourteenth. "You ever heard of a guy named Harold Sunday?"

"The lawyer?"

"That's right."

She shifted her feet. "He's been with a few of Walker's girls."

"Did he ever get rough?"

"Sure. But they all can be."

"Anyone like to strangle the girls?"

"Once in a while."

"What about Sunday?"

"I don't know. The girls don't talk that much. They're too afraid."

"I won't let him hurt you."

A bitter smile twisted her lips. "You can't make that promise. No one can."

He handed her his card. "If you change your mind and want to talk, call, okay?"

"Sure. Sure."

"Thank you for your time." He left her staring after him as he crossed the yard and got back into his vehicle. Casey had disappeared on April 13 or 14, and they were hard dates he could work from.

Spencer's next stop was the forensic department. Inside the building, he removed his hat and found Andy Lucas and an assistant looking into a microscope. Neither looked up when he entered the room, forcing him to clear his throat. "Officer Lucas."

The man shifted his gaze up. "Have you heard how Poe is doing?"

"No, but when she's awake, I'd like to take her status report. You have anything new?"

"We do." He pulled off his glasses, drawing attention to dark circles under his eyes. They were all putting in long hours. They had two, possibly three, victims and an injured cop.

"First to the Jane Does," Lucas said. "The first did not have any kind of dental, breast, or medical device I can track with a serial number."

"And the second victim?"

"The medical examiner was able to pull fingerprints, and we matched those to Tammy Fox's."

Jane Doe #2 had a name. According to Rivers's file, Tammy Fox had vanished five or six days ago. She had last been seen in a bar called the Saloon. Her employer had filed her report.

"Less than one week means there's a good shot at getting security footage," Lucas said.

"We already have the footage. Detective Poe spoke to Dustin Tate at the Saloon and requested it. Got a tech going through it now."

"Perfect."

"Now to the plastic found at the last crime scene." Lucas motioned him toward a light table. "We put it in a fuming chamber." When evidence was placed inside a fuming chamber, superglue was added to the heating element, and after a press of the start button, the vaporized glue adhered to latent fingerprints.

"And?"

"We found plenty of Detective Poe's prints around the face. Most were smudged but enough were clear. On the inside, we found more prints belonging to Casey Andrews. There is an assortment of partial and random prints, and we're running those."

So far, this guy had not been sloppy, and the risks he'd taken appeared to be calculated. It didn't make sense that he wouldn't have worn gloves.

"What else did you find on the plastic?"

"Detective Poe's blood. Casey Andrews's sweat and traces of urine. We also pulled several dark hair strands from inside the plastic. We're running DNA on that."

"The killer?"

"We can only hope that's a yes and his DNA is on file."

"What about the footprints found at each scene?" Spencer asked.

"Same set of shoes at all three sites."

"There was semen found in Tammy Fox."

"No hits in CODIS yet, but we're comparing it to the hair fibers found at the Andrews scene."

Legwork and good detective work identified an offender. When a cop had a name, then forensics could prove or disprove he had the right guy. "Keep me updated."

"Will do."

He left the building, settled his hat on his head, and as he crossed the lot, his phone rang. "Ranger Spencer."

"This is Dr. McIntyre. I was told to call you and remind you that I've scheduled the Walker autopsy for Saturday morning at nine."

"I'll see you then."

In his car, he tossed his hat on the passenger seat and sat for a moment. The image of Jordan lying in a pool of blood raced across his mind.

He gripped the steering wheel hard, wishing right now that he could rip it off the column and hurl it across the parking lot. When he was younger, his temper had ruled him. There had been fistfights as a teenager, too much drinking, and arguments with his superiors. He was older, wiser now, and thought all that had been under control for years. He had been wrong.

He rubbed his hand over his chin, the callus scraping over the stubble. He had not had the chance to shower or shave since he'd responded to Poe's call. He needed to get cleaned up, eat. If he did not refuel, he would not be of use to Jane Doe #1, Tammy Fox, Casey Andrews, and Jordan Poe.

As he pulled out, it occurred to him that Jordan would not like being on his list of victims. Going forward, he would be more careful. Important to keep treating her like a cop.

CHAPTER FOURTEEN

Thursday, April 15
11:30 a.m.

Jordan was aware of voices swirling around her. Her head was pounding. Her mouth felt as if it had been stuffed with cotton. And the room was so dark.

She thought if she could sit up, the pressure in her head would ease, but when she tried, someone pushed her back down. "Stay still, Detective Poe."

She had never been good at following directions, and so the order irritated her and made her more determined to rise. She needed to sit up. Clear her head. And get the hell out of here.

"Detective Poe. Do not move." The woman's sharp tone insinuated there was no room for discussion. It reminded her of Captain Lee when he ordered her to back off a case and move on to the next. He was better at recognizing when an investigation should be set aside and the detective needed to move on. Letting go of a case never got easy. Accepting this order was not, either.

She would have argued with the voice if her head did not feel as if it had been cracked in half. What the hell had happened? Her scrambled memory was so knotted up with the damn pain.

"Where am I?" She did not recognize her own voice, which sounded as raw as sandpaper.

"You're in the hospital, Detective," the woman said. "You have sustained a head injury. You underwent surgery."

"Surgery?"

"To relieve pressure on your brain."

Her arm rose, an IV tugged, and she brushed her fingers over the bandage wrapped around her head. "How did I get here?"

"You don't remember?" The woman's tone turned grave. Jordan had not given the right answer, which meant she was supposed to remember. She let her mind drift back, but the inky blackness was too damn thick.

"I remember," she said. She had bluffed her way out of tight spots on the job before.

"Do you really?" The woman did not believe her.

"I hit my head." Factually true, given the pain in the back of her skull. "Who are you?"

"Your nurse. And no, you were hit," the nurse corrected.

She had been hit. When? Who?

But the answers, like scrambled puzzle pieces, would not seam together. "Where's my sister?"

"She's outside. She wants to see you."

"I want to see her." For Avery's sake, she tried to open her eyes, but the lids were so damn heavy.

"Don't try to open your eyes," the nurse said. "It's better they stay closed."

"I need to see Avery. To show her I'm fine."

"The doctor is updating her now," the nurse said. "We'll let her in soon. First, you need an MRI."

"Avery has to go to work. And I have a new shift soon." What time was it?

"No one is going anywhere, Detective Poe."

***

Hours later, when Jordan opened her eyes, the MRI was an unpleasant memory. She had been too weak to argue about being put in the confining tube, so she'd pretended she was lying on the beach, canopied by blue sky and not the metal inches from her nose.

Now, back in her room, her brain was not slamming against the side of her skull like it had been. But it felt bruised and tender. Her tongue remained heavy and thick.

A hand rested on her arm. "Stay still, Jordan."

"Avery?" Jordan asked.

"Yep, it's me." She sniffed. Cleared her throat.

"You sound upset."

"Just a little rattled. You know I don't like hospitals."

"How did I get injured?" Jordan asked.

"You were attacked."

The memory danced on the edges of her brain. "By who?"

"They don't know. Ranger Spencer found a billy club near you. Your blood was on it. He's investigating."

"Spencer is a dick."

Avery laughed softly. "He seems okay to me."

"I should be investigating."

"Not this go-around."

"Why not?"

Jordan tried to sit up again. But whatever tentative agreement her body had brokered with the pain dissolved, and her skull throbbed in agony. She sank back against the pillows and kept her body steady until she could negotiate a new truce.

"Why is the room so dark?" Jordan asked.

Avery hesitated. "It's dark outside."

"How long have I been here?"

"Twelve hours."

"What? That can't be right." An IV tugged at her arm and a nearby machine beeped.

"You had to have surgery. You had a brain bleed," Avery said.

"But I'm okay, right?"

Avery's warm fingers gripped hers. "Yes. You're alive, and the rest will come in time."

"What *rest*?" Jordan asked.

"There's going to be rehab," Avery said carefully.

Jordan wiggled her toes and fingers. "I can move. Avery, turn on the lights so I can at least see what's going on," she said.

"They need to stay off for now," Avery said. "Doctor's orders. The darkness will help prevent the headaches."

She tried to sit up, and her effort was rewarded by a sharp jab inside her skull. The pain took her breath away, and she immediately eased back against the pillows. "Fair enough."

"Your body needs time to heal."

"It needs to heal fast," she said. "I've never been good with lying around."

Avery rested a steadying hand on her arm again. "Sometimes you have to surrender, Jordan. Sometimes patience is all that works."

"This isn't a counseling session, is it?"

She chuckled. "Sorry, I've been to so many the mantras come naturally."

"Can you get a doctor in here to see me?" Jordan asked. "I want a debriefing."

"That'll come in the morning when the doctors make rotations. And they're doing another MRI," Avery said.

"Why?" Jordan demanded.

"They want to confirm the swelling is going down," Avery said. "And you have a dozen stitches in the back of your head that need checking."

Stitches in the back of her head. "And when they do, can I get out of here?" she asked.

Avery drew in a breath. "Of course."

"What aren't you telling me?" she asked.

"Nothing," Avery said.

Jordan might not be able to see her expression, but she had known Avery long enough to recognize when she was lying.

CHAPTER FIFTEEN

Friday, April 16
9:00 a.m.

Jordan was about to lose it.

The nurses were insisting that her room stay totally dark. There had been a second MRI, and this go-around, she was not as dazed. She was fully awake and very aware that the tube the technicians had put her in was like a coffin. Suffocating.

Now she was back in her room. She had sent Avery home. Told her to shower and eat. Her sister needed a break, and so did Jordan. She required all her energy to brace for what the doctors were going to tell her, and putting on a brave face for Avery might just be too much.

There was a knock on her door, and she sat up. Automatically, she ran fingers through her hair to flatten out some of the tangles, but her fingers brushed the white gauze that wrapped around her head.

"Come in." The shadow that entered the room was tall, broad shouldered, and bore a familiar scent. "Ranger Spencer."

"That's right," he said carefully. "Doc said I need to keep the light off."

She sat a little taller. "That's what they're telling me. I should get the rundown on my status any minute."

"I can leave."

"No, I'd rather you stay. Distract me. Tell me about the crime scene." Self-conscious, she wondered what she looked like. She wanted to appear professional but knew hospital gowns made the strongest look weak.

A chair pulled up beside her bed. "You sure you want to hear about it?"

"Not sure what it says about me, but I would like nothing better." She held up a hand. "Skip the part about me rushing in alone. No lectures."

"None to give."

She arched a brow. "Really? You sure about that?"

"I'm too busy kicking myself for not being faster. What happened?"

"The details are still foggy."

"Tell me what you know."

A smile tugged her lips. "You're being too nice."

"Am I?" No hints of amusement in his tone.

"I figured you would read me the riot act," she said.

"I still might. For now, tell me what you remember. Start with the call from Casey Andrews."

"Did you find her in time? Were you able to save her?"

"No," he said. "The killer removed her from the plastic and took her."

"Took her?" Jordan shifted her body toward the sound of his deep voice.

"We found you on the floor beside the plastic. Casey Andrews's DNA and fingerprints were on the plastic."

"So, she really did call me."

"Sounds like you're doubting yourself."

"Too much time and too many drugs pumped into my system. A few times I couldn't tell you what year it was."

"Your mind is not playing tricks. Casey did call you."

The fact primed the pump, and more details rose to the surface. "Her mother told me she had two phones. She called me on the burner."

"What did she say?"

"She told me she was in trouble. That she needed my help. How did I find her?"

"Find a Friend. She accepted your request to track her."

His words primed more memories. "I wanted to break the case, but I wasn't going to approach the house until you or the deputies arrived. But all the lights were on in the house, and I had a bad feeling about it." Faint memories of Casey wrapped in plastic emerged through the fog. "I heard several thud sounds. I saw her wrapped up."

"And waiting for me would have been a death sentence for her."

"That's what I thought."

"I would have done the same."

"You said he took Casey," Jordan said. "Did he kill her and dump her body somewhere else?"

"We haven't found her yet."

"You didn't see him?"

"I saw you lying on the floor, and that was enough to stop me in my tracks."

"I wish you'd pursued him."

He cleared his throat. "I made the right call."

"What did you find at the scene?"

"The forensic team is still sorting through the evidence. We did identify Jane Doe #2."

"Tammy Fox?"

"Correct."

"Victim #1 is still pending," she said.

"Correct. Did you see anything? Hear anything?" he asked.

"I had tunnel vision." It happened when cops were in a hot pursuit. Their focus narrowed to only their quarry, and they missed what was happening around them. "The plastic was strong, and I was clawing at it. I reached for my pocketknife, cut enough so she could breathe, and saw the terror in her eyes. And then nothing."

"Okay."

"Is her phone still sending a signal?" she asked.

"No. I have an officer checking on the hour. Do you think it might have been a trap?"

"I don't think so. I think Casey really called for help."

"What if he made her call you?" Spencer said.

"It's a possibility. But I think I spooked the killer. He could have murdered Casey and me, but he ran."

"Maybe he thought he had killed you."

"But why take Casey? He would have been able to flee faster without her."

"Unfinished business. Maybe he's compelled to kill Casey in his same ritualistic style."

Suddenly she felt very tired and eased her head back against the pillows. She winced.

"How's the pain?" he asked.

"Creeping back."

"I'll ask the nurses to give you something for it."

"I'd rather not."

"You don't get extra points for suffering."

"Too bad."

"Seriously."

Her head sank deeper into the pillow. "Big substance-abuse problem in my family. Mother died in a car crash because she was drunk. Sister had serious issues with drugs."

"Avery?"

"You've met?"

"I notified her about you."

"How did she seem?"

"Tough."

"Mom could be like that, too. Seem tough, I mean. But inside, they can be fragile. Avery's been sober two years. I don't want my issues to mess her up."

"Don't underestimate her."

Outside in the hallway she heard voices. A man and a woman. And then the door pushed open, bringing with it a rush of air.

"Jordan Poe?" a man asked.

Whatever bravery she had mustered for Spencer evaporated. "That's right."

"I'm Dr. Sam Kensington," he said. "I'm your doctor."

"The man who likes MRIs," she said.

A chair scraped and the energy shifted. "I'll take off now," Spencer said.

Suddenly, her pride, always a sturdy shield, crumbled. She did not want to face this doctor's diagnosis alone. "Spencer, stay. I could use an extra set of eyes. And a second set of ears."

Spencer went silent for a beat. "As long as you need backup."

Dr. Kensington came to her bedside. His aftershave smelled expensive and his energy field, for lack of a better word, was smaller than Spencer's. "As you pointed out, we conducted three MRIs."

"Why three?" she asked.

"The one before your surgery was difficult to read. Once the blood was drained from your skull, we tried for a better picture. Which we got."

"And?" This was the part that was going to hurt. But unlike ripping off a Band-Aid, she feared the sting was going to be long lasting.

"You suffered damage to your ocular nerve, Detective Poe."

"What's that mean?" she asked.

"It's the nerve that translates brain messages into vision. Your brain hemorrhaged after the blow, and the subsequent swelling cut off blood to the nerve, which was deprived for too long. It means your vision is limited now and may be for a long time."

She gazed into the darkness, realizing with a sinking heart that the lights were not off in the room. Was she blind? Her heart rate kicked up several ticks as a chill shuddered through her body. This could not be right. There had to be a mistake.

Mentally, she scrounged for better news. "May be. Might *not* be?"

"Likely," he said carefully. "There's significant damage."

"How will you know for sure?"

"We'll turn the lights up in the room and evaluate what you see."

"So, they're off?" she asked with renewed hope.

"They're dimmed," Dr. Kensington said. "Anyone with normal vision can see fine."

"Spencer, is that true?" she asked.

"Yes," Spencer said.

"Why have the lights been lowered if my vision is impaired?" she asked.

"You might have light sensitivity," Dr. Kensington said.

"I can't see well, but the light could bother me. That's a hell of a contradiction," she said.

"It's not uncommon in people with some types of visual impairments."

Jordan plucked at a loose thread in her blanket. A weighty sense of dread burned through her. "Turn up the lights."

Dr. Kensington came up beside her. *Click.* "I've turned on a penlight," he explained.

A faint light flashed across her eyes. "It's very dim, but it's there. Does this mean I'll get better?"

"Maybe. What you see now could change," Dr. Kensington said. "We might not really know for months."

"I could see again?"

"Maybe."

"What does *maybe* mean? I want a yes or a no."

"I can't give that to you right now."

"Can I lose what little vision I do have?" she asked.

"Yes."

Spencer moved around the foot of the bed and now stood at her left side. The steel radiating in his body shored up her resolve. For the first time since she arrived at the hospital, she took a deep breath. Tears welled in her eyes, and when one spilled down her cheek, she wiped it away.

"Jordan, close your eyes for a moment," the doctor said.

Jordan closed her eyes. The rest of her life, her career . . . everything was on the line. She could not lose what she had worked so hard to build.

"What was Detective Poe struck with?" Dr. Kensington asked.

"We recovered a billy club on the scene," Spencer said. "It had traces of her blood and hair on it."

"He hit the first two victims in the back of the head," Jordan said. "Are there traces of their blood on it?"

"Yes," Spencer said.

"Who are you talking about?" Dr. Kensington asked.

Spencer hesitated. "Detective Poe was investigating two murders involving head traumas and suffocation."

She appreciated that he had not lumped her in with the victims. Knowing it was one thing, but hearing it from him was too much right now.

"Open your eyes slowly."

Her lids were so heavy when she opened them. She searched for the doctor's face, lost in a dense, dark fog. This time the penlight appeared in her line of sight like a distant lighthouse beacon. "I see the light. That's good, right?"

"It's a start," he said.

"When will I see faces? I need some kind of timeline I can hold on to." Her tone carried the desperation tightening in her chest.

The doctor hesitated. "It's impossible to say how long the healing process will take or how far it will go."

Why was getting a definitive answer so hard? Wasn't science supposed to have the answers? "I know. But when will it get better?" She could get through this if she had an end date.

"You keep asking me that, and I don't know, Detective Poe."

"Why don't you know?" The darkness tightened around her, revving up her fear and anger. She could deal with this for days, maybe weeks, but she needed to know when this all ended. "You're a doctor. You are paid to know."

"We'll recheck tomorrow." His voice attempted to be soothing. "I'll run more tests."

"Meaning, you are looking for improvement?"

"That's the hope."

"Hope is not a solid answer." She pressed for the response she really wanted, not the one he was giving her. "At least tell me this could get better."

"It's possible."

"That's what I say to myself when I'm trying to solve the murder case of a homeless junkie. It's conceivable but not likely."

"Detective Poe, you'll need to be in the hospital for a week, maybe longer, so we will continue to monitor you. Don't panic yet. This is only day one."

"Technically, it's day two, and I still can't see," she said. "I think I've got a right to be upset."

"Like I said, we'll do more tests tomorrow. Take it one day at a time." He spoke more about the eyes and the ocular nerve, but the mechanics meant little to her. Like her car engine, she did not care how the spark plugs fired. She just wanted her engine to turn over.

"How do we fix this?" she asked.

"For now, we don't," Dr. Kensington said. "Down the road there're experiments with stem cells."

"How long before I can get the stem cells?"

"It's not something I do, but I have names of doctors."

"Give me the list," Jordan said.

"Again, let's give your body more time to heal. And I don't want to give you false hope. Many of these therapies are experimental."

"What do I do in the meantime? What if I'm released from the hospital, and I can't see?"

"If that's the case, then I'll have an occupational therapist visit you."

"Why?"

"She can talk to you about training for people with vision loss," Dr. Kensington said.

"You mean like braille or a cane?"

"Yes."

"Those don't sound like solutions. They're adaptation strategies," she said. "I'm not going to adjust to this."

"You may not have a choice," Dr. Kensington said.

Life had taken away her ability to choose before when her family had moved from Boston, when her mother had died, and when her sister had gotten high. She had adjusted to it all, but each new forced path had been difficult. And she always mourned the life she'd had before the changes. But the idea that she would never see again was crushing. How could she keep her life and Avery's together if she could not see?

"Are there any questions?" Dr. Kensington asked.

Pressing him for details was like trying to squeeze blood from a stone. "No," she said bluntly.

"You sure?" he asked.

"Unless you have more information to share?"

"No."

"Then we've done all we can today."

"Call me if you need me," Dr. Kensington said.

"Will do." When he left, she gently ran her fingers over her flushed face, noting the knot on the right side of her forehead. She must have hit the floor hard after she had been struck. "You're still there, aren't you, Spencer?"

"Yes."

Having him here was keeping her from breaking down completely. "How does my face look? And if you say 'not bad,' I'll scream."

"Like you went five rounds with a boxer."

"You should see the other guy." The joke fell flat and sounded sad. "Bruises I can deal with. But nerve damage." She closed her eyes for a moment. "This scares the shit out of me, Spencer."

He eased closer to the bed. "One step at a time, Detective."

She wanted him to take her hand, tell her it was all going to be fine. Instead, she counted to three, hoping when she opened her eyes, she would see Spencer's frowning mug and realize all this had been a mistake. She raised her lids and stared into shadows.

"Any luck?" he asked.

Feeling Spencer's scrutiny, she raised her chin. "No."

The darkness shrank in around her, pushing all her fears and insecurities to the surface. She wanted to crumble. She wanted to give up.

"Detective Poe, are you all right?" Spencer asked.

Spencer's voice halted her descent. She swallowed and sat straighter. When this was over and she returned to work, she wanted everyone to acknowledge that she had handled this like a badass. "Yes, because I'm going to get my vision back so I can see this motherfucker's face when the judge sentences him to death."

"I'm going to catch this guy, Jordan." There was no false bravado. Just a brutal determination that almost brought her to tears.

"Cops should never make promises like that," Jordan said. "Didn't you learn that at the police academy?"

"In this case, I'm making an exception."

"And what if you don't catch this guy? What if he vanishes into the mist?" What if her sight never came back?

"He's not getting away from me."

***

Eyes. Panicked, desperate eyes encased in a film of plastic stared back at Jordan. Their watery blue depths pleaded with her for salvation. Jordan reached out to the woman, anxious to help her and free her from the shroud cutting off her oxygen.

"Hang in there," she said. "I'll get you free."

Jordan's fingertips were only inches from the woman's face, which was growing paler and bluer by the moment. However, the gap between them grew with each beat of her heart.

Help me! Help me!

The woman's plea etched deep into her features. Casey.

Jordan strained her muscles, trying to close the distance separating Casey from her. But each time she pressed her fingertips a fraction closer, the woman slipped out of range.

Heart pounding, head thundering, Jordan struggled to breach the divide, and just as she brushed Casey's hand, the woman vanished from sight.

Jordan's eyes opened to a darkened room, her pulse wild in her throat, her head hurting. She had had a dream. Just a dream. She fumbled around for her cell, hoping to figure out the time and date. But her cell was not on her nightstand, where she always left it. She was in bed. Not her own. Where was her own bed?

This had happened before. Always after she had worked several days in a row on a case. So tired, she would fall into bed only to wake disoriented and off her game.

"This happens," she whispered.

But the headache and the darkness were not right. There was always a light on in her house. And where was the ticking clock on the mantel in her den? Avery hated the clock because it made so much noise, but Jordan needed the sound to ground her during nights like this.

No ticktock. No light.

Her fingertips brushed well-bleached sheets and then skimmed a metal handrail. In the distance she heard a machine beep.

Hospital. She was in the hospital. Casey and her own desperation had been real. It had been not a nightmare but a memory. The woman had been taken. She remained lost or, worse, dead.

Jordan ran her hand over her hair, fingertips gently skimming over the bandage fixed to the back of her head. She was surrounded by shadows. She had hoped after a long rest her sight would return.

But the shadows did not brighten; if anything they had thickened. Her hands curled into fists, and panic-fueled adrenaline shot through her body as she stared into the darkness.

Rogan had taught her years ago to meditate when she felt off kilter and panicked. She began to breathe. Two-second inhales. Four-second exhales. Her heart slowed, and a fragile sense of control returned. Better.

As she exhaled, something in the corner of her room shifted. Adrenaline rushed her system again, scorching through her. She sat, her hand automatically fumbling for the service weapon that should have been in her nightstand. But this was not her room. It was the hospital.

"Who's there?" she asked.

Silence slithered around in the dark corner.

"I know you're there. I can feel you." She rooted through her sheets for the nurse's call button. The control panel was large and cumbersome and had multiple buttons that also controlled the pitch of the bed and the volume on the television. Which one summoned the nurse?

She could feel the gaze leveling on her. And then footsteps sounded quietly on the tile floor. The air shifted and a presence approached the bed. Whoever was there was not worried about trespassing. Or stalking.

She randomly pushed the buttons on the universal remote. The television turned on. The volume went up. Then down.

"Don't be upset." Harold Sunday's voice reverberated from the edge of her bed.

"What are you doing here?"

"Came to see how you were doing? I was concerned."

She sat, her heart beating, scanning the darkness with her ears. The early afternoon news blared loudly. "Get out of my room."

"There's the detective I know and love," he said smoothly.

"Get out!"

"Have a good day, Detective," he said.

The curtain blocking her open door shifted, and his footsteps feathered into the noise from the hallway.

She sat up in her bed, her brain hammering in her skull, her heart racing as she struggled to control her fury and fear.

"Detective Poe, what's wrong?" The voice was female. There were hints of annoyance. "What's going on?"

"Who is this?"

"Your afternoon nurse, Gina."

"Gina, there was a man in my room. His name is Harold Sunday," Jordan said.

"He said he was your friend." Gina pulled the controller from her hands and turned off the television.

"He is not my friend," Jordan said. "Never let him in here again."

"Of course."

"I don't want any visitors unless the hospital staff announces them, understood?" The streets had taught her long ago to listen to her gut. And her gut told her Harold Sunday had not come here out of the goodness of his heart.

Outside the room conversations buzzed, machines beeped, and carts rolled past. "What time is it?" she demanded.

"Two p.m." The nurse crossed the room and tugged at the sheets and blanket that had slipped to her waist when she'd sat up. "Can I get you anything?" she asked.

Her weapon. A ride out of here. Her vision. "Water."

"Sure."

A water tap turned on, and she imagined it streamed into one of those nauseatingly pink plastic patient cups. The nurse pressed it into Jordan's hand.

"There's a straw." She guided the tip to Jordan's mouth.

Jordan drank greedily, savoring the rush of water down her raw throat. "When does the doctor make rounds?"

"About five this evening."

"Good. I'll be more awake. And ready to grill him about treatment options."

The nurse's quiet was as unsettling as the inky blackness. The things people didn't say . . .

"I'm sure he'll be happy to answer your questions. Anything else?" Gina asked.

"No. Thanks."

"I'll be right outside," the nurse said.

Jordan wanted the nurse to stay close and monitor her hospital door. She wanted some kind of backup. But she was in this alone and had to manage her fear. She had never given in to anxiety before, and she would not now.

CHAPTER SIXTEEN

Saturday, April 17
9:00 a.m.

Spencer arrived at the Travis County medical examiner's office for Walker's autopsy. He had slept only a few hours over the last couple of days, and fatigue had put him in a sour frame of mind. He did not want to see Walker's dead body, a reminder of the failed drug investigation and the missing women. But his feelings did not figure into the equation.

He moved through the medical examiner's building, winding down stairwells and hallways until he reached the changing room for the autopsy. He quickly donned a gown and gloves and pushed through the doors into the autopsy suite, where he found Dr. McIntyre gowned up and ready to open Walker's chest.

"I was wondering if you were going to make it," Dr. McIntyre said.

"Been one of those days." Walker's head now rested on a block that exposed his bruised neck.

"Already?"

"Been on the phone with Captain Lee."

"How is Detective Poe?"

"Her vision remains compromised. Ocular nerve damage. The doctor is still being vague about her prognosis."

"Dr. Kensington and I went to medical school together. He's a sharp doctor, and if he's not being straight with her, then he doesn't know. The brain and the ocular nerve are very complex."

"I wonder how I'd function without my vision," he said. Jordan had to be terrified.

"I could ask myself the same question. I'd figure out how to function on a daily basis, but my career would be over."

"So is hers," he said.

Dr. McIntyre shifted her attention to X-rays on a monitor. "The X-rays show that Mr. Walker's hyoid bone was fractured, but there were also several other broken bones in his neck."

"Is that consistent with hanging?" Spencer asked.

"It can be. A study done about ten years ago found that twenty-five percent of men who hanged themselves had a broken hyoid bone. Other studies claim the bone is fractured in over sixty percent of the cases. He used a thin, hard rope, which increases the chances of the broken bone."

Spencer studied the neck. "There're multiple rope marks," he said. "Does the rope shift during hanging?"

"It can."

"And it can shift if he's being manually strangled and fighting. Broken hyoid bones are more consistent with strangulation than hanging, correct?"

"I did retrieve skin samples from under his fingernails. DNA might tell us who they belong to."

"He's a big man and strong, but according to the witness statement, he was also pretty high when he was last seen at four a.m. Walker might not have had the ability to fight back."

"A tox screen will tell us what's in his system," she said. "I've sent his blood off for extensive drug testing, so I'll have that answer in a couple of days."

"Good."

"Why do you suggest murder?"

"I revisited a witness who was with Walker his last night and who had also been interviewed by Detective Poe. The witness, Ms. Stone, placed another man in the apartment about four a.m. Snapped a partial picture of him. Jordan also said Walker was very pleased with himself in the courtroom."

"Maybe something changed for him. Maybe the drugs confused him."

"Marco Walker is not the kind of guy that loses his nerve," Spencer said. "He runs in very dangerous circles and easily holds his own."

"I did the autopsy of his late girlfriend."

"You determined her death was inconclusive."

Dr. McIntyre shook her head. "I can only state what I found. And I could find no recent evidence of trauma other than the blow she sustained in her fall. There were fading bruises on her body, but they were not recent."

"Witnesses stated he abused her."

"But that does not mean he killed her intentionally."

"He had a volatile temper, and a hard shove would have sent her tumbling backward into the hearth. He might not have meant to kill her, but he did."

"I agree, but I must back up my statements with medical facts."

She pressed the tip of her scalpel into the flesh and drew it over each side of his chest and down his midsection, creating a Y incision.

The doctor spent the next hour examining his organs, weighing and measuring them. His heart and lungs appeared normal. There was no internal trauma. In the end, she concluded that Walker had died from asphyxiation with manual strangulation as the cause. She marked the manner of death as suicide.

Spencer was frustrated that there had not been medical evidence to back up Jordan's theory. He had requested search warrants of Walker's financials and phone records. According to his financial records, he had less than $3,000 in hard assets. However, he was a drug dealer and traded strictly in cash. Phone records revealed multiple calls to his lawyer, several women he slept with, and a car dealer. If Walker used burner phones, which Spencer assumed he had, none had been found in the apartment where his body was discovered.

There were also deputies hunting down surveillance footage near the courthouse and apartment that might tell the full story of his last hours.

Spencer arrived at the hospital at noon, parked, and made his way to Jordan Poe's floor. He stepped off the elevator and came face-to-face with Captain Lee. The older man's face was usually grim, but today it telegraphed an unspoken rage.

"How is she?" Spencer asked.

"The doctor is in with her now," Captain Lee said.

"Where's her sister?"

"In the room as well."

"Have you seen her today?"

"No," Captain Lee said. "She doesn't need a bunch of cops breathing down her neck."

He was not so sure.

The door to Jordan's room opened, and Avery stepped into the hallway. Her eyes were red and her face damp with tears. She rolled her shoulders back and headed toward the family lounge.

"Is she going to be strong enough to get through this?" Spencer asked.

"I don't know. I hope so."

Dr. Kensington exited Jordan's room. His expression was grim, and there were hints of the emotion Spencer had seen in Avery's face.

Captain Lee glared at the door, like a man staring down the barrel of a gun.

"I'd like to go in with you," Spencer said.

"You barely know her."

But she had asked him to stay yesterday when the doctor delivered his initial assessment. She had needed a steady, even presence to keep her grounded. And given Avery's and Kensington's expressions, she was going to need more of it.

"I'm coming in," Spencer said.

Captain Lee stared at him. "Okay." He knocked hard once on Jordan's door.

Silence stretched before Jordan cleared her throat and said, "Come in."

The room was dimly lit, and the curtains were drawn. He could see her leaning against the pillows, staring sightlessly at the ceiling. Beside her bed was a large arrangement of bright, full flowers and a half dozen Mylar balloons. An oversize card read, "Get Well."

"Jordan," Captain Lee said.

Her head shifted in the direction of the captain's voice, but her gaze did not quite lock on his.

"It's Captain Lee."

"I could tell by the aftershave," she said.

A smile tugged at the edges of Captain Lee's mouth, but it held no humor. "My wife keeps telling me I need to change it."

"It's a classic," she said.

"As in old men wear it?" he quipped.

"You're not old." Her head shifted slightly in Spencer's general direction. "Who else is with you?"

"Ranger Spencer," Captain Lee said.

"I should have known. Hard to miss the large shadow you cast," she said.

Spencer traced the brim of his hat. "Poe, how are you?"

"I've had better days, Spencer. Harold Sunday paid me a visit on Friday."

"Why?" Spencer asked.

"Said he was checking up on me," she said. "Told the nurses we were friends."

"I'll pay him a visit," Spencer said.

Captain Lee glared as if he had crossed a line, but Spencer had learned long ago ignoring problems did not make them go away.

"On the bright side, today's MRI grabbed a better picture than the others," she said. "All four show ocular nerve damage."

"Will it improve over time?" Captain Lee asked.

Jordan smoothed a trembling hand over the white blanket covering her legs. "That's the sixty-four-thousand-dollar question. The doctors don't know. But there's a good chance that I'll have some vision damage."

She spoke carefully, as if delivering the news of an accident or death to a loved one.

Captain Lee rubbed the back of his neck. "One day at a time."

"That's not my forte, as you both may have suspected." Her hair hung loosely around her face. It was dirty and flat, and her pale skin looked sallow.

"When do you get out of here?" Spencer asked.

"Don't know. A few days, I guess."

"Focus on getting better," Lee said. "The office is covered." His phone buzzed, and when he glanced at the screen, he frowned. "I've got to take this."

"Please, take it," she said.

Captain Lee left and Spencer moved closer to the bed. Jordan was quiet for a moment. They had little in common other than the case. "You up for discussing business?"

"God, yes," she said. "If one more person tiptoes around me, I might scream." She reached for the control panel and pressed a button that gently raised her head.

"They're worried."

"I'm worried. In fact, I'm scared shitless. But I need a break from the fear."

"And Sunday did not say anything else?" Spencer asked.

"He didn't have to. He could have done any number of things to me while we were alone. He knows it and so do I."

"He won't bother you again here," Spencer said.

"You can't guarantee that."

"Let me worry about Sunday."

She tucked a strand of hair behind her ear. "Thanks, Spencer. Now tell me something about the case to distract me."

"I attended the Walker autopsy today. The doctor is calling it a suicide. She's waiting for the blood tox screens to come back before the final call."

"Any other injuries?"

"Neck injuries are consistent with hanging and manual strangulation."

"Did you recover his phone from the crime scene? Who had he been in contact with?"

"Phone was missing."

"He had plenty of time to get one after his bail hearing. And he always had one. Ms. Stone have it?"

"No."

"My money is on murder."

"You might be right."

She shifted and sat a little straighter. "Any word on Casey Andrews?"

"No sign of her."

"Her face is the last thing I really saw. There was so much terror and fear. Christ, it's a hell of an image to have burned in your memory. Makes my stomach hurt to think about her."

"I pulled Tammy Fox's police file. Like Casey, she has arrests for drugs and prostitution. She was eighteen the last time she was arrested. That was two years ago."

"What about family?"

"There's an uncle listed in Maryland. I've left him two voicemail messages but no callback yet. And a former boyfriend now in prison."

"Seems fairly hopeless now." Her fingers curled into a loose fist and relaxed. She did this over and over.

"I'll keep beating the bushes, and forensics has mountains of data to process. Even needles in haystacks get found eventually."

The door opened and Avery appeared, two cups of coffee in hand. Her gaze narrowed when she saw Spencer. "Jordan needs rest."

"I'm resting," Jordan said. "And it smells like you brought me coffee."

"You can't have it if you're stressed," Avery said.

"I don't function without caffeine or stress," Jordan said.

"You'll have to learn." Avery set her coffee cup down and pressed the other into Jordan's hand. "Got it?"

"Yeah." Her fingers skimmed the top of the cup, feeling for the spout opening. She carefully raised it to her lips. Coffee dribbled down the side, forcing her to swipe it away.

Spencer could not imagine his world shifting so drastically. "I'll get going."

"Wait just a minute. Avery, Ranger Spencer has news about Tammy Fox."

"Really?"

Spencer looked at Avery's inquisitive expression. "She was identified as one of the victims."

"Avery and Tammy are both artists," Jordan said. "They knew each other."

"Wow, I can't believe she's dead," Avery said. "When Jordan told me she was missing, I figured she had flaked."

"What can you tell me about her?" Spencer asked.

"Sweet, fragile. Very talented. After Jordan said she was missing, I checked my room and found a few of her small paintings that she had given me."

"Can you send me pictures of them?" Spencer asked.

"Sure." Avery absently sipped her coffee. "I asked around about her at group the other night. She was tense, agitated, having a hard time on the eighth or ninth."

"When did you do this?" Jordan asked.

"While you were sleeping here. I needed to get out. Went to a meeting and thought about Tammy. Kill two birds with one stone. And before you freak, I was careful."

"No freaking out," Jordan said.

Spencer was not sure he believed Jordan. "I better get going. When I know something, I'll contact you," he said.

Jordan retraced the rim of her cup's lid. "I'm counting on it."

***

Jordan fumbled around for the television remote for nearly two minutes before she found it lodged between her mattress and the rail. It was as satisfying as it was frustrating. A simple task should not be this hard.

She turned on the television. With the afternoon sunlight streaming into her hospital window, her vision did not equate to total darkness. To her relief, she could see light flicker by the window and could discern the outline of the television screen's glow. Still like driving in a thick, dark fog.

She listened to the television station, determined it was broadcasting news, and then switched to the sound of a man with a lively voice commentating on three cooks racing through a grocery store. Normally, when she decompressed after a long shift, she gravitated to reality shows like this. However, without her vision, she was missing so much.

A knock at her door had her fumbling for the power button. The first button she pressed jacked the sound up. Frustrated, she felt around the buttons for the one below it and pressed hard until the sound muted. "Come in."

"Jordan, it's Rogan."

Relief warmed her. A familiar voice. Unlike with Avery and Spencer, she did not feel as if she had to keep her guard up. "Hey. Thanks for coming by."

He crossed the room and took her hand gently. Spencer and Captain Lee had both seemed almost afraid to touch her.

"I spoke to Avery," he said. "I'm so sorry."

Tightness fisted in her chest. The tears she had refused to acknowledge bubbled to the surface, brimming in her eyes. "I'm not going to lie." Her voice broke, and she could barely whisper, "It sucks."

A chair scraped against the floor closer to her bed. "Avery is holding up well."

"Is she? I'm worried this might be too much stress."

"She seems to be handling it like a champ."

"Keep an eye on her for me, would you? She's not as tough as she looks." She swiped away a tear.

"How are you?"

"I'm terrible," she said. "I can only see shadows, and the doctors don't know if my vision will improve. I had a visit from the Austin Police Department personnel officer earlier. Nice lady. Assured me I'd be on full disability. All I wanted to do was punch her."

"Helpless is never a good place to be."

"One day you think you got your shit together, and the next you don't."

"I've made time for you in my schedule. We need to talk."

"What's there to talk about? My vision is messed up, and I'm likely to lose my job. Besides, we crossed a bridge that rules out therapy now."

"Your life has changed," he said. "We're friends, and as a friend I can help."

"I'm not sure what would make this better."

"These changes are coming with a lot of emotion."

"Grief, anger, bargaining, acceptance? I haven't accepted squat, but I ping between grief, anger, and bargaining by the minute. Amazing what you'll promise when you really want something."

"It's important to talk about it."

"Talk doesn't change anything."

"Talk will help you come up with a plan. There's always a way forward."

"I don't want to be on this new path," she said. "I don't *want* it."

He drew in a breath. "It's going to take time."

"What really sucks is that I've not only screwed up my life, but I didn't save Casey Andrews."

"The missing woman."

"Yes."

"The case is still open."

"If she's alive, can you imagine what her life is like? She's got to be suffering." Picturing the panic in Casey's eyes jacked her nerves.

"Jordan. This isn't helping." His voice sounded closer.

She could feel the air shift around her and knew he was right by her bedside. "If you can suggest something that'll help, I'm all ears."

"Give yourself time, Jordan," he said softly. "You aren't good to anyone if you don't take care of yourself. Your goal should be to get better."

"If bed rest would do the trick, I'd be all over it. But no one has any idea what will make my sight better."

"Time. Give it time."

"How long do I wait? How long before I accept that my sight is never coming back, Rogan?" She had not said the words out loud until this moment because the prospect terrified her so much.

"I'll always be here for you." He drew his fingertip gently down her cheek.

"I really need to be alone."

"Sure. Anything you want."

She listened to his footsteps cross the room, pause at the door, and then vanish into the hallway.

She was frustrated that she had not been able to see his face or read his expressions. He was a fine, caring man. But he was not enough for her. He never had been. And she had never lost any sleep over it. Her life had been on track this last year. Avery was stable. Jordan had gotten the promotion to homicide. It had all been good. And now her vision was gone. And she felt even more helpless than she had when her mother had died. At least then she could see the path forward. Now she was lost.

CHAPTER SEVENTEEN

Monday, April 19
9:00 a.m.

The list Spencer had created of Marco Walker's known associates was a short one. Walker did not have many friends. He had people who knew him from the streets. People who had bought drugs from him. Some who owed him money. Women he had screwed. But when his girlfriend died, the people who knew him backed off.

Spencer had gone looking for Alana Stone, but she had checked out of the hospital and was not at her apartment. With her missing, that put Harold Sunday, Walker's lawyer, at the top of his list. Sunday made a hell of a living keeping men like Walker out of jail. And Sunday had paid a visit to Jordan, which in Spencer's book had crossed a line.

He entered the glass-and-steel low-rise building on Congress Avenue. Removing his hat, he crossed the marbled hallway to an elevator and rode it to the top floor. When the doors opened and he stepped out, he had one of the best views of the city.

"May I help you?"

His attention shifted to a woman sitting at the reception desk. "I'm looking for Harold Sunday," he said as he held up his badge. "I have questions for him about a former client."

A frown knotted her brow. "I'll ring him."

"I would appreciate that."

She picked up her phone and spoke softly into the receiver as he walked toward the glass window and savored the crystal-blue sky, white clouds, and Austin skyline. His thoughts went to Jordan Poe. What she wouldn't give to see this view.

"Ranger Spencer."

He turned to see Harold Sunday wearing a pin-striped suit, a red tie, and his black hair slicked back off his face. "I thought you might stop by. I'm surprised it wasn't sooner."

"There a place we could talk?"

"Conference room is right here." He opened glass doors, and as he did so, the lights above flickered on. The room was outfitted with a conference table surrounded by ten smooth leather chairs and a big-ass television that dominated the back wall.

"Have a seat, Ranger."

Spencer sat, rested his hat on his crossed knee. "I'm here to talk about Marco Walker."

"I assumed as much. I can't discuss the work I did for him, even if he's dead."

"He was under investigation for drug trafficking at the time his girlfriend died."

Sunday steepled his fingers. "My relationship with him dealt strictly with the manslaughter trial. I had no knowledge of his other dealings, legal or otherwise."

"A man facing manslaughter charges would have been worried that his other business ventures could be exposed."

"I assume so, but I never asked, and he never offered."

"Why did you go see him the morning he died?"

"Who said I did?"

"Why did you go see Alana Stone in the hospital?"

"Just looking out for her."

"Why? You don't strike me as the caring type."

"You don't know me that well. I can be quite kind."

"Where is Ms. Stone?"

Sunday shrugged. "I have no idea."

"Walker is dead, but my investigation into his drug dealing is not. He was one link in a chain I'm going to climb."

Sunday's smile was relaxed as he tugged at the cuff of his shirt. "I commend your dedication, Ranger Spencer. Texas is lucky to have you."

Word games had never been Spencer's strong suit. And dancing around Sunday's polite conversation was already feeling like a waste of his time. "He sold drugs to all walks of life. Some were influential people." He let the silence settle. "I'm not after them, and right now I don't care how you handle your clients. But I want Walker's supplier."

"As I've said, our discussions centered only on the manslaughter charge," Sunday said. "By the way, how is Detective Jordan Poe doing?"

"You ever get within a hundred feet of her again, and you'll be dealing with me."

"That a threat?"

"I don't make threats."

"I broke no laws."

Spencer pictured her lying in a pool of her own blood at the old house. "Stay away from her."

"Like everyone, I look forward to seeing her back on the job again."

"Stay away from her."

A smile quirked the edges of Sunday's lips. "Ask her about her personal connection to Walker. You might find it interesting."

"What's that mean?"

"Ask her."

***

Spencer drove down to San Marcos and the Sanchez home. He parked in front of the modest house, and as he settled his hat on his head and strode toward the front door, he thought about the text Constance Sanchez had sent Jordan. We need to talk.

He rang the front bell, saw the flicker of curtains by the front door, and stepped back, hand near his weapon. The door opened to a woman in her midfifties with gray streaks in her dark hair and hesitation in her narrowing eyes.

"Ma'am, I'm Texas Ranger Carter Spencer," he said. "I'm looking for Constance Sanchez."

"I'm Constance." She glanced behind her toward an unseen room, where a television played a cable news show. She stepped outside and closed the door behind her. "Why are you here, Ranger Spencer?"

"I'm here to talk to you about your daughter, Elena."

"My Elena is dead."

"I know. And I'm sorrier than I can say."

"What do you want?"

"You sent a text to Detective Jordan Poe. You suggested you needed to talk to her."

"How do you know that?"

"Detective Poe was injured. She's in the hospital, and your text appeared on her phone when I was gathering her personal effects from the scene."

Constance raised her hand to her lips. "Is she going to be okay?"

"She'll survive."

"But—"

"I can't discuss her condition," he said. "Why did you want to talk to her? Was it about your daughter's connection to Marco Walker?"

The woman's worried expression soured to anger. "I hate hearing that man's name. May he rot in hell."

"What did you want to tell Detective Poe?"

"Elena was afraid of Walker. She planned to leave him the night she died."

"Why did she want to leave him?"

"He wanted her to do favors for him, and she couldn't bear it."

"What kind of favors?"

"He wanted her to go with one of his friends. Be nice to him. She understood what that meant and didn't want any part of it."

"Who was the man?" Spencer asked.

"She never told me his name. She said Walker considered this man important to his business."

"His drug business?"

"Yes."

"Did your daughter ever send you any texts or pictures of this man?"

"No."

"Was he the kind of man who would kill Walker?"

"I think so, yes. That's what I wanted to tell Detective Poe. I believe if she could find this man, she would learn a great deal."

Spencer nodded. "Did your daughter ever talk about a woman named Tammy Fox?"

"She was mentioned in the news. She's dead, correct?"

"Yes, ma'am."

Her folded arms tightened. "When you lose a child, you start paying attention to all kinds of things you never noticed before. I said a prayer for Miss Fox."

"Who were Elena's friends? She must have had many."

"She lost track of the girls from high school. The drugs became too much for them. The only person I heard her mention was Laura."

"Do you have any pictures of Elena or Laura?"

Mrs. Sanchez reached in her back pocket for her phone and opened the photos app. She showed him a picture of Elena and another smiling woman with blond hair.

Laura fit this killer's profile. "Have you heard from Laura since Elena died?"

"No."

"Do you have a last name for Laura?"

"No."

"What about a phone number?"

"I do have that."

Spencer added the number to his phone and then gave her his number. "Call me if you have anything that you think will help."

"Of course. When will Detective Poe be back on the job?"

"Not sure. Thank you for your time."

She nodded and disappeared into her house, locking the door behind her.

Back in his vehicle, Spencer called Laura's number. The call went to voicemail. "This is Texas Ranger Carter Spencer. I'm looking for Laura. She needs to call me." He left his contact information.

Laura was another needle in this growing haystack.

CHAPTER EIGHTEEN

Wednesday, April 21
9:15 a.m.

It was release day. The doctors had held Jordan for almost an entire week, and she was glad to leave behind the parade of doctors and their examinations that had not provided her with any new answers.

The swelling in her brain had finally healed, and the dozen stitches in the back of her head had been removed. The nurse said the spot they'd shaved was easily covered with the long strands of hair above it. No one would know she had been hurt. Other than the fact that she still could not see. Shit, they could have shaved her whole head if she could get even half her sight back.

There had been a nice woman, Sally Taylor, who was an occupational therapist. Jordan had no idea what Sally looked like but judged her to be about her age and a few inches shorter, given the sound and direction of her voice.

A few days ago, Sally had talked to Jordan about getting around in her home. Jordan had assured her she would be fine. Sally wanted Jordan to begin practicing with a cane. Jordan refused. Sally, in her sweet southern voice, said she could not okay Jordan's release until she at least tried. Sweet Sally was not above blackmail.

Only because the cane was a means to an end did Jordan agree to try it. It felt long and awkward in her hand. She hated it. Wanted to cry. But she sucked it up and made a show of giving it a go.

Jordan had showered with the nurses' help this morning. The stitches were out of her head, and it would be a few more days before she could wash her hair, but just the idea of it felt like progress. Next, she changed into sweats, a T-shirt, and athletic shoes Avery had brought her yesterday.

Jordan could not see her face. However, her fingertips confirmed that the knot on the side of her forehead had gone down, though she had no way of knowing how much bruising remained.

A knock on the door had her shifting to the approximate location. Her sensitivity to sound was improving, and her senses of smell and touch were stepping up.

"Ready to hit the road?" Sally asked.

Jordan smiled. "More than ready."

"Where's Avery?"

"Bringing the car around."

"Good." Sally was always pleasant and direct. "Seriously, how are you doing?"

"I'm terrified," she said. "I have no idea what I'm doing."

"Where is your cane?"

"In the chair across the room, I think." She did not like having it close.

"You have to keep it within arm's reach, Jordan." Sally's footsteps crossed the room and returned. She pressed the cane into Jordan's hand. "Have you considered the counseling I mentioned?"

"I'm not sure what talking will do about my condition."

"It'll help with the stress of the transition."

"*Transition.* Makes it sound like I won't get back what I had."

"It's good to be mentally prepared, regardless."

"Maybe. Right now, I'm focused on getting as much normal back into my day as I can. I'm on medical leave, and I don't want to waste it in the hospital."

Sally chuckled. "Fair enough. I've got your wheelchair and your discharge papers."

"Can't I walk out of here?" she asked.

"No. The hospital's policy is fairly strict. You know, the lawyers always get their way."

"I hear you." Jordan swung her legs over the side of the bed. And with Sally's help, she lowered herself into the wheelchair. Sally folded the cane, explaining what she'd done, and laid it across her legs.

Jordan absorbed the hospital's normal background noises. The beeps, buzzers, hushed conversations, and rolling carts were becoming her points of reference in this new world of shadows and light. From her hospital outings with Sally, she'd learned the man in the room beside hers had been in a car accident. He had been broadsided by a truck that had run an intersection. He had regained consciousness. "One lucky bastard," his father had said over and over as if he were muttering a prayer.

Down the hall was a young girl who had been thrown from a horse. Her neck injuries required surgery, and she was facing months of rehab.

"I'll be coming by your house later today," Sally said. "I can help you rearrange furniture and make it more accessible."

"No offense, Sally, but that sounds awful. I don't want to change a thing in my house. I like it the way it is."

"For now, you'll need to make modifications."

"I'll have to put it back when my sight returns."

Sally did not miss a beat as she guided Jordan's hand to the arm of the wheelchair. "If that day comes, I'll come by and help you do it."

If. Sally had never used *when*.

"You don't think it's going to happen," Jordan said.

"I worry about the evidence before me."

"You should be a homicide cop."

"You think?" she said lightly.

"I'm sure of it."

"Well, I'll keep that in mind. You never know."

She set Jordan's feet in the foot cradles and unlocked the brake. "What do you want to do with all the flowers?"

"Give them away."

"They're lovely."

"They smell nice, but honestly, they're wasted on me right now."

"You sure?" The wheels were rolling, and she could tell by the change in sound that they were in the hallway.

"Very."

The elevator doors dinged open, Sally asked a nurse to hold them, and the wheelchair rumbled over the ridge. When the doors closed, she sat straighter, finding low vision had not cured her agitation in confined spaces.

When the doors opened again, the air pressure shifted, and the room felt taller. "We're in the lobby?"

"That's exactly right. You're starting to be aware of echolocation."

"Sound waves are my new friend." Doors slid open, and the hot spring air rushed toward her. She inhaled. It was her first lungful of fresh air in a week. Sally tapped Jordan on the shoulder. "I have sunglasses for you."

"Why?" The last thing she wanted was to look as if she could not see well.

"Your eyes could still be sensitive to the light, and it's a bright day."

She fumbled with the glasses, which felt clunky and orthopedic, but she dutifully slipped them on, knowing she would do what she needed to get out of the hospital. At home, she would not follow any rules.

Savoring the heat soaking into her bones, she tipped her face toward the sky, imagining the vivid blue that came with low-humidity days.

Suddenly, loud clapping erupted. Several folks shouted, "Detective Poe," and she realized she had an audience.

"There're about two dozen officers here," Sally said softly. "A few have balloons."

"Balloons?" Jesus, she had wanted to slip out of the hospital, get home, and regroup.

"Smile," Sally said.

Jordan twisted her lips into a grin, shifting toward the sound of the revelers. She could make out faint outlines of people but could not see any faces.

"Detective Poe."

The spicy aftershave was a dead giveaway. "Captain Lee."

"I'm changing my aftershave next time," he said easily. He came up behind her wheelchair and asked Sally if he could drive.

It was a thing they did in their department. When an officer was injured, the guys and gals showed up to wish them well as they left the hospital. She had participated in her share but never once pictured herself on the receiving end.

"Captain, tell me there're no reporters here."

"A couple from the television station."

"I'm the feel-good story of the hour."

"Roll with it, Detective Poe." He sounded like he was grinning, but his smiles always looked a little forced.

Greasy hair and the Darth Vader shades must have made quite the sight. Normally, she was not vain, but she also did not go out of her way to look goofy.

Someone approached her and in a loud voice said, "Detective Poe, it's Detective Leo Santiago."

"I'm good."

"Glad to hear it." Again, the loud voice.

"My sight is compromised," she said. "I can hear fine."

"Right," he said quickly. "Sorry about that."

"No worries. And spread the word that I don't want any tiptoeing around me. If you have a question, ask it."

"How much can you see?" he asked.

They could ask, but that did not mean she had to be totally honest. "Not enough to drive or shoot my weapon."

"Fair enough."

More cops came up, shook her hand, introduced themselves. There were offers for grass-cutting services, grocery store runs, and chauffeuring. She should have been thrilled, but she resented being on the receiving end.

Finally, the welcome sound of Avery's clunky car engine rumbled near the curb. The freedom car had arrived. Captain Lee, however, was in no real rush to deposit her in the car, and as much as she wanted to demand he end this dog and pony show, she kept her cool. She might be a basket of nerves, but she sure as hell would not broadcast it.

The wheels rolled a few more inches toward the car. When she got home, she was going to lie on the couch and drink a cold soda. It was not on the outpatient protocol sheet, but she did not care.

"Detective Poe," Captain Lee said. "I would like to introduce you to Angela Richards. She's a local reporter."

Jordan stuck out her hand.

"Nice to meet you," came from the three-o'clock position.

Jordan shifted her hand and felt the reporter's firm grip. "You were at the press conference last week."

"That's right. I'd like to interview you," Angela said.

"I was telling her about the case you were working with the Texas Rangers," Captain Lee said.

So now it was *with* the Rangers. She wondered if Spencer was in the crowd. "Really?"

"Exposure will engage the public in your hunt for this killer," Angela said.

It would also engage the killer. "I need a few days to get settled."

"Sure, of course. If it'll help, I can email questions to you ahead of time."

And she would read them with what? "Perfect."

"Terrific." Angela sounded pleased with herself.

"Jordan," Avery said.

Thank God, the cavalry.

"I need to pull her away, Captain Lee." Avery spoke with authority.

Jordan remembered her fourteen-year-old self arguing with a four-year-old Avery, who always walked away with the victory, whether it was an extra cookie or another bedtime story. "Sorry. She's the boss."

"The doctor was clear about her getting rest," Avery said.

"Right," Captain Lee said.

Jordan held up her hand and waved to the guys, who she assumed were to her right and left. "Thanks, guys. I'll be back on the job harassing you all soon enough."

The cheer was filled with enthusiasm, but she was not sure if they believed it any more than she did. If she could see their expressions, she would have a better read of the crowd. But for now, her other senses would have to step up to the plate.

The wheelchair rolled forward on a downward grade, indicating they were approaching the car. Captain Lee set the brakes, and his unexpected touch made her stiffen, but she quickly forced herself to relax.

Avery came up on her other side and tapped her arm gently, as Sally had taught her. Jordan took it.

Jordan relied on them both, her legs still weak after the bed rest that had been broken only by the short walks in the hallway with Sally.

As she lowered herself into the car, Captain Lee put his hand gently on her head and guided her inside the vehicle. He tugged at the seat belt, handed the buckle to her, and she fumbled with it until it clicked into place.

"See you soon, Poe," he said.

"I'm planning on it."

As he closed her door, Avery slid behind the wheel, started the engine, and cranked the air-conditioning. "That was quite the show." The bracelets on her wrist rattled, clinking against each other. She was waving goodbye.

"Are you smiling?" Jordan asked.

"Like a crazed fool." She put the car in gear and slowly began to drive. "You do the same and throw in a wave."

Jordan did as she was told. More cheers from the crowd.

"There're so many officers here," Avery said.

"It's a good group of folks," she said.

"But it sucks to be you, right?"

"No truer words." She flipped her sunglasses up, shoving her hair back.

"You're supposed to be careful of light."

The sun's warmth spread across her face, easing the tension. "I've got my eyes closed."

"Not good enough. Seriously. Cover your eyes. I don't need a return trip to the emergency room."

Jordan slipped the glasses back on because the goal was to regain her vision and to stay out of the hospital. "Ten-four."

The bucket seat was not overly comfortable, and the car smelled of french fries and coffee. "Is there anything to eat at the house?"

"I ordered a pizza last night. There're a couple of slices left."

Normally that would have appealed to her frugal mind. "How about we stop for a burger?"

"You like fast food."

"If what's happened to me doesn't earn me a burger, fries, and a vanilla shake, I'm not sure what does."

Avery did not speak for several seconds. "You're being very chill about this. I would be freaking out."

Jordan ran her finger over a piece of duct tape covering the peeling vinyl on the passenger door. Her fingernail dug into the sticky edge. "I'm freaking out."

"You don't look like it."

She could go into the regular nightmares featuring Casey Andrews's panicked gaze or the sensation that someone was in her room, watching her. But upsetting Avery would not help either of them. "I'm going to stay focused on getting better."

Avery downshifted and slowed, presumably for a light. "You'll have to do exactly what the doctor says."

And she would. After the burger and shake.

Avery shifted into first and then up to second and third gears before quickly downshifting and turning. "We're at the Burger Barn."

"Burger, fries, and a vanilla shake."

Avery ordered doubles of both. Jordan rooted for her purse to pay. "Where's my purse, wallet, and cell?" In the confusion she had forgotten about them all, which was not like her.

"The nurse put all your stuff in a big plastic bag. It's in the back seat."

"Get my wallet."

"I can cover this. You get the next round."

"I can still pay my own way," Jordan said.

"I know." Avery placed the order, paid, and set the warm bags of food on Jordan's lap. Jordan fished for fries and grabbed a handful. The salty fried potato hit a happy spot in her brain.

"I could use a fry, too," Avery said.

Jordan handed her the half-empty fry bag. "You can also have the rest. Seeing as I won't be going on long runs for a while, it's better I don't get too well acquainted with the fries." She fumbled for the shake in the cup holder, dug out the straw, and tore the paper off with her teeth. It took a couple of jabs to hit the hole in the lid, but when she did, a sense of victory blossomed. She took a long pull.

"You're supposed to lie down when we get home. I'll hang out and keep an eye on things."

"What about your job?" Jordan asked.

"I took a couple of weeks off. The boss understands."

"I don't want you doing that for me. I don't need a babysitter."

"Actually, Jordan, you do need a sitter right now. Someone has to manage your pain meds, and someone has to make sure you don't fall down and hit your head or something."

"I've lived in the house for years. I know it pretty well." And she had stopped taking her pain meds days ago.

"I get it. And you'll get your independence back after some training."

"You sound like the occupational therapist," Jordan said.

"She has some good ideas and suggestions."

"She said something about coming around the house."

"It was a condition of your release."

Another condition. She sipped on the shake and turned to the window. She loved to drive. It was her escape when life got too tense. If she could not drive, she could not de-stress, work, or live.

Tears welled in her eyes, and she was glad for the Darth Vader glasses, which offered her some cover. She felt as if she were drowning. And an old familiar knot fisted in her chest. She pulled in a deep breath and slowly released it. Words like *transitions*, *therapy*, *conditions* brought with them a future she did not want.

CHAPTER NINETEEN

Wednesday, April 21
9:45 a.m.

Spencer stood back from the crowd dispersing from the hospital. He, along with the others, had been here to watch Detective Poe make her victorious exit, and while the crowd of officers cheered, he had watched. There were cases when the perpetrator returned to the scene of the crime. Some visited their victims' homes or called loved ones, inquiring about their status.

And it stood to reason that this killer, if he had gone out of his way to set up Jordan, would linger and be present when she left. He would want to see how she was doing. Confirm the swirling rumors that she had lost some or all of her vision. He would want to know.

No one stuck out in his mind as odd, but he had two officers recording the scene so that later he could go back and study it more closely.

Captain Lee approached Spencer. "That went as well as could be expected."

"If you say so." Spencer did not need to ask how Jordan was faring. Her unnaturally happy smile had said it all. "A few days at home with nothing but this case to chew on is going to have an impact."

Captain Lee drew in a deep breath. "You're saying she'll be in your office sooner rather than later."

"If the shoe were on the other foot, I'd do the same. And I do want to talk to her. We need to deconstruct what she saw in that house before she was attacked."

"Any word on Casey Andrews?"

"Nothing. I've also been in contact with Detective Rivers again and asked her to extend her search back a decade and to widen her search area. I want to know if any other women matching this killer's profile disappeared."

"You think there could be more?"

"This killer has honed his routine. His method of killing is highly unique, which I would argue he has perfected over time. I would bet his victim type has not changed that much. Many killers like him have specific preferences."

Spencer's phone rang. "Excuse me. It's Dr. McIntyre."

"By all means. She's the lady with the answers."

"Let's hope." He accepted the call. "Doc."

"Agent Spencer, I have a toxicological report back on Marco Walker."

"And?"

"There were so many drugs in his system it would have been darn near impossible for him to stand up, let alone hook a noose, climb up a chair, and hang himself," Dr. McIntyre said.

"Are you sure?"

"Very. In fact, if left by himself, he could very well have died of respiratory failure."

"What was in his system?" Spencer asked.

She listed several illegal substances, including lethal levels of crack and heroin.

"All that was in his system?"

"Yes. He either injected himself, or someone did it for him."

"He was using with a woman from his building, a Ms. Alana Stone. She swears she did not administer drugs to him."

"I requested the tox report on Ms. Stone's blood work done at the hospital," Dr. McIntyre said. "They were using similar substances. Unless Ms. Stone is a very strong woman, I doubt she strung Walker up. He would have been deadweight."

"Does this change your ruling on his death?" Spencer asked.

"I'm now classifying it as a homicide."

Alana Stone had vanished after he spoke to her. However, Stone was likely a creature of habit and would return to her apartment next to Walker's. He would keep checking back until they connected. "Thanks, Doc. Will be in touch."

"One more thing, Ranger Spencer. Tox reports on Jane Doe #1 and Tammy Fox came back. They both had heroin in their systems at the time of their deaths."

"A common drug."

"Maybe just a coincidence."

That damn word made the back of his head itch. "Thanks again, Doc."

"Good news?" Captain Lee asked.

Spencer slid the phone in his breast pocket and gave Captain Lee the rundown.

"Stay on top of it," Captain Lee said.

"Will do. And keep me posted on Detective Poe's progress."

Captain Lee regarded him. "Sure."

***

Avery's car jolted to a stop. "We're home."

Jordan released her grip on the door handle. She was always nervous during the rare times she let Avery drive. At least before she'd been able to see the trouble coming. Now she was at her younger sister's mercy, with only her ears to alert her of trouble. God only knew how many yellow lights they had run.

"You're alive," Avery said. "Stop deconstructing the drive."

"I wasn't."

"You were, and like it or not, you're going to have to get used to it. You won't be driving for some time."

The words *some time* held out the hope that she might one day, and she appreciated it. She was hanging on by a thread and would take any positive sign from the universe.

"I'll come around," Avery said. "Let me help you inside."

"I should be able to walk into my own house," Jordan said. Even if she could not really see, she had walked the stone path thousands of times. She opened the door and stepped out, her foot grinding against gravel. Rising, she shifted her body in the direction of where she thought the house was. "Where is my car?"

"The police have it."

"It's being processed as part of the crime scene." Crime scenes often extended beyond the room or space where the body was found. If a killer disposed of the murder weapon in a different location, it became part of the scene. Basically, anything touched by case evidence was part of the crime scene. And she had arrived at the murder house minutes before all hell broke loose.

"That's what Spencer said," Avery said.

"They find anything interesting yet?" Everyone's environment said something about them. What had hers whispered to Spencer?

"Probably that you're a control freak."

Jordan laughed. She took several steps forward, skimming her foot over the gravel and slate. She pictured the path that she had put down herself last year.

Avery hurried beside her, her bracelets rattling as she tapped Jordan's elbow. "Let me help you."

"I know every inch of this yard. I've spent enough time in it."

"I don't remember you out here in the middle of the night," Avery said.

Jordan quickened her pace to prove her point. She covered the next five or six feet fairly fast. And then her foot caught on a piece of flagstone. It tipped her off balance, and she could feel herself falling forward. Her hands went out in front of her as she braced for impact.

Avery grabbed her by the arm and yanked her back up. "Nice going."

Jordan jerked her arm away. "I would have been okay. A few falls are to be expected."

Avery took her arm again. "You just suffered a head injury. You don't need another one."

"Don't be dramatic." Jordan's heart thundered in her chest, but she still moved forward, at a more tentative pace.

"Shut up," Avery said. "And step up."

"What?"

"We're at the front porch. Three steps."

"I know that."

Avery sighed.

Jordan climbed the three, surprised that what had been so familiar was now awkward. She counted each step, sliding her foot forward until it touched the next landing.

They crossed the porch, and Avery's keys rattled as she shoved the house key in the front door. She pushed it open wide. "I moved my stuff back into your house. No sense in me keeping my apartment right now."

"You moved back?" It was the best news she had had all week.

"Temporarily."

"Right. Temporary," Jordan said.

"It'll be easier when you master your white cane."

Jordan gripped the cane. "Did you know only two to eight percent of blind people use a cane or a guide dog?"

"And the rest rely on usable vision."

"You've been doing homework."

"I have."

The floor under Jordan's feet was too smooth. "Where's the carpet?"

"It's a tripping hazard, so it's in the spare room." Avery guided her to the couch and helped her sit.

Relief washed over Jordan. For a moment, she felt like she had landed in a safe space. Right now, she was tempted to stay here until her sight improved. The doctor had said her ocular nerve was not likely to fully heal, but she was clinging to the hope that her sight would return.

"Where's my phone?"

"In your purse. Let me get it for you."

Seconds later, Avery set the purse in Jordan's lap. It was surprisingly light without her service weapon. Her fingertips skimmed the dimpled black leather, reached for the zipper, and tugged it open. Her fingers glided over her wallet, a packet of tissues, the notebook for case notes, and her phone. She thumbed through the case notebook, trying to recall all the details of the Jane Doe #1 and Tammy Fox murders. Her observations often felt random, but experience had taught her that the most important details could initially seem insignificant. And now they were lost to her. She ran her fingers over the phone's smooth surface. "I live and die by this phone."

"We can change that to voice activated," Avery said. "Sally said it'll enable you to use your phone."

Jordan pressed the home button. Experience told her the home screen had appeared, but she could not make out the icons. Voice activation had to be in Settings. Wherever the hell that was.

"You want me to do it for you?" Avery asked.

"Yes."

Avery took the phone and in seconds returned it to her. "Just talk to it. Ask it to 'Open email.'"

"Open email."

"You have two hundred unread messages."

"Doesn't take long for them to back up, does it?" Avery said.

"No."

"Do you want me to scan them and read them out loud? It might be faster."

"Maybe later." She ordered the phone to close. "My brain is scrambled. Do I smell roses?"

"You received a large vase of roses."

"Who sent them?"

"No card," Avery said.

Who had sent her roses? Who knew where she lived?

Avery retrieved something, sat next to Jordan, and placed her hand on a shoebox. "Feel all the 'Get Well' cards."

Jordan moved her fingers through the unopened envelopes, which came in varying sizes.

"Pretty touching, huh?" Avery said.

"Yes." She set the box aside.

"What's wrong?"

"I refuse to be a sick person who needs anyone's pity."

"No one pities you."

Jordan rubbed her hands over her thighs. "Of course they do. Every cop on the force said a prayer of thanks that they weren't the one that lost their sight. I know how it goes. Everyone visits at first. They cut grass, bring meals, help out where they can. But then life goes back to normal for them, and they stop coming as much and then not at all. In a month, they'll be back to their lives, and I'll be here. It won't be long before we'll be lucky to exchange cards at Christmas."

"It's not going to be like that."

"When you were struggling with the drugs, a few folks offered words of encouragement after the first emergency room trip. But by the third, it was just you and me."

Avery was quiet for an instant. "I'm sorry I put you through that."

"I'm not trying to make you feel bad. I'm just pointing out that I'm alone here."

"You aren't alone. You have me."

"You have a life to live."

"And you had one to live when I was using. And you gave it up for me. I'm going to do the same for you."

"What if I don't want you to?"

"Like I didn't want your help that last time I overdosed? Remember that day how we fought? And then I got into trouble. I was sure I was going to die. And then there you were holding me as I sucked in air."

"I keep thinking about that night. Your circumstance was very similar to the women who were murdered."

"Don't say that. Don't. You've had too much time on your hands to think the last week."

"Maybe, but it's getting harder and harder to ignore the similarities. You all were users, got clean, and slipped thanks to Walker. I found you with your hands and feet tied and plastic shoved down your throat. These women had the same experience, only this time he put a bag over their heads and wrapped them in plastic."

Rising, Avery took several steps away. "Why are you telling me this? I know you're scared, but you don't have to freak me out, too."

"I'm not trying to," she said. "Killers like this usually start somewhere."

"And you think he started with me?"

"Maybe you were the first. Predators like that often need to amp up the violence to get the same sense of satisfaction."

Avery stood silent, and Jordan could feel her staring. "Practice with your phone. I need to step outside."

"Where are you going?" Jordan asked.

"Just out in the front yard. I need air."

"I'll let it go now, but you need to think about that night and what happened. Whatever you can remember will be important."

***

Emma Powers knew about the other girls. Anyone who lived or worked in downtown Austin had heard whispers. Like her, they all had used, gotten clean, and then vanished.

She left the hospital after pulling a twelve-hour shift. The nurse's aide job had sounded like a step up when she had read the ad, but now she realized it was mostly babysitting. There was nothing cute about spoon-feeding adults or changing their soiled linens.

She was beat, her feet felt as if they were twice their normal size, and her back ached. Her boss had been promising her a schedule of four ten-hour days, but every time each new scheduling period came around, he could not make it happen. She was feeling like a putz and thinking maybe it was time to find a new job.

Emma shouldered her backpack and moved toward the bus stop in front of the hospital's truck delivery bay. She was craving a coffee, but it would keep her awake most of the night, and what she really needed was sleep.

At the bus stop, she sat on the bench. Five minutes until the bus arrived. She slipped off her shoes and wiggled her toes. Cars passed. Hospital staff were ending and starting their days.

As she leaned back against the bench, she saw a man cross the street toward her. He wore a black hoodie, dark jeans, and athletic shoes. It struck her as odd that anyone would be wearing a jacket. Even this late in the day, it was warm and was going to be hot as hell. Lucky for her, she would be in her air-conditioned home soon and sleeping.

As he paused by her, he dug a fresh pack of cigarettes out of his pocket and lit the tip of one with a lighter. Inhaling, he clearly savored the smoke. The sulfur scents made her crave a cigarette herself. When she had first stopped using, she had smoked heavily because it calmed her and kept her mind off the constant craving that never really left.

But lately, she had been trying to taper off. Her asthma was getting worse, and the nurse at the urgent care had told her to choose between her lungs and the butts. So, she had only three cigarettes in what would be her last pack.

Emma moistened her lips, watching as the smoke curled around the man's face. As if sensing her, he looked down, and their gazes met. He grinned. It was not a leering kind of look but friendly, even understanding. Sort of like, "I get you."

He raised the pack and shook it gently. He was offering. She checked her watch. Four minutes until the bus came. Plenty of time to grab a smoke.

"I know the look," he said. "Trying to quit."

"Almost finished with my last pack."

"That's good. Three weeks is my record." He shook the pack enough to jostle loose a cigarette. She took it and accepted the blue plastic lighter.

"I swore I had bought my last pack." Even as she spoke, the lighter's flame touched the tobacco's edge.

"You didn't really buy this pack, though, right?"

She inhaled, held the smoke in her lungs for a beat, and then slowly released it. "Technically, that's true."

"Always got to find a loophole."

"Sometimes you have to look hard," she said.

"Nah, it isn't that hard."

She laughed, inhaled.

"Good to hear laughter," he said. "I've been at my mother's bedside all day."

"What's wrong with her?"

"Cancer. She's dying." He stared at the glowing tip and then inhaled as if trying to reclaim his peace.

"Sorry to hear that." The hoodie now made sense. It could get cold on the critical care units.

"It's not a new story, is it? You a nurse?"

"No, just an aide."

"Don't say *just*. It's important work."

"Thanks."

He finished his cigarette and handed her the pack. "You look like you could use this."

"No, man. I can't take your pack. It's barely opened. Plus, I'm finishing my last pack."

"You said you wouldn't buy any more. And you still haven't bought a pack. So theoretically you're free and clear."

She grinned. "Are you a lawyer?"

"Just play one on TV."

As she laughed, the rumble of a bus had her turning in time to see her bus come to a stop. "Shit, that's my bus."

"Want to grab a coffee?" he asked.

"I don't think so," she said.

"I get it. Black hoodie. Lurking. I must look like a serial killer. Sorry, it's been a long couple of weeks with Mom."

His soft words carried hints of apology. "It's not personal. I don't know you."

"The café is across the street. Let me at least treat you to breakfast or dinner. We can kill time while you wait for the next bus."

She had eaten in the shop often enough. It was public. And he was good looking. "Sure."

"Great. It's going to be my treat," he said.

She tossed her cigarette on the sidewalk and ground it out with her toe. "You don't have to do that."

"Sure I do. You're the best thing that's happened to me today."

CHAPTER TWENTY

Wednesday, April 21
5:15 p.m.

Jordan sat in the bathtub, her chin hovering over the waterline, her eyes closed. She tried to imagine how she had lived in this house when she had twenty-twenty vision. The sounds were all familiar. The hum of the air conditioner. A neighbor's dog barking. The drip of the water from the faucet. The tick of her clock. It was all normal, until she opened her eyes.

She rolled onto her stomach and pressed her face into the water. It would be so easy to dip below the water and just not come back up. Her mother had done essentially the same. All the anxiety, fear, and anger would wash away. So easy. So tempting.

And if she did end it, what would happen to Avery? Would her sister stay clean? Or would she fall apart and end up on the streets again. How many times had Jordan railed against her mother for leaving them?

She sat up, wiped the water from her face, and gingerly rose out of the tub. She grabbed the towel Avery had laid out for her and dried off and dressed in jeans and a pullover shirt, also chosen for her by her sister. She ran a comb through her hair, careful to avoid her incision.

As Jordan slowly moved down the hallway, the front doorbell rang, and Avery, who was more cheerful than she had ever been in her entire life, hurried to answer it. "Hey, come on in." Avery turned to Jordan. "Sally is here."

Like it or not, her life without vision was racing toward her at full steam. "Hey, Sally."

"I live close by and thought I'd check in." Footsteps crossed the bare hardwood floor. "Are you getting settled in?"

"I've barely left the couch. Avery voice activated my phone, but so far practice has not made perfect. I'm lost. And pissed."

"Which is about right at this stage of the game," Sally said. "Losing your sight is like a death. You're grieving."

"I'm still holding out hope for my sight."

Several plastic bags rustled. "Well, hope is a good thing. But until it pans out, I'm here to teach you how to live your life. You can't spend forever on a couch."

"Technically, I could," Jordan said. "What's in the bag?"

"More cards you left behind in the room."

"Don't need them."

"I'm sure they're very touching. It's always good to know when people care."

"More psychology?"

"It's only the first of many tools in my tool kit," Sally said. "There's also guilt, shame, and peer pressure."

Her straightforward honesty softened Jordan's resistance. "Sally, this really sucks."

"I know it does. But you're a fighter, Jordan. I can see it in your demeanor."

"I wasn't counting on this fight."

"We rarely count on the ones we're forced to face."

Jordan shoved out a sigh. "So, now what?"

"First, we're going to practice more with your white cane. It'll be your ticket off the couch and around your house. And after that, it'll get you to the curb, into an Uber, and around downtown Austin."

"For what purpose?"

"That'll be for you to decide. I can't do all the work, Jordan. But I promise you, there's a good life waiting for you, if you're willing to adapt."

How many times had Jordan said the same thing to Avery? *Just muscle through the pain and the cravings. Just keep putting one foot in front of the other.* She was suddenly aware that Avery was now paying close attention. And one day, her sister might face a battle with drugs again, and she wanted her fight to be the example. "Fine, let's give the cane a whirl."

"Excellent."

***

Emma relaxed against the 1972 sedan seat. Stan, the guy from the hospital, had a slight smile as he drove south on I-35. Though they had not eaten at the diner because the line was too long, Stan had suggested another place. She had agreed, and dinner had been fun.

"Thanks again for the ride," Emma said.

"Least I could do after you missed the second bus."

"Still, there's another one in an hour."

"Which is silly."

"You sure this isn't a problem?"

"Not at all." He switched on the radio. She let her thoughts drift, thinking what had started as a bad day was now pretty good.

When he drove past her exit, she sat forward. "You missed my exit."

"Did I?" He seemed confused. "Sorry. I'll turn around."

She smiled. Didn't think twice.

He appeared to move toward the right side, ready to take the next exit. She let her gaze drift out the window.

When she heard the snap of electricity, she looked at him just as he pressed metal prongs to the side of her neck. Energy snapped through her, sending bolts of fire through every muscle. She spasmed several times, and her jaw clenched as her head fell backward.

"We're going to have a little detour," he said. The stun gun sounded as if it were recharging.

"No," she whispered.

"Sorry, Emma, but we're on my timeline now." He pressed the stun gun to her side, and she jolted again. Her body seized, and she lost control of her bladder. Humiliation and fear burned through her.

"Please."

"Junkies like you get what they deserve."

"I stopped. I haven't used in months."

"It's a matter of time before you use again. You all go back eventually. I should know. I can't seem to control myself."

"No, I'm not using again."

"We all say that."

"It's true for me! I'm clean!"

"Be a good girl, or I can keep shocking you for hours. The stun gun is better than the club. And I like the way your tits twitch when your body spasms." He turned up the radio louder, the pulsing rock music scraping over her shattered nerves. "We're going to have a good time."

She pressed against the passenger-side door, doing her best to put as much distance as she could between them. When they arrived at an old house, he shut off the engine and powered up the stun gun.

"No, please," Emma said.

"Be good and I won't."

He followed her into the house, several times pressing the power button on the gun so it snapped with electricity. Inside, he locked the door. "Take your clothes off."

She faced him. "Why?"

He pushed off his hoodie. "You know why."

"I'm not doing this," she said. "I want to leave."

He closed the gap between them and pressed the stun gun to her neck. Her body convulsed, and she dropped to her knees.

"Take your clothes off."

With trembling hands, she reached for the hem of her blue scrubs.

"The white cotton bra is a disappointment, and your hips are too round for me."

"Then let me go."

"Your look isn't exactly right, but you'll do for tonight."

He ordered her on the floor, and then he tied her hands. For fun, he pressed the stun gun against her naked flesh. She screamed and her body convulsed.

Stripping, he turned to a cabinet and grabbed a plastic bag. "Put this on your head."

"Why?"

"It'll be fun."

She slid the bag over her head and stared up at him through the clear barrier.

"I have a job for you."

Her breath fogged against the plastic, and the air quickly grew stale. Her panic sharpened.

He lit up a cigarette and inhaled. "If you do this, I'll set you free."

Hope softened some of the fear. "What?"

"I need you to make one phone call," he said.

"To who?"

"A cop."

"The cops? Why would you want me to call the police?" Her eyes and nose were red from crying.

"Just one cop. She'll be very interested to know that we're together."

"And then you can let me go?"

"Yes." *Go. Free. Dead.* Basically, they were interchangeable.

"Why would you let me go? I saw your face."

"But you said you won't tell anyone, right?" he asked smoothly.

She shook her head. "No. Never."

He smiled. "Then we're all set."

"You really will let me go?"

"Why would I lie?"

CHAPTER TWENTY-ONE

Thursday, April 22
4:00 a.m.

Jordan's sight was perfect as she looked up at the bright-blue sky filled with white, puffy clouds. The sun shone on her face as she savored the hues, the gentle folds of the clouds, a plane racing to its destination, and a bird perched on a branch.

She had had a nightmare. She had lost her sight and was now dependent on her sister and strangers. She could not do her work. She was trapped. That was the nightmare, but this was the reality.

A phone rang in the distance, pulling her attention away from the sky. She did not want to look away, fearing if she did, she would lose it.

The phone kept ringing.

The sound sliced across the sky, erasing the clouds, the plane, and the birds, and washed out the blues until it was a dingy black.

Jordan stared into the darkness, her heart racing, her mind clawing back the memory of color and sunshine. She sat up, tears streaming down her face. She shifted her body to the nightstand and fumbled for the light switch. A click told her it was on, and for a brief second she thought she might need a new light bulb.

And then she remembered. She was living the nightmare, and it was not going to fade like her now-imaginary blue sky.

Would she ever switch this lamp on again? As she groped for the phone, she knocked over a bottle of sleeping pills she had refused because she feared if she took one, she would never stop.

As her fingers brushed the smooth surface of her phone, it stopped ringing. "Shit."

She raised the display to her face, trying to shift the screen so she could make out who had called. But the haze and darkness were too thick.

The voice activation had become so annoying to Jordan she had asked Avery to turn it off before she went to bed. Now, her once-valuable phone was little more than a paperweight.

Jordan swung her legs over the side of her bed. Her feet touched the blue area rug that extended roughly a foot beyond her bed. Rising, phone in hand, she moved slowly, her hands outstretched. Sally had told her to use the white cane, but she could not remember where she had set it down. If she did not get more organized or develop a sharper memory, her injury was going to swallow her whole.

The carpet shifted to the cool tile, and she guessed she had another five feet to walk to reach the door. The house was quiet, the silence broken only by the shuffle of her feet and the *ticktock* of the clock.

Her phone dinged with a voicemail, drawing her attention back to the screen as if she could somehow magically see it now. Middle-of-the-night calls generally were attached to a case, and in her situation a homicide. The word had spread about her disability, but she had scattered her business cards around the city during so many investigations that she knew there were plenty of people unaware of her situation.

She shuffled her feet across the great room that separated her room from Avery's. Crossing with confidence, she believed her many years in this room had armed her with enough familiarity to pass safely.

Jordan's knee slammed into a coffee table.

Muttering an oath, she drew back, rubbing her bruised skin. Had she drifted that far to the right, or was this from Avery's apartment? She would pay better attention to the tour today.

She crossed over the east side of the house. To her left was her home office, and across from it was Avery's room. She skimmed her fingers lightly along the walls and, when she felt Avery's doorframe, knocked. At first, she heard nothing, so she knocked harder.

"What?" The word rushed over Avery's lips, breathless and slightly frantic.

"It's Jordan."

"Is everything okay?" Avery asked.

This was too much work and effort for a phone call that she once could have processed in seconds. "I received a phone call."

"Okay, who was it?" Her voice was heavy with sleep.

"I don't know." Her adrenaline had ebbed, and in its wake flowed frustration. "If I knew, I wouldn't be here. I would be in my room dealing with it."

"Don't get bitchy with me."

Jordan gripped her phone. "I'm sorry. It's just really frustrating."

A light switch clicked. "Let me look."

Jordan held out the phone. "And did you move a table?"

"I told you I moved some of my stuff back."

"I wasn't listening."

"And you couldn't find your cane as well?" She snatched the phone from Jordan's grip.

"I could not."

"Today, maybe you'll be a better student when Sally comes by and offers helpful tips."

Jordan gritted her teeth, resisting the urge to shout. "Can you just play back the message?"

"Because you're going to be a better student, right?"

"When did you become such a hard-ass?" Jordan snapped.

"I remember a moment when I was doubled over with cramps while I was detoxing. I don't remember a lot of sympathy from you."

"I didn't intend to lose my vision."

"I didn't intend to be a substance abuser."

An edgy silence filled the space between them. Avery had moved home, and Jordan did not want them to be fighting. "You're right. That was a shitty thing to say. I should have been nicer to you when you were using and nicer to you now."

Avery grunted. "You're feeling trapped right now. I know how that feels. And if you'd been nice to me two years ago, I'd be dead."

"Which means you're going to ride my ass until my sight comes back."

"*If* it comes back, Jordan. We both heard what the doctor said."

"I'm staying positive. He said there was a slim chance. And slim is better than none."

"Staying sober comes with the same odds."

"You're beating the odds, and I'll do the same," Jordan said. "Now play my message."

Avery typed in Jordan's passcode and opened the voicemail.

"Detective Poe, this is Emma Powers. You don't know me, but he wanted me to call you. He's going to let me go. He told me so. But he wanted you to know he's sorry he hit you so hard. He didn't mean to hurt you. Also, he hopes you like the roses." Emma hesitated and then added, *"Casey is alive and doing fine."*

The call ended. Jordan's adrenaline rushed through her body with such force her temples pounded. "It's him."

"How did he get your number?"

"I called Casey. She called me back on a second phone she carried. That's how I found her. The phone's not putting off a signal, so he must have discovered and disabled it."

"Does this mean he has this Emma girl?" Avery asked.

"Yes."

"She said he wasn't going to hurt her." Avery's optimism was almost childlike.

Jordan shook her head. "Don't believe it. And don't believe that Casey is still alive."

"Why is he doing this?"

"It's a game to him. He's having fun. I stopped his last murder, and he wants me to know he has found another victim."

"He's having fun? What the hell is *fun* about this?" Anger strained Avery's voice.

For the first time since Jordan had been attacked, she had a sense of purpose. She remembered why she was a cop. Why she loved the job. "Help me figure out this voice-activated thing on the phone again."

"What are you going to do?"

"Call Ranger Spencer. He's going to want to hear this."

***

Spencer was on his morning run when his phone rang. He paused, wiped the sweat from his brow. "Jordan, is everything all right?"

"I have a situation."

"What is it?"

"A potential victim just called me."

Turning back toward his house, he said, "Hold tight. I'll be there as soon as I can."

When he reached his house, he called his office and asked for a search of Emma Powers's name. By the time he had showered and dressed, his phone rang. "Spencer."

The officer explained that Emma Powers had an arrest record for drugs and gave him the name of her parole officer.

"Do you have a picture?"

"Yes, sir. Sending now."

Spencer glanced at his phone, and as soon as the text arrived, he opened the image. Emma Powers had light-blond hair and was twenty.

As he moved toward his car, he called Emma's parole officer, landed in voicemail, and left a message. "I'm going to need current employer, address, and anything you have on her."

He arrived at Jordan's home at five minutes to 6:00 a.m. He knocked and heard unsteady footsteps moving toward the door. When it opened, Jordan stood there, wearing jeans and a light-blue pullover blouse. She had brushed her hair, stood straight, and, to his relief, looked more like her old self.

"It's Spencer," he said.

"Avery told me," she said. "Otherwise I wouldn't have opened the door. But audio cues are much appreciated."

"Consider it standard protocol going forward."

"I'll take the help wherever I can get it right now."

"Where's Avery?"

"Making coffee." She stepped aside, hesitantly, as if feeling her way. "Figured we both could use a cup."

"I never say no." As he removed his hat, he noted her gaze did not quite reach his eyes, the only visible sign that she could not see him clearly.

"Follow me. But if you see a coffee table or a chair in my path, say something. Avery's moved back home, which is great, but I've already earned a couple of bruises on my toes and the sides of my legs because of it."

"How's it going?" he asked.

"Nice to have Avery back. But the other stuff ain't so great."

"If it were me, I'd be pounding my fist on the wall and flipping furniture."

"Flipping furniture could be on my afternoon agenda."

The dry sarcasm was a good sign. "And the vision?"

"No improvement. The doctor said it could be weeks, maybe months."

Or never. "If I ever ask a question that bothers you, just tell me. My questions can be blunt."

"A hazard of the job."

"Exactly."

"I appreciate the directness. Walking on eggshells never works well. And if you cross a line, I'll let you know."

"Understood." In the kitchen, Avery stood behind the counter, setting out cream and sugar. She was dressed in athletic shorts, a shirt, and shoes. Hints of tension strained her features. "Avery."

"Ranger Spencer. Glad you could join us. We're having quite the morning."

"Your sister told me." Jordan did not appear rattled, but Avery was a different story. She was not used to this kind of stress.

"The coffee is ready, Jordan," Avery said.

"Why don't you go for a run?" Jordan asked. "It'll give the ranger and me time to discuss the case. And you really don't need to hear this."

"Are you sure?" Avery asked.

"He's capable of pouring coffee, and I don't think we'll be getting into a case turf war today. Right, Spencer?"

"If we do, we'll keep it bloodless," he said.

Avery studied him, trying to judge whether this was a brand of humor or he was serious.

"He's kidding," Jordan said.

"How do you know?" Avery asked.

"His tone of voice. Spencer, you're going to play nice, right?"

"Yes. Cop humor sometimes falls flat," he said.

"I can handle whatever you two are going to discuss," Avery challenged.

"I know. But I don't want you to," Jordan said. "Remember, I'm still in charge in this house."

"Debatable." Avery clunked down two empty coffee cups on the counter. "Spencer, I leave it to you."

"Ten-four," he said.

When she exited out the back door, he moved to fill the cups. In the corner of the kitchen was a white cane. "How do you take it?"

"Cream and sugar."

"I wouldn't have figured it."

"I treat myself to both when I'm under stress or tired. And I've checked both those boxes this morning." She felt around for the barstool in front of the kitchen island and sat.

He set the cup in front of her. "Cup is at twelve o'clock. Six inches from your right hand."

"I appreciate specifics more than ever."

He sipped his coffee, savoring the flavor. "It's good coffee."

"Avery works in a café. Which I consider a real perk."

He stood on the other side of the island. "Can I hear the message again?" She had played it for him over the phone, and he had called dispatch and reported the possible kidnapping.

She fished her phone from her back pocket and opened it with her thumbprint. "Have at it."

He hit play and listened. *"Detective Poe, this is Emma Powers. You don't know me, but he wanted me to call you. He's going to let me go. He told me so. But he wanted you to know he's sorry he hit you so hard. He didn't mean to hurt you. Also, he hopes you like the roses."* Emma hesitated and then added, *"Casey is alive and doing fine."*

"It could be a hoax. Both you and Casey Andrews have been mentioned in the news."

"Maybe. But it shouldn't be hard for you to track down Emma Powers in Austin."

"Did you receive roses?" he asked.

"Yes. Avery said it's a dozen yellow roses."

"Where are they?"

"On the back porch. I didn't want them in the house after I heard the message. No surprise, there's no card or florist's name attached."

The killer knew where Jordan lived, and he wanted her to know it. Spencer suspected any warnings to Jordan now would fall on deaf ears. Instead, he recapped for her what he knew so far about Emma Powers. "She has light-blond hair and a small frame like Tammy Fox and Casey Andrews."

Jordan nodded slowly, but it was hard for him to read her expression. She raised the cup to her lips and gently sipped. "Good work."

"This killer is keyed in on you, Jordan. Do you think he knows about your vision?"

"Anyone hanging around the hospital could figure it out. My occupational therapist walked me around the halls. Lady likes her tough love."

"Did you hear anything that might have troubled you during these walks? Did your OT mention anyone suspicious? What about Sunday?"

"Sunday never came back. And honestly, I wasn't on my game at the hospital. It was all overload for me."

"Fair enough."

"Any other odd things happen?"

She tapped her finger against the side of her cup. "At the hospital, I had a couple of nightmares and woke up. I kept dreaming someone was watching me. But when I questioned the nurses, none of them saw anyone."

Twenty-four-hour, around-the-clock police protection sounded good, but the reality was that the city budget did not have the funds to guard Jordan's room. "I'll pull the surveillance footage from the hospital and see if there's anything that's off base while you were there."

She rubbed her temple. "I'll take any lead at this point."

"You said the roses are on the back porch?"

"We didn't toss them. Just in case there're prints or a card we missed."

"I'll have a look." Spencer's phone rang, and he glanced at the display. "It's Emma Powers's parole officer." He accepted the call. "Burt, thanks for getting back so early. I'm here with Detective Jordan Poe. I'm putting you on speakerphone."

"No sweat," Burt said. "You don't call just for the hell of it."

"Do you have anything on Powers?"

"As of her last visit with me four weeks ago, she worked at Dell Seton."

"Really?"

Jordan's gaze had shifted in his direction.

"She's a nursing assistant. She's been on the job for six months. Did time for drugs, as you confirmed. She was released from parole a month ago, but I still have the name of her boss. It's a place to start."

Spencer fished a notebook and pen from his breast pocket. "Shoot." Burt relayed Powers's home address and the name of her boss. "Thanks, Burt." He hung up and checked the time. "I need to confirm her work schedule and if she's missed a shift."

"These kinds of victims often share the same traits. Drug abuse. Same look. Young. All lived within ten miles of each other."

Spencer picked up the cream and turned toward the refrigerator. As he opened the door, he saw a picture of a young woman with two girls in her lap. The kid on the right could not have been more than twelve, but he recognized Jordan. The toddler had to be Avery, and the woman their mother. It struck him that their mother, Jordan, and Avery looked a lot like Laura, Tammy Fox, Casey Andrews, and Emma Powers.

"Why are you quiet?" Jordan asked.

He replaced the cream and closed the refrigerator door. "This picture of you, Avery, and your mother."

"It's one of our favorites. It's before she really started using so much that she couldn't function. And in the interest of full disclosure, I have never taken a drink or used a drug in my life."

"You said your mother died in a car crash, right?"

"I was twenty-two when her car drove off a bridge and landed in Lake Austin. She drowned."

"I'm sorry."

"She was intoxicated at the time." Jordan drew in a breath. "You see the similarities between the victims and my sister and me, right?"

"Yes."

She sat silent, and he sensed she was debating whether to open up. "Two years ago, I found Avery in an apartment. Walker had sold her drugs. She was high and her hands bound. There was also plastic shoved in her mouth. If I'd not arrived when I did, she would have suffocated."

That explained Harold Sunday's comment about Jordan's personal connection to Walker. "Does she remember anyone else being with Walker?"

"She doesn't remember much. Whatever he gave her that night knocked her out so well."

"And she never had any other issues?"

"That night scared the hell out of her. She sobered and so far has stayed clean. It might not have anything to do with this, but keeping it hidden won't help anyone now."

"How did Avery hook up with Walker?" he asked.

"She was young and struggling. Barely got out of high school and didn't want to go to college. Worked odd jobs and then started to drift. He showed up and said all the right things, and she fell under his spell. When they were getting serious, I did a background check on him."

"Did you really?"

A grin tugged her lips. "I did. And then I found drugs in her room. Immediately, I connected him to the drugs. We had a terrible fight, she stormed off, and I got worried. Like I said, I followed, found her in his apartment, suffocating. Five more minutes and she would have been dead."

"You've good instincts."

"Maybe. Or maybe I just got lucky."

"I appreciate your trust."

"I should have told you sooner, but I did not want to believe these two murders were attached to Avery. It's been two years, and this killer's MO is different." She shoved out a sigh, and her frown suggested she already regretted her honesty. "But killers evolve."

"Yes."

"Where do we go from here?"

"I'll call the hospital," he said. "And hope Emma Powers showed up for work today."

***

While Jordan and Spencer waited for a callback from Emma's supervisor, he updated her on his visit to Sunday's office as well as the findings from the medical examiner. Standard investigative information, but it felt good to think about the case and not herself.

"I've never been crazy about Harold Sunday," she said. "If Satan paid Sunday's price, then he'd represent him. But he's good at what he does, and if there's a loophole to crawl through or leverage to be found, he'll take advantage of it."

"How many times have you gone against him in court?" Spencer asked.

"Five or six times. He and I share a mutual dislike for the other."

"Has he made any threats?"

"No, but while I was in the Walker hearing, someone keyed my car."

"Sunday?"

"I can't prove anything."

"He's too smart for that."

"Exactly."

At 7:15 a.m., the hospital administrator, Ben Barnard, called Spencer. He put the call on speakerphone and asked again about Emma Powers.

"How did you know she didn't show up for her shift today?" Mr. Barnard asked.

Instead of answering, Spencer countered with, "Is it like her not to come to work?"

"Some in the beginning, but in the last few months she's fallen into a good routine. She's turning out to be one of my best nursing assistants."

"Do you have her current phone number?"

The man recited the number, which matched the number that had called Jordan's phone this morning.

"Thank you," Spencer said. "Call me if she comes in to work."

"I sure will, Ranger Spencer."

He hung up. "I'm going by Emma Powers's apartment."

"I want to come with you." The words rushed out before she considered she could be a liability.

"Think that's a good idea? You've only been out of the hospital a day."

"If I sit around here and practice using that white cane all day, I might go crazy."

"Have you used the cane at all?" he challenged.

"I have the basics down. Enough to get around a little."

"You won't know what you're stepping into or disturbing at a potential crime scene."

"You can park me in a corner, and I promise not to move around unassisted. Even though her apartment isn't officially a crime scene, I'll treat it as such."

The back door opened. For an instant, Jordan tensed, realizing she had only Spencer to depend on.

"It's me," Avery said.

As her sister moved closer, Jordan caught a whiff of perspiration and sunshine. Runs always left Avery pink faced and relaxed in an endorphin high.

"How was the run?" Jordan asked.

"Quick. Did the ranger behave?" A cabinet opened; water rushed from the kitchen faucet and shut off.

"I'm no worse for the wear," Jordan said.

"I was a gentleman," Spencer said. "Did you find any of Tammy Fox's art?"

"Yeah, I did. It's just two small paintings. Be right back." Avery returned less than thirty seconds later. "I kept them out for you."

"What do they look like?" Just having to ask the question was frustrating.

"It's mixed media," Avery said. "Lots of dark tones, rough edges, and streaks of red."

The description reminded her of some of Avery's work. Not the brightly colored landscapes she sold to tourists, but the ones she kept for herself.

"Very modern looking," Spencer said.

"Does it tell you anything about her?" Jordan asked.

"It suggests she was struggling," he said.

Avery gulped water. "That's fairly accurate. She hated being sober."

"What are you going to do with the paintings?" Jordan asked.

"Keep them," Avery said. "It's good to remember."

"Okay."

"What are you two up to today?" Avery asked.

"We're now leaving to investigate a lead," Jordan said.

"No." Avery set her glass down hard on the counter. "That's the craziest thing you've said in a long time, Jordan. You were released from the hospital yesterday."

"I'll be fine, Avery," Jordan said. "Ranger Spencer will drive, escort me, and then deliver me back home."

"Is that true, Spencer?" Avery asked.

His silence telegraphed indecision and perhaps a little frustration. "I'll make sure she doesn't overdo it, and I'll bring her back safe and sound."

"I cannot believe we're having this discussion," Avery said.

"Avery, I need to do this," Jordan said. "If this is my new life, I've got to figure out how to navigate it."

"This crazy guy out there almost killed you," Avery said. "He's delivered flowers to our house!"

"And we'll both be safer as soon as Spencer and I find him," Jordan said.

CHAPTER TWENTY-TWO

Thursday, April 22
7:30 a.m.

Jordan stepped out of her house, searching the shadows and shards of light for any landmark or anchor. She felt Spencer stand beside her and imagined him slipping on his Stetson, his crow's-feet deepening as he glared at the morning sun. She liked the look of his face and missed seeing it.

"How do you want to do this, Detective Poe?" he asked. "I can offer you my arm. I can offer verbal directions or let you go it alone."

"I want to do it myself." She fumbled in her purse for her sunglasses. The sun was not at its peak, but already the light bothered her.

"I want to be on my new land north of the city, sipping coffee and enjoying the morning. But it's not likely to happen anytime soon. What I need is to stay in the game and find this killer."

"I need that, too."

"Then we're both putting our wants aside and doing what needs to be done. After the killer is caught, I'll head to the ranch, and you'll do whatever you want. But for now, we suck it up."

She could not imagine what *want* would make sense without her vision. "I'll take your arm and all the verbal cues you think I need."

The air shifted as he held out his arm.

She laid her hand on it. The cotton shirt was a fine weave and stiff with starch. Under the fabric the muscles of his forearm felt like corded steel. "Let's do this."

"All right then."

He guided her down the front steps along her walkway toward the curb. "My SUV is parked at eleven o'clock."

"Understood."

He paused, reached, and opened the door.

She climbed inside, fumbled for the seat belt, and when it clicked in place, he closed the door. The seat leather warmed her back. She breathed in what she now recognized as a mixture of Spencer's soap and his natural scent.

The driver's-side door opened, and the leather seats creaked as he settled behind the wheel. Again, the energy shifted, and she could almost feel the tension rippling from his body. He was as unsure of this adventure as she was.

"Thank you." Her gruff tone scraped rust off the words.

"Call it self-interest," he said easily. "Two heads are better than one."

The engine roared to life, and the gear shifted into first. Spencer seemed to be in his element behind the wheel of the car. So was she. She loved driving. She loved independence.

The police radio squawked a couple of times, but none of the messages were directed at him.

"Why did you want this case?" she asked.

Silence wrapped around him, a turn signal clicked, and the tires slowed as they were likely approaching an intersection. "I was married once. We were young, excited, and idealistic. I wanted children. She wanted to wait, so we did. I was working a lot in the early days and missed a few clues I should have caught. Turns out Vickie had always been a drug user but hid it well. Then she started injecting heroin. We fought. I took her to rehab a couple of times, but we always ended back at square one. I never could bring myself to divorce her. Two years ago, she was found dead in an El Paso alley. She had been sexually assaulted and strangled to death."

She did not speak, sensing he had more to say.

"DNA was recovered from her body, but it never matched any in the system. I decided to move back to Austin, hoping to put it behind me."

"Do you think Vickie's death is connected to these killings?"

"No. But the recent murders hit a nerve with me."

"If you'd told me that, I would have given you the case. I know what it's like when a case strikes close to home."

"You have a reputation for being a pit bull."

Her lips quirked. "I'll take that as a compliment."

"It's meant as one." He pressed the accelerator, and the car started moving.

"Takes one to know one?"

Hands tightened on the steering wheel. "That's about right. I saw us butting heads, and I didn't want to waste time arguing."

"Then we better get it right this time," she said.

"We owe it to the dead women. I owe it to you."

"Are you taking pity on me because of the attack?" she asked.

"Not pity. But you've earned your place on this case."

She turned her face toward the sound of his voice. "I'll have to make hay, as the saying goes, while the sun shines. If my vision doesn't come back, this will be my last case."

"Then we better solve it." He slowed, took a sharp right and then a left.

She shifted her line of sight to the windshield, searching the perpetual fog for anything that might tell her what the place looked like.

There was nothing but gray haze and what looked like a blinking light. "Is there a marked car here?"

"There is. At two o'clock."

"I've been here before, but it's been several years. Still gray with a faded terra-cotta roof?" she asked.

"That's correct. Two stories, rooms face outward."

"Rents by the week if my memory serves."

"Correct."

He shut off the engine. "I'll come around."

"Let me get out of the car. If the uniforms see a ranger opening my door, I'll never hear the end of it."

"Sure."

He exited his side as her fingertips fumbled for the door handle, and the door swung open. She got out, taking note of the wind on her face, the growing warmth of the sun, and the asphalt under her feet. Carefully, she closed the door as Spencer came up beside her.

"Arm?" he asked.

"People are going to talk."

He chuckled. "It won't do either of our reputations any good if you fall."

"True." She could endure these indignities and frustrations because they were temporary. Hurricane winds that swept over the Gulf Coast left behind destruction, but after the storm passed, people rebuilt. So would she.

"Do you have gloves?" she asked.

He handed her a set. The latex felt familiar in her hands, and she pulled them on as she had so many over her career.

She laid her hand on his arm, and they walked ten paces forward before he noted a curb and then indicated they would be climbing ten steps to a landing. His precise navigation made the journey palatable, and as his pace slowed, she surmised they had arrived.

"Officer Ruiz, any word from the apartment manager?" Spencer asked.

"He just went down to get the master key," Officer Ruiz said. "Should be back in a few minutes."

"Good," Jordan said.

A silence settled over the officer, and she felt him staring.

"Excuse me for asking, Detective Poe, but I heard you had been hurt pretty badly," Officer Ruiz said.

"That so?" she asked.

"They said you were blind."

"You mean low vision? Who said?" she asked.

"Everyone."

She grinned. "And yet here I am."

Keys jangled behind her, and she turned toward who she assumed was the apartment manager. As he reached around her, she noted he smelled of breakfast sausage and stale cigarettes. He unlocked the door.

"Let Ruiz and me go in first," Spencer said.

A rebuttal was on the tip of her tongue, and then she remembered her promise. "Sure."

Her hand lowered to her waistband, and automatically it slid to where she holstered her service weapon. Of course, it was not there, and its absence left her feeling naked and exposed. The indignity was magnified by the fact she was standing outside the apartment with the manager, waiting on Spencer's search results. A month ago, she would have been the one in that apartment, searching for a threat.

"What's going on with Emma?" the manager asked.

"We received a tip that she might be in distress. We're following up," Jordan said.

"She's a good kid."

"Is she dating anyone? Does she have any close friends?" Jordan asked.

"Emma has brought a few guys to her place but never the same one twice."

"You keep a close eye on your tenants?" Jordan asked.

He cleared his throat, shifted his stance. "I make it my business to see who's coming and going. No one wants trouble."

"And Emma Powers had no trouble?"

"None."

"When she applied for the apartment, did she put down any references?"

"Her parole officer and drug counselor vouched for her. Taking her on was a risk, but that's the way it is in places like this. We don't get the folks who fly the straight and narrow."

"What are the names of her references?" Jordan asked.

"I'd have to look them up."

"Do that."

Heavy footsteps approached seconds before Spencer announced, "Clear. There's no one here."

"Thank you for your help," Jordan said to the manager. "Ranger Spencer and I will lock up when we leave."

"I should stay."

"Not necessary," she insisted.

Steps approached, and the creak of Ruiz's gun belt gave him away. "Ranger Spencer asked me to stand outside. He said you'd call if you needed anything."

"Perfect." Jordan hesitated, oriented her body toward the smoky scent of Emma's apartment. She slowly stepped inside, noting the shag carpet under her feet.

Spencer moved beside her. "It's basic. Couch, chair, television, and kitchenette. Fairly neat."

"There has to be a full ashtray here somewhere."

"On the coffee table."

"Any signs of struggle?"

"No." They moved several steps forward, and the carpet changed to linoleum. She kept moving until she bumped into a refrigerator. She skimmed her fingers over the front, felt different textures of paper. Judging by the size and weight, she guessed, "Take-out menu, business card, and several photographs."

"Mexican takeout, the business card of her parole officer, and the pictures are of Emma with a group of other young girls."

"Key in on the females. Anyone familiar?"

"Interesting."

"What?"

"One could be Tammy Fox. The hair is different, but it looks like her."

"How many females in the picture?"

"Four. Emma on the end and beside her the Tammy look-alike, and two other unidentified females."

"Any notes on the back?"

"Yes. Emma, Tammy, Sarah, and Amy."

"Sarah or Amy. Could one of them be Jane Doe #1?"

"Don't know."

"Where was the picture taken?" It was frustrating. There was so much to be learned from settings as well as facial expressions. Body language represented about 90 percent of communication.

"A bar. I can't tell you where."

"We need that DNA from Jane Doe #1 and to confirm her identity." She opened the refrigerator door, caught a whiff of garlic. Spencer inventoried the contents: creamer, Chinese takeout, eggs, and a head of lettuce past its prime.

They moved to the bedroom, and she skimmed her fingertips along the wall until she felt a light switch. She flipped it on, hoping it would help. It did not.

"There're clothes and shoes on the floor," Spencer said.

"Bed unmade?"

"It is."

"What about bathroom trash can? Anything of interest?"

"Tissues, aspirin bottle, and an empty box of condoms. No condoms in the trash."

Emma was living her life just like any other person trying to get on after a setback. The woman received points for that in Jordan's book. Life could humble your ass.

"Ranger Spencer," Officer Ruiz said.

"Yes?" Spencer asked.

"Just received a call. A woman's been found dead. She was wrapped in plastic."

"Where?" he asked.

"Ten miles north on I-35. Found in a vacant house."

"I'll take you home," Spencer said to Jordan.

"No way," Jordan said.

"It's one thing to check out an apartment. It's another to take you to an active crime scene."

"I've worked enough scenes. I know my way around."

"With vision," he said carefully.

"I'll take your lead. Stay out of the way." Before, she would not have been forced to justify her presence.

"I won't have time to babysit."

The last word stung. "I'm not a child, Spencer."

"I didn't mean it that way."

"Sure you did. I'd have said the same to you if the shoe were on the other foot."

"You understand where I'm coming from then?"

"Yes, but I don't care," she said carefully. "Emma called me. This killer hurt me. He knows where my sister and I live. I want in on the crime scene."

His exhale advertised his frustration, and she imagined the lines on his face deepening. "You'll do everything I say. Do you understand? And like it or not, I'm the lead on this case."

"I'm not a rookie."

"Those are the terms, Detective Poe. Do as I say, or your next ride will be home."

She rolled her head from side to side. *Be nice. Make nice. Remember the real goal.* "Sure. Fine. Understood." She was not sure how much value she was going to add, but she could not let this investigation go. She needed to prove to herself that she still had value as some type of investigator. If she could not be a cop, she could be totally lost.

CHAPTER TWENTY-THREE

Thursday, April 22
9:00 a.m.

Spencer needed only a glance to see Detective Poe was nervous. She was quiet, her face tense, and her gaze directed ahead. She wanted this to work so badly he could feel her urgency. But wanting was not enough. Bringing her along was going to stir unnecessary questions and distract from the case.

And yet here they were.

In the older neighborhood, he spotted the flash of cop car lights. At first, they did not register on Jordan's radar, but as they rolled closer and the tension in his body increased, she shifted forward in her seat.

"Who's on scene?" she asked.

"Four marked cars and the forensic van. Also looks like Captain Lee's vehicle is here."

"He won't be thrilled to see me."

"No, he will not."

"Don't sound so tense. I'll be as quiet as a church mouse."

He snorted, knowing she did not believe that statement any more than he did. "Sure you will."

"You better start trusting me. We're partnered for the duration of this case."

"We're not partners."

"I'm good at what I do, Spencer. I have an instinct for the work."

"And you're visually impaired." He dealt with the facts presented to him, not with the ones he wanted.

"Well, you're direct, and obvious."

"Do you want me to put on the kid gloves, Detective Poe? You don't strike me as the type who wants to be treated like a child."

"No, I do not. Being a cop is not for the faint of heart. Neither is losing your vision. If you ever do patronize me, I'll know it, and I'll be pissed."

"Good, because I don't know how to soft-pedal."

He parked behind a deputy's patrol car. Shutting off the engine, he handed her gloves and got out. She slid on the gloves and hovered close to the vehicle, appearing to listen to the sounds of the officers' voices, car engines, and the rattle of the forensic team tent currently being set up.

He came around and offered her his arm, and this time she took it instinctively. As they moved toward the house, Captain Lee spotted him and then Jordan. The older man's face soured, and he was mumbling as he strode toward them.

"Detective Poe, this is a surprise," Captain Lee said.

"Is it?" she asked. "I know Ranger Spencer forwarded Emma Powers's call to you."

"All the more reason for you not to be here. This killer has targeted you."

"Not the first time a murderer has resented my presence," she said.

Damn but the woman had a brass set. Hard not to admire it, but there was a fine line between bravery and foolishness. "I'll escort the detective inside just this one time," Spencer said.

"It's your case," Captain Lee said.

"And mine," Jordan added.

Spencer tugged her forward, knowing at the rate she was going, she would talk her way out of this investigation. As they moved away, he said, "I thought you weren't going to say much."

"I've lost my sight, not my intelligence. And I refuse to think of myself as helpless."

"You are."

"When push comes to shove, I could hold my own."

He did not doubt she could handle most civilians. But this killer was not like most people.

As they approached the front door, the faint scent of death reached out immediately. Jordan's head cocked, and she looked in the direction of the bright forensic lights set up in the living room.

"Her hands and feet are bound," Spencer said to Jordan. "There's a bag over her head, and the outer layer of plastic is wound tightly around her body."

"Is it Emma Powers?"

"She matches the picture, but identity will need to be confirmed." He moved them closer and studied the victim's features. Panic imprinted on once-smooth skin, and a gag filled her mouth. However, there was a marked difference. "She's like the others, but her eyes are taped closed."

"Eyes taped closed?" Jordan asked. "This is a first."

He studied Jordan's face, watching as she stared in the general direction of the body. Her brow furrowed.

"She can't see. Like me," she said.

"If that's true, then he knows your injury status." He thought about the unknown person in her room at the hospital and the vase of roses.

"Why me?" she asked, more to herself.

"You were featured in the media."

"So were you. So was Captain Lee."

"You're the only female," he said. "And you are Avery's sister."

Neither of them had to say it, but she and Avery fit the victim profile.

Footsteps approached, and then Lucas's voice said, "Ranger Spencer. Detective Poe."

"Lucas," she said.

Lucas stared at her, his face reflecting too many questions. "How are you, Detective Poe?"

"I've had better days," she said.

"Sorry to hear what happened."

"Yeah, it sucks."

"Lucas have a look inside?" Spencer asked.

"Right."

Footsteps crossed the apartment, and they quickly returned to the door. "In the bedroom. There's something that you need to see." As soon as the word was out of his mouth, his frown deepened. "Sorry."

"You can reference sight," Jordan said. "I'm not going to fall apart."

"Right. I know that," Lucas said.

"Can you tell if her eyes have been physically damaged?" Jordan asked.

"They don't appear to be," Lucas said. "But I'll let the medical examiner remove the tape."

"I don't think his intention was to attack me," she said. "Emma said the assailant apologized for hitting me so hard."

"Why didn't he kill you?" Spencer asked.

"Maybe he thought I was dead," she said. "Maybe he didn't have time. You were close to the driveway as I entered the house."

"Why did he take Casey?" Spencer asked.

"He didn't get a chance to finish the job," she said. "Seeing his victim die is an important part of the ritual."

"So, he takes her somewhere else, repeats the process, and kills her," Spencer said.

"He might not kill her immediately, but he won't keep her alive for long." Jordan's sightless gaze shifted in the direction of his face. "Have you considered another press conference?" she asked.

"Not with you."

"He's already sent me a message with the tape and roses. Give me a chance to send a message back to him."

"No."

"Why not?"

"Because I won't take that risk."

CHAPTER TWENTY-FOUR

Thursday, April 22
3:30 p.m.

Jordan felt helpless. She listened to the sounds of the crime scene technicians and officers, but without her vision to process the sights, she was not receiving enough data to make a difference. Using the voice-activated software on her phone, she called her sister, and when the phone actually rang, she felt a sense of victory.

Avery picked up on the second ring. "How goes it?"

"Not great," Jordan admitted as she turned her back to the scene. "Could you come and pick me up?"

"Sure. Where's Spencer?"

"Knee deep in the investigation. I'm of no use to anyone here."

"I don't think that's true."

"I know my limitations. But if you pick me up, we can visit Casey Andrews's mother."

"She's the girl that's missing."

"Correct."

"Of course. I've been tracking you on Find a Friend just in case, so I can be there in twenty minutes."

"You've been tracking me." Jordan was annoyed and impressed.

"You used to track me."

But that was different. She was the older cop sister. Was. Now she was the older sister with limited vision that might not ever improve. "Fair enough. See you soon."

Jordan slid her phone in her pocket as a new vehicle arrived. Doors opened and closed; feet thudded onto hard-packed dirt as the pair moved around to the back, opened another door, and gurney wheels jangled. The medical examiner's team had arrived to collect the body.

Spencer and Lucas spoke to the medical examiner attendants in subdued tones that she might not have noticed before. It was not like she had superpowerful hearing now, but she was already keying in on sounds, smells, and textures more.

Spencer was explaining the location of the body and its condition. He wanted the plastic maintained. Lucas had photographed the wrapped body, but Spencer wanted detailed photos taken as the body was transported.

Approaching boots struck the earth, the air shifted, and she detected Spencer's now-familiar scent. "The medical examiner is here."

"Do you have a time yet for the autopsy?" she asked.

"Tomorrow. It'll take time to unwrap the victim and photograph the body."

"I'd like to attend."

His silence was bursting with unsaid thoughts, and his long stares were palpable. "I'll see you at nine tomorrow."

"Great. Avery's on her way now."

"A deputy can drive you home."

"Foolish to pull someone away." And because it was basically true, she said, "Besides, Avery has agreed to be my driver for the foreseeable future."

"Okay."

The gurney wheels rolled, growing distant as the team moved into the house. "Go on, get back to your crime scene. I'll be fine."

"I'll see you in the morning."

"Will do."

He turned, moved away slowly.

"Hey, Spencer," she said. "Stop beating yourself up."

He retraced the steps and moved closer to her. "I could have prevented it."

She stared in the direction of his voice. "The only one who could have prevented it was the man who hit me. We both are cops, and we do the very best we can, but sometimes it's not good or fast enough. We both knew the risks."

"We also can't save them all," he said carefully. "You understand there's a good chance Casey Andrews is also dead."

"I won't accept that until her body is found. Until then, I'll be like you and berate myself for not saving her."

"You came closer than anyone."

"Close doesn't count."

She laid her hand on his forearm and offered the best smile she could muster. Tension rippled through his arm. The touch was not in the normal bounds of two cops at a crime scene, but her normal had shifted for now. Maybe forever. "I'm not angry with you."

He cleared his throat. "We're quite the pair."

"Yes, we are."

***

Jordan had always been good at guessing the time. She would glance at her wristwatch or phone if a report needed an exact time, but in everyday life and on the job, she used her own internal clock, which was rarely minutes off. This knack had become a bit of a parlor trick for the other cops, who placed bets on how close she could get to central daylight time. Thankfully, this gift was holding strong.

When Avery pulled up, Jordan knew it had been approximately twenty minutes since she had placed the call. The medical examiner had loaded the victim on the stretcher, and the technicians were at their vehicle's back bay and ready to hoist it aboard.

Car wheels rolled in slowly beside her. A window rolled down. "Your ride is here," Avery said. "Passenger-side door is three steps to your left."

She reached out until her fingers brushed the warm metal of the door handle of her SUV. Pulling it up, she opened the door and climbed into the passenger seat.

"You have my SUV." Closing her door, she fumbled for her seat belt. She had never ridden in the passenger seat of her own car and found the reverse location a little off putting.

"Just back from the forensics. I figured if I'm driving you, we might as well have the best ride. Your AC is better than mine."

"You can consider it your AC now," Jordan said. "Until I get my sight back, the car is yours."

"Thanks. Don't mind if I do. By the way, I brought your cane."

Her sister's way of saying this vision thing was here to stay. Jordan refused to accept the prognosis. This all still felt like a nightmare that would eventually end. But until it did, she would use the cane.

"If it'll get you motivated to use the cane and work with Sally, then so be it. Why are we going to see Casey Andrews's mother again?"

"It's been eight days since we spoke, and Mrs. Andrews might have remembered something that'll help me find her daughter."

"And the killer?"

"Nothing would give me greater pleasure than to bury him."

Avery chuckled. "There's the Jordan I know and love."

***

Jordan called Mrs. Andrews, asked her if she could visit, and when she received the go-ahead, Avery and she set out. The drive in the SUV with Avery behind the wheel was no less harrowing than it was in Avery's small four-door sedan. There had been a couple of quick stops, a "Watch out!" from Avery to another driver, and a gunning of the accelerator, a sign she had run a yellow light. But the armrests in Jordan's SUV were sturdier, giving her more to grip.

Avery slowed, took a sharp right, and the tires glided over a slightly rougher road. "We're in her neighborhood."

"Good." Routine questions would at least get the conversation started.

The car stopped. "Arrived," Avery said.

Jordan savored the stillness as her heart rate slowed. "What's the yard look like?"

"Flat, grass is brown and brittle, and there's a stone path that leads to a black front door."

"Is the brick painted? How's it maintained?"

"No paint, and the maintenance isn't great," she said. "Looks like it hasn't been taken care of in years."

Casey's mother worked long hours, had a child with a substance-abuse problem, so the house suffered.

"Let me get your cane," Avery said.

Jordan got out of the car and listened as Avery opened the back door and unfolded the cane. She slipped the wrist strap over Jordan's hand and wrapped her fingers around the leather grip. The weight of the cane still felt strange, and as she stood there, her world shifted closer toward forever darkness. Her old self was fading, and this new person emerging was a stranger to her.

"Ready?" Avery said.

She drew back her shoulders. "Yes."

"Do you want me to come inside?" Avery asked.

"It might help Mrs. Andrews relax if you're there. Your presence might shake something loose."

"People do like to talk to me," she said easily.

Jordan placed her hand on Avery's elbow, and using her cane, she moved slowly forward. She paid close attention to the ground under her feet, which normally would have been a nonevent. But rocks, roots, and clumps of dirt were now obstacles to negotiate.

Avery pointed out the two steps at the porch stoop and estimated there were three paces to the front door. Doorbell was at three o'clock, and she allowed Jordan to fumble around for it. Her fingertips skimmed the smooth button, and when she pressed it, a bell chimed in the house. Victory.

"Should we stand to the side?" Avery asked. "You always said domestic calls can be dangerous."

Remembering her training, she tugged Avery to the right side of the door with her. "You should be a cop."

"That's what I was thinking."

Jordan imagined her sister in the police academy, her wild blond hair tied back, a uniform on her slim body, and heavy laced-up boots on her feet. She shifted to Avery running down an alley at night, alone, chasing a guy accused of assault or rape. Or storming into a house where an enraged husband held his wife at knifepoint. "That's for another day."

Footsteps inside the house silenced Avery's response, but Jordan knew this topic would come up again. The door opened, and Jordan shifted in the general direction of the noise. A familiar scent of plywood and oil reminded her of the hardware store where Mrs. Andrews worked.

"Detective Poe," Mrs. Andrews said.

"Thank you for agreeing to see me. This is my sister, Avery Poe."

"I heard you were hurt pretty bad," Mrs. Andrews said.

"Yes."

"You look okay now."

"I can't see." Jordan raised her white cane. "That's why my sister is here. Do you mind if we come in?"

"Sure. Come on inside. Just got off from work, so the house is a bit of a mess."

The walls in the house felt close, and judging by the sound and space, she sensed there was a good bit of furniture and knickknacks. The air smelled dusty. Avery guided her toward a couch that smelled faintly of cigarette smoke.

Jordan settled, felt the cushion beside her dip as Avery sat. A chair to her left squeaked as Mrs. Andrews took her place. Jordan laid her cane on the floor over her feet.

"Can I get you two anything?" Mrs. Andrews asked.

"No, thank you," Jordan said.

"I heard from the cops you saw Casey in that house."

"I did see her." Images of the young woman's terrified eyes rushed her brain. "I'm sorry I couldn't help her."

"You did what you could. You tried. And I am grateful."

"Have you heard from anyone about Casey?"

"No. No one has called. And I keep my cell phone with me all the time. It's even on the bathroom counter when I shower."

"Did you go through her room?" Jordan asked.

"The police did. They said they didn't find anything."

"What about you? Have you searched it?" Jordan asked.

"I haven't had the heart."

"Go through the room. Tear it apart if you have to. If there's anything in there that might tell us who took her, we need to know."

"But the police did," Mrs. Andrews said.

"No one can go through a kid's room like a mother. You'll think of places to look the cops wouldn't."

Avery shifted. "My mother was good at finding anything. No secrets stayed secret long if she wanted to know what was going on."

The springs in Mrs. Andrews's chair squeaked. "Sure, if you think it'll help, I'll rip it apart. Casey won't be happy."

"I promise you she won't have a problem with it," Jordan said.

A back door opened and closed, and she was aware again her waistband felt light without her gun. "Who's that?"

"It's my youngest daughter, Cloe. She's sixteen."

"I'd like to talk to her," Jordan said.

"Cloe? Come in here, honey," Mrs. Andrews said.

Jordan reached down for her cane and rose. Sitting put her at a greater disadvantage. Avery stood as well.

"Whose car is that, Mom?" Cloe asked.

The footsteps were sharp, impatient, and stopped abruptly when they reached the carpeted living room.

"The police are here," Mrs. Andrews said. "They're still looking for Casey."

"Really?" Sarcasm laced the word. "It's been eight days since she was seen."

"We haven't given up," Jordan said.

"Who are you?"

"Detective Jordan Poe." Technically, they had not taken her badge away yet.

"You're that cop," Cloe said.

"If you mean the one who saw your sister, yes, that's me."

"The one that didn't save my sister," Cloe corrected.

"What can you tell me about Casey? Who knew her best? Was there anyone who ever said they wanted to hurt her? Anyone that watched or followed her?"

"No."

The too-crisp response caught Jordan's ear. "You're only three years younger. You went to the same high school for at least a year."

"Sure. But that was high school."

"What about when Casey started using drugs? Was there anyone who bothered her?"

Cloe's stillness harbored unspoken secrets. "I don't know anything."

Jordan turned to Avery, hoping she could follow a ruse. "Avery, could you take Mrs. Andrews out to the car and show her the mug shots?"

"In the blue binder?" Avery asked.

Leave it to Avery to embellish the story. "That's the one."

"Sure. Would you come with me, Mrs. Andrews?" Avery asked. "It won't take long."

"What about Cloe?" Mrs. Andrews asked. "Shouldn't she come?"

"We like to show images to witnesses separately," Jordan said. "Prevents one person from unduly influencing the other."

"Okay. Sure," Mrs. Andrews said.

When they left the room, Jordan turned to Cloe. "Tell me about your sister. Your mother is not here to listen, so you can be candid."

"I told you, I don't have anything to tell you."

"I think there's more you can add to the story."

"Why do you say that?"

"I can hear it in your voice," Jordan said.

"Hear what?"

She deflected the girl's question with one of her own. "Was Casey using drugs again?"

"How would I know?"

"Sisters know a lot about sisters."

Cloe grew quiet, but it did not feel defiant. Instead she sensed the young girl was balancing different bags, both filled with trouble.

"I don't care about the drugs," Jordan said. "I just want a tip that'll lead me to your sister."

Cloe sighed. "When she came home that last night, she was really nervous and jumpy. Got defensive when I asked her about where she'd been. That's the way she used to act."

"Did she look high?"

"No. But she wasn't acting like herself."

"So maybe she was carrying drugs and was self-conscious." Jordan asked, "Who would have sold her drugs?"

"I'm not sure."

"I hear hesitation," Jordan said.

"I don't want to get anyone in trouble."

"You must have heard something."

"I just heard her mention a guy's name once. Marco, I think. I asked her who it was, but she said he was just a friend."

Marco Walker. That sure as hell would be an odd coincidence. "Marco have a last name?"

"Started with a *W*. Wallace. Wilson. Something like that."

"Marco Walker is a drug dealer who was found dead about the time your sister vanished."

"I don't know about that."

The front door opened, and Mrs. Andrews and Avery reappeared. Avery said quickly, "We couldn't find the book, Jordan. We searched all through the back bins."

"That's okay," she said. "Thanks for trying."

"I want to help in any way I can," Mrs. Andrews said. "And so does Cloe."

"Go through Casey's bedroom," Jordan said. "And call me if you can find anything."

"You won't give up on my sister, will you?" Cloe asked.

"No." Jordan tightened her grip on her cane's handle.

"You can't even get here without help," Cloe said. "How are you going to find Casey?"

"I'll work the evidence like I always have done," Jordan said.

***

When Jordan angled into the passenger seat of her car, her nerves were humming. Walker had a connection to all the women, but he was dead, so he could not have attacked her or taken Emma. Who had he been working with?

Avery started the engine. "What was that all about? Did you get anything out of it?"

"I don't know, maybe." The car slipped into drive and moved forward down the street. "If you started using again, you would tell me, right?"

"What brought that on?"

"Cloe said her sister was acting like she did when she was in trouble."

"You mean using."

"Yes."

"I don't talk around your vision, so don't substitute euphemisms for my prior drug use. Ignoring ugly doesn't make it go away."

"Point taken. And when did you get so wise?"

"I've always been wise," Avery said. "But you never saw it."

"That's not true." Avery was right. Jordan had always seen her sister as the little kid, the wounded dove.

"Bull. And I'm stronger than you think."

"You're right. I'm sorry."

Avery's tone softened. "I swore I would never go back to that life, and I won't."

"My sight is putting you under a lot of pressure," Jordan said.

"I can handle it."

"Okay."

"What do you want to ask me?" Avery asked.

"Did you know Walker is dead?"

"Walker? Are you sure?"

"You really didn't know? None of the cops in the café talked about it?"

"I haven't been to work since your attack. How did Walker die?"

"He hanged himself."

"Are you sure? It doesn't sound like Walker. He said he was going to live forever. What brought his name up?"

"Cloe thinks Casey bought from a guy named Marco with a last name that started with a *W*."

"That world is very, very small."

"The other victims of this serial killer also used drugs or had used drugs."

"If it was heroin, it was Walker or someone who worked for him. He controlled a big chunk of the downtown area. But you said he's dead, so he couldn't have killed the last one."

"Who did Walker hang out with? Was there anyone that could have killed him?"

"Plenty of people."

"Who did he trust?"

"No one. But he used to be tight with his attorney."

"Harold Sunday." The man seemed to be in her path these days.

***

When Avery pulled in the driveway, she said to Jordan, "Well, that's a surprise."

"What?"

"Dr. Malone is here."

After Rogan had drawn his finger over her cheek, Jordan had decided to keep her distance. She had told the nurses to keep him away, or she pretended to be asleep when he came into her room. The reality of her disability was too raw now, and the idea of dealing with his feelings as well was too much.

"Don't look so worried," Avery said.

"I don't want to deal with him now," Jordan said honestly.

"Why not?"

"It's hard to explain."

"Is this about you two sleeping together last year?"

"You knew?" Jordan asked.

"I figured it out. And you can't run from your past. Face it."

She gripped her cane. "Right."

Avery got out of the car. "Hey, Dr. Malone!"

Jordan listened as her sister chatted and walked away from the car. Reaching for the door handle, she opened it, got out, and used her cane as she worked her way toward her house.

Rogan's steady footsteps moved toward her. "You're a hard lady to find."

"What can I say?" She grinned. "I keep busy."

He didn't touch her, but she could feel that he wanted to embrace her. Her sense of spatial awareness, or whatever it was, was sharpening. "I've been worried about you."

"I'm figuring it out, just like I always do."

"Headed inside," Avery said. She hurried ahead, but neither of them moved.

"You've been avoiding me," he said.

"I know."

"Why?"

"I have a lot to figure out."

"I can help you."

"You really can't," she said. "I have to do this on my own."

A heaviness lingered between them. "I'd like to take you out to dinner. We could drive to Fredericksburg like we used to."

It had been over a year since they had made that drive. "I don't think so."

"We're friends. Friends help each other." He leaned forward and kissed her on the cheek. It would be so easy to lean into his embrace, ask him to hold her and just take care of everything that was so terrifying right now.

However, as much as she wanted her old life back, getting back with him would be backtracking. He wanted more than she could ever give, and to lean on him now would give him hope for something that would never happen.

Her body remained rigid as her fingers curled at her side. "Thanks, Rogan. Really."

"You don't have to do this alone." His voice was deep, soothing.

"I'm not alone. I have Avery."

"Can she handle this?"

"She's stronger than she was. She's different."

"I hope you're right, Jordan."

CHAPTER TWENTY-FIVE

Thursday, April 22
5:30 p.m.

Spencer pulled up in front of Jordan Poe's house, dog-ass tired and carrying the crime scene scents with him. Out of the car, he surveyed the dimming light, trying to imagine what Jordan saw on a day-to-day basis. He found himself doing that frequently, especially when he woke up in the middle of the night, unable to sleep.

Resting his hat on his head, he strode across the yard and rang the bell. Inside, he heard hesitant footsteps, what sounded like a body bumping into furniture, and then a few choice curses.

"Identify yourself," Jordan asked on the other side of the locked door.

"Carter Spencer."

Security chains scraped, and the door opened to Jordan. She wore yoga pants and a V-neck sweater and had pulled her hair back into a loose bun. Barefoot, she gripped the handle of her white cane. Her gaze rose, her eyes searching. "Spencer. Thanks for coming."

"You said it was important."

She stepped aside. "Come inside."

He removed his hat and stepped over the threshold. "Everything all right?"

"Good as can be expected. Can I get you something? Just made a pot of coffee."

"Sounds good."

"Follow me at your own peril," she said. "My sister did more rearranging, thinking she was helping, but it's driving me crazy. Nothing is as I remembered."

"You look like you're managing. You held your own today at the crime scene."

"I'm the proverbial duck. Floating on top, paddling like mad under the surface."

"Aren't we all."

She smoothed her fingertips along a wall and rounded the corner to the kitchen. On the other side of the island, she reached into a cabinet and located two mugs. "Now the trick will be to pour and not spill."

Instinct pushed him to help, but he held back. This was her journey, and he would help only if asked.

She poured two cups, filling them two-thirds full, and then set one out in front of him. "Progress."

He sipped the coffee. "And you make a decent cup of coffee."

"A talent I have not lost."

"I bet there're plenty you haven't lost."

"I hope so."

So did he. "Why the call?"

"I went by Casey Andrews's mother's house this afternoon. Avery drove me."

A smile tweaked the edges of his lips. "I could say I'm surprised you're still working the case, but that would be a lie."

"Leopard can't change his spots."

"What did you learn?"

"Not much from Mrs. Andrews. I did ask her to go through Casey's room."

"I had officers do that."

"She told me. But she wants to find her girl, and who knows what she'll uncover." She turned the cup, slipped her finger through the handle, and cradled it. "Casey's younger sister, Cloe, had more to say."

"She barely spoke to me when I was at the house."

"She's not an easy kid. And I think it helped that I had Avery along with me. Seeing my family humanized me. Anyway, she told me she thinks Casey bought drugs from Marco."

Energy snapped through him. "That's not a surprise."

"No. We know Tammy Fox tested positive for heroin. Tox screen on Jane Doe #1 back yet?"

"It is. She had heroin in her system. Also received a call from Dr. McIntyre on the way here. Jane Doe #1 has been identified. Her name is Laura Davis, age nineteen. Her mug shot matches the picture Mrs. Sanchez gave me."

"Laura knew Elena?"

"Seems so."

"What was she arrested for?"

"She was arrested last year for prostitution. Served a few months in the county jail and during that time got herself cleaned up. She had a job working as a waitress in an outdoor café in Austin until she vanished two months ago. No missing person report was filed, and if not for the arrest record, she could have gone unidentified."

"What did she look like?"

He almost reached for his phone to show her a picture. "Blond. Petite. Pretty. Young."

"Elena Sanchez had dark hair and olive skin," Jordan said.

"Maybe Walker wasn't looking to traffic Elena but her friend Laura."

"I spoke to Elena about five weeks ago. I tried to convince her to leave," Jordan said.

"She made a choice," he said.

"Yes."

He understood the blame game too well. Best way to end it was to shift the thoughts. "We have three dead women, possibly four, and this killer isn't shy about placing his bodies where he knew they would be found. Have you talked to Avery more about that incident two years ago?"

"She said Walker tied her up, but beyond that she says she doesn't remember."

"What do you think happened?"

"I think Walker either sold her to someone or was planning to."

"Someone like Sunday?"

"They were tight. And Sunday has a taste for young women."

"I spoke to him last week. He's clever. Dances right up to the line but never crosses it."

"He knows more about Walker than anyone. If Walker was killed, Sunday would have an idea of who did it."

"He'll never tell unless his ass is on the line. What does Avery say about Sunday?"

"She didn't have much interaction with him."

He faced a tough question he did not enjoy asking. "You sure she's still clean?"

"We just had this talk. She says she is."

"And you believe her?"

"I made a deal with her two years ago when I paid for her treatment. Going forward, I could demand a drug test at any time. And I've done it at least seven or eight times each year since then. They've all been clean."

Vickie had once been clean over a year, and he'd thought they were out of the woods until they were not. "Two years of sobriety is an accomplishment."

"I worry about her all the time."

"She seems pretty tough to me."

"You know how the drip of stress can take a toll. We see it on the job all the time."

"Does Avery have plans for the future?"

"She said she wants to be a cop."

"With her record that's not likely to happen. But there's plenty of good she can do without wearing a badge."

The front door opened and closed. "Jordan, I'm home."

Jordan stood a little taller. "In here with Ranger Spencer."

Avery came around the corner, her hands filled with paper grocery bags. "Look at you two, sharing a cup of java like you are best friends."

"I wouldn't go that far," Jordan said easily.

Her teasing was welcome. He wanted them on the same side. "Coffee cures a lot of ills."

"Good thing I brought more home from the café," Avery said.

"Please tell me it's not decaf," Jordan said.

"No, still feeding you the real stuff. But you're going to need to get off of it," Avery said. "It's a stimulant."

Jordan sipped from her cup. "One day, I'll give it up."

"Right." Avery set her bags on the island and began to unload.

He noted an assortment of vegetables and vegan meat substitutes. Only possible in Austin. He wondered if Avery considered meat on Jordan's no-consume list. "We were just talking about you."

Jordan set her cup down carefully.

"Why?" Avery asked. "Is there a problem?"

"The murder cases we've been working," Jordan said. "You bear a striking resemblance to the murdered women."

"I know," Avery said.

"They also had drug problems," Jordan said. "All went into rehab, and all had a relapse shortly before they died."

"I have not relapsed in over two years," Avery said.

Avery's tone was firm, but her word choices held no fillers, extra facts, or long-winded explanations that hinted at deception. "I didn't say you had."

"But you wondered," Avery said. "You know what? I'll take a drug test right now."

"It's not necessary," Jordan said.

"Yes it is," Avery said. "The test strips are still in the bathroom. I'll pee on one right now."

"I can't see the strip," Jordan said.

"Spencer can," Avery countered. "Be right back, kids."

Footsteps moved at a clipped, irritated pace that reminded Spencer of Jordan. "She's convincing."

"She takes a lot of pride in her sobriety. I'm sorry the question came up."

"To ignore it would be worse. You said yourself you've worried about her, so now you'll know Might help you sleep better at night."

"How do you know I don't sleep?" she asked.

A grin tugged at the corner of his mouth. "Because few cops do."

The footsteps returned, and Avery moved toward the trash can. "Unless you want my pee stick by your coffee, you'll have to come toward the trash can and have a look."

Spencer rose and with no fanfare crossed the room and looked at the stick. It was white.

Avery held up the test jar with the color bar on the side. "As you can see, white is negative."

"How do I know you peed on the stick?" he asked.

"I'll do the next one right in front of you if that's what it takes to prove I'm clean."

He had no doubt. "Not necessary."

She dropped the stick in the trash can, crossed to the sink, and washed her hands. "Now that we've cleared that up, you can rule me out as a potential victim."

"Did you ever know Marco Walker's girlfriend Elena Sanchez?" Spencer asked. "Or her friend Laura Davis?"

Avery folded her arms and leaned against the counter. "Unless they were around Walker two years ago, I didn't know her. Back in the day, Walker had several girlfriends at a time. None of them, including me, lasted very long."

"Because he was violent?" Jordan asked.

"Yeah. And he liked to farm his girls out to his friends," she said. "If he owed anyone a favor, he got one of his girls to pay the debt back. I always refused. Pissed Walker off, and he told me to get out. I did and got clean for a couple of months. It was harder than I realized, and I returned to him that last time."

"Any of Walker's friends have an obsession with strangulation?" he asked.

Avery studied him closely. "Jordan told you how she found me that last time, didn't she?"

"She did," he said.

"It's too close to the current cases to ignore, Avery," Jordan said.

"Are you saying I could have been this guy's victim?" Avery asked.

"I don't know," Jordan said. "But I can't rule it out."

"What do you remember about that night?" Spencer asked.

Avery's cheeks flushed. "Not much after I got high. It was powerful stuff."

"Who tied your hands?" Spencer asked.

"Walker. Like I said, the rest was all a blur." Avery rested her hands on her hips and tipped her head toward the ceiling. "If I had more to tell you, I would. But I don't remember. Is there anything else you want to ask me?"

"No," Spencer said.

Jordan raised her chin. "Know that I trust you. But I had to ask."

"You sound like Rogan," Avery said.

"Who is Rogan?" Spencer asked.

"I saw him for a few therapy sessions when Avery was struggling," Jordan said. "I needed someone to talk to, and he encouraged me to talk through what I was feeling. Can't say I've mastered the talent."

Jordan's expression told him sharing feelings was about as pleasant as walking on broken glass. If anyone understood that one, he did. "Jordan, thanks for the update. And Avery, appreciate the conversation."

"What's next?" Jordan asked.

"The uniforms have rounded up surveillance tape from the hospital. The hope is to see Emma Powers and whoever she spoke to."

"I wish I could help," Jordan said.

"You've been a big help," Spencer said.

"And I'm ready to pee on a stick anytime," Avery quipped.

"Good to know," he said.

"I'll walk you out." Rising, Jordan reached for her cane and moved around the island to join him. As he crossed through the great room, he glanced toward the mantel and saw Tammy Fox's paintings. He wondered if that was what it had been like in Vickie's mind—dark and disturbing.

Jordan opened the front door. "That turned into a family-airing-our-dirty-laundry kind of moment."

"Every family has it."

"You talked a little about Vickie. What about brothers and sisters?"

"Two younger brothers. One is a lawyer, and the other is in med school. I'm the black sheep," he joked.

"And your folks?"

"Both passed. A decade ago. Cancer, heart disease. Since our folks died, the Spencer boys have scattered to the wind." When his parents were ill, he had been in the throes of dealing with Vickie's drug problem. His brothers had seen what it was doing to him, tried to get him to leave her, and they had fought. If he could go back, he wondered if he would have done it differently.

He was not sure why he was sharing his personal résumé with her. In fact, he made it a habit not to share much about himself.

"You'll have to step up your game if you want to compete with the Poe family."

He chuckled.

"I'll see you at the medical examiner's office in the morning," Jordan said.

"I can pick you up."

"Avery can drive me."

"Fair enough." The urge to touch her was strong. If she could see, he might have. But it felt wrong. "Until tomorrow, Detective Poe."

CHAPTER TWENTY-SIX

Friday, April 23
6:00 a.m.

Waking up was turning into a daily disappointment for Jordan. Her dreams were filled with familiar faces, the vivid colors of everyday life, and the rolling landscapes of the Texas Hill Country she loved to take in on long drives.

However, when her eyes opened to shadows, hope and optimism stripped away, exposing the real fear she would never get her old life back. Tears brimmed in her eyes, and all she wanted to do was pull the covers over her head and cry.

"You can't," she said. "You can't give up. Not now."

She sat up, swung her legs over the side of the bed, and pawed at her nightstand until her fingers brushed the smooth surface of her phone. She held it up and touched the screen toward the top. *"Six o'clock."*

She blinked, dragged her fingers through her hair, and then reached for the nightstand lamp and turned it on. A faint light appeared, much like a distant lighthouse trying to cut through thick fog. If she leaned close to the lamp, the brightness increased but offered her no details of her hand inches from her face.

"Another day in paradise."

The morning routine still took five times as long as it once had, but she was better about getting Avery to help her lay out her clothes. Dark jeans, a black V-neck sweater, and low-heeled boots was her standard uniform. And wearing work clothes made her feel more in control.

In the shower, she turned on the hot spray, closed her eyes, and stepped under it. In these moments she felt normal. That her life was her life. She lingered until the water began to cool. Out of the shower, she reached for the towel that now always hung on the towel rack and dried off.

Makeup remained a daunting task, but she could brush out her hair and dry it with a dryer. She wiped the foggy mirror near her face and peered close, hoping to see something. When she did not see her reflection staring back, the disappointment punched like a prizefighter. "This has to end. It has to get better."

Finally, squaring her shoulders, she turned from the mirror, dressed, and grabbed her cane by the foot of her bed.

The house was quiet. Avery was still asleep. A good thing, really.

She made her way to the kitchen. She stood for a moment, orienting herself, and then felt for the stove, moved her fingers to the left, and fumbled for the buttons on the coffee maker, which Avery had preset. The buttons felt surprisingly similar, and she pressed several until she heard the machine gurgle.

She touched the screen on her phone and dragged her finger toward the general location of her email icon. She tapped and it indicated it was open. As the voice read back what was mostly junk mail, she grew impatient with the pace. It suddenly sounded slow. "Siri, speed up voice-activated software by twenty percent."

She processed the emails faster, but a couple of times she had to slow down to make sure she had not missed something critical. The next email was from the Austin Police human resources department. They were requesting a meeting to discuss her disability.

"Disability," she whispered. The brutally honest word irritated her. "I don't want to be disabled."

She sat for several minutes, considering blowing off the HR department. Wishes were not going to change her current situation. She would need the money to support herself and Avery until she got better or was forced to find the next step on the path.

Jordan dictated a response. Several times she stopped and redid her sentences, cutting out extra words. She was accustomed to seeing the computer screen, and visualizing the words in her mind was a challenge. Finally, satisfied, she hit send.

"Is that coffee I smell?" Avery asked.

"It is."

"Did I hear you talking?" Avery yawned.

"Dictating an email."

"Really? Using the accommodations like Sally taught you?"

"Yes. And I'll have to see her soon to learn a few new tricks."

"And you'll pay attention this time?"

"Yes."

Avery hugged her. "I feel like my little girl is all grown up."

"Very funny."

The sound of coffee pouring and then the refrigerator door opening and closing had Jordan turning toward the counter. She felt for her cup, discovered it was still empty. "No coffee?"

"You can pour."

She filled the cup, sticking her finger inside and pouring until the heat reached her fingertip. The cream was a little more of a challenge, but in the end, another functioning cup of coffee. Hope. "We're going to have to leave here by seven thirty. Morning traffic slows the commute."

"I can't remember the last time I drove in morning traffic. I either left really early to open the café or stayed late."

"Triple whatever time it took on the off hours."

"Will I have to go into the autopsy? I mean, if I have to I will."

"No. Just get me to the autopsy suite, and I'll take it from there."

"Can you do it alone?"

"It shouldn't be too difficult to slip on a surgical gown and gloves."

"While I'm waiting, I can swing by the café and check in on the guys."

"Great. I'll call when we're finished."

***

At 7:00 a.m. they were on the road. Avery switched on the radio, a country-and-western station featuring several songs highlighting deep bass tones that thudded in Jordan's chest. She had always enjoyed music but now seemed to feel the notes more.

Based on a few quick stops, horn honks, and lane changes, Avery's driving remained bad, so whatever joy Jordan might have derived from the music was overridden by the fear that they would not make it to the medical examiner's office alive.

Avery found parking easily, surprising since Jordan often had to circle the lot. "That was quick."

"I applied for an accessibility sticker for you," Avery said. "Captain Lee helped expedite the process."

"Seriously?"

"I know. Another change. But it's either use it or hoof it across the lot."

"I used to park in the last row all the time. I liked the walk."

"Well, then next time, we'll park far away."

She thought about tapping her way across this lot at a snail's pace. "Maybe one day."

"Right. I can't believe there're so many people here this early."

Out of her car, cane in hand, Jordan waited for Avery to come around and offer her elbow. Like it or not, the new routine burrowed deeper into her life.

The *whoosh* of revolving doors announced their approach to the front entrance. Avery led her to the single side door reserved for anyone not able to use the revolving door.

Inside, the familiar sounds of chatter, footsteps, and ringing telephones echoed in the main lobby.

"Where do we go now?" Avery asked.

"We stop at information and get a badge for you."

"What about you?"

Jordan removed her police badge from her pocket and slung it around her neck. "They still haven't taken it, yet."

At the information desk, Jordan showed her badge and explained that Avery would need to escort her to the autopsy suites. Avery produced a driver's license, but the receptionist did not sound happy about this exception.

"I'm not sure that'll be enough," the receptionist said.

Jordan recognized the woman's voice. It was Marge, a sixtysomething woman with graying hair and a stern face. She had always been a stickler for rules.

"I'm a detective," Jordan said. "She's my sister. Her identification will confirm that."

"But she's a civilian," Marge countered.

Steady, determined footsteps moved toward them. Most cops exhibited a commanding air because the ability to take charge could deescalate tense situations or neutralize potential threats. Some cops, like Spencer, dominated the space around them.

"Sounds like the cavalry has arrived," Jordan said.

"I can take it from here, Avery," Spencer said.

"Agent Spencer," Marge said. "I wasn't sure how to handle this one."

"It's an unusual circumstance," he said.

Would Marge have questioned Jordan being here a month ago? The thought put her on defense. "I'm still me, and my badge is still good."

"I didn't realize you were still active duty," Marge said.

"I have my badge," Jordan pressed.

"But you are . . . blind," Marge said in a lower tone.

"Low vision but still on the team," Jordan said through clenched teeth.

"Marge was trying to figure out how I fit into the big scheme of things." Avery's tone was light.

Her sister's words carried a bigger message: *Lighten up.* If Jordan was forever pissed and defensive, she was going to have a long row to hoe.

"She's right. Thanks for the help, Marge," Jordan said.

"I'm the one that's sorry, Detective Poe," Marge said. "No one likes seeing a cop's career end."

Jordan straightened, her fingers tightening around her cane. "It's not over yet."

"Maybe Avery will get her guest badge another day," Spencer said.

Like her sister, Spencer was reminding her to be cool.

"Okay, if you two kids are all set," Avery said, "I'll be off to play in Austin. Jordan, call me when you're ready to be picked up."

"Will do, Avery," Jordan said. "And thanks."

"Aim to please."

As Avery's footsteps grew more distant, Jordan shifted her gaze toward Spencer's face. "If you can offer me your arm, I'll take it."

"Ready and waiting."

She laid her hand on his arm. All muscle. "Lead the way."

"Glad to."

The elevator doors dinged open as they approached, and he mentioned the small gap between the elevator and the first floor. She stepped over the threshold, sensing one, maybe two more people in the car. The space felt crowded, and not knowing who else was with them had her taking a step toward Spencer. He did not speak, but again his quiet energy was a rock she anchored to.

The doors opened, two people stepped off, and then the doors closed again.

"Two more floors," Spencer said.

"Thanks." She'd hoped her compromised sight would have abated some of the unease she felt when she was in an elevator, but the darkness tightened the already confined space. The doors opened, and Spencer's arm moved close to hers, signaling she could take it. She did, knowing navigating once-familiar halls without sight cues was going to be a challenge.

"Still smells the same," she said. "No amount of air freshener can quite hide the antiseptic scent."

"I remember the day I got used to the smell of decomposition," he said carefully. "I was working a case outside of Houston. Responded to a tractor trailer loaded with a dozen undocumented women. Six were dead and the others barely holding on. I worked the site for nearly twelve hours and didn't think twice about the odors. It wasn't until I got back to the office. My coworkers chased me out of the building and told me not to return until I'd cleaned up. Hell, how could I not notice?"

"When I first started patrol, there were many nights I couldn't sleep. I was just too amped up replaying the day and what went down. But over time, I couldn't box up all the memories, but I came pretty damn close. We develop calluses."

And those calluses made everyday relations harder.

Spencer paused to open a door, and she guessed they had arrived at the changing room beside the autopsy suite.

"Lockers to the right," he said.

Turning, she sensed the proximity of the wall. Moving slowly, her cane in front, she halted when the tip touched metal. Experience reminded her that the clean scrubs were to her right, so she trailed her fingers along the lockers until she touched the plastic-wrapped gowns.

She carefully unpacked one, slid it on, and fastened the ties around her waist. Spencer handed her gloves.

"Thanks," she said.

"Dr. McIntyre is waiting for us."

"Right."

He pushed through the doors into the autopsy suite. The overhead lights were brighter in here, which helped a little. And she remembered enough of the room's layout to know that Dr. McIntyre's exam table was the first of the four in the room.

Normally, she stood back from the table and approached only when the medical examiner wanted to show her something. Today, she moved up to the table until her gloved fingertips glided over metal and then the edges of the sheet covering the body.

The door opened, and Dr. McIntyre's expensive perfume announced her arrival. "Detective Poe. I had heard you were working the case."

The doc's husband had no doubt spoken to Spencer. Law enforcement was a fairly small community. "I don't know how long they'll let me work the case, but I'll stay until they kick me off."

"I understand completely," she said easily. "We all have those cases that get under our skin."

"Yes, we do."

"Detective Poe, why don't you stand to my left," Dr. McIntyre said. "I'll talk you through the autopsy."

"Sure." She moved along the edge of the table, drawn by the crunch of plastic as the doc opened the instrument bag. The door opened again, and this time she guessed it was one of Dr. McIntyre's lab assistants.

"Detective Poe, it's Deb. We worked together on a case about a month ago."

God bless the audio prompts. "Good to be working with you again, Deb."

The sheet covering the body rustled, and a faint chill rose from the exposed flesh. For the first time, she did not regret her loss of sight.

Witnessing how death savaged the human body always left an unpleasant lasting image. Those sleepless nights she had mentioned to Spencer generally came after an autopsy.

A camera lens clicked several times; then she heard the slap of a gloved hand against the naked flesh and knew Deb was working the victim's limbs, likely still stiff with the remnants of rigor mortis. Breaking up the rigor in the muscles allowed the doctor to move and manipulate the body more easily during the autopsy. It had been more than twenty-four hours since Powers's approximate time of death, so the body would be in full rigor mortis, and the victim's youth and increased muscle density meant the rigor would be more pronounced.

Metal measuring tape slid from its case, and then Deb stated the victim had been five foot, two inches tall. The tape snapped back into its case.

The boom supporting the microphone above the table squeaked as Dr. McIntyre pulled it toward her mouth, as she always did. For the audio record, the doctor introduced herself and noted who was present in the room. "Today is the autopsy of Emma Powers, age twenty. Ms. Powers was found yesterday wrapped in plastic." The doctor detailed the facts of the case for the record, then shifted toward the head of the table. "The victim's eyes have been fastened closed with surgical tape. I'm removing it now to examine the eyes. I'm bagging the tape so the forensic team can analyze it for prints."

Jordan stood still, praying the young woman's eyes had not been damaged. The fact that she had to wait to be told fueled her frustration. She wanted to contribute but now realized she was of little use.

"The eyes are intact and appear to have suffered no trauma," Dr. McIntyre said.

Jordan rolled her shoulders, releasing some of the tension banding the muscles.

The doctor moved around the body, noting three tattoos, what appeared to be old and very recent track marks, and a pierced belly button. "I'm rolling her on her side so I can get a good look at her back." After some shuffling: "There's significant lividity on her back, buttocks, and legs, indicating she was supine when her heart stopped pumping."

Next came the rattle of metal instruments and the almost-silent tug of the scalpel through flesh. Always distracted by the visual, Jordan had never noticed the subtle sound of the knife tip, the tearing back of the flesh, the snap of the ribs with bone cutters, and the sucking sound of the rib cage rising off the body cavity.

Dr. McIntyre inventoried the organs, which were all of normal weight and size. Finally, she packed the organs in the body cavity and sewed the flesh back together. She next confirmed that the victim had been sexually assaulted, likely several times given the vaginal bruising. She collected semen.

In the end, the cause of death was asphyxiation, as it had been with the other victims. "I'll have a full report in a few days. Tox screens will take a little longer."

"Thanks, Doc," Jordan said.

"Call me if you need anything." Dr. McIntyre's tone sounded genuine and heartfelt.

"Will do, Doc."

Spencer offered his elbow, she took it, and he escorted her to the changing room. "What do you think?" he asked.

"I'm operating on the assumption that the surgical tape was a message for me."

"Okay." He stripped and wadded up his gown. It *whooshed* across the room and hit the disposal bin. A nothing-but-net dunk.

She stripped off her gloves and gown, balled them up, and aimed toward the bin. The bundle hit the ground. "So much for basketball."

Chuckling softly, he crossed the room, and seconds later the discarded garment swooshed into the basket.

Jordan turned toward Spencer. "What if there were other messages to me at the other crime scenes? What if they were subtle enough that I didn't pick up on them?"

"That's pressing it, don't you think? You were interviewed in the press several times, and guys who kill like this generally pay attention to the media. They like the attention. They follow the cops who are tracking them."

She reached for her cane, opened the locker, and grabbed her purse. "Avery is my sister. Laura Davis knew Elena Sanchez, a woman I met with once. Tammy Fox knew Avery. Emma Powers worked in the hospital where I stayed."

"Let me look over Laura Davis's and Tammy Fox's files again. I'll read them with your theory in mind."

"I know it's a long shot," she said.

"At this stage, it's all a long shot." A locker opened and closed, and she imagined he'd grabbed his Stetson.

"If you can get me to the lobby, I'll call an Uber. Easier for me to meet Avery downtown at her café."

"I can drop you."

"It's tempting, but I've got to figure this out. Getting around is a fact of life unless I want to stay in my house forever."

"Baptism by fire?" he asked.

"They're the most effective kind, aren't they?"

"Let me at least get you to the curb," he said.

"Fair enough."

They moved through the building and out the front door into the bright sunshine. Sliding on her sunglasses, Jordan tipped her face toward the sun and savored the warmth. The air was crisp and the humidity low, so she guessed the sky was a clear blue. She tried to picture the shade of blue and finally decided it was azure. Nothing worse than leaving an autopsy and being met by gray skies and rain.

She fished her phone out of her purse and touched the screen. Using her voice-activated software, she asked the Uber app to open, and she summoned a car.

"High tech," Spencer said.

"I'm a novice," she said.

"You're a quick study. You're adapting well."

"I'm hoping all this darkness is a temporary setback. Knowing I'll get past this keeps me going."

"And if your vision doesn't improve?" No softening the question's sting.

"Ouch. You don't pull any punches."

"You wouldn't, either, if the shoe was on the other foot."

"Honestly, Spencer, I have no idea what I'm going to do. I feel like I've got my leg in a snare. Right now, I'm just gritting my teeth and hoping the trap springs open."

"Even if a trap opens, they always leave a mark."

Her grip tightened around her cane. "Did you know that almost seventy percent of low-vision people are not in the workforce?"

"Sounds like you were practicing your internet skills last night."

"Maybe. But it's a real fear. And what will I do if I'm not a cop? The work gets in your blood."

"I know that."

"What does a thirty-four-year-old former cop with poor vision do?" So far, she had not come up with any answers. Maybe he had one.

"I really hope you do get your sight back. I do. But you're smart, adaptable, and should consider a plan B."

"Such as?"

"Prosecutor. Advocate. Teacher. The academy needs good training instructors."

"When you decided to be a ranger, did you have a plan B?"

"No, but I'm hardheaded with more nerve than common sense." A smile softened the words. "You're a woman who knows better. You've been challenged before and come out on the other side."

His ideas all required extensive thought on her part. Sally had mentioned braille, but that would be like learning a new language.

Right now, the future was too much to consider. "First, let me put this case behind me. Then I'll think about the future."

"Cases can drag on. Life won't wait for you."

Again, more she did not want to consider.

A car pulled up to the curb as her phone chimed with a text. This was her first Uber ride since the attack. Another one for her Book of Firsts. "Looks like my ride is here."

Spencer checked the app on her phone for the car's make and model, confirmed the driver's name and also Jordan's. "Yes, this is your car." Spencer offered his elbow and guided her to the vehicle. "I'm still happy to give you a ride."

"I need to do this alone because, believe it or not, I'm just as hardheaded as you."

"Help me." Spencer patted her on the shoulder. "Ryan, you make really sure this lady gets to where she needs to go, or I will hunt you down."

She heard the man shift. And she had to smile. "Thanks, Spencer."

"Will keep you updated, Detective Poe."

CHAPTER TWENTY-SEVEN

Friday, April 23
9:30 a.m.

Avery's first fifteen minutes at the café were fun. She liked catching up with her former coworkers and favorite morning customers who recognized her and being in the place that had helped stabilize her two years ago after rehab.

But after the initial meet and greet, she and the coworkers ran out of things to talk about. Beyond bitching about the small break room in the back, the lousy parking, and the pros and cons of the latest flavor of coffee, they did not have so much in common. Since she had sobered up, she recognized that daily chatter created the illusion of closeness, but it was smoke and mirrors.

Avery took her coffee, sat in the corner by the window, and ate a blueberry muffin. How many harried mornings had she wished she could do just this? Sit, relax, savor instead of rushing to fill the morning orders.

The café staff, like her, often grew annoyed when a customer hogged a prime table and stayed way past their expiration time, which for them was about thirty minutes. Eat, drink, move on.

"Avery?"

She looked up to find Detective Leo Santiago approaching with a cup of coffee in hand. "Let me guess, a triple espresso."

"You know me well." He nodded to the seat opposite hers. "Mind if I sit? I have a few minutes before my shift starts."

"Please, have a seat."

He pulled out the chair, smoothing his dark tie flat as he sat. He was clean cut, detail oriented, and disciplined. "What brings you here?" he asked.

"Killing time. Jordan has a meeting, and I'm waiting on her." She was not sure how much the Austin Police Department knew about Jordan's continued involvement in the current murder cases.

"How's she doing?" he asked.

"Getting along."

He set his cup down, looking at her with an intensity that made her uneasy. Cops were not supposed to have X-ray vision.

"Santiago," she said.

"How did you know it was me?"

"Neighbor described a guy who looked like Chris Evans."

He shook his head, grinning. "Hardly."

"It's appreciated," she said. "Life's been hectic."

"If there's anything else I can do, just say it. All the guys and gals in the department want to lend a hand, but Jordan's not the kind who asks for help."

"She's softening. She'll need help to figure the rest of her life out."

His jaw muscle clenched. "The Rangers have the Mummy case. Spencer is one of their best."

"Good to know. Have you heard anything about the case's progress?" She dabbed a blueberry muffin crumb from her plate, doing her best to look like someone who knew less than they let on.

"The forensic department is still combing over all the materials found with the bodies. They've pulled hair and cloth fibers, so both might give up DNA. And there were a few partial fingerprints. Lots of pieces but no full picture yet."

Memories of a man with a hoarse, low voice swirled in her mind. Had Walker given her to the man who shoved plastic in her mouth? Had this faceless man been developing his obsessions? If the answers were buried in her memory, they remained out of reach.

Avery had listened so many times when Jordan expressed her frustration over an investigation. Jordan wanted justice for the victims and their families, but it rarely came as fast as anyone wanted it. Now on the other side of the equation, Avery experienced the same irritation.

"What cases are you working now?" Though she was only mildly curious, she liked having the company.

"A couple of homicides from last week. We have persons of interest in both cases, so it's a matter of getting the forensics team to confirm evidence. I miss having Jordan to bounce ideas off of. She's a hell of a detective."

"She loves the work."

"Yes, she does."

Santiago's phone chimed with a text, and he glanced at the screen. "Speaking of the job, it's calling. I've got to go."

"Sure. Back to work."

"Are you coming back to work here?" he asked.

"Soon," she said. "Maybe. It depends on Jordan."

"Jordan doesn't like anyone hovering."

She laughed. "Very true."

"That tells me I'll be seeing you around here soon." He rose and dutifully pushed his chair under the table. "Stay safe."

"You too."

Through the front window she watched Santiago stride down the street to an unmarked car. He got in. After flipping on his blinker, he pulled into traffic.

Though tempted to stay put, she tossed her trash, waved to her friends, and left the café. She had no idea where she was going. It had been a long time since she'd had extra time in her schedule. She sometimes logged sixty hours a week at the café, and then there was her art and the NA meetings she attended sometimes twice a week. She checked her watch and knew there was a midmorning meeting down the block in a restaurant that did not open until the afternoon.

She had missed too many meetings the last few weeks because she had been consumed with Jordan and now knew the extra time could not go to waste.

Down the block she looked across the street to an alley where she used to hang out. How many times had she gotten high there? How many stupid choices had she made?

That last time she had gone to Marco, her sobriety, like a wool sweater that was three sizes too small, had scratched her skin and constricted her lungs.

It had been easy to find Walker in those days. A few questions lobbed to the right people had been rewarded with directions to his latest apartment. When she'd knocked on the door, she had not been nervous. She'd been sure of what she wanted—needed. But the instant the door had opened, and Walker had grinned down at her, she had questioned her decision.

"Been a while," he said easily.

"I've been busy." If she told him she was struggling with sobriety, he would have seen it as a challenge.

"Glad you're not too busy for an old friend now." She stepped inside the apartment. This did not feel right. But her cravings silenced all the doubts. Walker closed the door and locked it. "What can I do for you?"

She had been so determined to get high after she had fought with Jordan. Now, she could not bring herself to say the words.

Grin widening, he wrapped his arm around her shoulder. "There's no shame. No shame at all. I remember exactly what you like."

Trepidation gave way to well-being. He understood her. He knew what she wanted. The last few months had been filled with people telling her what she needed. "Thanks. I don't have much money."

"Your money is no good here, sweet Avery. I'm going to hook you right up."

Her next memories were muddled by the drugs she'd taken that night. She remembered the first rush of relief that had whisked through her system as the drugs took effect. *Her vision blurred. And then came a tremendous sense of regret. She had worked so hard and had tossed it away. She wanted to leave. But as she tried to stand and move toward the door, Walker stopped her and tied her hands. She blacked out.*

Avery stood very still, allowing herself to really peer into the darkness and remember what had happened to her. For so long, she had avoided it, but she knew now doing so could mean a killer went free.

From a distance, she heard men talking and then felt a rough hand move over her body, squeezing her breast, and she pushed it away. "Get off me."

"Not yet, Avery."

She'd barely had time to sort out the stranger's voice before Walker said, "This one is better than the other one I promised. This should square us up."

"Yes, it does."

"I'll leave you two alone." A door opened and closed. Walker had abandoned her.

The man held her face in his hands, and when she opened her mouth to scream, he shoved plastic in her mouth, cramming the wad to the back of her throat before he tied a gag around her mouth. "No, no, no," he said.

Her nostrils flared. She shook her head as her breathing quickly grew labored.

"Relax. Save your breath."

Avery's heart beat hard against her chest as she stared up at his masked face. He pushed up her dress, shoved inside her, his excitement growing as she weakened. When he had finished, he quickly dressed and left her. She tried to control her nostril breathing. Tried not to panic. But she hyperventilated. Grew dizzy. Began to choke. Die.

"Avery!"

Avery coughed, and when she focused on Jordan's face, tears welled and spilled down her cheeks. "I'm sorry."

"I know. I know. I'll call an ambulance. Who put the plastic down your throat?" Avery could see Jordan struggling to contain her anger. Jordan's little sister needed help, and someone had taken advantage of her weakness.

"I don't know." Her voice sounded hoarse, scratched.

"Did Walker do it?"

"I don't know. Maybe. Maybe a friend of his."

"Did you get any names?"

"No," she cried. "I just remember Walker handing me the needle and tying me up. I'm sorry. I'm so sorry."

Jordan pulled Avery into an embrace. "Okay. It's okay."

Avery's body shuddered with sobs as she gripped the sleeves of Jordan's T-shirt. "I'll never do this again."

"I know. I know."

Jordan had saved her. Again.

Maybe that was why she had pulled away from Jordan after that night. She needed to prove she could be sober. And if she stumbled again, there would be no disappointment to face other than her own.

However, in her struggle, she had distanced herself from the one person who had her back.

She fought the creeping guilt as she quickened her pace. She arrived at the Italian restaurant and entered the front door. Inside, a dozen people milled around by the bar that now sold only coffee.

"Avery?" The question came from Rogan Malone. He donated spare time to treating substance abusers.

"Hey, Dr. Malone."

He came toward her, taking her hands in his. "It's good to see you. How is Jordan? Is she with you?"

"No, attending an autopsy," she said before she thought. "An old case she wants to solve."

"Really? How is she able?" Dr. Malone asked.

"She has enough connections, and she's determined. You know how she is."

"She's stubborn. Maybe too much." He grinned. "But aren't we all lucky she is? Join us. We're about to start. Would you like a coffee?"

"No, thanks. I drank my fill at the café. Dropped in on old friends." She pictured Jordan with Dr. Malone but did not like the image. She was sorry now she had come to this meeting.

"That's always good." He nodded toward the empty chairs arranged in a circle. "Have a seat."

Unease crept up her back as she reached for a chair and pulled it a few inches out from the ring. Her regular meetings felt like family, but this was a new group. She was not interested in telling these strangers about herself.

As the people sat and got comfortable, she silenced her phone but left it on her lap in case Jordan called. Everyone in the circle introduced themselves by their first names.

The meeting went as most did. People shared their troubles and struggles. As she listened, the knot in her chest that had coiled tight the last few weeks eased. This was not her group, but they were her people.

Malone listened to each story, and no matter how hard someone said they had fallen, he showed compassion and warmth. It was the kind of understanding that came from not a textbook but life. Though he had never shared his story, there had to be one. Like her, the man was entitled to his secrets.

After the meeting, she put her chair back behind a dining table and shifted her purse to her shoulder. "Thanks, Dr. Malone."

"Don't be a stranger," Dr. Malone said.

"Never."

Outside, she noticed several shops were open, and she spent the next hour moving from window to window. Lots of cool stuff. Her former self would have whipped out the credit card and bought a few things. But debt, like the drugs, always took more than it gave.

She slipped into Thompson's grocery store. Jordan had been here shortly before her attack and had picked up the best roasted potatoes. Avery might not be willing to splurge on a new blouse, but good food was always worth it.

At the back deli, she waited in line until her number came up. Mr. Rawlings smiled at her from behind the counter. "Avery, how are you? Haven't seen you at the food bank lately."

The food bank had been a staple for her when she was trying to get back on her feet. "Been working steady and making enough money."

"Good to hear it. How is your sister? You and your sister are my two favorite customers."

"You're our favorite takeout."

"I saw in the news that Jordan was injured."

"She's out of the hospital and home. Doing well."

"Great."

He leaned forward on the counter, the muscles of his thick arms straining the sleeves of his short-sleeved T-shirt. "What can I get you?"

She chose the macaroni and barbecue. Not healthy by just about any standard but the kind of comfort food that made life better.

He ladled double helpings into the take-out container. "Thanks for shopping Thompson's," Mr. Rawlings said.

"I'll be back soon." She grabbed a few paper napkins and plastic forks. Maybe she could talk Jordan into a field trip to a park.

He wiped his large hands on his white butcher's apron. "You're always welcome."

At the front register, when she looked up from her wallet, the kid was staring at her. "No charge."

"That can't be right."

"Says no charge."

She put her credit card back in her wallet. "Thank you."

"You work in the café, don't you?" the guy asked.

"I do."

"I always get a black coffee with a blueberry muffin."

"I remember," she said. "Take care, Mr. Black Coffee."

Grinning, he handed over her bagged meal. "Come back."

"Of course."

She left the shop and checked her time. It was after noon. As she headed back toward the café, she saw an SUV pull up. Jordan got out, cane in hand.

As tempted as Avery was to rush toward her, she hesitated.

Jordan tapped her cane awkwardly from side to side, and when a door opened to her right, she moved toward it. She stepped inside the dress shop, and Avery wondered why she had chosen a store filled with pastels and monogrammed bags.

Seconds later, Jordan reappeared with a young clerk, who walked her up to the entrance of the café. Jordan's tight smile telegraphed her frustration.

It hurt Avery to see her very strong sister struggle, but the fight was part of the healing process.

CHAPTER TWENTY-EIGHT

Friday, April 23
12:30 p.m.

"Jordan." She heard the approach of footsteps and recognized the scent of Avery's organic soap. Relief soothed her tense muscles.

"Avery."

"You made it," Avery said easily.

"Barely. I just walked into the wrong shop."

"A little detour. Nothing that can't be overcome." The bangles on Avery's wrist jingled seconds before her elbow gently brushed Jordan's arm, a signal that it was there if she wanted it. "I bought us lunch from Thompson's Market."

"Terrific. I'm starving."

"We can sit in the car or find a park."

"How about the car? Less distractions there." Her nerves were on high alert, and lowering the volume was a priority.

"Perfect. We're parked about a block and a half from here."

Jordan laid her hand on her sister's arm. "Lead the way."

"How did the autopsy go?" Avery walked a slow, steady pace, giving Jordan time to maneuver down the street.

"More productive than I thought it would be. Dr. McIntyre is good with narration."

"Good."

As they moved down the busy city street, Jordan was more in tune with the sounds of cars rushing past, the thud of footsteps on the sidewalk, and the opening and closing of shop doors around her.

Avery stopped. "Street corner. Waiting on the light."

When Jordan heard a pedestrian crosswalk sign beep, she began to walk. A car rushed past, coming close to the curb, and Avery backed them up a step.

"Asshole," Avery mumbled.

Jordan hated feeling vulnerable. In her old world, she would have memorized the license plate and called it in.

"Okay, clear," Avery said.

The two crossed the street and walked the length of the block. "We're here."

Jordan located the curb and fumbled for the door handle. When it clicked open, she folded her cane, sat, and pulled the passenger door closed, grateful for the familiar smells and feel of her car.

Avery slid in behind the wheel. She rustled paper and handed Jordan a fork and napkin wrapped in plastic. Next she pried off a container lid and placed the warm to-go box in her hands. Fork and napkin removed from their wrapping, Jordan inhaled. "Smells like barbecue and mac and cheese?"

"Bingo. Hope it tastes as good as it looks."

Jordan scooped up cheesy macaroni. It tasted of butter and cheddar. "Fantastic."

"Good. Glad you like it. I figured neither one of us would feel like cooking today."

"You said this was from Thompson's?"

"It is. And he refused to charge me."

"He's a nice guy." She poked around the barbecue. "I should get back in the kitchen. It would be good life-skills practice."

"You used to be a great cook."

"Life and the job don't leave much time. But looks like I'll have plenty of it."

"Have you thought about going back to school? I see you as a lawyer."

Jordan laughed. "Spencer said the same thing. Not sure if I'm ready for three more years of school and all that it takes to get into law school."

"I'm pretty sure with your connections, any school in Texas would love to have you."

"One step at a time."

"Sure. But I'm going to keep pushing."

She took a bite of barbecue. Again, moist and delicious. "What about you? You can't spend the rest of your life taking care of me."

"I'm here for the duration."

"That's okay for now. But I'll kick you out if you get stagnant and don't attempt something new," Jordan warned. "I won't hold you back."

"And I'll kick you in the ass if you don't move forward."

Jordan chuckled, and the two ate in silence. When they were finished, Avery collected the empty containers and dumped them in the grocery bag.

"Where to next?" Avery asked.

"Back to the crime scene where I was attacked," Jordan said carefully.

"Why?"

"I want to experience it again."

"Where's the value?" Avery challenged.

"Maybe I just need to put a few memories to bed. Either way, I need to visit the place."

"Do you have the address?"

Jordan recited it. "Burned in my brain."

"Okay. Should we tell Spencer we're doing this?"

"He would just get worked up and tell me not to."

"Wise man."

"Maybe, but he's not in my shoes."

Avery started the engine. "Okay, you're the boss."

The drive to the house where she had found Casey Andrews took twenty minutes. When Avery pulled up, she shut off the engine. "There's still time to change your mind."

Jordan reached for the door handle. "Nope."

Out of the car, she opened her cane and faced the direction of the house. When she had originally come, she had parked about fifty yards away. All caution had deserted her when she had seen the lights.

"It's not public knowledge, but the last victim's eyes were taped closed. None of the other two or Casey Andrews had their eyes taped closed."

Avery's bracelets jangled closer. "He wanted you to know he's aware of your vision."

"I think so."

"What about the first two victims?" Avery asked. "What, if anything, do they have to do with you?"

Jordan explained her theory. "Too close for comfort for me."

Avery drew in a breath. "I'd say six degrees of separation, but it's less than that."

Anxiety vibrated in her sister's tone, suggesting there was more she wanted to say. Jordan waited, but Avery did not offer more. "Let's go inside."

"There's crime scene tape on the door."

"I'm a cop," Jordan said. "At least for now."

"Okay."

Jordan took Avery's elbow, and the two crossed the lawn she had raced across just over a week ago. Avery cued about small stone steps, and then they climbed.

"Do I take the tape off?" Avery asked.

Jordan pulled latex gloves from her pocket and handed a set to Avery. "Just in case."

"Where did you get these?"

"I keep a stash in my room in case I'm called out unexpectedly."

Jordan worked her fingers into the gloves, reached out, and skimmed her fingers over the crime scene tape, which had grown slack in the heat. She ripped it down and then reached for the front door. It was locked.

"If memory serves, there's a window to the left and right of this door," Jordan said.

"Yes. So? The door is locked."

Jordan ran her hands along the side of the wall until she felt the window sash. She pushed up. It was locked. She moved left to the other side of the door and again found a window. She shoved upward and it gave way.

"We're not breaking into a crime scene," Avery said.

"I am," Jordan said. "And because you're my eyes right now, so are you."

"This seems like a bad idea on so many levels."

Jordan widened the window opening and folded her cane. "I can go first."

"No, I'll go first," Avery grumbled. "God only knows what is left behind, and I don't need you falling or getting hurt again."

Jordan grinned. "Thank you."

"Just be sure to call in all the favors owed you when we get arrested."

"Absolutely."

Avery's leg scraped over the windowsill, and her body slid through the opening. She brushed her hands against her jeans and walked into the room. A switch clicked. "The lights work," she said.

"The house was lit up when I approached it eight days ago."

Avery advanced toward the open window, and Jordan sensed her sister's hand reaching toward her. "Let's do this before I return to my senses."

Jordan took Avery's hand, ducked, and climbed in through the window. The room smelled dusty and dank. "What's left behind?"

"Lots of yellow tents, fingerprint powder, and discarded latex gloves." Avery drew in a breath. "And there's a large bloodstain on the floor."

"Mine, I suppose."

"Jesus, Jordan. The stain is so big."

"Head injuries bleed a lot." She followed Avery toward the room's center. "Casey was lying near the kitchen. She was struggling, and her face was covered in a plastic bag."

"She was suffocating," Avery whispered.

As she stared into the darkness, Jordan's mind drifted back to the house filled with so much light. She had wanted a better look. Just a look. Backup was coming. And then she'd seen Casey.

"When you found Casey, what did you see?" Avery asked.

"She was struggling, thumping her bound feet against the floor," she said. "I crossed to her immediately. Normally, I would have secured the scene, but she was turning blue. Her time was almost up. I cut the plastic from her face, and she sucked in a breath. It reminded me so much of that day I found you."

"I remember seeing your face, and all I wanted to do was cry." Avery rubbed her palms together.

"Did Walker do that to you?" Jordan asked.

"I was thinking about that night this morning. I never heard a name, but I think there was a second man. His voice was a hoarse whisper. I think he's the one that shoved the plastic in my mouth."

"You refused to go to the emergency room. I wanted a rape kit done."

"I know, and I couldn't face that."

"Where was Walker when this second man might have been there?"

"He'd split. And then you showed."

"Do you remember anything else?"

"No."

"You sure?"

"Yes."

"Okay."

"If this is the same guy, why didn't he kill you? Your death would have solved a lot of potential witness problems for him."

"If he's been sending me messages, murdering me would end the game."

"What game?"

"No idea." Jordan turned toward the room, inhaling and exhaling as she listened to the drip of water from a pipe, a scurrying mouse, and the creak of floorboards as Avery shifted her weight from foot to foot. She opened her cane and moved across the room, noting the wood floor changed to a cracked laminate. The kitchens in houses like this were generally small, so it took only six steps to cross the length of it. She ran her hand over the wall until she felt the door handle.

Jordan opened the door. "What's out back?"

"A shed."

It had been too dark for her to see that night, and any outbuildings had been the last thing on her mind.

"Did you know he was there before he struck?" Avery asked.

"I assumed, but I didn't see him. The panic in Casey's eyes tipped me off."

"Did you hear anything?"

"Footsteps."

"Smells?"

Jordan closed her eyes, allowing herself to relax.

"Did he say anything?"

Jordan tapped her finger against her thigh. "He said, 'Too smart.'"

"He wasn't expecting you to find Casey so soon?"

"I drove like a bat out of hell, but I wouldn't have found her in time if I didn't have Find a Friend," Jordan said.

"He expected you to discover Casey's body, eventually."

"Yes."

"If he holds to his pattern, then he'd leave Casey's body where it will be discovered, but so far she's not turned up," Avery said.

"Instead, he killed Emma Powers." Was Casey still alive? Was this killer keeping her somewhere, expecting to use her again?

"Do you think Casey can identify him?" Avery asked.

"If he was careful, and she hasn't seen his face, maybe not. But I suspect if he hasn't killed her, he's going to, so he doesn't care what she's seen."

"But she's heard things. She must know something that would lead to his identification, so why keep her alive?"

"She reminds him of somebody."

"Me?" Avery asked.

"She looks like you," Jordan said. "The other three victims also resemble you. But unlike them, you have not used drugs recently. That seems to be a trigger for this guy."

"If there was ever a reason to stay sober, it's that."

For the first few years, the foundation under sobriety was brittle. It did harden over time, but there would always be cracks that left the entire structure vulnerable.

***

When she and Avery arrived home, Jordan could not shake a sense of unease as she walked herself to the front door, fished keys from her purse, and after some fumbling, opened the door. Inside the house, she kicked off her shoes and took a moment to set them by the entryway table. Keys in purse, she put both on the same table. Sally had said, during their hospital walks, that organization was important.

Avery's phone rang, and her voice dropped low. Judging by the sound, she had turned away. Jordan moved into the kitchen, washed her hands, and set up a pot of coffee to brew.

"Hey, do you mind if I duck out for a while?" Avery asked.

Jordan did not want her leaving, not for her own sake but for Avery's. But if she had learned anything with her sister, holding on too tight fostered resentment. "No, not at all."

"I shouldn't be gone more than a couple of hours."

"I can survive." For a long time after Avery's first overdose, Jordan had grilled her sister constantly about her comings and goings. She could not relax until her sister returned and she was satisfied she was sober. Two years ago, after Avery's last hit, she had refused to come home after treatment because the pressure of facing Jordan had been too great.

Though twenty-five months of sobriety was not a record, it was a solid base. And Jordan needed to give her sister space. "Have fun."

"Thanks."

"Be careful."

"I'll be fine."

"I'm not talking about the regular kind of danger," Jordan said. "Until we figure out this case, you need to be extra careful."

"I will."

Jordan reached in her back pocket and dug out a penknife. "Take this."

"It's a knife."

"I always carried it on the job. Came in handy a few times. Saved me once. Carry it, and if you need to use it, do it."

"But this is yours."

"I've got another one."

Avery did not fire back her normal quip. "Okay. I'll keep it close."

When Avery left, Jordan stood alone in the kitchen, listening to the gurgle of the coffee maker.

"What do you want?" She closed her eyes and listened, hoping information about this killer was buried somewhere deep in her brain and would wiggle its way to her consciousness.

Smoke. Athletic shoes. Intelligence. She repeated the details over and over.

But no replies whispered in her head. There was only the coffee maker, the tick of a clock, and the hum of the air-conditioning. Jordan's phone rang. *"Dot Andrews,"* the mechanical voice said.

She answered the call. "Mrs. Andrews."

"Detective Poe. I went through my daughter's room like you told me. I didn't find anything there."

Jordan leaned forward. "But?"

"I found a crumpled-up piece of paper in Cloe's car. She borrowed her sister's car from time to time."

"And?"

"It was a job application for Thompson's Market."

"Thompson's on Sixth Street?"

"That's what it says on the top of the form. Casey had started to fill out the form but stopped."

"Did she date it?"

"Yes, it's dated the day before she vanished."

"Can you hold on to the copy? I'll have an officer pick it up."

"It's a job application," she said. "What does it mean?"

"It fills in another piece on the timeline before she was taken. All the pieces matter."

"Okay."

"How are you doing?" Jordan asked.

"Not well. I can't sleep. I'm always worried about her."

"I think about her all the time as well."

"Do you think that she's alive?"

"As a police officer I won't speak in absolute terms. Not yet. I'm moving forward assuming she's alive."

Mrs. Andrews drew in a quick, sharp breath, as if trying to hold back tears. "Thank you."

"I'll find out what happened to her," Jordan said.

When she hung up, she cradled the phone close to her chest. She had been within inches of Casey. She had nearly saved her. And then the blow to her head, and her world had gone dark.

Tears welled in Jordan's eyes, and several spilled over her cheeks. She had faced frustration many times before, but without her sight, the problems felt insurmountable. How was she going to find Casey when she could barely get around in her own home?

Of course, if a solution was out there, it would not be discovered while she wallowed in self-pity. After Casey was found, she would curl up in a ball, pull the covers over her head, and embrace all the sorrow and defeatism. Until then, she did not have the luxury.

On her phone, she carefully maneuvered her way through her contacts until she found Spencer's information. She dialed, anticipating the sound of his voice.

On the third ring he picked up. "Jordan."

"I just received a call from Dot Andrews, Casey Andrews's mother." She spent the next several minutes detailing what she had learned.

"Thompson's Market on Sixth Street?" A chair squeaked in the background, followed by a rustle of paper.

"Someone should talk to him about Casey and also Tammy Fox, who worked at the store," she said. "I can do it. I'll Uber to his store."

"I'll do it," he said quickly. "Do not go to his shop or engage. Understood?"

"I know how to handle myself."

He swore. "Jordan, no. I'll talk to him."

It made sense. Spencer did not know Rawlings, and he might get a more objective read on him. "Sure. Fine."

"Are you doing all right?"

"Never better. You?" she quipped.

He chuckled softly. "That's the spirit. I'll be in touch."

"Roger."

CHAPTER TWENTY-NINE

Friday, April 23
2:30 p.m.

Spencer strode into the grocery store on Sixth Street. He showed his badge to the cashier and asked to speak to the owner or manager. The boy, wide eyed, nodded quickly and hustled to the back of the store.

Seconds later a midsize man came toward him. Spencer introduced himself and discovered he was speaking to Rawlings.

"What can I do for you?" Rawlings asked.

Spencer showed him a picture of Casey Andrews. "Do you remember this woman?"

"Sure. She applied for a job here."

"She's been missing over a week, and we've been trying to find her."

"I haven't seen her since I gave her the application. She seemed really excited about the job and said she would bring it back in a day or two. She never showed. That happens sometimes. Kids get a better offer and don't circle back to close the loop on another job possibility."

"How many times did she come into the store?"

"Just the once. She was motivated and ready to get to work."

"Anything strike you as odd about her?"

"Nothing."

"You also employed a young woman by the name of Tammy Fox."

"That's right. Worked here about two months. She quit and took a job in a bar."

"Did you know her before she started working here?"

"She was recommended to me by her drug counselor. Said she was worth taking a chance on."

"Who was the counselor?"

"Rogan Malone. He runs several meetings near here each week. And for the record, I go to meetings as well."

"When's the last time you saw Ms. Fox?"

"Whenever she left. Six months ago."

"Did you ever know a Laura Davis?" He showed him a picture.

"No. Should I?"

"Not necessarily."

"What's all this about? Do I need an attorney?"

"Tammy's dead and Casey's missing."

Rawlings ran his hand over his head. "I didn't have anything to do with that."

"That's what I'm trying to determine."

"I might give my attorney a call after all."

"That's your right." He handed the store owner a card. "Call me if you think of anything."

"Sure. Of course. I'm really sorry to hear about them both. A girl can't be too careful."

"No, sir, they cannot."

On the drive back to the office, Spencer requested any background material on Rawlings. By the time he arrived at his office and hung up his hat, he had promises for a quick follow-up. He sat at his desk and discovered an email message waiting for him regarding security recordings at the hospital.

When the hospital footage of Emma Powers had arrived early the previous morning, Spencer had assigned the task of reviewing it to two forensic technicians, who had spent yesterday combing through it. When his phone rang, the technician reiterated the highlights in chronological order.

Spencer opened the attachments and noted the time stamp from two days ago, when Emma Powers had walked into the hospital at 4:00 a.m. Coffee in hand, she'd paused to show her badge to the security guard and then vanished inside.

There were several instances when Emma had been spotted in the hospital that day. She had been carrying in meals to patients, delivering water and sodas. Once she had been on Jordan's floor. She had often paused at the nurses' station to chat. She'd spent time in the break room, eating a burger and watching an afternoon talk show.

And then later that afternoon, she had emerged from the hospital. The grainy image showed her burrowing her hands into the pockets of her scrubs as she ducked her head and moved to the bus station and sat on the bench. She checked her watch once or twice. And then something distracted her.

He zoomed in on the image and saw the outline of a figure standing in the shadows. He crossed the street, lingered near her, and then started a conversation with her.

The two lingered for several minutes, her bus came and went, and then they crossed the street out of the camera's range. He pulled up Google Maps and saw the diner. A woman would not feel threatened to visit a diner with a stranger in the late afternoon.

Spencer scribbled down the name of the restaurant and then picked up his phone and dialed. On the third ring, he heard, "Jordan Poe."

"It's Spencer. How would you like to go out to a late lunch?"

"I can always eat, but why?"

"Surveillance footage of Emma Powers shows her possibly going into a diner across the street from the hospital."

"McKenzie's Diner, right?"

"That's the one."

"Great french fries. Sure, I'm in."

"I'll pick you up."

"It'll be faster if I Uber over there. I'll see you in about a half hour at the diner."

"I can get you."

"Really not necessary."

Her determined tone told him she needed to do this. "Okay."

He hung up and, knowing he had about fifteen minutes to kill, watched the tapes featuring Emma again. She was relaxed when she walked out of the frame with the man, who was careful to keep his head down.

Spencer focused on the man. He wore all black, a hoodie, and jeans. He appeared to be about five ten, which coincided with the athletic shoe prints found at the Laura Davis, Tammy Fox, and Casey Andrews scenes.

Checking his watch, he grabbed his hat. Fifteen minutes later he arrived at the diner as Jordan was getting out of an Uber.

As he approached, her head swiveled toward him, and she braced.

"Jordan, it's Spencer."

The tension in her shoulders relaxed. Being a cop came with its own set of challenges, and her vision added extra layers of vulnerability.

Jordan had plenty of reasons to request help, but asking for anything did not come naturally to her. Maybe that was why he wanted to help so much. His late wife had always been dependent on him, and when they had first married, he had seen it as a form of love. But after a while, her constant need for reinforcement created friction between them. Maybe if Vickie and he had both been more mature, it would have turned out differently between them. Maybe not.

"Spencer," she said. "Your soap has faded from this morning."

"I didn't realize it was that noticeable."

"Not overly strong. And I'm always on the hunt for identifying clues."

He put out his elbow just close enough for her to sense it, and she took it. "I've not eaten here before."

"If you have work tonight, avoid the chili cheese dogs. Indigestion city."

He laughed and opened the door. "I'll keep that in mind."

A hostess smiled at him, and then her gaze shifted to Jordan and her cane. Smile fading, she guided them to a booth and handed him a menu.

"Hon, what can I get you?" The woman's voice rose several notches, as if speaking louder would help.

Jordan smiled. "You still have the grilled-chicken sandwich with melted provolone?"

"We do."

"I'll take that, fries, and a soda."

"Will do. And you, sir?" the waitress asked.

"The same," Spencer said.

"Will do," the waitress said.

As the waitress walked away, Spencer asked, "Have you been getting a lot of that?"

"Some. My Uber driver offered to turn the radio up, thinking it might make me more comfortable." She turned toward the window and the afternoon light before she faced him again. "I suppose that's part of it. Though it's already getting old. So, Emma Powers came in here with a man she met outside the hospital?"

"She did. I have an officer collecting footage from all businesses around the diner. ATMs, gas stations, retail shops. If they came here, then we might be able to track their path."

"I don't suppose you have a good picture of him."

"No clear shot of his face. He wore a hoodie and seemed aware of the cameras."

The waitress returned with their drinks and promised to have their meals in a few minutes. Spencer sipped his soda, watching as Jordan felt for her straw, opened it, and put it carefully in her cup.

Spencer had first taken note of Jordan the moment he saw her in the courtroom. After the bail hearing, it had been a pleasure to watch her walk across the courthouse parking lot. As she moved with confidence and purpose, he had found himself admiring her ass. If her life were not in one hell of a transition, he might have asked her out.

"Do you have a picture of Emma Powers?" she asked.

"I do."

"Our waitress notices the details, so she might have seen Emma."

"That's the hope."

She pulled her straw up and down in her cup, crunching the ice. "I had Avery drive me by the house where I was attacked."

"Why would you do that?"

"I hoped being there would jog my memory."

"And did it?"

"Right before he hit me, I smelled cigarette smoke. No aftershave. He moved so fast."

Spencer imagined the killer wrapping up Casey Andrews and pausing to have a cigarette while he watched her suffocate. "The forensic team found two cigarette butts by the back door outside."

"I should have been more careful." She sounded weary. "I didn't save Casey, and I've not only ruined a career I love, but my life is never going to be the same."

"You will find ways to adapt, Jordan."

"I don't want to adapt," she said. "I resent the hell out of all of this."

"You must pivot and find another way to serve the law."

The waitress returned to the table with their meals, setting Jordan's plate off to her left. The move struck him as careless.

"Ma'am," he asked as he pushed the plate closer to Jordan. "Did you work the afternoon shift here the day before yesterday?"

She reached in her apron pocket, removed silverware wrapped in paper napkins, and placed both in the center of the table.

"Worked a double the last two days."

Spencer opened the photo of Emma Powers on his phone. "Was she here?"

The waitress studied the image. "I've seen her in here before. She'll stop in for coffee after she's worked a long shift. Nice gal."

"Was she here two days ago?" Spencer repeated.

"She might have been. It was real crowded, and we were understaffed. Several folks came in the front door, saw the line, and left."

"Does the diner have security footage?" he asked.

"We have cameras," she said. "But you'll have to ask the manager if they're working."

"Who's the manager?"

"Dave. Dave Paulson. He just left for the day. He'll be back in the morning."

"Does he have a cell number?" Spencer asked.

"Unless the place is on fire, he won't respond to messages. He'll be in by seven tomorrow morning. What's this about?" the waitress asked. "That woman in trouble?"

"She was murdered two days ago," Spencer said. "We're retracing her steps."

"Murdered?" Her lips thinned into a grim line. "How?"

"I can't discuss it. Call your manager and leave him a message. Tell him the place is on fire if that's what it takes for a return call."

"Yeah, sure."

"And if you run across anyone who might have seen Emma Powers Wednesday, let me know." He handed her his card. "I'll want to talk to them."

The waitress glanced at the card. "Yeah, sure." A bell rang at the cook's station behind the counter. "I've got to go."

"Sure."

Spencer moved the silverware, brushing the tips of Jordan's fingers. "What do you think?"

She nodded her thanks and carefully opened the utensils. "In all my years, I've had one or two cases almost solve themselves. The rest came down to assembling bits of information. That's the way this one is going."

"What about Rawlings?" he asked. "Did he say or do anything that caught your attention?"

"Not really. He always gave me a discount on the takeout. Last couple of meals from him were free. Did you check to see if he had a police record?"

"He was arrested twenty years ago for assaulting his girlfriend. In the police file it mentioned that his attorney was Harold Sunday."

"All roads keep leading back to Mr. Sunday."

"Rawlings never served time and was ordered into counseling by the judge. Tammy's doctor recommended the group meetings. Stands to reason they met."

"Rawlings said he didn't know Laura."

"How well does Avery know Rawlings?"

Her gaze lingered in the direction of his voice. "They knew each other via the food bank."

"Rawlings has a connection to all the women."

"Just like Sunday."

"Looks like it."

She reached for her grilled-chicken sandwich. "I'm worried about Avery. I don't think she appreciates the danger. She was in Thompson's Market today. She knows Rawlings. She knew Walker."

He cleared his throat. "That's why I called Detective Santiago. Asked him to bump into her from time to time."

Jordan's gaze met his. "Did you?"

"I might have overstepped." But he would not apologize.

"I could kiss you."

The suggestion was a shot to his loins. He cleared his throat.

She smiled. "Are you blushing, Ranger Spencer?"

"I am not."

"Then I'll have to try harder."

***

Casey heard footsteps in the hallway and drew back against the wall behind her. She hated these visits. They were tests of her strength.

The door opened, and she winced against the light from the hallway that left his frame shadowed. "I've brought you dinner."

She did not respond. From the moment he had brought her here, she had never once thanked or begged him.

He set it on the floor inside the door. "I'm doing you a favor. You know that, right?"

"A favor?"

"I've kept you alive."

She raised her chin and pushed back her greasy hair. "Why?"

"Because you're going to help me catch someone."

It took every bit of control not to yell at him and demand to know what else he planned. But she kept silent, not giving him the satisfaction of knowing how terrified she was. "Why would I help you?"

"Because I can make it a lot harder on you."

"I don't see how."

He took a step toward her. His face was covered in a mask, but she saw the challenge in his gaze. "Maybe you need another demonstration."

CHAPTER THIRTY

Friday, April 23
7:30 p.m.

Jordan wanted to Uber home, but Spencer had insisted on driving her. He was protective by nature. A trait that not only explained his loyalty to his late wife but would have chased Jordan off six months ago. But now, she was practical enough to accept any help until her vision returned. Once she was back to her old self, she would stand on her own again.

He parked. "We're here."

She reached for her purse and her folded cane. "Thank you. I never appreciated driving as much as I do now."

His heavy silences remained hard to decode. "I'll walk you to the door."

"That's not necessary." She reached for her door handle.

"It is when you're a good ol' Texas boy." He was out of the car before she could protest, and when she lowered her feet to the ground, he was there waiting. Not touching or grabbing an elbow. He was willing to let her figure this out.

"This has been above and beyond the call of duty, Ranger." She liked having him around. God, how she wished she could see his face.

"Not really."

When she had joked about kissing him, she had not really been kidding. She shifted her focus. "Is my car in the driveway?" she asked.

"It is. But Avery's car is gone. She at work?"

"I'm not sure. She went out to see a friend. I thought she'd be back by now."

"Where was she going?"

"I didn't press."

"Can you find her with Find a Friend?"

"My new phone skills aren't that advanced yet."

"Want me to check?"

She hesitated, understanding she was asking Spencer to help her spy on her sister. "Under normal circumstances, I'd say no." She handed him her phone. His fingers brushed hers and sent a jolt of energy through her. "But these times aren't exactly normal."

"No, they're not." He opened the app. "She's in downtown Austin near Thompson's Market."

"Rawlings's place. Why would she be back there?"

"Did you tell her about Rawlings?"

"No." She accepted the phone back.

"I can call Santiago."

"This kind of micromanaging drove her away from me the last time. She needs me to trust her."

"Do you?"

"Yes."

"Look at it this way: if she's alive and well and pissed at you, it's better than feeling good about you and dead."

"You're right."

"I'll have Santiago appear. He's good about that."

She dialed Avery's number. It rang twice and went to voicemail. "Avery, this is Jordan, just letting you know I'm home. We've also had a red flag come up on Mr. Rawlings. Be careful around him." She gripped the phone, hoping she would get an immediate callback. Finally, she ended the call and said, "Do it. Call Santiago and ask him to drive by the area."

"Consider it done."

***

Avery moved down Sixth Street toward the alley that had once been her refuge and her prison. The streets remained full of tourists and shoppers, but some of the girls who worked the street were already out.

She had not spoken to Stacey or any of the other girls in two years. Nowadays, she walked these streets while the sun was shining but refused to linger once it set.

On the corner, she spotted a woman dressed in tight jeans and a halter top. She wore a red wig and was lighting up a cigarette. Stacey.

Avery hurried down the block toward her. "Stacey."

The redhead regarded her with a narrowing gaze. There were no hints of recognition, and then Avery detected a knowing nod. "Well, well. Thought I'd seen the last of you. How long has it been?"

"Two years."

"You look clean," Stacey said.

"I am."

"Then why are you here?"

"I was looking for you."

"I don't have any supply on me right now. Inventory has been spotty since Walker offed himself."

"I'm not looking for that."

Stacey inhaled, exhaled smoke slowly. "What do you want?"

"You heard about the Mummy murders?"

"A few tidbits."

"I knew Tammy Fox. We met in group and did art together."

A car drove by Stacey, and a window rolled down, but she waved the driver on. As he drove past, Avery glimpsed the man's face. He looked like Rawlings. She was not totally surprised. All kinds drove these streets.

"Talk fast, Avery. You're costing me money," Stacey said.

"Did you ever see anyone bothering her? Anyone watching her?"

"It's all I can do to keep up with myself."

"What about Casey Andrews?"

"Is she dead, too?" Stacey asked.

"Still missing."

"She hooked up with Walker about ten days ago. I saw her go into one of the abandoned buildings. She looked ready to fly high."

"What happened to her? Did she leave with Walker?"

She flicked an ash. "Are you working for your sister now?"

"Working for myself. I want to know what happened to these women."

"Why?"

"Maybe I see a lot of myself in them."

"Don't we all."

"Who did Casey leave with?"

Stacey inhaled. "He was a friend of Walker's. He's been around for years. Likes to play rough."

"Do you have a name or a description?"

"Even if I did, I wouldn't tell you. I don't need the trouble. Get back to your clean-and-sober world."

"You need to tell me more about this guy. He's killing women."

Stacey sniffed. "He wore a nice suit. Flashy watch."

"That's it?"

"All I know."

Avery had been part of Stacey's world just two years ago. But now the distance between them was immeasurable. She scribbled her number on a piece of paper. "Call me if you change your mind."

Stacey inhaled deeply as she tucked the paper in her purse. "Sure, you'll be the first person I call, Nancy Drew."

"What building did Casey go into?"

"A block east. It's real popular. You can't miss it."

As Avery moved east down the street, she spotted a familiar car. It belonged to Leo Santiago. "Shit."

She ducked in an alley and watched as the vehicle passed. Santiago looked annoyed. She stepped back into the shadows. Santiago was the last guy she could afford to be seen with. Finally, the vehicle rounded the corner.

As she stood alone, her phone rang. She did not recognize the number and considered letting it go to voicemail. But there were so many people who were helping Jordan, it was possible one might be trying to get ahold of her.

"Hello?"

"Hey, Avery, this is Maisy from the café."

"What's up?" She kept her gaze on the street, making sure Santiago did not double back.

"You'll never guess what I found? Your old phone."

"Seriously."

"Yeah. It was in the pocket of your jacket, the one that I borrowed. If you want to come and get it, I'm home now."

Santiago's car again drove slowly by the alley. She pressed her back to the wall. "Sure. I'll be by in a few."

***

Jordan opened her cane and slow walked to the front porch. At the front door, she groped for her keys. Inside the house, Jordan listened for Spencer's car. She heard the engine roar to life but noticed his car was not moving. He was making sure she was okay.

She turned on the lights, hoping each one would reassure him. Spencer drove off, but the darkness remained.

Moving to the kitchen, she reached for the coffeepot. It was not there. She patted around the counter, searching, and finally found it about four feet to her right. The coffee jar was where she had left it, but the mugs in the cabinet above were not in their place. She found them on the third shelf.

"Avery, I swear you better not be reorganizing."

She pulled the machine back to its rightful place and plugged it in before setting it up to brew. She moved down to her bedroom and crossed to her dresser. Third drawer down was for workout wear, including sweats and T-shirts.

Instead of her workout clothes, her fingers skimmed over bras, panties, and camisoles. "If this is a joke, it is not funny. Or if it is a test, whoever did this sucks."

She searched each of the drawers until her fingers brushed soft, worn cotton. She selected a pair of sweats and a T-shirt, but as she turned, she suddenly did not feel comfortable stripping. She thought about the roses. This killer knew where she lived.

"What the hell is going on?" She pulled her phone from her pocket and dialed Avery's number. The call went to voicemail again. "Avery, this is Jordan. Call me right now. Either this is April Fools' Day and no one told me, or there's some weird shit happening in this house."

She moved to her nightstand, opened the top drawer, and fumbled in the back for her spare knife. She opened the blade, touching the point with her fingertip. Carefully she closed it and slid it in her front pocket. Maybe she was being paranoid, and there was a logical explanation for this. But she was still a cop, and she was paid to question what did not feel right.

***

Spencer was thinking about Jordan. He had watched as she dropped her purse and seemed to kick off her shoes by the front entrance. She had proceeded to turn on all the lights. And he knew she was challenging her blindness with every bit of light at her disposal. Trying to turn the no into a yes.

"Got to love that." He pulled away and was taking a right out of her neighborhood when his phone rang. "Spencer."

"It's Captain Lee. There's been a development in your case."

"Another woman's been found dead?"

"No. A local man shot himself. Officers responded to a shot fired and found a room full of pictures filled with your victims. There're also personal items that appear to have belonged to each of the dead women."

"Who is it?" He flipped on his overhead lights. Blue and white flashed.

"The man's name is Rawlings. Seth Rawlings. I know you requested surveillance footage around his store and his police records."

"I did." Rawlings's death was too convenient. "Did he leave a note?"

"We've not found one yet. But we've only been on scene an hour."

"I just spoke to him hours ago. He was a little uncomfortable but nothing noteworthy."

"Your presence could have been enough."

Spencer doubted it. "Text me the address."

"Hold off informing Detective Poe," Captain Lee said. "She'll learn about this soon enough."

"This is her case."

"No, it's yours. And she'll want to be on scene, and given her vision impairment, she'll be in the way now."

It was true. There was not much she could do now. "You call her, or I will."

"Are you sure?"

"Yes."

"Sure, I'll handle it," Captain Lee said.

Spencer arrived twenty minutes later. The entire store was now roped off with yellow crime scene tape and surrounded by a half dozen police cars. He parked in the small lot behind the shop next to the forensic van. Lucas and two technicians were unloading equipment.

Out of the car, he went to Lucas, who handed him full PPE gear. Every bit of evidence would need to be protected, and no one was taking any chances.

He pulled on gloves, moved to the back entrance, and showed his badge to the officer controlling the scene. After giving him his name for the log, he climbed the back staircase to the apartment above the store. He took his time, making note of the walls, the stairs, and even the banister, looking for anything that might appear to be off.

The walls were painted white and were covered with framed black-and-white pictures that covered the last fifteen or twenty years of the store's existence. Rawlings appeared in all the images, and as Spencer climbed the stairs, Rawlings grew younger and younger. The last picture featured twentysomething Rawlings standing with a smiling, petite blonde.

He pushed through the apartment door and again was met by another officer, who directed him to Captain Lee in the back bedroom.

The lights of a camera flashed as he approached. When he stepped inside, he saw Rawlings lying on his bed, a single gunshot wound to his right temple. His gun, a .45, lay in his limp hand. The back of his head had exploded on the pillow behind him. How a bullet could ravage a human body never ceased to amaze him.

Captain Lee turned to Spencer. "There's a large closet to the left. Have a look, but don't enter yet."

Spencer moved toward the closet and studied the collection of photos filled with pictures of Laura Davis, Tammy Fox, Emma Powers, and Jordan and Avery Poe. "Jordan needs to be told about this."

"I've sent a car for her. She's on her way. I don't want her up here. But she'll stay by the command center."

Spencer returned to Rawlings's body. "Why kill himself? He was getting away with it."

"You were getting close."

"Maybe." He drew in a breath, finding he had no pity in his heart for the man.

Spencer descended the stairs in time to see Jordan rise out of a squad car. Her gaze was wide, searching, and unseeing. He crossed directly to her. "Jordan."

"How long have you been here?"

"Thirty minutes. I checked the scene out so I could brief you."

"Did Rawlings really shoot himself?" she asked.

"He did. Single gunshot to his right temple."

"Are you sure?"

"Yeah."

"I don't believe it," she said.

"There's a closet full of pictures of women, including you and Avery, and all the Austin victims," Spencer said.

Her head turned in the direction of the forensic team, whose evidence-collection kits rattled slightly as they crossed the lot.

"What about Casey? Anything linking him to Casey?"

"No. What do you know about Rawlings?"

"Always friendly. Like I said, gave me a discount because I was a cop. I went by his store at least once a week. I also know he supplied food to a homeless shelter. Said it was a waste to throw out unused food."

"He could have met all the women at the shelter."

"Avery lived there for a while."

"Did he ever say anything to you that gave you the creeps?"

"The last time I was in, he asked how I was doing and wanted to know if Avery was well." She shook her head. "It sounded so innocent."

"How did he know you two were sisters?"

"I brought her into the store several times over the years." She shook her head. "None of this fits the guy I knew, nor does it tell us what happened to Casey."

"This scene is going to take days to process," Spencer said.

"And it'll be weeks of evidence handling after that." She shook her head. "There has to be something in that apartment that connects to Casey."

"As soon as I know, you'll know," he said.

"Christ, Rawlings was in my life weekly. You would think after all this time I would have gotten some kind of vibe off him. But never once did alarm bells sound."

"Guys like him don't always look like the bogeyman. They're the nice guy next door."

CHAPTER THIRTY-ONE

Friday, April 23
10:30 p.m.

Jordan was bone-tired when she pushed through the front door of her house. She knew instantly that she was not alone. Keys gripped in her hand, she called out, "Avery?"

A beat of silence and then Avery called back, "Yes, it's me!"

The pump of adrenaline slowed, but these days it never fully eased. She lived on edge. On high alert.

"Where have you been?" Avery asked.

"A crime scene." She toed off her shoes by the front door and set her purse on the table.

"Again?" Footsteps moved down the front hallway. As Avery approached, she carried with her the strong scent of her favorite jasmine shampoo. She had showered.

"Mr. Rawlings, the owner of Thompson's Market, shot himself in the head. It's an apparent suicide."

"What? That can't be right. I just saw him. He seemed in high spirits."

"You and I both know that's not always the best predictor." She had learned many suicide victims felt a sense of peace and happiness just knowing their life was going to end soon.

"I know. But I just didn't see that one coming."

"There's more. His apartment was filled with pictures of the women who were suffocated to death in plastic. There were also trinkets from each woman. Personal items, jewelry, and driver's licenses." Jordan shrugged off her jacket, and Avery took it. "Please hang it in the same spot in the hall closet. I'm learning my lesson about organization."

"I know."

"Speaking of which, the coffeepot was in a different place on the kitchen counter, and the clothes in my drawers were rearranged. Did you do that?"

"No, I did not," Avery said. "Are you sure you didn't move it and forget?"

"I didn't forget," Jordan said. "I'm blind, but my memory is as sharp as ever. Has anyone else been in this house?"

"No one I've let in."

Jordan rubbed her hand over the tight muscles banding her neck. "Then who moved my stuff? If it's meant to be a joke, it's not funny."

"No, it's not."

"Do me a favor and check all the windows and make sure they're locked. I'll check the doors."

"Sure."

Jordan carefully ran her fingers over each lock, searching for scratches or imperfections hinting of a break-in. She found the doors were all locked and unmolested by an intruder.

Several minutes later, both reconvened in the living room. "All the windows are locked."

"And none look like they've been tampered with?"

"No." Avery laid a gentle hand on Jordan's arm. "You've been under a hell of a lot of stress since your attack."

“Do not tell me this is in my mind,” Jordan said.

“Let’s be realistic. With all that’s going on, it’s easy to move something and then forget you did it.”

“I did not forget.”

“Okay, let’s assume you didn’t.”

“I don’t assume. I know.”

“Then what do you propose to do about it?”

“I want to get a camera in the house. Whoever was here moved my shit around to get under my skin.”

“Who would do that, Jordan? How did he get in?”

“I don’t know, hence the camera!” Since she had lost her sight, she had been patronized far too much. She had lost her ability to see, not her mind.

“Okay, okay!” Avery countered. “I have a friend at the university who sells reconditioned nanny cams. He hides them in stuffed bears, clocks, and shit. We’ll go see him in the morning.”

Having an action plan calmed Jordan’s nerves, but it did not banish her worries. Someone had been in her house, and despite what the cops thought they knew about Rawlings, until she figured out who had invaded her space, she would remain on edge.

“Where were you?” Jordan asked.

“Remember I said I lost my cell phone?”

“You bought the disposable phone until you found it.”

“Because I knew it would turn up. My friend Maisy found it. Nice to have it back. God only knows how many messages I’ve missed. It’s charging now.”

“You were gone for hours.” She sounded like a mother, but given her state, she did not care.

“We lost track of time. Maisy was telling me about her recovery. Wanted to talk to someone who’d been down that road.”

“And?”

Avery sighed. “Before that I went to find my old friend Stacey.”

"I remember Stacey."

"I wondered if she had seen anything that might connect to the dead girls."

"And?"

"She said there was a guy who worked with Walker. He took the girls as a form of payment. Stacey said he could be rough."

"You need to be more careful now, Avery."

"I was careful. I know these people. It was my world."

"Not anymore."

"You were at a crime scene, Jordan. Talk about being careful."

"I'm a cop. And it might not be safe now."

"You just said Rawlings is dead."

"From an *apparent* suicide. Nothing about Rawlings's death has felt right to me. Walker's death could also have been a setup. Nothing is a given right now."

"I'm not going to stop living because there's a nut running around. Because honestly there're always crazy people on the streets."

"This one kills women that look like you. Big difference."

"We look alike, Jordan."

Jordan drew in a breath, trying to find the words that expressed the frustration chewing her alive since the day of her attack. Before, she was fearless. Other than losing Avery to the drugs, she was not afraid of much. Now fear was always present, and it took effort to keep it away.

"I don't want to fight," Avery said.

"Please be careful. Text me when you're gone for more than a few hours."

"Text me when you go to a crime scene."

"I will as soon as I master this damn phone."

"You're smart, Jordan. And if I can stay sober, you can learn to use your phone and tackle braille."

"Has it been hard for you to stay sober since my attack?"

Avery did not speak immediately. "I've always had days that are harder than others, but the last few weeks have been tough. And in full disclosure, I've missed a few meetings lately."

"That's not good." She pulled her phone from her pocket. "You keep going to meetings, and I'll figure this out."

"Teamwork."

"Something like that."

Avery hugged her, holding her close. And for once, Jordan relaxed into the embrace.

"We'll be okay," Avery said.

Jordan wanted to believe that. But until she had surveillance on the house and the police proved Rawlings had indeed shot himself, she would not let her guard down.

CHAPTER THIRTY-TWO

Saturday, April 24
8:00 a.m.

Dr. McIntyre had several questions for Spencer when he called her about Rawlings's body. Was there a note? Prolific killers often had an agenda known only to them, and if they did opt for suicide, they often shared their motives in a note or video message. Had Rawlings fired a practice shot in the ceiling? Suicides by handgun were not as easy as most thought. If the bullet was not properly angled, it did a good job of maiming the individual but did not kill them. And the practice shot into the ceiling allowed them to judge the gun's recoil and sound.

Spencer noted her questions and replied negative to both. When he hung up, he stood in the hallway outside Rawlings's apartment. When the medical examiner's office arrived and removed the body, he followed it down to the street.

Lucas approached Spencer. "I'll call if I find anything. No sense in you hanging around."

"Right." None of this felt right. None of it.

Spencer went home, closed and locked the door behind him. He unfastened his gun belt and locked his weapon in a secured box before he sat and pulled off his boots. Needing to wash the crime scene smells and memories away, he undressed and turned on the shower. Stepping under the hot spray, he leaned against the tile wall, savoring the hot water as it pummeled his back.

According to Rawlings's neighbors and associates, he had operated his store for twenty years at this location. He always took a week off in the spring to go fishing. He never took his phone with him, telling everyone he needed time off the grid to decompress. He was friendly and kept his store and the sidewalk in front of it clean, and he regularly donated food to the local shelter and food bank. It all fit Jordan's assessment of Rawlings, who appeared to all to be a hardworking man. Serial killers could hide in plain sight, but in retrospect there was always something that someone thought was off. It was still very early in the investigation, but something about this didn't sit right with him.

He turned and faced the spray, letting it bead on his face. He had promised Jordan an update, and in all honesty, he wanted to see her.

Out of the shower, he toweled off and stepped up to the steamed mirror. As he stared at his distorted, nearly invisible reflection, he tried to imagine what Jordan saw all the time. He wiped his towel over the mirror until his reflection reappeared. How many times had she done the same in the last week and a half, only to find that no amount of wiping brought her vision back?

Twenty minutes later he was shaved, dressed, and ready to leave. Out the door, he drove to a favorite coffee shop, ordered a bag of bagels and three cups: one for him, Avery, and Jordan. Back in his vehicle he called Jordan.

"Spencer." Her voice rumbled with sleep.

"Did I wake you?"

"No, just got up."

"I can bring coffee and bagels, and we can go over what's been found so far at the Rawlings scene."

"That's music to my ears," she said.

"See you in fifteen?"

"I'll be ready-ish. The wheels of progress still don't move fast. But I'll be decent."

For a flash, he imagined her indecent, and the image triggered a bolt of desire. "See you soon."

When he arrived, there was only Avery's car in the driveway. He crossed to the front door and rang the bell. Footsteps mingled with the steady tap of a cane. The door opened to Jordan.

"Spencer," she said.

"What gave me away? The soap?"

"And the large shadow you cast. You take up all the space directly in front of me."

"Interesting."

"Come on inside. I smell coffee and bagels."

"I brought three coffees," he said. "I thought Avery was going to be here."

"She took an early shift at the café. We're trying to get back to the new normal."

"And what about you? If this case is truly solved as we thought, then what?"

"Then I work with Sally and the eye doctors and try to make the best of what I have." She led him to the kitchen island. "Did you find any trace of Casey Andrews at Rawlings's house?"

"We found her driver's license. But nothing to tell us where she might be."

She frowned. "A souvenir is not a good sign. Men like him keep the collectibles so they can relive it all."

"I'm afraid that one day we'll find her body in an old house, a shallow grave, or in the woods."

"I thought I could save her."

"You did more than most."

"But not enough."

He set the cup in front of her along with two creams and a sugar. "Coffee, sugar, and cream at three o'clock."

"Thanks." She carefully pried off the lid and poured in both creams and the sugar. "I'm going to have to call on her mother this morning and tell her what was found."

"Let's do it together. It'll mean more if it's coming from you, and it'll be official if I'm present."

"Not relishing the task, but it has to be done."

He opened the bag of bagels. "I didn't know what kind you liked, so I got cinnamon raisin, plain, and sesame."

"Cinnamon raisin." She turned to the kitchen cabinet and retrieved a couple of plates and two knives. She set it all on the island.

He placed a bagel on her plate and pried open the tub of whipped cream cheese.

"Why do you think he killed himself?" she asked.

"I can only think my visit triggered something in him."

"Seems like he would have been tougher than that. He's killed at least three women. He's seen me almost weekly for years."

"I don't know," he said. "I'd feel better if I did."

"Can anyone place him with Walker?" She felt for the cream cheese, found the tub, and scooped out a generous serving with her knife.

"Not yet. There're a lot of puzzle pieces that'll have to be pasted together."

They both ate in silence for several minutes, each lost in their own thoughts. He felt a kinship with her. When she wiped a bit of cream cheese from her lips, his gaze was drawn to the simple action that suddenly felt very erotic. He wondered if her lips tasted as good as they looked.

"I can feel you looking at me," she said.

"That so?"

"Beams of energy radiate from your eyes," she said. "It's almost tangible."

"I'll remember to be more circumspect."

"Don't change on my account." She set her bagel down and wiped her fingers with her napkin.

He had never had a solid read on Jordan. He wanted her right now, but that was a complication neither one of them needed.

"You're thinking so hard I can almost smell the smoke coming from your brain," she said.

He chuckled. "I'm not a deep thinker."

"Neither am I. That's what I like about you. You act and don't hesitate."

She came around the island and moved within inches of him. He swiveled around on his barstool so that he faced her. It was one of the few times they were eye to eye.

"When I saw you in the courtroom that first time, I thought you were hot," Jordan said.

"That so?" As tempted as he was to touch her, he kept his hands at his sides.

A small frown furrowed her brow. "Not being able to see your face now makes it hard. I can't get a read on you. I can't tell if you might be a little into me or not."

"What if I am?"

"It would feel like the most normal thing that's happened to me in the last few weeks."

His hand rose to her side. He could feel her muscles tense at his touch, but he held steady, waiting for her to either relax or pull away.

She leaned forward and kissed him gently on his lips. He did not deepen the kiss or pull her toward him—as far as he was concerned, this had to be her show.

She drew back and regarded his face with a mixture of curiosity and amusement. "Was that not what you wanted?"

"It was mighty nice."

"If you would rather not, no harm, no foul. I don't want to mess up whatever professional relationship we have or had."

His hand remained on her side. "Had?"

"Sounds like the case is behind us."

"A kiss isn't going to ruin anything," he said carefully.

Jordan kissed him again, this time injecting more passion, which sent desire surging through him.

"I feel like myself when I kiss you," she said. "I like it a lot."

"Same."

"I'm tired of death and loss," she said. "I want to feel alive." Her hand slid to the one pressed to her side. "My bedroom is down the hallway."

"That's a bigger step than a kiss."

"Like I said, if you don't want to, no harm, no foul."

"I want to."

"But?" she asked.

"I don't want to take advantage."

"If I didn't want this, this conversation would have been handled over the phone."

He rose, and she tipped her gaze toward him. He cupped her face and kissed her. Since the first moment in the courtroom parking lot when they had gone toe to toe, she'd had the ability to make him rock hard. Jesus, he had not wanted a woman like this in a very long time.

"I want this," he said. "Maybe too much."

She grinned, took his hand, and led him toward a hallway. "I promise to be gentle."

He chuckled, following her. "Ma'am, don't hold back on my account."

She glanced back at him, her grin wicked. "I won't."

***

Avery stood on the street corner near Thompson's Market. The building remained surrounded by cops, techs dressed in space suits, and miles of yellow crime scene tape. As she cradled a cup of coffee, she thought back to that night when the stranger's hot breath had puffed against her skin as he shoved the plastic in her mouth. When she had seen Rawlings the other day, she had not gotten any vibe or hint that he had been that man.

"What brings you here?"

Leo Santiago's familiar voice startled her.

"What are you doing here?" she countered.

"I'm a cop."

"You keep popping up," she said.

"I could say the same for you," he said. "Why are you here?"

"Rawlings, I suppose. I can't picture him doing what's being said about him. He was a nice guy."

"Not from my perspective."

"You didn't know him."

Santiago slid his hand in his pocket, turning his back to the market and focusing on her. "What did you know about him that made you like him so much?"

"He boxed up his unsold food at the end of the day and delivered meals to the homeless. Why do something like that and then kill those women?"

"People are complicated. Good can coexist with the bad."

Her life had been a study in extremes. "Maybe."

"Are you off to the café?"

"I don't work there anymore." And then catching herself, she said, "I haven't told Jordan yet. I quit after her attack. She was there for me when I needed her, and now it's my turn."

"That's good."

This should square us up. She remembered the words she had heard Walker utter to the shadow man. What could Walker have owed Rawlings?

"I guess the more you dig into Rawlings's past, the more you'll learn," she said.

"Anywhere in particular I should be looking?" Santiago asked.

"I'm not really sure."

She met his gaze and realized he was studying her intently. She was not sure how much Jordan had told him about her past. She hoped her sister had not said anything about the drugs because, for some reason, she did not want to disappoint. "I've got to go."

"I won't judge you, Avery."

"You wouldn't mean to, but you would. I know because I judge me every day."

CHAPTER THIRTY-THREE

Saturday, April 24
11:00 a.m.

Jordan lay on her side, her naked body close to Spencer's. She savored the feel of his corded muscle pressed against her breasts and belly. He was a powerful man but had proved he had a real capacity for tenderness.

His breathing was even, relaxed, and she sensed that his eyes were closed, because when he looked at her, her skin tingled as if snapping with electricity.

Her phone rang, and with her eyes still closed, she quickly snapped it up before the second ring as she rolled on her other side. Without thinking, said, "Detective Poe."

"This is Casey."

The woman's shaky voice sent a jolt of energy through Jordan's body, and she quickly sat up. She felt Spencer's muscles tighten and attention sharpen. "Who is this?"

"Casey Andrews," the woman replied.

"Casey?" she asked. There had been enough media coverage for her to doubt the claim.

Spencer sat up and turned her hand to see the phone's display. "That's not the name on your screen," he whispered.

"Casey. This isn't your number."

"He left me a phone. And Max was my teddy bear."

"Where are you?" Jordan asked.

"I don't know. It's dark."

"How did you get this phone?"

"He left it with me. It took time to find it in the dark. He programmed your number into it."

Jordan swung her legs over the side of her bed, her heart pounding in her chest. Had Rawlings left the phone for her to find, knowing he would soon be dead?

Spencer rose, reached for his own phone, and dialed. "I need a call traced. Ready for the number?"

As he recited the number, she said calmly, "I need you to stay on the line, Casey. We need to keep talking so the police can find you."

"I don't know where I am."

"The phone signal will lead us to you," Jordan said.

Spencer pulled on his pants, boots, and shirt, all the while talking softly on his phone.

"Casey, do you know who took you?"

"No. I never saw his face." Her voice broke and she started to weep.

Jordan rose and glided her fingers over the chair near her bed, where she had left her clothes. She had dressed enough in the dark over the years, cradling a phone as she received pertinent information on an incoming police call. "Casey, we're headed your way now. Don't hang up. I'll keep talking to you."

"I don't think I have much battery time left."

"We're on our way."

Spencer took her by the arm and picked up her cane. The time to practice navigation skills was not now. Speed was the driving factor.

The two hurried out the door and toward the driveway. His firm, steady grip gave her the confidence to rush across terrain that normally now made her cautious. He opened his car door, she climbed in, and as she fastened her seat belt, he closed it.

"Casey, are you still there?" Jordan asked.

"Yes."

Spencer angled behind the wheel and fired up the engine. In direct, clear tones he spoke to dispatch, urging them to rush the signal's triangulation.

"I'm sorry," Casey said through tears. "He hit you so hard. I thought you were dead."

"Don't cry. I'm alive and well. I've met your mother and your sister, Cloe."

"Mom and Cloe?" She cried harder. "I want my mom."

"We're going to get you to her as fast as we can," Jordan said.

Spencer pulled into the street and made his way toward the main road. When he received the phone's location, he pressed the gas and flipped on his lights.

"We've got your position," Jordan said.

"Be careful," Casey said. "He's a liar. He promised me over and over that he would let me go. But he never did."

"Is that what he did in the house where I found you?"

Casey drew in a ragged breath. "He said he was setting me free. Said I was going home. And then he tied me up and made me put the plastic over my head." Her voice broke. "He likes seeing me struggle to breathe. It excites him."

"Is there anything you can tell me about him? His height, muscle tone, the sound of his voice."

"He felt massive when he was on top of me. His chest and hands were smooth."

Rawlings's body was at the medical examiner's office, and she would have Spencer check both descriptors, but Jordan did not connect Casey's description to Rawlings.

"He shut the lights off after that day he hit you."

"What do you mean?" She heard the vehicle accelerate as the car wove in and out of traffic.

"I can't see anything," Casey said.

"Why did he turn off the lights?"

"I don't know."

The killer had already hinted that he knew Jordan's vision was impaired. "Okay."

"We're less than a minute out." Spencer slowed the car and took a hard right. The new road was rougher, and she guessed narrower, as many of the side roads on the fringe of the county could be.

"What does your room feel like, Casey?" Jordan asked.

"The walls feel like cinder block. There's a toilet in the room and a sink, but nothing else. No windows."

"Seconds out," Spencer said.

"Almost there, Casey," Jordan said.

The wail of police sirens mingled with the odd flashes of lights as the other cops joined them. Spencer slowed and pulled sharply to the left before bringing the car to a stop.

"Where are we?" she asked.

"It's another old house," Spencer said. "One story, looks as if it were built in the nineteen forties. There are no other vehicles in the area. It's within three miles of where we found you unconscious."

"He has a favorite area," Jordan said.

"We're all creatures of habit," Spencer said.

Jordan unlatched her seat belt and reached for her car door handle.

"Stay in the car," Spencer ordered. "Keep talking to Casey."

"I want to be there when you find her."

"No. Your vision impairment makes you a liability. I wish it didn't, but it does. The goal is to get Casey out of the house alive. Stay put. We haven't confirmed that we're even talking to Casey."

She had dismissed all thoughts of a fraud when she'd heard the name Max. From then on, she'd been so focused on keeping the woman on the line her thoughts had narrowed, edging out the possibility that this was a fraud or a trap. "Understood."

He was out of the car, and seconds after he slammed his door, he opened the SUV's back hatch. Like many cops, he kept his tactical gear in the back for cases just like this. He slammed the hatch closed.

"My battery is—" Casey's last words ended, and the line went silent.

More cars rolled onto the site, surrounding Spencer's vehicle. Jordan gripped the phone and listened to the cops assembling. In her mind's eye, she pictured the grouping of officers dressed in black, ready to breach the house. She imagined their tactical discussions and the gear checks.

Too anxious to sit, she opened her car door and slid out, careful not to close it for fear she would attract attention.

She shifted her face toward the palpable energy swirling among the officers, as it did before a raid. A silence settled. A breeze caught a wind chime somewhere in the distance.

And then footsteps thundered upstairs, and a crash signaled that the front door had been breached. Gripping her phone, she took a step toward the house.

"Detective Poe." The male voice sounded young. "Ranger Spencer issued orders for you not to leave the car."

"Who is this?"

"Deputy Menendez," he said.

"Have we met before?"

"No, ma'am."

"Look," she said, masking the tension humming under her voice. "I have been a part of this case since the beginning."

"I've heard."

"I need to know Casey is all right."

The shouts of the cops reverberated from the house. Jordan stepped forward, but her path closed as the deputy stepped in front of her. "Can't let you do that."

"Are you going to arrest me?"

"Ranger Spencer said to put you in cuffs if I have to. You and Ms. Andrews are safer if you stay here with me."

She flexed her fingers. The logic did little to quell her agitation. Casey's fate was in the hands of one of the best lawmen in Texas, but Jordan desperately craved the action. She missed it. Missed her job. Missed her life.

The house's front door opened, and Spencer called out, "We have her."

Emotion banded around her chest. "How is she?"

Spencer's footsteps grew louder as he approached. "Alive. Well. We have her out of the house."

"Can I talk to her?" Jordan asked.

"Paramedics are with her now."

"What's wrong with her?"

"She's been in total darkness for over a week, she's malnourished, and she's been sexually assaulted multiple times. They're getting her on a stretcher and an IV in her. She's also in drug withdrawal."

"Drugs?"

"He's been injecting her since the night he took her."

"Did she say why?"

"She doesn't know."

Jordan folded her arms over her chest. "He didn't have to leave her the phone," she said. "He could have let her die in that basement."

"I don't begin to understand Rawlings's motivation on this one. Hopefully, Casey can shed some light. She was with him for ten days."

The wheels of the paramedics' stretcher rumbled, and she knew the rescue team was on the move with Casey. "Can I see her?"

"It'll have to be quick. Her eyes are covered and protected from the sun, so she can't see you." Spencer offered her his arm and guided her across the dried, brittle terrain. She wanted to run but knew a root or rock was waiting to trip her up.

When they approached the rescue squad, she was struck by the strong scent of body odor and urine. She conjured memories of Casey and stripped away weight and skin tone. The young woman's features drew inward, her hair lost its luster, and her eyes hollowed.

"Casey," Spencer said. "This is Detective Poe."

Casey reached out a hand. "Detective."

Jordan took her hand in both of hers, feeling the torn fingernails gritty with dirt and grime. "You made it."

"Yeah." Casey's voice sounded rusty, like a wheel that had not turned in too long. "Is he really dead?"

"Yes," Jordan said. "Mr. Rawlings shot himself."

"It doesn't seem right that he would just die after what he did. It's not fair."

Thin fingers gripped Jordan's hand tighter. The woman's physical nightmare was over, but there remained months, if not years, of work to help her move past what had happened. "Let the doctors take care of you. I'll visit you at the hospital as soon as I can."

"Thank you."

"Of course."

The paramedics counted to three, lifted the stretcher, and pushed it into the rescue squad's back bay. She did not remember when they had loaded her up in one over a week ago. Her head pounded as her graying vision quickly narrowed.

Spencer laid his palm on Jordan's shoulder. "She's in good hands."

"I know."

"Let's get back to my car. The officers are still going through the house and the outbuilding."

"Why didn't he kill her? Why leave her a phone, knowing we might find her? I don't understand this man."

"In time we might piece together his motives."

Or they might not. Death had silenced Rawlings, and unless they found written notes or recordings, she would never be fully convinced that he was the killer.

Back in Spencer's SUV, she relaxed against the seat, feeling energy escape her body. Finding Casey had kept her going. It had motivated her to get out of bed in the morning. Now, she had found the woman, alive, and the killer was dead.

So now what? Now how did she find a reason to face the darkness?

CHAPTER THIRTY-FOUR

Saturday, April 24
10:30 p.m.

The hospital sounds drifted around Jordan as she sat in the waiting room down the hallway from Casey's room. She had drunk too much coffee, filled up on vending machine candy, and practiced with her phone in the three hours since Spencer had brought her to the hospital. He had promised to return when he could. She understood that he had a job to do. Once she talked to Casey, maybe more of her questions would be answered.

"Jordan." Rogan's voice drifted from the waiting-room door.

"Rogan." She was so drained and spent, his familiar voice was welcome.

He crossed the room and sat in the seat beside her. "I just heard."

The words *How are you doing?* lingered in the space between them. "That frown line on your brow must be getting deep."

"It's hard not to worry about you," he said. "You keep charging forward when you should slow down. You need to give your body time to heal."

"That's what I'll be doing very soon," she said. "Casey has been found, and the killer is dead."

"Dead?"

"It'll be released to the news today." She did not tell him more, knowing despite all the information the police had, they were still in a very active investigation.

"Good. Now that you don't have this case dogging you, you can rest."

"What am I going to do with my life?" she asked.

"You'll find another purpose."

"No one needs a detective who cannot see well."

"There's a chance some of your vision will improve."

"You and I both know it won't return to what it was."

"Then you'll reinvent yourself," Rogan said.

"Everyone keeps saying that. Sounds easy, doesn't it?"

"I know it's not," he said. "But if anyone can, it'll be you."

"Let's hope."

"Detective Poe." The voice belonged to the charge nurse on the three-to-eleven shift.

"Sandra?" Jordan said, looking up. "Can I see Casey?"

"Yes, but just for a few minutes."

Jordan reached for her cane and rose. Rogan did as well.

"I'll only allow one visitor, Dr. Malone," Sandra said.

"I understand, Sandra. I'm just here to give the detective a few good words."

"If you'll follow me," Sandra said.

Jordan opened her cane, and moving slowly, she noted the change of carpeting in the visitors' lounge to tile floor in the central hallway. The lights seemed brighter, and the noises of machines grew louder.

"She's in room 309," Sandra said.

"Thanks. I wasn't sure."

"There's braille on the room placards and in the elevators."

"Haven't learned braille yet. One mountain at a time, Sandra. Has Casey's mother been to see her?"

"She's come and gone. She was very upset, so we thought it best she didn't stay too long. Casey needs to stay calm until we can evaluate her."

"Sure. I get that." The nurses had said the same to Jordan, but she had hated the quiet and the calm. She wanted her family and friends around her.

"Let me guide you to the chair by her bed. Don't want you tripping."

"That would be appreciated."

Sandra guided her across the room to a chair. "Casey, Detective Poe is here."

Casey drew in a deep breath as if she had just woken up.

"She's had a sedative," Sandra said.

It would take time to peel back the layers of Casey's ordeal. Jordan stretched her fingers forward, brushing the smooth cotton of the bedsheets. "Casey."

"Detective. I've been asking for you," Casey said.

"I know you've had a lot of people in and out of here today. I won't stay long."

"It's okay." Tubes shifted, and the mattress creaked as Casey adjusted her body. "Can you press the button to raise me up?"

Jordan felt for the control panel she had never mastered when she had been here. "You'll have to press the up button. I can't see it."

"It's dim in here," Casey said. "I can turn up a light."

"I'm afraid that won't help." Jordan held out the control.

Casey took the device, and soon the bed was rising. "Why can't you see it?"

"My vision is messed up." The descriptor still did not fit.

"How can you . . ." Casey shifted her body against the mattress, and Jordan could feel her scrutiny intensify.

She did not flinch or look away. "You saw him hit me on the back of the head."

"Yes."

"Long story short, the blood supply was cut to my ocular nerve. It caused damage."

"Will it get better?"

"I don't know." She smoothed her palms over her legs. "Tell me what you saw that night."

"I saw you rushing into the room, then your face and the knife. I just wanted air. And then I saw him racing toward you. I tried to scream, but my throat was so dry. And then it was too late. You were on the floor."

"And then?"

"He grabbed me by the arms. Said he'd kill me if I made a sound. He dragged me out of the room and threw me in the bed of his truck, covered me with a tarp. We drove around for hours."

"He's been operating in a ten-mile radius," she said.

"In the darkness it's impossible to tell," Casey said.

"It's very disorienting."

"He came back more times than I can remember." A sigh shuddered over her lips. "Each time he had a bag and told me to put it on my head."

"The nurses told me you were sexually assaulted."

"I lost track of how many times." She began to cry.

Jordan sat silent, waiting. Fear and shame were powerful demons that could make life damn near impossible.

Casey sniffed, cleared her throat. "I was so afraid each time that this would be the time I suffocated. The more I struggled, the more excited he became. The last time, he told me he wasn't coming back, and if I could find the phone, I could call you."

"He must have decided then he was going to kill himself."

"The last time, he called me by a different name."

"What was the name?"

"Avery."

Jordan stiffened. "Are you sure?"

"Yes."

"Do you know Avery?" Jordan asked carefully.

"No."

Jordan moved to the edge of her seat, staring into the darkness and willing her eyes to work. But the shadows did not dissipate. Christ, what she would not trade right now to have her sight back for just a few hours.

She fumbled in her pocket for her phone. She needed to call Avery immediately. "Thank you, Casey. I'll come back."

"I'm so sorry, Detective Poe." She began to weep.

"It's not your fault. All the blame lies with him."

Using her cane, she made her way past the curtains pulled in front of the door and pushed them back. In the hallway, the air lightened, and the sound of the nurses' voices at their station anchored her location. "Call Avery."

Her phone dialed and quickly rang one, two, three, and four times. The call went to voicemail. "Avery, this is Jordan. Call me. Now."

If Avery was working late at the café, she could still be behind the register or busing tables. "Call Austin City Café."

The phone rang, and a young man picked up on the second ring. "Austin City Café."

"This is Jordan Poe. I'm looking for my sister, Avery Poe."

"Oh, hey, Jordan. It's Matt."

She pictured a tall skinny kid who was studying premed at the University of Texas.

"Jordan, Avery's not worked here in over a week. She quit to take care of you."

"I must be confused. Avery said she was still working at the café."

"Not here. Maybe she got a gig somewhere else."

"Okay. Thanks, Matt." She ended the call and pictured Avery in a dark alley, exchanging cash for heroin; then she rejected the image. She redialed Avery's number. "I don't know what the hell is going on, but you need to call me. Matt said you quit your job."

Jordan had once known all of Avery's favorite spots. The alleys, abandoned houses, and lots where she bought and used. Christ, they had come so far, and now it was all sliding backward. "Avery, I can't do this without you."

***

When Avery arrived at the house, she was surprised it was dark. She pushed through the front door. "Jordan?"

She flipped on a light, grateful it chased away the darkness. She had spent the evening in the shadows, asking the women on the street if they knew of a guy who had a thing for asphyxiation. A couple of the sex workers mentioned a few guys drawn to choking, but no one remembered anyone using plastic bags.

Kicking off her shoes, she dropped her purse and keys by the door. Moving down the hallway, she looked in Jordan's room. The sheets and blankets were rumpled, and both pillows were creased.

Avery reached for her phone and checked for messages. The most recent were from Jordan, and she heard her sister's frantic tone. She dialed Jordan's number.

"Where are you?" Jordan asked.

"I'm home. I'm safe," Avery said.

"Where have you been?"

"On the streets, asking around."

"Why would you do that?"

"I don't know. I thought there was something the cops were missing. But maybe not. I came up empty."

"Stay at the house. I'll be there soon."

"Where are you?"

"Leaving the hospital. Casey was found. She's alive. I'll fill you in when I get home."

"I want to hear it all. Not going anywhere."

From her nightstand, she picked up her old phone, now fully charged, and saw that she had twenty messages. A few were old messages from Jordan, several from work, and one from a number she did not recognize. She hit play.

"Help me, please. He's going to kill me. Please save me."

Avery stilled as she listened and then replayed the message. She double-checked the date and realized the call had come in on March 23. When had Laura Davis vanished? Late March.

"Why would she call me?" she whispered.

Floorboards shifted behind her, and when she turned, she saw the man standing in her doorway. He was wearing black jeans and a hoodie, and his face was covered with a ski mask. "Because I asked her to call you."

Hands trembling, Avery dialed 911 as panic burned through her body. The man crossed the room in seconds and snatched the phone from her before she could hit "Call." "No!"

"You don't want to call anyone, Avery," he said. "You only just arrived, and we have a lot to do together."

Her mind tripped back to Walker's apartment two years ago. He grabbed her arm and she remembered the stranger's grip on her arm and the intense fear. She tried to break free, but his fingers tightened with bruising strength. "Let go of me."

"You have a lot more fight in you than I remember," he said.

"Who are you?"

He grabbed her chin and yanked her face, forcing her gaze to meet his. "You must remember. We had some fun together a couple of years ago."

Avery stared into the eyes that sparked like shards of dark glass. Again, she was back in Walker's apartment.

"I'm not doing anything like that again." Her skin crawled at memories of that man sliding his hands up under her dress and over her bare legs.

He dragged her out of the bedroom and toward a chair sitting near the kitchen. He forced her into the chair, and when she tried to get up, he struck her hard across the face. Her head snapped sideways, and pain rocked through her body. Duct tape ripped from a roll and bound her wrist to the chair arm. As he pulled more tape, she clawed at her bindings, but her fingernails simply scraped over the slick tape. He grabbed her second hand and attached it to the chair.

When he stepped back, he looked pleased, excited. "I've waited for this for a long time. When Jordan gets home, we're going to have a real party."

"Jordan is too smart for you."

He reached in his pocket and pulled out a syringe and rubber hose. "I don't think she is."

As he moved toward her, she pressed her back into the chair. "What is that?"

"A little something to help you relax."

"I don't want it! I don't do that anymore. *Please.*" Her voice broke as panic scraped her insides.

"Oh, come on, Avery, you've missed it. I know you must lie in bed at night and dream about getting high again."

She had. Some nights in the early days the temptation had been almost painful. But she had resisted. And for him to put that poison in her now could unchain a beast she might not ever tame again. "I don't want it."

"Sure you do."

She shook her head from side to side. "No!"

He tied the rubber hose around her arm, and when the vein in the crook of her arm bulged, he flicked it with his fingertip. "Pretty vein."

"Don't do this. Please don't do this."

He pressed the needle to her vein. "This is just a start. Once I've taken care of Jordan, you and I'll find a quiet place. By then, you'll realize how much you want this, and you'll do anything I want to get it."

She winced as the needle pricked her skin. The warm liquid streamed into her vein, and almost immediately, the tension and worry melted. "I don't want this."

"You don't know what you want. But I do." He leaned close to her ear and pulled his mask up. "I'm going to show you things you never dreamed possible when I put the plastic bag on your head."

Tears rolled down her cheeks as her eyelids grew heavy. "No."

He chuckled softly. "This is going to be fun."

CHAPTER THIRTY-FIVE

Sunday, April 25
12:00 a.m.

The Uber driver dropped Jordan off, and she quickly crossed her yard and pushed through the front door of her house. Switching on lights as she moved down the hallway, she called out Avery's name, not concerned if she sounded worried or upset. She needed to know her sister was okay. "Avery!"

The silence was broken by only the hum of the air conditioner and the clock's *ticktock*. She caught her shoulder on the doorframe of Avery's room. Pain rocketed through her; she cursed and stumbled over a pair of discarded shoes by the bed.

Quickly she rummaged through the rumpled sheets, searching for Avery. The bed was empty. "Where the hell are you?"

She sat on the bed, lifted her phone, and said, "Call Avery."

The phone rang four times before it went to voicemail. *"This is Avery. Leave me a message!"*

Jordan closed her eyes, summoned a calming breath before saying, "Avery, this is Jordan. I thought you were at home. I'm worried."

When her mother had died, she had endured crushing loneliness. There was no one to call or talk to about what it was like to be twenty-two and suddenly in charge of a grieving twelve-year-old sister. But she had rallied, found a way forward. When Avery overdosed, that same loneliness had nearly suffocated her. But she had been so engaged in fighting for her sister's life that she did not dare entertain it.

There was a ripping sound and an anguished cry. "Jordan!"

Avery's voice echoed from near the kitchen. It sounded strangled, strained. "Avery?"

Rising, she moved across the room, tripping over the same shoes. Righting herself, she kept rushing into the living room and searched the shadows.

"Avery, where are you?" She struggled to keep her voice calm.

"Jordan," Avery whimpered softly.

Jordan visualized the corner nook by the side patio door off the kitchen. She had never felt so helpless, never angrier that she couldn't see. "Avery."

"Don't come closer." Avery's voice was slurred, but panic twisted around the words. "He's going to kill us both."

Jordan stretched out her hands, moved forward until they brushed Avery's torso. Her sister was sitting, and her wrists were lashed to the arms of a chair.

"Get out of here," Avery whispered. "He's going to kill you."

"What did he do to you?"

"Shot me full of H." Avery began to cry. "He's ruined me forever."

"No, he has not. I'm not leaving you." Her fingers dug into the tape, discovered it was wrapped several times and would require a knife to cut. She fished her knife out of her pocket.

"Please," Avery begged. "Leave and get help."

Jordan pressed the knife's tip to the tape. "I'll try not to cut you."

"Get out," Avery said. "He's here somewhere."

Jordan worked the knife blade under the tape and sawed upward. She cut through the binding and freed Avery's first hand. "Take the knife. I'll be right back."

"Where are you going?"

"Keep cutting."

In the academy, she had been trained to neutralize the threat. And right now, the only advantage she had was the darkness. She could not see, but that did not mean she could not even out the playing field.

She hurried into the kitchen pantry, fumbled with the latch on the metal circuit breaker box, and opened it. Her trembling fingers groped along the straight-row circuit breaker switches. At first, she lost track of what lever controlled what, and then she realized she had to shut it all off. She counted down fourteen spots to the master switch. She flipped it off.

What little light her eyes processed completely vanished.

"Very clever, Jordan." The man's voice was barely a whisper, but it carried familiar notes from the living room. She pictured him sitting on her couch, enjoying this drama playing out. "Do you think we're now on an even playing field?"

"It's flatter than it was."

***

Spencer pulled the surveillance tapes from Thompson's Market and had been reviewing them for nearly two hours. The guy showed up at his store at 6:16 a.m., which witnesses said was about an hour later than normal. He had made excuses about his alarm clock, but his two morning employees had thought that odd. The man had woken up before his alarm for almost two decades.

Customers began arriving at the store at 7:00 a.m., seconds after he flipped the sign from CLOSED to OPEN. He served up breakfast sandwiches that a young kid made on the grill and by 11:00 a.m. was taking deli orders. When he scribbled his first note on butcher block paper, Spencer noticed he used his left hand. He replayed the scene, and as he watched again, he remembered the gunshot wound on Rawlings's right temple. A left-handed man could shoot himself in the right temple, but it would be awkward, and the angle of the wound would reflect it.

Jordan had said Rawlings's suicide did not feel right to her.

His interest sharpening, Spencer fast-forwarded through several more hours, pausing each time Rawlings wrote a note. He used his left, never his right.

Spencer sat back in his seat. He had not received any preliminary forensic reports from the Rawlings crime scene, and the autopsy would not be until late tomorrow. Until then, he would not know which of Rawlings's hands had gunpowder residue.

Why would a left-handed man use his right hand to kill himself? He could have used both hands to steady the gun. That would have made sense if he had placed the gun barrel into his mouth or under his chin.

Spencer swiped through the pictures on his phone until he found the image that he had taken of Rawlings's face at the crime scene. The entry wound was indeed on his right temple.

He knitted his fingers behind his head as he stared at the image of Rawlings's face.

Back to the security tapes, he fast-forwarded to the last two hours of the day. The stream of customers peaked around 6:00 p.m., but after that, the traffic ebbed with each quarter hour until minutes before 7:00 p.m., when the cashier flipped the sign from OPEN to CLOSED, removed his smock, and left through the back entrance. Five minutes after closing, Mr. Rawlings was straightening stock on the shelves when someone approached the front door.

The person was male, midsize, and wore a dark hoodie that obscured his face from the camera. He knocked on the door. Rawlings opened it.

Many would have sent the late customer away, but Rawlings seemed to recognize the individual.

The man nodded his thanks as Rawlings pointed toward the back of the store. Rawlings nodded and motioned to aisle three. The stranger vanished.

Minutes passed, and there was no sign of the newcomer. Rawlings traced the man's steps into the store. Seconds later, the lights went out, and there was no other sign of Rawlings or the stranger.

"Rawlings, you didn't kill yourself, did you?" Spencer said.

As he watched the tape, Spencer reached for his phone and dialed Jordan Poe's number. Even if she was asleep, she needed to hear this.

The phone rang once. The call went directly to voicemail. "Jordan, this is Spencer. You were right. Rawlings did not kill himself. Call me."

He hung up and stared at his phone, expecting her to return the call in seconds. He imagined she had put the phone down and was searching for it.

Spencer shifted to security footage from an ATM located south of Rawlings's store. As he watched people pass, he waited for a man in a dark hoodie. The man may have kept his face covered at the store, but a block away, it was possible he had let his guard down. No figure matching the man's description passed, so Spencer shifted to a restaurant camera that was positioned a block north of the store. He spotted a man without a hoodie who walked down the block and then quickly crossed the street toward a woman standing on the street corner. He paused to speak to her. She shifted her stance, looked down, and nodded. She followed him to a late-model navy-blue four-door.

The man kept his face tucked, clearly aware of the camera. Spencer called dispatch. When the operator answered, he identified himself. "I need plates run ASAP."

"Yes, sir."

Spencer read off the plates and, as he waited, checked his watch. It had been ten minutes since he had called Jordan. The hair on the back of his neck rose. Why did this not feel right? He reached for his hat. It would take him fifteen minutes to drive by her house and confirm she was fine. He was hurrying across the lobby of the Rangers' headquarters when the dispatcher got back on the line.

"Ranger Spencer, I have a name."

"Who?"

"Rogan Malone."

***

As total darkness surrounded Jordan, she listened for signs of movement. She advanced a step, her arms stretched out in front of her. "Who are you?"

Footsteps shifted in the room as the man crossed back toward Avery. Her sister whimpered.

"Turn the breaker on, Jordan," he whispered.

Whenever she felt cornered, she knew only pushing back worked. She was not armed, but she and the darkness had been getting acquainted for more than a week now. "Why? If I can't see, why should you?"

"I want your sister to see what's going to happen to her."

The ragged whisper was so familiar she immediately rejected the connection her brain made. "Is that supposed to convince me?"

Plastic rustled near Avery. "I've done this enough. I don't need that much light," he said. "And in case an audio cue is required, I'm putting a gag in her mouth."

His familiar tones hit Jordan hard. It could not be him.

Her sister's cry was cut off and muffled. Jordan imagined a gag being jammed in Avery's mouth as it had been two years ago.

"Men who prey on women half their size think that they're strong and dominant," Jordan said. "But they're exactly the opposite. They're weak cowards. If they were real men, they'd say what was on their minds, face-to-face, isn't that right?"

Avery's muffled screams mingled with the rustle of plastic.

Jordan's resolve wavered, and she nearly begged him to let Avery go. Instead, she pushed back. "You're worse than a coward. Avery's small. I can't really see. What next? Puppies and children?"

"Turn the breaker on," he repeated.

"Why should I do that, Rogan?"

His silence confirmed the truth. The realization that her ex-lover and confidant had betrayed her cut deep. The man she had kissed and trusted was a monster. She nearly crumbled under the weight.

"She's going to suffocate," Rogan said. "It'll take a little time, but she'll die."

Her anger reignited. "You're going to kill us anyway. Why should I make it easy?"

"Hearing her die will make you suffer."

"Rogan, why hurt me after all we shared?"

"You were so overwhelmed when you first came to me for counseling," he said. "You were so worried about Avery, and helping you became a calling for me."

"You saved my sanity," she said honestly.

"And you saved mine. I drew strength from you. Seeing you overcome your struggles helped me with mine. I could control all my darker desires."

She thought about all the counseling sessions with Rogan and then later the nights lying in bed, their bodies intertwined. She had shared so many secrets with him. He knew more about her than anyone.

"And then I stopped seeing you as a counselor."

"Yes. And I went back to my old ways, only this time I wanted more. I reached out to Walker."

"Did you kill women when we were together?"

"No. I was able to control myself."

"Why Walker?"

"We had an understanding. I told him who was most ripe for using again. And if I needed a woman, he found one for me. When he told me that he had Avery in his apartment, I rushed over." He hesitated, as if remembering that night. "When I was with her, it was fantastic. If I'd had more experience, I would have made the encounter last, but I had never killed before, and I was nervous."

"She ended up in your treatment program."

"It's a small world."

"And then I came to you. Our random meeting after Avery's attack wasn't an accident, was it?"

"No. I worried Avery might remember me, so I made a point to see you."

He had said all the right things, and she had fallen into bed with him. He had been a tender, patient lover, and Jordan struggled to reconcile those memories with this raw violence. "And then I left you. Again."

"Yes, you did."

Aware of each passing second, she pushed aside this deep betrayal. "Were there others before Laura and Tammy?"

In the silence she felt his gaze burrowing into her. "Maybe."

"Who? Where are they?"

"It doesn't matter."

"Why did you keep Casey alive?"

"You tell me."

"To torture me," she said.

"Yes. That was a big part of it. But she also looks the most like you."

"The tape on Emma's eyes was meant for me," Jordan said.

"Did you pick up on my clue? I wasn't sure."

"Why me?"

"You're an amazing woman, Jordan. You have a strength few possess. I still dream about being with you, being inside you. I thought maybe with you, I could be a better man. And after you lost your sight, I even thought we might have a second chance."

A chill slithered down her spine. "You killed Walker."

"He threatened to tell the police about my connection to Laura, Tammy, and the others. Tried to bribe me. I couldn't let that stand."

The seconds ticked by. Avery's breathing grew slower, shallower. She was preserving her oxygen. "And Rawlings?"

"Rawlings and I had a good working relationship through the food bank. He was an easy mark." More silence, but this time delight mingled with arrogance. "Turn on the breaker, Jordan."

"It won't take the police long to figure out you killed those women," she said. "Your DNA was on two of them. Sooner or later it'll be traced to you. And the police already have their doubts that Rawlings killed himself."

"Cops give themselves too much credit. Besides, I can justify the DNA. I can admit to consensual affairs with the women. All the real evidence linking Rawlings to the killings is in his apartment."

"Why kill him?"

"He was a means to an end. By the way, your sister's head tipped forward. She's losing consciousness."

Jordan moved toward the sound of Rogan's voice. She curled her fingers into a fist and hoped Avery still had access to her knife. "You're attracted to addicts who are like you. Your drug is killing. Sexual heroin."

Footsteps advanced quickly toward her, but she was able to sidestep, and his wild swing missed its mark. Still, even in the darkness, he had the advantage. He reached out, but she dodged his hand.

Avery had grown too silent, and Jordan's hope that she could provoke Rogan was crumbling.

"Let Avery go. Work out whatever shit you have with me. And stop hurting the innocent."

"They aren't innocent. They gave in to weakness, and now they're dead because of it."

"You give in to weakness!"

"It's ironic, isn't it?"

"Avery isn't using drugs. You forced her."

"How do you know she wasn't high when I arrived?"

"Because I know my sister."

This time his arm shot out with lightning speed. He grabbed her right arm and then her left. He roughly hauled her toward him, his familiar scent warring with this reality. He dragged her toward the fuse box and switched on the main breaker.

Faint flashes of lights appeared around her.

He yanked her into the living room, and she tripped over a strip of plastic. Shoving her down, he drove his knee into her chest and anchored her to the ground. She struck out aimlessly, hitting him on the legs, belly, and arms.

"Showing me how much you love me?" Jordan demanded.

He grappled for her left hand. "No more love here, Jordan. I'm truly going to enjoy watching you die."

Jordan swung her fist, connecting with his jaw. He howled a curse, but the blow was only enough to enrage him. She drew her knee up, tried to connect with his groin, but missed.

Out of the darkness that was always with her came a rush of energy and mass. "Bastard!" Avery howled like a wild animal.

Rogan yelled, "Bitch, you've cut me!"

Avery grunted and then her knees dropped to the ground. A knife clinked against the floor and was swallowed by the shadows.

***

When Spencer pulled up to Jordan's house, all the lights were glowing bright. She had said she liked to keep the lights on so if she woke up with sight, she would know it.

So why didn't it feel right?

His phone rang. "Spencer."

"This is Santiago. I couldn't find Avery."

"I'm at Jordan's house," Spencer said. "Avery's car and Jordan's SUV are in the driveway, but this doesn't feel right."

"I'm on my way." Santiago ended the call.

Out of his car, Spencer settled his hand on his weapon. As he moved toward the front door, he heard Jordan's anguished cry of pain. Standing back, he unholstered his weapon.

He stepped back and kicked the front door hard with his booted foot. The hinges gave partway. He kicked a second time, and a third, and then the doorframe cracked, and the door fell inside the house.

He saw Jordan on the ground, covered in blood, Rogan Malone straddling her and raising a knife above her as she raked her hand down his cheek. Lying nearby was an unconscious Avery. He drew in a breath, praying he was not too late.

Spencer fired, hitting Rogan in the shoulder. The bullet tore through his body and threw him off balance. He struggled to right himself as he scrambled for the knife.

Jordan rolled to her side, drew her fist back, and struck Rogan. The blow grazed his jaw. Not enough to stop Rogan but enough to distract him.

Spencer fired a second round. This one struck Rogan at center mass in the chest. He stared down at his injury with a mixture of shock and fury. The man fell backward, hitting the floor.

Spencer was on top of him immediately, rolling him to his belly. He unhooked his cuffs and clicked them on Rogan's wrists.

"She needs to die," Rogan wheezed.

"Jordan, are you okay?" Spencer asked.

"I'm fine." Her voice sounded ragged.

Her shirt and pants were covered in blood, and automatically he ran his hands over her body, searching for injuries. "The blood."

"It's his."

Spencer reached for his phone and called for backup.

"I need to get to Avery," Jordan said. "He hit her. She's on the floor."

Jordan tried to rise on wobbly feet and then fell to her knees. Her face tightened with frustration as she fought against her body's weakness.

Moments like this for any cop passed in painfully slow seconds as they struggled to overcome an injury. "Stay," he said. "I've got this."

He gently rolled Avery on her back and pressed his fingers to her throat. Her skin felt hot to the touch, and her pulse was weak but present. He pushed open her eyelids and stared into oversize pupils. She was high.

"Avery," he said. "Can you hear me?"

She did not respond to his voice, prompting a fear that she had overdosed. He rubbed his knuckles into her breastbone. The distant sound of sirens grew louder. "Avery!"

Jordan crawled toward them, and she took her sister's limp hand in her own. "Is she okay?"

He did not have the heart to tell Jordan he was not sure. "Avery!"

Jordan squeezed Avery's hand until her own knuckles whitened. "Open your eyes. Look at me!"

Avery's eyes slowly opened. Black pupils swallowed up blue irises. She stared at him blankly.

"Can she see us?" Jordan asked him.

"Avery," Spencer said. "Can you see?"

"I'm not sure."

Jordan cupped her sister's face in her hands and turned it toward her own. "Avery!"

Avery's gaze focused, and she sat up suddenly. "Where is he? He's going to kill us."

"He's cuffed, Avery," Spencer said. "He can't hurt you or Jordan anymore."

Avery's eyes filled with tears of anger and defeat.

"What did you take?" Spencer asked Avery.

"I don't know. He shot me up." Her gaze dropped to the needle mark at the crook of her arm, and she shut her eyes. "He's killed me."

"No, he has not," Spencer said. "Jordan, take care of Avery. The cops are here."

When he turned back, Jordan had dropped her tear-streaked face to her sister's. "It's okay. It's okay. We will survive this, I swear."

EPILOGUE

Thursday, July 1
1:30 p.m.

Jordan stood in the lobby of the medical building. Today her neurologist had evaluated her recent MRIs and brain scans and updated her on the status of her ocular nerve.

She had not needed a doctor's test to tell her what she knew. A small amount of vision had returned in the last couple of months. Some of the shadows were not as dark, she could make out people if they were standing in front of a bright window, and her sensitivity to light had diminished. But her vision was not what it had been, and the chances of it improving enough to get back on the force were slim.

She could hope for a miracle. And maybe one day there would be more progress in nerve regeneration. But for now, that was not an option for her.

The front door opened, and determined footsteps moved toward her across the medical building's lobby. Spencer. He always walked as if he were racing toward a crime scene.

He had offered to attend this meeting with her. "Two sets of ears are better than one" had been his justification. Avery had also offered, but Jordan wanted her sister's focus to remain on her new fight to remain sober. The poison Rogan had injected in her was a challenge to overcome, and it was taking all of Avery's mental strength to stay the course.

In the end, Jordan had decided to take Spencer up on his offer. He'd listened to the doctor's prognosis, asked questions, and held her hand when the answers were not what she wanted to hear.

Spencer kissed her on the lips. "I've pulled the car around. It's out front."

"Thanks." She hooked her arm in his. Outside, the hot summer sun warmed her skin, chasing away the chill of the doctor's office. She tipped her face to the sky.

They crossed the sidewalk toward the idling engine of his vehicle. Now familiar with its layout, she reached for the handle, opened the door as Spencer moved around to the driver's side. That had been a number one rule when they'd both agreed they were in a relationship. She did not want to be babied. Sally certainly had not cut her any slack during the months of therapy sessions, and she appreciated that.

She closed up her cane, climbed into the front seat, and shut the door. She hooked her seat belt with relative ease.

As Spencer began to drive, the seat's warmth, coupled with the cool air-conditioning, allowed her mind to wander back over the last couple of months. It was not good to live in the past, but Rogan Malone had been impossible to forget.

Rogan had survived his injuries and was in jail. Bail had been denied, and he would wait in jail until his trial later this summer. So far, Rogan had refused to speak to anyone about any other possible victims.

Jordan had worked with Spencer over the last month to unravel Rogan Malone's killing spree. The therapist had put the women in Walker's path, knowing the temptation of using was too much for them to resist. After Jordan had broken up with Rogan, he'd taken only the women who looked like her.

When Walker had accidentally killed his girlfriend, his hold on his drug operation had started to slip. His money had dried up, and he had tried to blackmail Rogan. Rogan had realized if he wanted to continue, he needed to kill Walker and find other sources for his victims. He had shot the drug dealer up and hanged him from the light fixture. He had also admitted that Emma had been clean when he'd taken her. He had injected her as he had Avery.

He had not expected Jordan to find Casey alive the first time, and his attack on Jordan had been unplanned. They believed he had kept Casey alive, realizing she satisfied his relentless addiction.

The forensic evidence backed up this theory. Not only had Rogan's DNA matched all the samples that had been collected from the victims, but he had been spotted near Jordan's hospital room multiple times. No one had noticed him because he was on staff, and he knew Jordan. When Spencer had reviewed more recordings, he'd spotted Rogan in the crowd the day Jordan was released from the hospital, and an eyewitness placed him near the hospital in a hoodie around the time when Emma was taken.

When Spencer had dug into Rawlings's past, he'd also discovered that Rogan had been his counselor years ago. Rogan had built a connection with Rawlings via the food bank, and he had sent Tammy and Casey to interview at Rawlings's store, knowing he might one day frame the man. The world of addiction was a small one.

Spencer slowed, shifted gears. "How are you feeling about the appointment?"

"You heard as well as I did. My sight might be as good as it gets."

"And?"

"It stinks," she said. "I want to see again. I want my old normal again." She smoothed her hands over her jeans. "But I'll deal with what I have in front of me, not what I wish was there."

The car accelerated again. "Did Captain Lee speak to you about the new job?"

Captain Lee had called her this morning. He was transferring her to victim assistance. The idea had appeal, but she had asked to consider the offer.

"You're well connected, Ranger Spencer. I only received the captain's call this morning."

"I didn't mean to pry. But he ran it past me when he first came up with the idea."

"I'm really considering it. I love working, and this job would allow me to use what I know. It'll mean getting a master's in social work, but that's doable." She had already looked into returning to school and learned that until she mastered braille, she could use audiobooks and readers.

"You haven't said yes yet?" he asked.

She shrugged. "It's always best not to say yes right away."

"That the way it is with us?" he asked.

"My life is changing faster than even I can process," she said. "I don't want you making a promise that could end up being a burden to you."

"There's nothing burdensome about it, Jordan. I know what I'm getting into."

"I'm not sure I do, but I'm stuck with it. You're not."

"I'm not going anywhere, Jordan," he said.

"You're a good guy, Spencer, and you're loyal to a fault. Even if I became a burden, you wouldn't leave." His loyalty to Vickie was the proof.

"I'm crazy about you." His voice was rough, heavy with emotion.

"I'm crazy about you," she said.

"Then why are you worried about burdens? I'm exactly where I want to be."

She knew he believed that, but she did not want his future self ever looking back on this moment with regret. "Why don't we take it one day at a time? That's about all I'm really good for right now."

"I'm in it for the long haul, but I'm patient. And I'll wait."

She turned toward him, feeling that rock-hard determination that etched the deep frown lines she still remembered on his forehead and around his mouth. However much time they ultimately had together was incentive enough for her not to waste a second of it. "Seeing as we both have today off, it would be a shame to waste it."

"What would you like to do?" he asked easily.

Grinning, she smoothed her hand over his thigh. "I have a few ideas."

ABOUT THE AUTHOR

Photo © 2015 StudioFBJ

New York Times and *USA Today* bestselling novelist Mary Burton is the popular author of more than thirty-five romance and suspense novels, as well as five novellas. She currently lives in Virginia with her husband and three miniature dachshunds. Visit her at www.maryburton.com.